THE SECOND CRUSADE

BY DANIEL MITCHELL

THE SECOND CRUSADE

Managing editor - Amanda Meuwissen
Associate editor - Michelle Kisbee

Book layout/Cover design - Mario Hernandez

ISBN-13: 978-1943619399

Second U.S. Edition: August 2018
Printed in the United States of America

To my sisters, Jennifer, Leah and Diana.
Well, maybe not Jennifer. …alright, even Jennifer.

And to anyone who has ever sat around a gaming table
with me, for that is truly where the first ideas for this
world began.

AUTHOR'S NOTE

WARNING: I'm going to proceed as if you've already read The Vlishgnath Chronicles, so if you haven't, you may want to skip this introduction as it contains some references that you may not understand.

Towards the end of The Dark Elf Rebellion, BigWorldNetwork.com Managing Editor Amanda Meuwissen asked me if I was planning on doing another Vlishgnath story or if I had something else in mind. Initially, I was thrilled that they were going to let me keep writing and posting it on the website, but once the initial awe wore off I actually got to thinking, and decided I wanted to do something a little grittier this time. Something darker. Something where the church of Mithos didn't necessarily comprise the largest religious denomination in the western kingdoms. I had mentioned the church's second crusade in The Frost Giant War, when Vlishgnath was explaining to Aevana how the deeds of his father overshadowed him at times, and at one point during my deliberation it occurred to me that I had already referenced the story I wanted to write.

I had always envisioned Roningus as a sterner, more aggressive style of paladin, which manifested itself in his dual-sword fighting style. In fact, in an email exchange with Amanda, we were discussing the differences between the two, and I referenced the second confrontation between Vlishgnath and Halbryn Demtor during The Dark Elf Rebellion, stating that (and I'm paraphrasing here), "while Vlishgnath was content to simply swat at her with the flat of his blade to prove he could have won, Roningus would have simply hamstringed her so that she was unable to ever threaten him again." It was this stark contrast in philosophies that set the tone for Roningus as a character, and would ultimately determine how I wrote him.

As always, a tremendous thank you goes out to all of the hard working individuals at BigWorldNetwork.com that put their time and effort into polishing this story and making it better than it actually was, and to you, the holder of this book, whether you're a returning reader who enjoyed The Vlishgnath Chronicles or even if The Second Crusade is your first venture into the western kingdoms. I sincerely hope you enjoy the darker, grittier world it takes place in as much as I enjoyed writing it..

THE SECOND CRUSADE

BY DANIEL MITCHELL

CONTENTS

(1) 1
(2) 10
(3) 20
(4) 29
(5) 37
(6) 45
(7) 53
(8) 62
(9) 70
(10) 79
(11) 87
(12) 95
(13) 104
(14) 112
(15) 120
(16) 128
(17) 136
(18) 144
(19) 152
(20) 160
(21) 169
(22) 177
(23) 185
(24) 194
(25) 204
(26) 214
(27) 223
(28) 232
(29) 241
(30) 250
(31) 260
(32) 269
(33) 278
(34) 288
(35) 297
(36) 306
(37) 315
(EPILOGUE) 329

As the rain began to fall lightly from the dreary, overcast sky, the tall, broad-shouldered squire stepped out into the sparring ring. Nineteen years of age and standing a full three heads above his peers, Roland turned and flexed to the boys behind him, grinning and nodding as they made japes about how easily his pending victory would be. Clad in a chain shirt over a leather jerkin, he donned a wooden shield, grabbed his training sword and moved to the center. He stared down at his opponent, who had dark brown eyes and shoulder-length raven black hair.

Roland chuckled with a predatory glare, noticing that the other boy hadn't brought his shield with him but was gripping a wooden training sword confidently. The boy was of an average height, but Roland had seen him in the training yard before. This one was in peak physical condition; always running, often with sacks of flour slung over his shoulders.

"What, is your left arm crippled or something?" As Roland spoke, he turned, smiling boastfully to his friends back at the fence, all of whom hooted and hollered their approval. But when he turned back around, the boy continued to stare at him with the same hungry look in his eyes, continuing to stare even as the weaponmaster approached to explain the rules of the match.

"First rule! No biting! Second rule! No shots to the groin! Third Rule…"

But as the weaponmaster spoke, the boy simply continued to stare, his eyes boring into Roland, and for the first time that he could remember, Roland felt his confidence leaving him. Jarred by the sudden thought, Roland realized the absurdity of it and smirked, shaking his head to clear such nonsense from it.

"…and lastly, keep in mind this is a practice fight, boys. You're of no use to the church or High Priest Argos if you cripple each other. Now, cross swords and—Remn, where's your shield?"

The black-haired boy shook his head, his eyes still fixed on Roland.

The weaponmaster furrowed his brow, but continued. "Cross swords and begin on my command."

Roland held his wooden sword out, the boy Remn doing the same, crossing them as instructed. Once the weaponmaster was out of earshot, Roland spoke in a muffled tone.

"If you think I'll go easy on you because you're too dull to use a shield, you're wrong."

"I don't need a shield. Soon I'll have another sword."

When Roland squinted in confusion, Remn glanced down at Roland's sword, then looked back up at him. His serious eyes unsettled Roland, and he barely heard the weaponmaster call out to them.

"Begin!"

Immediately, Roland drew back his sword, swinging out with a powerful shield bash aimed to knock Remn off-balance. But the other boy's reaction came instantly, leaning back and allowing the shield to sail over him. His back nearly parallel with the ground, Remn righted himself just as quickly, his hands still hanging at his sides. Roland growled, and lunged forward with a powerful front kick meant to put distance between the two of them, so he could follow up with a powerful downward stroke. But instead, Remn turned and pivoted to his left, his eyes locked with Roland's as the kick missed completely.

Anger beginning to swell within him, Roland lashed out again, bringing the top of his shield around in a horizontal swing aimed to catch Remn in the chest and take him off his feet. Again, Remn ducked, but this time, he spun out of the way, and before Roland could see where he'd gone, his sword arm was bent up behind his back, a practiced application of a wrist lock forcing his hand open and allowing the sword to fall right out of it.

When his arm was abruptly released, Roland spun around again, putting all of his weight behind the shield in an attempt to catch the other boy off guard and send him sprawling. It wasn't until he missed that he saw Remn again, standing a foot out of the way and gripping a wooden sword in both hands. Roland stopped for a moment, gawking in disbelief at the boy, who in turn responded with the same cold stare he'd maintained the entire time, voice disturbingly serene.

"I'll not make this offer again: yield now."

Roland's friends were howling wildly, calling out to him to make an end of it. With a sneer, Roland spat at Remn's feet, clenching his right hand into a fist and deciding that he was going to have to hurt the boy to teach him a lesson.

Remn stared down at the saliva near his foot, shaking his head before looking back up to Roland. When Roland chuckled condescendingly, Remn leapt forward, launching a barrage of slashes and thrusts with blinding speed and surgical precision.

Roland reeled backwards, unable to get his shield up until several hits hand landed. Remn's onslaught was merciless, cowing Roland further and further until he was practically hiding behind his shield, the wooden swords falling on him as steadily as the light rain that fell from the sky. Realizing his predicament, Roland roared angrily, planting his feet and swatting away one of the wooden swords before reaching out to grab at the boy, his hand grasping the front of Remn's jerkin and chain mail.

In a flash, three sword strokes flew out, the first one catching Roland on the wrist, the second on the back of his knuckles, and the third driving the point up into Roland's armpit. The result was instantaneous: as his hand and wrist began to throb and turn red, his arm went numb and fell limp at his side. Roland's eyes widened in horror as he struggled to try and move it unsuccessfully. The rest happened quickly, a deft spinning pivot and a pair of well-placed slashes at the back of Roland's legs brought him to his knees, Remn taking his time in moving around in front of him before crossing the wooden training swords at Roland's throat. Roland looked up in shock and awe at the boy.

"Remn! Disqualified! What did I tell you, boy?!"

As he spoke, the weaponmaster rushed over, and Remn immediately stepped back and dropped down to one knee, laying the weapons on the ground and bowing his head. As the weaponmaster walked past Remn, he cuffed him on the back of the neck. Remn neither moved nor made a sound. Then, hurrying over to Roland, the weaponmaster pulled him to his feet and inspected his arm.

"Let me see here, Roland...can you move it at all?"

Still too stunned to speak, it wasn't until the weaponmaster said anything that Roland realized feeling was gradually returning to his arm, and with some effort he was able to twitch his fingers feebly. As it happened, the weaponmaster turned to Remn, frowning and shaking his head, but was unable to hide how relieved he sounded.

"You're lucky, boy! Mithos knows what High Priest Argos would have done with you if you'd cost Roland his sword arm!" Then, turning to the gaping crowd of onlookers, "That's enough for today, boys. Turn your gear in and get to your chores."

As the crowd dispersed, Roland approached Remn, and as the other boy stood, he caught Roland's gaze.

"…how did you do that?" Roland asked, undoing the buckles of his wooden shield.

For a moment, Remn said nothing, until finally a faint grin formed on his lips. "Maybe I'll show you some time."

Roland continued to stare for several long seconds, until finally he began to laugh, slowly at first but increasing in volume and intensity, reaching out and putting his arm around Remn's neck and walking towards the quartermaster's with him. "I'm going to hold you to that! From now on, you're sitting with us in the mess hall!"

"His prowess in the sparring ring is unmistakable, but the boy is out of control. Did you see how aggressive he was with Roland this afternoon?" Arch Cleric Brogam said, his eyebrows furrowed in concern.

High Priest Argos, once a fiery red-haired man with a robust constitution and an imposing build, sat slumped in his chair, the sagging frame of a tired old man vaguely reflecting the once proud and mighty battle cleric that led the crusades to conquer the demon-conjuring wildlings. His faded hair, now interspersed with strands of white, had thinned considerably on top, though his beard remained as long and full as ever.

Argos yawned, repositioning himself in his chair and glancing over to the robed arch cleric to his right, speaking in a voice that had gone hoarse with age. "Vogoth, you've remained silent thus far…tell us, what do you make of all this?"

Middle-aged but young by arch cleric standards, Vogoth sighed heavily, meeting Brogam's gaze as he answered. "Remn Drakmahr must be anointed."

Brogam scoffed, shaking his head and answering Vogoth in a rebuking tone. "We *must* do no such thing! Or perhaps you've forgotten that he almost crippled one of our most promising squires?!"

Vogoth shook his head sternly. "Roland is skilled indeed, but he lacks Remn's ability to control a battlefield. Remn knew exactly what he was doing when he put the point of that wooden sword to use under Roland's arm; the boy recovered full range of motion within moments, did he not?"

"Yes, but the fact still remains! The boy has been unstable ever since his father passed away." As Brogam spoke, everyone in the room winced.

The death of Sir Berengir the Herald of Mercy had been a tragic loss, and many who knew him personally still grieved for him, including each of the arch clerics in the room. Nonetheless, Brogam remained resolute, but Vogoth spoke with increasing persistence.

"All the more reason to allow the Drakmahr line to continue. The boy still grieves for his father, as do we all. That's no reason to cut off a line of successive church knights that goes back more generations than any other surname in active service."

When Brogam opened his mouth , but found himself unable to speak, High Priest Argos smiled, looking to Vogoth. "Well then, it seems all that's left is to come up with a title befitting our wrathful young squire, one that the church's enemies might hear and grow wrought with fear, as if he were a tempest on the horizon."

Vogoth chuckled, placing a gentle hand on the elderly arch cleric's shoulder. "High Priest, I believe you've just named him already."

"And do you swear, before Mithos the All Father, to uphold the tenets of our faith, defending the church from her enemies, and vanquishing evil from the realm of men, so that good may flourish?"

"I swear it on my life," the two said in unison, clad in full suits of plate mail.

Roland, on the left, wore his longsword belted at his waist, his unadorned kite shield strapped to his left arm. Remn, on the right, wore the Drakmahr family armor, an adamantine suit of full plate with enameled black leather laid over the breastplate, the surface made smooth from meticulous buffing. At the chest, the leather gave way to the Drakmahr coat of arms which rose up through it: a seven-pointed asymmetrical sunburst with an angelic female holding a sword to her body with both hands in the center. Remn wore a pair of longswords crossed at the back of his waist, his left arm devoid of a shield.

Both paladins kept their helms tucked under their left arms, baring their heads for anointing. Their devotions spoken, High Priest Argos reached over and grasped a vial of holy water, approaching Remn first. Pulling out the glass stopper, he tilted the bottle and gently sprinkled some of the holy water on Remn's head, mouthing the words to a silent prayer and closing his eyes. He then did the same for Roland. The gathered congregation of clerics and paladins, as well as a few commoners from the city, watched the ceremony in a reverent silence.

When it was done, Argos returned to Remn, handing the bottle off to an attending cleric, who returned the stopper and took it away. Putting his hand on Remn's head, Argos spoke, and as he did, Remn stood.

"Rise, Remn Drakmahr, as Sir Roningus the Wrathful Tempest, that your oathbrothers may cloak you."

Remn stood and a black-caped paladin approached, draping a dark brown cape over his shoulders and fastening it to his pauldrons. Argos approached Roland next.

"Rise, Roland Ubarian, as Sir Ionnus the Righteous Shield, that your oathbrothers may cloak you."

As Roland rose, another black-caped paladin came up to drape a brown cape over his shoulders, and when it was done, the two turned to face Argos. The high priest smiled proudly at both of them.

"Go forth, in the name of Mithos. Your oathbrothers will want to congratulate you."

That said, the entire congregation burst into applause, Ionnus and Roningus turning in unison and marching behind the black caped paladins that had cloaked them to join the ranks of their oathbrothers. They shook hands as the crowd began to disperse.

Another brown-caped paladin, a young man no more than a year older than the two of them, grinned as they joined in the ranks, reaching out and shaking hands with them as well. His dark brown hair was cropped short, a neatly trimmed beard with connecting moustache adorning his face. His steel gray eyes were vibrant with excitement, and his tone of voice reflected it.

"Welcome to the order, oathbrothers. I am Sir Grisbane the Herald of Justice. You two couldn't have picked a better time to swear your oaths."

Roningus furrowed his eyebrows, turning to glance at Ionnus for a moment before returning his gaze to Grisbane. "What exactly do you mean by that?"

Seeing the puzzled expression on Roningus's face, Grisbane quirked a brow. "You hadn't heard? Sir Lothran the Vengeful Blade is taking several brown capes out on a field excursion come morning. There've been reports of activity concerning the dead god in one of the outlying villages, and we are to investigate."

"And they hadn't heard for a reason, Grisbane. I was going to deliver the news to them myself," came a voice, followed by a paladin clad in a royal purple cape with threads of gold embroidering along the edges. His straight blond hair was carefully combed back, his sky blue eyes peering over a long hook shaped nose.

Lothran grinned at Grisbane and shook his head, his long and pointy chin looking as if it were almost close enough to brush against the collar of his breastplate.

"My apologies, Sir Lothran…" Grisbane said, bowing his head respectfully.

Lothran chuckled, his voice noticeably high-pitched for a male yet well-enunciated and of a polite tone. "It's quite alright, Grisbane, although I wouldn't want you filling our newest oathbrother's heads with notions of valor and battle just yet; more often than not, these excursions turn up little more than the drunken ramblings of the common folk."

That said, Lothran turned to Roningus, looking him up and down for a moment before tilting his head at him in confusion.

"Where is your shield, Sir Roningus?"

Without so much as a smile, Roningus stared back into Lothran's eyes, his words spoken plainly. "I do not require one, Sir Lothran."

Roningus continued to stare as Lothran chuckled and turned to walk away. "Not that it matters, I suppose…we aren't going to need them, anyway."

The small, nameless farming community was two days' ride out of Ascention, into the sprawling countryside where the majority of the bustling holy city's produce was grown. As Sir Lothran led the four brown-caped paladins in an orderly procession atop their armored war horses, the simple farming folk looked up from their daily labors with confused, wary expressions. Most of them had never seen a church knight from afar, let alone watched one ride past within arm's reach.

As they proceeded down the only road that ran through the cluster of homes, Ionnus leaned over and spoke to Roningus quietly, his tone sounding highly disappointed. "This is almost insulting… two days' ride for what? To come listen to a bunch of dirt-encrusted farmers' tales? It's likely just a dire wolf that's eating their cattle."

For several seconds, Roningus said nothing, continuing to look down at the apprehensive expressions of the field workers they passed. He answered just as Ionnus was about to lean away. "Something's wrong. Look into their eyes. I know fear when I see it, but this is something more. These people have seen an evil they can't fully comprehend."

For a moment, Ionnus contemplated Roningus's words. Then, looking over to his left, he caught the anxious stares of a woman, bent over a basket of long beans she was preparing. Her sea green eyes were distrustful, the way a beaten animal looks when it has finally submitted.

Looking back to Roningus, Ionnus spoke quietly again. "They do appear more introverted than your usual farming community."

Grisbane leaned back and silenced them with a raised finger, as Sir Lothran approached a man who had just stepped away from his harvesting work. He wore a brown vest over a well-worn white shirt, his rough-spun pants ending just above his ankles. He wore a pair of leather shoes that had begun to fall apart, and carried a long-handled scythe, planting the blunt end into the ground as he faced Sir Lothran. His unkempt gray hair was chopped short, and his wild black beard was also heavily streaked with gray. Staring at Lothran with a complete lack of reverence, the man simply nodded his greeting as the church knights approached.

"Dismount!" came Lothran's command, and on his word all four of the brown-caped church knights dismounted in unison with him, standing beside their animals patiently while Lothran approached the gray-haired man to shake his hand.

As they did, the man looked over the others, his eyes stopping to linger on Roningus a moment, before looking back to the purple-caped church knight as Lothran began to speak.

"Greetings. I am Sir Lothran the Vengeful Blade. By chance, is there somewhere we could stable our horses? We've had a long ride from Ascention, and a bit of rest and refreshment before we begin our investigation would be greatly appreciated."

The gray-haired man nodded, and for a moment, it seemed as though he was going to remain silent before he finally spoke up. "You can hitch them up over there, or let them run free in the pen, whichever you'd prefer." As he spoke, he pointed towards a large penned-off area hosting various animals; mostly pigs, several geese, and a few cows.

Sir Lothran nodded, reached up, and pulled his helmet off, tucking it under his left arm. Smiling pleasantly, he bowed his head as he spoke. "Thank you kindly, mister…?"

The man gave Lothran another distrustful glance, looking the other paladins over once more before responding. "Harkon. I'm the closest thing to someone in charge we've got around here."

Once more Lothran bowed his head. "I thank you for your hospitality, Harkon. But where are my manners? Allow me to introduce my oathbrothers: this is Sir—"

Harkon shook his head, cutting Lothran off. "No need to learn their names. Chances are they already know you're here, so more'n likely they'll come for you next. Tonight, probably."

That said, Harkon turned and headed back to his field, at which point Ionnus looked over to Roningus, Roningus standing stoically and staring straight ahead.

Lothran blinked, then turned to address the other paladins. "Hitch up your horses, and seek shelter for the evening. Use copper pieces if you don't find them hospitable towards the church; a single gold piece could very well collapse their entire economy. Speak with anyone who will talk, and report anything suspicious to me. These are your orders."

With a nod, Lothran dismissed the church knights, the four of them leading their horses over to the pen to tie them up.

As the sun began to set, Ionnus found Roningus seated in front of one of the small cabins that comprised the majority of the housing within the village. One of his longswords lay in his lap as he carefully rubbed oil into the blade, the other still sheathed at the back of his waist.

As Ionnus approached, Roningus looked up, removing his helmet from the chair next to him and setting it on the ground, offering the seat up without a word. Ionnus grinned, gently lowering himself into the chair and testing its load-bearing capabilities before fully committing to sitting in it. Once he was certain it wasn't going to collapse underneath him, he spoke.

"Did these people take you in?"

Silently, Roningus nodded, holding his blade up to inspect his work. Satisfied, he sheathed it and withdrew the other, going to work on it as well.

Ionnus laughed, shaking his head. "I don't suppose you've spoken so much as a word to any of these people since we've arrived, have you?"

For a long while, Roningus said nothing, and simply continued to carefully rub oil into his second longsword with the soft cloth.

Ionnus looked around and listened as the sound of frogs and crickets began to swell up all around them, until finally Roningus spoke up.

"Someone has been murdering villagers and making away with the corpses."

Ionnus looked over suddenly, furrowing his eyebrows and staring at Roningus in confusion. "They've been what?!"

Roningus nodded, continuing his work. "Several villagers told the same stories and gave the exact same details, independent of one another. They're all consistent."

Ionnus's eyes went wide, his voice a mixture of shock and disbelief. "Did you report it to Sir Lothran?"

In response, Roningus nodded again, and when it was apparent he wasn't going to say anything, Ionnus spoke again.

"Well? What did he say?"

"Nothing," Roningus said as he shook his head.

"What do you mean nothing? Wait…how did you get anyone to talk to you? I had to give the family I'm staying with a handful of copper pennies just to get them to speak, let alone allow me to stay under their roof."

Roningus glanced over at Ionnus for a moment, chuckling once silently before beginning to look his sword over. "You underestimate the value of silence."

Ionnus scoffed, shaking his head at Roningus as he spoke. "What's that supposed to mean?"

For a few seconds, Roningus said nothing, until finally he nodded in satisfaction at the second sword, sheathing it as well before looking over to Ionnus. "It means close your mouth, and open your eyes and ears. People are more likely to offer up information if you don't accost them and try to press them into a conversation they aren't ready for."

Ionnus quirked a brow, giving Roningus a quizzical expression. "So how did you get them to talk, then?"

With a faint grin, Roningus looked over to Ionnus once more. "I didn't. I let them come to me, and when they did, I listened."

Ionnus rolled his eyes, sat his helmet down on the ground next to him, and unsheathed his own longsword. "Let me use some of your oil. So what did Lothran really say?"

With a heavy sigh, Roningus handed the oil over, watching as Ionnus took the soft cloth to his blade as he replied. "He said he'd take it in to consideration. I do not think he truly believes there is any real threat. More than likely, he believes the 'abductions' to be no more than the presence of some wild animal that has grown bold and developed a taste for human flesh now. More than likely, he'll have us riding for Ascention at dawn so he can inform the Journeymen and they can dispatch a few of their Rangers to deal with it. Use a circular motion; it spreads the oil out more evenly."

Nodding, Ionnus began to do as Roningus had said, and was about to speak when Sir Grisbane came hurrying up to them. He spoke in bursts between deep breaths, his voice with a great sense of urgency.

"Have…either…of you…seen…Sir Lothran?!"

Ionnus and Roningus glanced at each other, the two of them looking up to Grisbane and shaking their heads in unison.

"No, why?" Ionnus asked, tilting his head inquisitively.

"Sir Resmeron hasn't…seen him either!" Grisbane huffed, catching his breath gradually.

For several seconds the two contemplated this, until Ionnus spoke up again, sounding unperturbed. "Has anyone asked around? He may have simply turned in for the night. Probably wants to get an early start tomorrow morning on our trip back to Ascention."

Grisbane shook his head, his eyes wide with concern. "We checked in with the family that was hosting him, and they said he hasn't been back to the house since he first approached them and paid them to stay under their roof."

Immediately, Roningus reached down, snatching up his helmet and standing from his seat. "Where was Lothran staying?"

Taken slightly aback by Roningus's sudden commanding attitude, Grisbane had to think for a moment before turning and pointing towards a house. "That one, there. With the Royce family."

"Come with me," Roningus said, his cape whipping behind him as he strode towards the small house confidently.

When Grisbane looked down to Ionnus, Ionnus simply shrugged, scooping up his helmet and falling in behind Roningus next to Grisbane.

When the door swung open, a leery-eyed man glanced out at them, his expression immediately growing worrisome when he saw the three church knights standing at his door. Roningus stood with his helmet tucked under his arm and stared sternly back at him.

In a quivering voice, the man spoke. "L-look, like I already told your companion there…I don't know nothing about where the one with the purple cape went…if it's about the coppers, you can have them back if it's that impor—"

"Keep the pennies. We just want to ask you a few questions," Ionnus said, doing his best to sound comforting.

The man stared at him for a moment, then meekly shook his head. "N-no, it's getting late, and I'd prefer not to disturb my wife and children…so if you would, please clear out, alright?"

Just as he was about to close the door, Roningus reached out, grabbing hold of it. For several long seconds, he simply stared into the man's eyes, his expression hard and his gaze cold. When he spoke, his voice sounded gruff as it always did.

"Invite us in. Our oathbrother has gone missing, and you were the last one to see him. Or should we force our way in and conduct a full search of the house to make certain you haven't detained him?"

The man's mouth dropped open, and for several long seconds one could practically hear the wheels turning in his head, trying to decide whether or not Roningus would make good on his threat. When Roningus gave a hard pull on the door as if to wrench it from his hands, the man released it immediately, averting his eyes from Roningus's gaze.

"Y-yes, of course…c-c-come in…we can sit at the table, but like I already told you, I don't know nothing…"

"Thank you," Roningus said, entering the small house.

The man continued to hold the door, Grisbane and Ionnus entering somewhat timidly and awkwardly nodding both their thanks and their apologies for Roningus's behavior, the man avoiding their eyes the entire time. Once they were inside, the three of them took their seats at the table, the man shuffling in behind them. His wife, a portly woman with dirty blonde hair dressed in a long-sleeved white blouse with a shawl draped over her shoulders and a rough spun skirt, looked up from the fireplace, stirring something in a pot. Her eyes grew wide at the presence of the church knights, and her husband shrugged helplessly to her, at which point she plodded barefoot over to the table, doing her best to sound brave and polite.

"Would m'lords care for some supper?"

Looking up to her, Roningus spoke in a firm tone, yet not without a sense of genuine appreciation. "No, but thank you for your hospitality."

Then, without another word, he looked to the man and pointed at the empty seat across the table from him, the man obeying and taking his seat without looking up from the table.

That done, Roningus addressed the woman without looking up. "Would you care to join us, my lady? Your husband was just about to tell us about the last time he saw our oathbrother Sir Lothran, and perhaps you could help him fill in some of the gaps."

Tentatively, the woman sat next to her husband, meeting eyes with Roningus and speaking in a pleading tone. "Please, m'lord, you must believe us...we didn't do nothing with your friend!"

Roningus nodded silently, staring quietly at the two of them.

"Tell us what you—" Ionnus began, but Roningus quickly raised his hand and silenced him, cutting him off. For several moments, none of them said anything, Grisbane and Ionnus watching on in fascination as the husband suddenly began to speak.

"It was shortly after he'd approached us about staying here... paid us eight coppers for room and board...then he said he was going out to talk to some of the other families about the...the disappearances..."

Roningus nodded again, remaining silent, and after a few seconds the wife spoke up again.

"He asked us if we knew anything, and truth be told, we didn't…none of us do, really, and that's the honest truth…people disappearing, and no one knows where or why…some folks say they heard things at night, unnatural noises coming from the woods…usually on the nights people go missing…"

When neither the husband nor the wife said anything else, Roningus sighed deeply. "Anything else?"

When both of them shook their heads, Roningus nodded one last time.

"Thank you for your time."

The husband nodded, the wife speaking up again. "Are you three going to…to catch them? Whoever's out there, that is?"

"We are," Roningus said, with such conviction that even Grisbane and Ionnus felt the chill of his words. But just then, a blood-curdling scream shattered the tranquility of the small village, and immediately the three church knights rose from their chairs, Roningus bursting through the door with Grisbane and Ionnus right behind him.

Wide-eyed villagers leaned out of their doorways, and when Roningus looked to the nearest one, a horrified looking man pointed his bony finger at a house near the edge of the village. Rushing towards the house, Roningus kicked in the door without so much as breaking his stride.

A woman was huddled in the corner with her arms wrapped protectively around her two children, sobbing uncontrollably and pointing towards the side window, when she looked up and saw the three church knights. Blood ran down the wall from the windowsill, spreading out on the ground in a wide pool.

"What happened?!" Grisbane cried out, pushing past Roningus and rushing over to the woman and her children.

"They took him!" the woman wailed hysterically, fighting just to maintain enough composure to speak. "They came in the window and took the other church knight!"

At once, all three paladins drew their swords, Roningus brandishing his with a flourish and approaching the window aggressively. Ionnus stepped over to the woman and her children, putting himself between them and the window, keeping his shield raised defensively and his sword held in a low back position. Grisbane stood in the middle of the room, facing the door with his own sword and shield at the ready.

As Roningus reached the window, he stopped, listening for a moment before leaning out and looking around. It was then that he spotted the tip of a plate mail boot, disappearing behind the house as if it were being dragged.

"Outside!" Roningus hissed, planting his left hand on the windowsill and vaulting through it.

Grisbane turned, pointing at the woman and her children as he spoke hurriedly to Ionnus. "Stay with them!"

That said, Grisbane rushed towards the window, climbing through as quickly as he could, looking left then right before spotting Roningus's brown cape whipping around the corner behind the house. Taking off after him, Grisbane rounded the corner, nearly crashing into Roningus who had come to a sudden halt.

Before them stood a man with skin as pale as the moon, his ghastly complexion possessing an eerie, unnatural looking glow. His eyes, narrowed at Roningus and unblinking, had no irises, the large black pupils nearly comprising their entirety. His long, bone-white hair hung down his back in waves, and tight-fitting blue velvet nobleman's clothes clung to his slender frame complete with a half-cape. In his right hand, he held the limp figure of Sir Resmeron up by his throat, keeping him close as if holding him hostage.

Sir Resmeron gasped weakly for breath, blood running down his face freely from a large gash in the side of his head. The pale man's fingers were tipped not with nails, but with sharp, animalistic claws, the points of which dug into Resmeron's neck. When the pale man spoke, his voice was high pitched, unusually calm, and with great precision in his enunciation.

"Church knights."

"Vampire," Roningus said, giving his swords another flourish and standing at the ready.

The pale man grinned, showing his red-stained teeth to be razor-sharp jagged points. Glancing back at Grisbane, the pale man spoke again. "Oh my. Two against one. This hardly seems fair."

"Let him go…" Grisbane said in a dangerous tone, moving to stand next to Roningus and gripping the sword in his right hand tightly.

The pale man chuckled silently, the heaving motion of his chest looking forced and unnatural, as if he'd forgotten how to laugh properly. As he spoke again, he tilted his head inquisitively. "And if…I refuse?"

"Find out," came Roningus's response, drawing his left sword back by his right side and holding his right sword up behind his head parallel with his shoulders, preparing to strike.

"I see…" said the pale man, watching Roningus with an amused expression.

But then, drawing a deep rasping breath, Resmeron spoke in a pained whisper. "Kill…me…"

It was then that Grisbane looked down, taking in Resmeron's condition for the first time, and spotting the bite marks half-concealed by his plate mail.

"He's been bitten!" Grisbane cried out, the pale man's sickening grin widening into a full smile.

Immediately, Roningus lunged forward. The pale man tossed Resmeron aside like a rag doll, dashing backwards out of the way of Roningus's swords. Grisbane hurried forward, kneeling down next to Resmeron and helping him sit up a bit. Resmeron reached up weakly with his hand, grabbing hold of the front of Grisbane's plate.

"Kill…me…don't   want…to   bec-come…must…..with Mithos…" Resmeron's breath grew shallower by the second, and within minutes, Grisbane knew he'd begin to turn. A slow, gradual process that lasted almost an entire night, but if the victim's life was cut short before it could begin, they would be spared vampiric affliction.

Grisbane set his sword down, then reached back and retrieved a dagger sheathed near the back of his waist. With a trembling hand, he brought it around, his voice quivering with fear and anger all at once as he spoke. "Mithos's blessings be upon you, oathbrother… may you find the All Father's eternal embrace."

With his left hand, Resmeron mustered what little strength he had left, reaching out and grabbing hold of Grisbane's hand. "Do it…"

Grisbane sniffed loudly, tears welling up in his eyes as he brought the dagger up, putting the point just under Resmeron's throat pointing down towards his heart. Then, summoning all of his will power, he thrust the dagger down forcefully, the blade sliding behind Resmeron's collarbone. When Resmeron coughed, blood spattered from his mouth onto Grisbane's arm, and with a sharp twist to the left and right, the main arteries were severed. Then, pulling the dagger out and laying it aside, Grisbane held Resmeron in his arms, tears streaming down his face as he held his dying oathbrother in his arms for the final moments of his life.

Meanwhile, as Roningus slashed out in a rapid chain of fluid swings, the vampire continued to dash backwards out of the way, the grin slowly fading from his face as Roningus's swords got closer and closer. Realizing Roningus was rapidly learning his pattern of movement and adapting, the vampire planted himself, and when Roningus swung hard with his left sword, he pivoted to the right, then spun and dropped down into a leg sweep meant to bring the church knight to the ground. But Roningus reacted just as quickly, jumping into the air to avoid the maneuver and spinning in a full 360 degrees, extending the swords and slashing at the vampire as he did. The carefully honed edges of the swords cut deep, the left one leaving a long open gash in the side of the vampire's face while the right one caught him in the back of the head, a wide length of severed hair falling from his head as the blade opened a wound in his skull. No blood spilled from the wounds, and the red gashes almost immediately began to close up.

The vampire reeled back, staggering to his feet just as Roningus landed, immediately following up with a hard downward cleave from his right sword that nearly split the vampire's face in two, the force of the swing so strong it bent the vampire forward. From there, Roningus pivoted to the left, and with a fluid motion swung both swords up above his head, bringing them down on the back of the vampire's neck in tandem. The blades cleaved clean through flesh and bone and sent the head rolling away from the vampire's body as it collapsed in a heap on the ground, the dark red muscles of his neck wet with blood.

Roningus walked over to the head, rolling it over so that it was staring up at him, the vampire's eyes still blinking as it glared at him furiously. Roningus reached down, putting the point of the sword in his right hand into the vampire's right eye, the vampire's reflexive reaction of closing his eyelids doing nothing to prevent the sharp point from passing easily through the thin layer of skin and on into the gelatinous mass of his eyeball. Once he had done this, Roningus spoke in a voice with a calmness that surpassed even the vampire's.

"When the dead god asks, tell him the Wrathful Tempest sent you."

That said, Roningus lifted the head upright with the point of his sword so the vampire could watch what he was about to do. Leaving the head with a clear view, Roningus casually strolled over to the crumpled body that lay on the ground, kicking it over onto its back. The vampire's remaining eye widened in horror, its mouth opening in a silent scream as there were no lungs to push air over its vocal chords. Then, sheathing the sword in his left hand with a casual flourish, Roningus planted his feet shoulder width apart, standing over top of the body and taking his right sword in both hands, moving the point over top of the chest. Glancing over to the vampire's head one final time, Roningus thrust down hard with his left hand on the pommel, then abruptly twisted left and right for good measure.

The body convulsed wildly, Roningus planting his left foot on the stomach to hold it down, the vampire's one good eye rolling into the back of his head. When the body finally went still, blood began gushing out of the neck, the vampire's mouth falling open as a pool began to form around it as well. That done, Roningus turned and walked over towards where Grisbane knelt, still holding Resmeron in his arms.

Grisbane shook with silent sobs, and when Roningus saw the bloody dagger lying on the ground, he immediately understood. "I had no choice…I couldn't let him turn…" Grisbane said, looking up to Roningus afterwards.

Roningus nodded silently, pulling out a cloth and wiping the blood off his sword.

Back inside the woman's house, the three paladins sat around her table, all of them staring solemnly into the bowls of hot stew she had insisted on making them. Outside, the fire they had built to burn the vampire's corpse had begun to die down; the creature's remains had created a flame that burned white hot for nearly an hour, and provided the light to dig Resmeron's grave.

Roningus sat with his helmet and gauntlets lying on the table, his hands wrapped around his wooden bowl, while Grisbane sat with his hands on his knees, his eyes still bloodshot and bleary. Ionnus sighed heavily, sipping at the contents of his bowl before speaking in a reverent tone.

"The woman has asked that one of us stay here for the night to put her children at ease."

Roningus glanced over at Grisbane, who had been silent ever since Resmeron died in his arms. Grisbane gave no indication of having heard what was said. When it was clear that the now highest-ranking church knight among them was not going to assign one of them to the task, Roningus looked over to Ionnus.

"Go ahead."

Ionnus nodded, going silent again for a few seconds before speaking in a tentative voice. "Actually…I believe she requested you…"

Roningus looked back over to Ionnus again for a moment, then wordlessly nodded his consent, his eyes returning to his bowl of stew.

"M'lords…is there anything else I can get you?" the woman asked sheepishly, appearing from the only other room in the small cabin.

Ionnus turned, smiling reassuringly and shaking his head. "No, but thank you, milady. Your hospitality is tremendously appreciated. It isn't often we are treated to such fine home cooking."

The woman smiled, lowering her eyes and visibly embarrassed by the compliment. Appearing to be no more than perhaps a decade older than them, her attractive features were done no favors by the simple garb she wore: rough spun clothes and a hooded shawl that hung down past her waist to help keep her warm, her dark brown doe-like eyes glancing up and looking almost hesitant to pose her next question.

"Begging your pardon, but…will one of you be staying this evening, in case one of those…those things…comes back?"

Ionnus nodded, taking another sip from his bowl before replying. "Sir Roningus will be staying here this evening to safeguard you and your children."

When Roningus looked up to her and nodded solemnly, a look of relief washed over her, the sound of one of the children whimpering calling her away with a polite curtsey. Once she was gone, Ionnus turned to Roningus.

"I'm going to get Grisbane back to his host family's home. Want me to stop back afterwards?"

Roningus shook his head, to which Ionnus nodded, reaching out gathering up his helmet as well as Grisbane's, taking him by the arm, and helping him up from the table.

"Come, oathbrother. Let us take our leave. Roningus will handle it from here."

Wordlessly Grisbane stood on unsure footing, allowing himself to be lead from the house.

For several minutes, Roningus sat silent and motionless, staring at the surface of the table, his eyebrows furrowed as if in concentration. Then, finally, with a heavy sigh, he raised the bowl to his lips, taking his first sip of the stew and chewing on it thoughtfully.

"How does it taste?" the woman asked, standing half-concealed by the doorway and looking out at Roningus.

Roningus looked up, finished chewing, and swallowed, nodding his silent approval. As he did, the woman slowly made her way out towards the table, taking a seat across from him. Folding her arms under her bust, the two met eyes and continued to stare for a few seconds, until finally she broke the silence again.

"That thing you fought…it was a vampire?"

Roningus said nothing, but when he nodded slowly again the woman trembled slightly at the thought.

Forcing herself to be strong, she nodded once, speaking again. "Do you think there will be more of them?"

Roningus looked down at the table again, hesitating for a moment before looking back up, his eyes meeting hers as he frowned and nodded a third time.

The woman let out a small gasp before burying her face in her hands, sobbing quietly. Wincing at the sight, Roningus set his bowl down, rising slowly from the table and making his way around to her, the woman rising from her chair and wrapping her arms around him the moment he was within reach. For several minutes the woman clung tightly to him, Roningus wrapping his right arm around her waist and holding her gently, patting the small of her back with his left.

"My husband…he was the first to go missing…" she said in a quiet, sorrowful voice, her eyes wet with tears. "Tell me…he didn't turn into one of them, did he?" When Roningus didn't speak, she leaned back a bit, looking into his eyes and pleading silently with him for an answer.

Roningus looked away for a moment before meeting her gaze again as he spoke. "I wish I could tell you he hasn't, but the truth is I simply don't know."

Nodding, the woman pulled away, wiping her eyes dry and sniffling. "I'll bring you some blankets and a bedroll…you must be weary after all you've done tonight…"

Shaking his head, Roningus returned to his seat at the table. "That will not be necessary. But thank you, all the same."

The following morning, Ionnus and Grisbane met Roningus at the door to the woman's home just as he was emerging, the sun already three finger widths up from the horizon. Grisbane had dark circles beginning to form under his eyes, but he no longer stared catatonically at the ground as he had before. Ionnus looked only slightly better, and as the two approached, Ionnus smiled sadly as he looked over at the mound where Resmeron was buried, the fire that had consumed the vampire's remains having long since died out.

"What do we do now?" Ionnus asked, looking over to Grisbane.

Grisbane looked at him blankly for a moment, then turned and stared at Roningus.

"Are you willing to voluntarily relinquish command of this unit, Sir Grisbane?" Roningus asked after a moment of silence.

When Grisbane nodded, Roningus turned to Ionnus.

"We hunt them down, we put them to the sword, and when it's done we watch their lair burn to the ground. These people deserve no less."

Trailed by Grisbane and Ionnus, Roningus approached the small house of the old man Harkon had directed him to at a brisk pace, his helmet tucked under his left arm. The old man seated next to the door eyed him suspiciously, frowning distrustfully before leaning over to spit out of the corner of his mouth. He wore a simple pair of rough spun coveralls, a long-sleeved white shirt, and a straw hat, his bare feet caked with mud. Lying on the ground next to him, a red-eyed bloodhound raised its head, sniffing at them and letting out a half-hearted bark as they approached. The old man folded his arms, and squinted at them from under the brim of his hat.

Ionnus spoke in a polite formal tone. "Greetings, sir. I am Sir Ionnus the Righteous Shield. Your friend Harkon told us—"

"He ain't my friend," the old man said, his frown growing sourer as he spat again.

Ionnus hesitated for a moment, glancing over to Roningus.

Roningus simply stared at the man with a cool expression, his eyes narrowed slightly.

"Yes. Well, at any rate, Harkon told us you and your hound have been known to do a bit of tracking. Would you be willing to assist us in a matter of church business?" Though it was Ionnus that spoke, the old man met Roningus's gaze as he replied, speaking to Roningus as if he were the one who had asked.

"Might be that I could. What's in it for me?"

Just as Ionnus was about to open his mouth, Roningus interjected. "The safety of your village. If you wish to put a price on your life, however, we can pay you in coppers."

The old man chuckled once silently, still frowning as he did so. When he said nothing in response, Roningus knelt down, setting his helmet down and removing his right gauntlet, holding it out towards the dog as he spoke again.

"What's the dog's name?"

"Sebastian, but he doesn't take kindly to strangers."

It was just then that Sebastian let out a light whine, pushing himself up off the ground and plodding over to Roningus. After sniffing the church knight's hand for a moment, the large bloodhound licked it a few times. Roningus reached up and scratched behind Sebastian's ear as he looked back up to the old man, who watched on in disbelief.

"Seems friendly enough to me. Will five coppers for a few hours of your time be sufficient?"

The old man stared at Roningus, his mouth moving silently as he tried to form words, until finally he nodded his head. "When are we heading out?"

Standing, Roningus gave Sebastian a final pat before donning his gauntlet and scooping up his helmet. "As soon as possible."

Using one of Lothran's personal effects from the saddle bags of his horse, Sebastian took to the scent quickly, and in no time was dragging the old man along behind him with the three paladins closely following. It wasn't far in before Sebastian led them off the beaten path, however, leading them further and further in until suddenly the dog stopped short. Turning and looking back to the old man, the blood hound whined loudly, heading back in the direction they had come from and tugging at his leash.

"Sebastian, what's gotten in to you?" the old man said, kneeling down and petting Sebastian comfortingly. Yet still, Sebastian persisted, anxiously pulling on the leash as he tried to double back. Shaking his head, the old man reached back with his free hand and scratched his neck. "I ain't never seen him act like this."

Roningus glanced in the direction they were headed, rising up on the balls of his feet to get a better view. Then, turning to the old man, he reached into a belt pouch, producing a handful of pennies and handing them over. "Leave a trail for us so we can find our way back."

The old man nodded as Roningus knelt down and petted Sebastian one last time.

"Good boy."

Sebastian whined, longer and louder this time, as if pleading with Roningus to return with him. When he stood, Roningus nodded to the old man, who in turn headed off with Sebastian, breaking sticks and shuffling his feet as he went.

Once they were gone, Roningus turned to Ionnus and Grisbane. "Swords," he said calmly, drawing his weapons from the back of his waist.

Grisbane and Ionnus followed suit, and the three paladins proceeded forward.

As the three stepped cautiously through the forest, Grisbane spoke in a quiet tone. "I had no idea you're so good with animals."

Roningus glanced back at Grisbane, who'd barely spoken a word since the death of Resmeron,. "I've always liked dogs."

With a gesture from Roningus, they fell silent, approaching what appeared to be an embankment that overlooked a clearing. Coming to a halt at the edge of it, the three leaned over the edge, peering down at the grizzly scene below. Trees jutting up from the ground all the way down the moderate incline were strewn with bones strung together, the various shapes and sizes recognizably human in nature. So numerous were they that each tree had enough lines hanging from its branches to make it impossible to traverse the slope without disturbing them, the lines clattering gently when the breeze picked up as they collided against each other rhythmically.

Where the ground evened out, a large cavern entrance formed naturally from a cliff side was seen. It was there they spotted Sir Lothran; stripped of his armor and all clothing, he appeared to have been tortured to near-death before being crucified, his arms and legs outstretched and nailed to the two thick wooden beams that had been pieced together in an X formation jutting from the ground.

"Sir Lothran!" Ionnus cried, rushing forward and sliding down the embankment without a moment's hesitation as Roningus reached out in vain to grab him.

Hacking his way through the bone rattles, Ionnus quickly sheathed his sword as he reached Sir Lothran. Roningus and Grisbane made their way down, cursing with every step.

"Sir Lothran...can you hear me?" Ionnus said apprehensively, immediately gasping as he drew close enough to assess the condition his fallen oathbrother was in. Tall as he was, Ionnus came up only to Lothran's waist due to how high up he was on the cross.

Glancing up, it was seen that large spikes had been pounded between the bones in his forearm just beneath his wrist to nail him to the wood. A matching pair was driven through each of his feet as well, and a spiked metal chain securing his waist where the two wooden cross beams dug into his flesh. Strips of his shredded skin hung lose all over his body, and his hollow eye sockets dripped with the oozing remains of his eyeballs where they appeared to have been burnt out with a hot poker.

As Roningus and Grisbane approached, Grisbane immediately looked away, removing his helmet and doubling over before retching violently. Roningus stood next to Ionnus, staring up silently at the disfigured corpse of Sir Lothran for several seconds.

"Help me get him down."

Working together, the three of them pulled the cross down, carefully lowering it to the ground. Once it was on the ground, they found the spikes were too long to be pulled out with the means at their disposal, and Roningus was the only one capable of bringing himself to pull Lothran's limbs up off of the spikes. Once it was done, he removed the chain, and Ionnus helped him lift the body and move it away from the area. That done, the three knelt down before their fallen oathbrother, Grisbane shaking slightly and Ionnus visibly troubled.

Glancing over at Roningus, Grisbane spoke in a tone of disbelief. "How can you be so calm?! Look what they did to him!"

Roningus sighed heavily, a moment's silence preceding his reply, and when he spoke, his tone was pensive. "As with Sir Resmeron, this man's death pains me a great deal. But now is not the time to grieve our fallen oathbrother." Then, Roningus looked up to the cavern entrance as he continued. "What does the final line in the code of conduct tell us, Sir Grisbane?"

Glancing over to Roningus, Grisbane pondered his words for a moment, answering in an increasingly assured tone. "Face evil with no fear in your heart, for the All Father guides your blade and watches over you."

With a nod, Sir Roningus stood, reaching back and drawing his swords once more. "Come, oathbrothers. Let us avenge our fallen comrade, and drive out this darkness that plagues these farmers."

As the three made their way into the entrance of the cavern, they silently drew their weapons. Taking a moment to allow their eyes to adjust, they followed the cavern until the rough walls took on a hewn look, the uneven floor smoothing out considerably. Just as the light began to grow too faint to see, torch sconces appeared along the walls, lighting the way. Then, after venturing in further, the hall opened up into an enormous cavern, a large wooden altar at the back erected with the dead-god's effigy, the human skull with curled ram's horns unmistakable. Two large iron braziers stood on either side of the altar, their fires providing an eerie illumination in the room. To the back of the altar, the cavern continued on, lit by a continuing series of torch sconces.

"Necros," Ionnus said, his voice dripping with enmity.

A row of stone benches lead up to the altar, the altar room large enough to host a small number of the dead-god's followers. Roningus strode up to the altar, staring up at the banner bearing the ram-horned skull and glancing over at the brazier to the right of the altar for a moment, but turning as Grisbane spoke.

"We should report back to Ascension. Let them send in a unit of black capes and clerics to properly dismantle and hallow this place."

"We will," said Roningus, turning and heading towards the entrance at the back of the room. "As soon as we retrieve Sir Lothran's sword and armor."

Further down the hallway, the corridor grew narrow, forcing the paladins into a single file, until it split off in two directions, the left inclining upwards slightly and appearing to wind around while the right continued on straight, then opened up into a pitch black room.

Sheathing the sword in his left hand, Roningus took a torch from its sconce and stepped in, holding it out. Ornate wooden coffins lined the floors in two rows of three. Immediately, Roningus stopped in his tracks, backing slowly and silently out of the room, motioning towards Ionnus and Grisbane to move out of his way. Once they were back at the divide, Roningus breathed a quiet sigh of relief.

"What is it?" Ionnus asked.

"Vampires."

"What should we do?" Grisbane asked, glancing down the corridor at the dark room.

With a nod of his head, Roningus motioned towards the left path, and the three made their way up and around the winding incline.

Coming to a large wooden door reinforced with iron, Roningus stopped outside, leaning in close to listen. For a few seconds he stood and listened as a pair of voices was heard coming from within.

"...how many are left?"

"Three of them. I suspect they slew Cedric; he did not return before sunrise."

"It is only a matter of time before they come for us."

"I am well aware, but first they will return to Ascention to call in reinforcements. Followers of the false father are nothing if not predictable."

At that moment, Roningus leaned back, then lunged forward and put his shoulder into the door, ramming it open. Immediately, two men robed in black stood from a table, their expressions horrified as the three paladins rushed into the room, Roningus pointing the tips of his swords at one while Grisbane and Ionnus forced the other to his knees. The room was luxuriously decorated, the ornate wooden table laid out with a map of the surrounding area, as well as a map of the Western Kingdoms.

Glancing around the room, Roningus spotted Lothran's gear heaped on top of a pile of the personal effects of countless other victims. Looking back to the black robed man, when Roningus spoke, his voice was icy cold.

"The punishment for practicing necromancy is immediate execution. Speak your last words, heretic. The judgment of the All Father is upon you."

The robed man smiled wickedly, showing his crooked, bony yellow teeth. "My death will stop nothing, church knight. Followers of the false-father are hopelessly outnumbered. You cannot hope to—"

With a flash of Roningus's longswords, the robed necromancer's head rolled from his shoulders onto the ground, his face frozen in a mixture of derision and despair. As the body crumpled to the ground, Roningus turned and pointed to the remaining necromancer, speaking in a commanding tone.

"Bind and gag him. We're bringing him back to Ascention for questioning. Grisbane, gather up these maps and notes."

As the two went to work binding the man's wrists with strips of sack cloth, Grisbane turned to Roningus. "What of the coffins downstairs? Leaving them behind would be unwise, lest they come for us again in the night."

For a moment, Roningus thought silently. Then, glancing at one of the torches sitting in its sconce, he sheathed the sword in his left hand and lifted it from the wall. Approaching the terrified man that was being bound, Roningus knelt down and addressed him calmly.

"Where do you keep your sacramental spirits, heretic?"

As the rain grew from a light drizzle to a steady fall, the city guard assigned to the gate huddled closer to the large metal brazier, pulling his cloak more tightly and feeling an increasing sense of appreciation for the small canopy roof over his head. Being in the early hours of the morning, it came as a great surprise when there suddenly came a shout from the front of the gate. The guard stepped out into the rain and peered down over the edge.

"Identify yourself!" he shouted, glancing back at the inviting blaze of the fiery brazier, promising warmth and dryness.

"Sir Ionnus the Righteous Shield!"

Doing a quick count of the figures he could make out, the guard spotted two others on horseback, and a fourth man who appeared to be bound by the wrists. "Who are the others, then?!"

"Sir Grisbane the Herald of Justice, and Sir—"

"Open. The gate. NOW. Or answer to High Priest Argos for delaying us," came a second voice, the stern tone and forceful delivery jarring the gate guard from his bleary state.

Leaning over further and squinting his eyes, it was then the guard was able to make out who they really were. "Church knights? What are you doing out in the middle of the night?"

Yet even as he spoke, the guard began turning the winch, opening the gates just wide enough for the three men and their guest to pass through. Once they had, he cranked the gates back shut, returning to his fire and watching as the three paladins trotted down the wide street that lead to the main cathedral, practically dragging the sopping wet man behind them as he struggled to keep up.

"His methods are unacceptable. You read Sir Ionnus' report: the man forced himself into a civilian's home and proceeded to intimidate them into telling them what he wanted to hear." Brogam frowned as he spoke, his eyebrows furrowed as he looked across the room at Vogoth.

Vogoth sighed, tilting his head in admission as he began to reply. "It is true, his ways were not entirely within the code of conduct, but were it not for him, we would be blind as to the threat that has been rallying against us right in our own back yard. Not only that, but he dismantled a heretical church and—"

"By burning it!" Brogam cried, his voice bordering on hysteria. "Imagine what would have happened if the fires had spread!"

Vogoth narrowed his eyes on Brogam, struggling to hide the irritation in his voice. "You're over-reacting, Brogam, and your bias against the Wrathful Tempest is clearly clouding your judgment. The simple fact of the matter is he eliminated an entire den of vampires, retrieved the arms and armor of Sir Lothran, and put the minds of an entire farming village at ease by taking command of his unit and upholding the firmest tenants of our faith."

"Whatever came of their prisoner?" came High Priest Argos's voice, weary and tired sounding.

"You mean the man Roningus dragged behind him from his horse?" Brogam said, leveling his gaze on Vogoth and speaking in a triumphant tone, as if he'd just proven his point.

"Yes, the necromancer. One and the same," came Vogoth's reply, in a flat voice that yielded nothing.

"That's still no way to treat a captive," Brogam said defensively, sitting upright in his chair as if he'd taken offense.

"Compared to what they did to Sir Lothran, it is downright merciful."

Brogam scowled, at which point Argos interjected once more. "The captive?"

Looking to Argos, Vogoth took on a respectful tone as he responded. "My apologies, your holiness. The captive is in one of our penitent's cells, awaiting judgment and sentencing."

"I see…and where is Sir Roningus now?"

"Presently? I would imagine he's at breakfast, your holiness."

Argos nodded, then turned and pointed to a young acolyte standing near the door. "You there, young lad…go and fetch the Wrathful Tempest for me, won't you? I'd like to hear his account first hand before I make any rash decisions."

"…so then Roningus, he takes the torch, turns to the heretic, and says, 'Watch closely, heretic, for this is what awaits you in the afterlife', then tosses the torch inside, and within minutes the whole place was ablaze! And then, the heretic…BEFOULS his robes, falls to his knees, and starts begging Roningus to have mercy!" As Sir Ionnus spoke, his eyes were wide with excitement, grinning as he recounted the tale, and almost as eager to tell it as the table of paladins that leaned in and hung on his every word were eager to hear it.

A burst of laughter erupted from the gathered crowd. Most of them wore brown capes, but here and there a few blue capes were seen, and a pair of purple caped church knights stood on the fringes of the group, grinning in amusement. From a nearby table, a large gathering of black and purple caped paladins broke their morning fast as usual, pretending not to be interested yet incidentally staying quiet enough to hear all the same.

It was at that moment a young acolyte approached, the young boy no older than eight or nine stepping forward timidly. "I'm looking for Sir Roningus...the Wrathful Tempest?"

Still chuckling, Ionnus turned and looked over to the boy. "What do you want with Roningus, lad?"

The boy looked around nervously at the table of men, who had all gone quiet yet still grinned as they turned to look at him. "High Priest Argos wishes to see him."

With a nod, Ionnus answered in a kindly tone meant to put the boy at ease. "Thank you for the message, lad. He'll be along as soon as he's finished eating."

The boy paused for a moment, then spoke up just as the table was about to return to their food and conversation. "My apologies, Sir Roningus, but...you're supposed to come at once. The council of arch clerics is waiting."

Looking to the boy again, Ionnus chuckled and shook his head. "I'm not Roningus, boy. This here's the man you're looking for." Then, placing his hand on the shoulder of the man seated next to him, he said, "Hear that, Roningus? You'd best get going, then."

Standing from his seat, Roningus scooped up his helmet under his left arm, stepping away from the table and walking briskly past the boy, the young acolyte turning and hurrying after him.

Once they were out of the mess hall, the boy bolstered enough courage to finally speak. "Is it true what they said? Did you really slay a vampire?"

Roningus turned and glanced down at the boy for a moment, looking forward again and saying nothing for several seconds before finally answering. "It is."

"How'd you do it?" the boy asked, gleaming with admiration and curiosity.

"Mithos favors the just."

It wasn't until they reached the doors to the council chambers that the boy spoke again, rushing ahead and pushing the doors open for Roningus. "Good luck in there…"

Just as he was about to walk past the boy, Roningus stopped, turning and kneeling down in front of him. "Luck is just a word invented by those without faith for divine intervention." That said, Roningus grinned slightly, patting the boy on the shoulder as he stood and strode into the council chamber.

"Ah, Sir Roningus…how kind of you to join us," Brogam said in a less than pleasant tone, his frown quickly intensifying as Roningus walked right past him to genuflect before High Priest Argos.

"What would your holiness ask of me?" Roningus said, his head bowed reverently.

Argos smiled, looking over to Brogam and shaking his head. Brogam rolled his eyes, and begrudgingly nodded his approval before Argos turned back to speak with Roningus.

"Stand, Sir Roningus…I would first have information from you."

Doing as he was bid, Roningus rose from the ground, meeting Argos' gaze and standing at full attention with his helmet tucked under his left arm.

"Tell us, what exactly did you find within that cave?" Vogoth asked, and it wasn't until Argos nodded his permission that Roningus turned to face Vogoth.

"A church of heretics, and a den of vampires enthralled in service to the dead god."

"These documents…the ones you say you took from their church…according to these, there are churches to the dead god sprouting up all across the Western Kingdoms. You say you found these in the necromancer's quarters?"

When Roningus nodded, Vogoth looked over to Brogam. For a long moment Brogam regarded Roningus, until finally he spoke.

"What possessed you to burn the majority of the evidence to support your claims?"

After getting another nod of consent from Argos, Roningus turned his attention to Brogam, calmly meeting the arch cleric's gaze and speaking in a perfunctorily polite tone. "Without farmers there would be no food, arch cleric. I thought it a service not only to the farmers but the city of Ascension itself to put the dead god's abominations to the fire, while at the same time dismantling a place of blasphemous worship."

"What, so we're to thank you for your rash behavior?"

As Roningus answered, he turned his attention back to Argos. "The farmers did."

Argos smiled, speaking in his tired sounding voice. "I've heard all I need to hear. Sir Roningus, step forward please."

Stepping forward, Roningus dropped to one knee before the high priest as Argos spoke again.

"It is not often that Mithos calls upon one of his servants so hastily, but you have answered that call with unsurpassed devotion and bravery."

As Argos spoke, a black caped paladin entered with a blue cape draped over his left arm. When Roningus rose, the paladin unclasped the brown cape from his pauldrons, removing it and handing it off to the young acolyte who rushed forward from the door, and as he clasped the blue cape to Roningus's shoulders, Argos continued.

"Therefore, it is the decision of the church that you be recognized for valor, and promoted to reflect your newfound position within the order. You will assemble a unit comprised of your oathbrothers, accompanied by a battle cleric, and will investigate the information you have uncovered. These are your orders."

Looking to either side at the blue cape that now hung from his pauldrons, Roningus bowed his head reverently. "As you command, your holiness."

That said, Roningus turned and left on the heels of the black caped paladin and the young acolyte. It wasn't until they were gone that Brogam spoke up again.

"I still do not approve of this."

At that, Argos turned to him and smiled once more. "The records shall indicate as such, one way or the other."

Crouched down, a man in black plate mail grasped a handful of ashes in his right hand, letting it fall through his fingers pensively. The entire cavern still smelled strongly of smoke, but with some work, they had been able to air it out sufficiently enough to enter.

"Our informant within the village said it was knights of the false father. They came as five, but left as three...and took Meliachus captive." A black robed man spoke in an apprehensive tone, as if fearful of the plate mailed man's reaction.

With a heavy sigh, the armored man slid his gauntlet back on, lifting his skull-shaped helm with rams horns from the ground. Slowly stepping over the ash remnants of the vampires' coffins, he stepped back out into the scorched cavern that was once the altar room.

"Half-fiend," he said, his voice cold with anger.

Leaning against a wall in the corridor that lead outside, the half fiend stepped forward, pulling back the hood of his cloak. His eyes, crimson red and dotted with black pupils, narrowed on the plate mailed dreadknight. Crowning his head were bone-like horns, growing out from his skull through his dark blue skin. His fists were wound tightly with rope gloves in the bare-fisted fighting monks' fashion, and a quarterstaff was slung at his back. Clad in customary monk's garb that had been dyed black and with the sleeves ripped off, his face was tattooed in sharp, angular designs, and when he spoke, his purplish-blue tongue flicked over pointed teeth.

"My name is Asmodeus."

The dreadknight smirked, looking Asmodeus up and down as he spoke. "I'm well aware. We're moving ahead with your assignment early."

Frowning, Asmodeus tilted his head. "Necros would not be pleased to hear that you are altering his specific orders to—"

"But you don't answer to Necros in this world, do you, half-fiend?!" The man spun around, staring Asmodeus down with a pair of icy blue eyes. His head was shaven completely bald, his face somewhat gaunt and his skin of a pale complexion.

Asmodeus clenched his fists, and as he did, the bald dreadknight chuckled.

"There's a good dog. Now…as I was saying, I think it's time we sent the church of the false father a message…"

"Of course I'll go along. It isn't like you have any other friends, anyways," Ionnus said, smiling and sopping up brown gravy from the bottom of his wooden bowl with a chunk of bread before stuffing it in his mouth.

Grisbane sat next to him, his hands wrapped around a cup of water that he stared into thoughtfully for several seconds before looking up finally, nodding with a stern look of consent. "I'll go."

That said, Roningus grinned slightly, nodding once.

As Ionnus finished chewing and swallowed, he reached over as if to take Grisbane's water. Grisbane pulled it away defensively, and Ionnus chuckled.

"They're sending a battle cleric with us," Roningus said. His words brought both Grisbane and Ionnus up short, and they turned to gawk openly at Roningus.

"Wait…what? Battle cleric? What exactly are you signing us up for?" Ionnus said, Grisbane reflecting his sentiments in his own concerned expression.

"We're investigating one of the locations mentioned in the notes we uncovered in the caverns. I've already told you this."

"Right…that would be the generalized version of it…" Ionnus said as he leaned back from the table, clasping his hands behind his head, "…but you still haven't given me any real details, and if things are serious enough that they're sending one of those…"

For a moment, Ionnus closed his eyes, as if refraining from speaking what was on his mind and searching for a better way to phrase it.

"Lunatics!" Grisbane cried out, albeit quietly enough that his voice didn't travel too far.

Glancing over at Grisbane, Ionnus nodded, looking back to Roningus and leaning forward as Grisbane continued.

"Don't get me wrong, I admire the intensity of their faith, but those men actively try to get themselves killed!"

Frowning, Roningus shook his head. "They're no good to the All Father dead, and they're well aware of it. Not to mention their undeniable attunement with the divine makes them indispensable in the field."

Ionnus shrugged, and began to put his gauntlets back on as he spoke. "Fine. Bring him along. But I'm not digging his grave when the fool gets himself killed."

As the three paladins entered the nave, they stopped for a moment to look around and immediately spotted their man. Openly kneeling in the middle of the main aisle near the foot of the dais that lead to the altar, he wore a simple blue and white tabard belted around his waist. It hung down to his knees with the symbol of Mithos displayed proudly on the front, his muscled arms bare and his hands folded in front of him clasping a holy symbol that hung around his neck from a silver chain. White leggings and leather boots comprised the remainder of his attire, and long flowing blonde hair hung down to his mid-back.

As the three approached him slowly, Roningus cleared his throat quietly as if to speak, but was instantly cut off by the cleric's light, almost musical voice.

"Kneel with me, brothers, and pray for safety in our journey."

Glancing at one another, the paladins shrugged, seeing no harm in doing so. Kneeling down next to him, the three said their silent prayers, and were about to rise when the cleric held out a hand to stay their position.

"Remain kneeling…"

Looking over to Roningus, Ionnus frowned, to which Roningus responded by narrowing his eyes, then focusing his gaze on the cleric.

Opening his mouth, the cleric cut him off once again. "Surely three anointed knights of the church would not pass up one last opportunity to spend a few minutes in the All Father's holy presence?"

Grisbane dropped his head dejectedly. Ionnus closed his eyes, sighing quietly and folding his hands again. Roningus frowned at the cleric once more, then stared at the altar. It was in this manner they passed the next several minutes, the cleric remaining still as a statue with his hands folded in front of him.

Finally, the cleric blessed himself quietly, then rose from his knees, the paladins doing the same. Turning to face Roningus, the cleric's eyes were seen to be a deep blue in color, the shade constantly moving as if comprised of a blue fire. Smiling warmly, the cleric reached out, taking Roningus's hand in both of his and shaking it as he spoke.

"Mithos's blessings be upon you, Sir Roningus. I am Osric, and I will be accompanying you and your oathbrothers."

"You will be a welcome addition to our unit, Cleric Osric."

"Osric will suffice," Osric said, still smiling brightly.

"Very well, then. This is Sir Ionnus the Righteous Shield…" As Roningus introduced Ionnus, Osric moved over, taking Ionnus's hand in his and shaking it in the sincerest display of genuine pleasure at being introduced that any of them had ever seen.

"Sir Ionnus. Mithos's blessings be upon you."

Ionnus stared blankly at Osric for a moment before bowing his head appreciatively. "A-And you as well."

Nodding once as if to confirm what Ionnus had said, Osric turned his attention to Grisbane before Roningus had even begun speaking.

"And this is Sir Grisbane the Herald of Justice."

Taking Grisbane's hand, Osric immediately looked down, turning it over in his own hands a few times before looking up at Grisbane, his smile returning. "You have the hands of a healer. Perhaps it is that you've missed your true calling. Tell me…have you ever considered the clerical path?"

Looking down at his hands for a moment, Grisbane looked back up, shaking his head and unsure of what to say.

In response, Osric simply chuckled once silently, his smile widening as he spoke. "Your honesty is a true virtue. Mithos's blessings be upon you."

"Yes. Well then, our orders are to gather our things and head out as soon as we can. If the notes we uncovered are true, we know where another church of the dead god might be found."

At the mention of Necros, Osric's warm, genial expression suddenly grew cold, turning to level his narrowed eyes on Roningus and speaking with a newfound sense of purpose backed by a divine calling. "I shall gather my belongings at once."

Outside in the stable yard, the three paladins were filling their saddle bags with necessary provisions and gear when Osric reappeared, leading the most pristine white mustang the three of them had ever seen. What drew their attention more, however, was Osric's weapon: a studded two-handed club wrought from solid adamantine, with leather wrapped around its handle and a single short, wide-based spike on the top. Osric had it holstered at his back, as unaware of it as if it weren't even there.

"HOLY—do you SEE that thing?!" Ionnus cried, Roningus immediately silencing him with a gesture.

"Yes, now keep your voice down," Roningus replied, casually climbing up onto his horse. Riding over to Osric, Roningus looked over the cleric's belongings with a puzzled expression, while Osric smiled brightly back at him.

"Where's your armor?" Grisbane asked, approaching Osric as well, with Ionnus riding along beside him.

In response, Osric smiled brightly, his flickering blue eyes fixing on the paladin. "I have no need for armor, Sir Grisbane. I armor myself in faith, and the might of the All Father shall be my shield."

As he spoke, Ionnus looked over to Roningus, widening his eyes and smiling as if to gloat about the odds of his previous prediction. In response, Roningus closed his eyes and sighed, and didn't open them when he spoke.

"Mount your horse, Osric. We're heading out."

The ride took several days, which seemed longer due to Osric's insistence upon stopping for half an hour of prayer twice per day. By the third day, the paladins' legs no longer fell asleep from the prolonged periods of kneeling. When the village appeared in the distance early one evening, Ionnus leaned over to speak to Roningus.

"What's the name of this place?"

In response, Roningus shook his head. "It doesn't have a name."

Ionnus sighed, rolling his eyes. "You're kidding me. What do farmers have against naming their settlements?"

"You know how they are. If they don't see a need for something, they don't bother with it," Grisbane replied, bringing his horse up next to Ionnus.

"Just because they don't see the need doesn't mean there isn't one," Ionnus said, to which Grisbane nodded in agreement.

"Their hard work and devotion to a simple life is admirable. There is much to be learned from an honest day's hard work," Osric said, to no one in particular.

"I'm sure there is. As it stands, I sincerely hope this one at least has an inn. We didn't exactly receive a warm reception last time, despite our good intentions," Ionnus said, to which Grisbane responded by smiling.

"Don't count on it," came Roningus's response. "Not only is it unlikely, but keep in mind we're telling these people they could all be in grave danger. We may very well end up sleeping on the floor in the small church they've built. You all brought your bedrolls, right?"

"I have no need for such amenities…I shall find comfort in the presence of the All Father, that surrounds us constantly and watches over us," Osric said, his voice full of conviction.

Roningus nodded once as he replied. "You do that."

As their horses carried them into town, however, it became immediately clear that something was wrong. Doors stood open, carts full of produce were abandoned in the streets, and not a single person nor light within one of the homes that lined the road were to be seen. The only noises to be heard were those of the frogs and the crickets, and a foul, sour stench filled the entire village.

Osric frowned, sniffing the air and looking around. "This town smells of death."

Dismounting from their horses and hitching them in front of the small wooden building that served as a church, Roningus stepped forward and pushed the door open, his eyes going wide as Osric gasped in horror at the sights within.

A cleric, likely one who had been stationed there to say masses and tend to the church, was pinioned to the wall with numerous iron spikes, his body stripped bare down to his waist and his face and chest flayed open with multiple rending wounds. The altar had been pushed over, shattered and burnt, the charred remains sitting amidst a pile of ash. Strewn about the aisles of pews were several corpses, each one looking to have been bludgeoned to death, the pews and floor spattered with their blood. A long, white banner hung from the ceiling above the deceased cleric, its words written in jagged black letters.

BEHOLD THAT WHICH AWAITS THE FALSE FATHER'S WORSHIPPERS

Immediately, Osric pushed past Roningus and rushed forward, beginning to pull spikes from the cleric's body as he turned and spoke to the paladins. "I'll need one of you to assist me!" He spoke with a sense of urgency, and Grisbane nodded, stepping forward and aiding him.

In the meantime, Roningus and Ionnus checked on the bodies of the fallen villagers, studying the corpses for clues as to what had transpired.

"Blunt weapon. Mace, perhaps?" Ionnus said, to which Roningus replied by shaking his head.

"Too clean. Maces do more damage to the skin than this. This looks like the work of a club, or perhaps a quarterstaff."

Nodding, Ionnus looked around for a moment, then up at the banner that hung from the ceiling, watching as Osric and Grisbane got the cleric's body down and laid it on the ground. "Looks like we know why they all left in such a hurry. Whoever did this probably did it in plain sight, and they did it to send a message: this is what happens when you let the church of Mithos into your village."

Roningus sighed, closed his eyes, and rubbed the bridge of his nose between his right thumb and middle finger. "We could have saved them if we'd gotten here sooner."

Ionnus frowned, lowering his head. For several moments they said nothing, while Grisbane and Osric went to work pulling the banner down from the ceiling. Then, a noise came from outside…a low, prolonged moan, human-sounding, and male at that.

Immediately all four looked up, glancing to each other, before rushing to the door and pushing it open. It was then that the source of the sound was seen: a man, his clothes covered in dirt and looking well worn, slowly shuffling towards the doors of the church as if he were in tremendous pain, his gaze cast downward at his bare feet.

"Sir! Are you alright?!" Ionnus shouted, but before he could rush forward, Osric reached out, grasping him by his shoulder and holding him back. "What are you doing?" Ionnus cried, to which Osric responded by silencing him with a gesture, then pointing to the man.

As the farmer continued to move towards them, he slowly raised his eyes up…a pair of glassy white spheres in sunken black eye sockets staring blankly at them, his mouth hanging open to reveal a set of red stained teeth.

"Undead," Osric whispered, his eyes narrowing intensely.

"Swords…" Roningus said, the four of them reaching for their weapons.

The undead farmer let out another long, loud moan, reaching out towards them with clumsy hands, this time his voice being joined by a multitude of others issuing the same mindless groan, coming from all around them.

As the three paladins quickly drew their longswords, Osric calmly stepped forward. Reaching behind his right shoulder, he grasped the handle of his two-handed mace and lifted it from its holster as he approached the undead farmer, the corpse continuing its slow shuffle towards him with outstretched arms.

"Osric, what are you doing?! We're falling back into the church to fortify our position!" Roningus shouted, just as countless more shambling bodies of fallen villagers started coming into view, all of them converging on the spot where the four of them stood.

Stopping, Osric turned back to face Roningus, smiling serenely as his eyes lit up in a divine blue fire. "Do not fear for me, brothers. I am armored in faith."

Then, as the corpse reached Osric and began to put its hands on him, Osric retrieved the holy symbol from under his tabard and pressed it into the corpse's forehead just as it was about to sink its teeth into him. The metal hissed and sizzled, as if it was burning hot, and the corpse let out a mindless, blood-curdling howl, dropping to its knees and struggling to get away from the cleric. With a complete lack of any sense of urgency, Osric let the holy symbol drop to hang from his neck, taking his weapon in both hands and adjusting his grip firmly around the handle. Then, with an almost regretful expression, he brought it up above his head before bringing it down hard on the corpse's head, spattering bits of skull and blood on the front of his tabard as the body slumped to the ground.

In response, the undead farmers that surrounded them let out angry sounding animalistic roars, approaching the paladins and cleric with a renewed sense of purpose. Glancing around at the advancing horde, Osric turned to the others, remaining as unfazed as if they were simply carrying on a conversation.

"I can turn them all, but I'll need a moment brothers. Would you be so kind?"

With a grunt, Roningus lunged forward. "Make it quick! Just half this number could overwhelm us in seconds!"

As he moved so did Ionnus and Grisbane, the three of them forming a defensive perimeter around Osric. Ionnus and Grisbane brought their shields up, drawing their swords back and poising them to strike as the horde drew nearer. Roningus flourished his blades at his sides, crossing them in front of him before drawing them back to attack. Meanwhile, Osric reholstered his weapon at his back, taking his holy symbol in both hands and mouthing his silent prayers.

"Here they come!" Grisbane cried, as the first corpses on the edge of the horde extended their arms and reached out for the armored church knights.

Roningus struck first, lashing out with his longswords and catching an undead woman in the jaw, then following up with a vicious downward stroke that caused her to stumble to the ground. Ionnus and Grisbane took to leading with their shields, swinging hard and bashing into the corpses then following up with powerful overhand strokes from their longswords.

As Roningus continued to spin and slash away with his weapons working in perfect tandem, the bodies quickly began to pile up around him, some still pulling themselves forward until their fingernails were torn out.. The stench of rot and decay grew increasingly overwhelming, and before long, Grisbane and Ionnus were fighting back the urge to double over and retch as they fought on.

"Is there no end to them?!" Ionnus cried, plunging his longsword into the chest of a wide-set corpse with an eyeball dangling by its optic nerve from the socket, and following up with a front kick to knock it back into a few others as he withdrew the blade.

"Tell Mithos we can't keep this up much longer, Osric!" Grisbane shouted, punching a short, squat farmer's wife hard in the bridge of her nose with the edge of his shield and knocking her back before turning and cleaving into the collarbone of what appeared to be the town oaf, his rough spun pants down around his ankles as he grasped at Grisbane's left pauldron.

"Hold position!" Roningus barked, sweeping his blades towards each other in front of him and clipping the head off of the stable master.

As the head fell from the corpse's shoulders and rolled to the ground, however, the volume of Osric's voice suddenly rose drastically. "Abominations of the dead god! Hear my voice and despair, for mine are the words of the All Father!"

Even as he spoke, the shuffling horde slowed to a halt, seeming repulsed by Osric's mere presence, the cleric holding his holy symbol up above his head. Though it was in the twilight hours of the evening, the holy symbol gleamed brightly, shedding a radiant white light upon the area. Every corpse it touched immediately began to decay rapidly; skin wrinkled in mere moments, and then flesh began turning to ash as if consumed by a fire from within. Most corpses shielded their eyes from the light, only for their hands to be eaten through as a flame consumes paper, and where the light shone through the holes in their hands it burned there as well.

"In the name of Mithos, I COMMAND you! BE GONE from this realm of the living, and embrace true death that the All Father may judge you kindly in the afterlife!"

As his voice reached its highest volume, the light shone its brightest, and in that instant, the surrounding corpses erupted into sudden bursts of white flame before falling to the ground as piles of ash. Even the ones who had stopped moving were consumed, and within seconds the entire village had gone silent again.

"…is it over?" Ionnus asked, looking around frantically as if expecting one to pop up and latch on to his neck.

In response, there was a sudden fluttering noise as a winged figure descended from the sky, catching Ionnus square between his shoulder blades and knocking him prone before landing, spinning around, and catching Grisbane with a spinning back kick that took him in his blind spot. As the two paladins staggered and fell over, the leathery bat-like wings slowly dropped, revealing a blue-skinned man with sinister full-body tattoos and a ring of jagged horns crowning his head.

Turning around, he narrowed his crimson red eyes on Roningus, his voice full of contempt as he spoke. "Church knight."

"Half-fiend…" Roningus said through gritted teeth, flourishing his blades at his sides and lowering his stance.

In response, Asmodeus grinned, reaching back and retrieving his holstered quarter staff, giving it a graceful spin in front of him before bringing it around to hold it in his right hand, resting lengthwise across his shoulders with an ease of motion that only comes from years of practice, holding his left hand out and beckoning Roningus forward.

But just as Roningus was about to leap forward, Osric reached out, placing a gentle hand on his shoulder. His eyes, still ablaze with flickering blue fire, met Asmodeus' crimson stare and held it as he spoke in a tranquil tone.

"You're responsible for all of this?"

Asmodeus chuckled once and shook his head in response.

Osric contemplated this for a moment, then continued. "Where is your master?"

A scowl slowly formed on Asmodeus' face, and just as he was about to reply, Osric cut him off.

"The dead god does not unleash one such as you upon this world to simply do as he wishes. You were summoned here, and I want to know by whom."

Asmodeus' temper flared, and as he spoke, he held out his hand and clenched his clawed fingertips together for emphasis. "Watch your tongue, cleric, or I'll rip it from the back of your throat."

In response, Osric smiled and tilted his head. "I am armored in faith, half-fiend. You cannot harm me."

Beneath his helmet, Roningus rolled his eyes, preparing for the inevitable attack on Osric. Gradually, Ionnus and Grisbane began to recover, struggling up onto all fours as they began to rise from the ground.

Asmodeus shook his head, chuckling silently and spreading his wings wide as he dropped down into a low stance, readying his quarterstaff. "Come, cleric, and put your faith to the test."

"What are you doing?!" Roningus shouted, as Osric stepped forward and readied his two-handed mace.

Asmodeus' attack came swiftly, leading with his wings to daze and befuddle Osric before following up with a powerful forward thrust of his quarterstaff. But Osric simply continued to advance forward, and when the thrust missed the side of his neck by mere inches, Asmodeus' eyes went wide in disbelief. Pulling back quickly, he brought it above his head in a spin before swinging down in a diagonal stroke that would have caught Osric on the collarbone, but when the end of the staff merely grazed Osric's shoulder, Asmodeus howled in frustration.

"The might of Mithos is my shield…so long as I stand on this hallowed ground, you cannot harm me, half-fiend." That said, Osric took his weapon in both hands, and began a barrage of powerful swings that forced Asmodeus on the defensive.

Expertly ducking, weaving, and tumbling out of the way, each time Asmodeus lashed out with the end of his quarterstaff it always seemed to be just as Osric was unintentionally stepping out of the way to line up his next strike, and before long it was becoming obvious that Asmodeus' frustrations were getting the best of him. The third time Osric caught him with the studded two-handed mace, it was just under his left arm in the ribs, the half-fiend wincing and tumbling away swiftly.

Spinning around and backing away from Osric defensively, Asmodeus snarled at Osric as the blond cleric began advancing on him again, holding his weapon casually in both hands at his right side. "You have not bested me, cleric…the favor of your deity is all that saves you…"

His smile widening, Osric drew his weapon back as he continued to advance. "The All Father's blessing is all I need."

Asmodeus glanced over at Grisbane and Ionnus, who immediately brought their shields up and drew their weapons back, before looking back to Osric, the cleric furrowing his brow slightly as he spoke.

"Throw down your weapon, and you will be spared."

Asmodeus let out one last growl of anger, then turned and took off running straight at Ionnus, who brought his shield up and prepared to counter. But instead of attacking, Asmodeus simply used the sturdy church knight as a spring board, leaping up and planting a foot on his shield before taking to the air, spreading his massive wings and flapping them furiously as he pushed himself skyward.

Once he was a considerable distance up, he turned and sailed over to where the paladins' horses were hitched, landing on the back of Osric's white mustang. The animal bucked and panicked, but in one swift, sure movement, Asmodeus reached down, rending its throat open. He leapt into the air to take flight before the horse had even collapsed to the ground, his wings carrying him swiftly away.

"That was uncalled for," Ionnus said, sheathing his longsword with a sigh and stepping over towards Roningus while stretching out his back.

"The journey back to Ascention will take considerably longer with one of our horses carrying two riders," Grisbane said, kicking piles of ashen corpse into the air and watching it as it was swiftly carried away by the slight breeze.

Meanwhile, Osric walked over, kneeling down next to his horse, closing his eyes, and placing a hand on it silently.

"Things are worse than we realized if they're sending a half-fiend after us," Ionnus said.

Roningus nodded in agreement as he responded. "There's nothing left here. We should head back to Ascention at once and report what we've found."

"What about the bodies inside the church?" Grisbane asked, looking towards the door that was still hanging open.

"We must bury them," Osric said, breaking his silence suddenly and walking towards them as he holstered his weapon at his back again. "Lest they one day rise up as the others did, and be used against us. I will not see a priest of the All Father's remains desecrated in such a manner."

Looking to Osric for a moment, Roningus turned then to Ionnus and Grisbane, nodding. "Start digging."

"I liked you better when you still wore brown," Ionnus said, looking around for something that might be used to dig with.

"If you'd like, you can go with Osric in my stead and investigate these homes to ensure that none of the undead remain."

"Sorry, but I've got graves to dig or I would."

Grinning, Roningus turned to Osric. "You're with me. Let's do a sweep of the village and make sure there aren't any more locked in a cabinet somewhere. I'm not leaving any behind."

Osric nodded, and the two headed off.

The first several houses revealed nothing, though in one they did in fact find a lone corpse clawing at a bedroom door that had been closed, its fingernails long pried off and the stubs of the bone beneath the flesh of its fingers scraping against the wood. A swift application of Osric's holy symbol left the corpse writhing as the divine flames consumed it from within, its hollow eyes glowing brightly. But it was as they were standing in the middle of a particularly well-decorated home that Roningus found it... in the middle of the main room, beneath a large carpet, a subtle bump that nearly tripped him as he was in mid-step.

Pulling the carpet aside revealed a trap door, leading down into a small room. There, a small altar to Necros was set up, designed for no more than two or three at a time to say their prayers to the dead god. Osric frowned, going to work dismantling the shrine room, leaving Roningus to look around. It was then that he found something particularly disturbing sitting neatly atop a small writing desk shoved into a corner: a carefully rolled parchment, tied in a fancy red ribbon and sealed with the insignia of Necros. A tag hung from the ribbon, the intended recipient of the letter written in plain handwriting.

TO THE HIGH PRIEST OF THE CHURCH OF MITHOS WHOEVER THAT MAY PRESENTLY BE...

Osric quirked an eyebrow when he joined Roningus, reading it over a few times before speaking. "What do they mean, 'whoever that may presently be'? Everyone knows Argos is high priest in Ascention…"

For several seconds, Roningus contemplated the writing on the tag, until suddenly it dawned upon him. "Finish up immediately. We ride for Ascention tonight."

Speeding through the gates and having nearly ran their horses to death, the four handed over their heavily lathered mounts to the care of the stable master at the front doors of the church. Without breaking stride, Roningus threw the doors open wide, Ionnus, Grisbane and Osric hurrying behind him. Stepping in to the council chambers of the arch clerics, as Roningus looked up and saw the high priest's throne empty, he came to an abrupt halt, interrupting Brogam just as he began to rebuke the four of them for barging in unannounced.

"What is the meaning of th—"

"WHERE IS HIGH PRIEST ARGOS?!" Roningus shouted, turning and looking to the gathered arch clerics anxiously.

For several seconds they all regarded Roningus with confused expressions, glancing to each other as if trying to decipher the meaning behind his question. When he looked as if to storm out and find Argos himself, it was Vogoth who answered.

"The high priest is in his office, no doubt sitting in his chair taking his customary afternoon nap. Why do you ask?"

Without so much as bowing, Roningus answered as he turned and exited the room with urgency in his step. "I have a letter to give him."

Taking the sealed letter and laying it on his desk, Argos looked up at Roningus with a tired smile, folding his hands and resting them on his stomach as he leaned back in his chair.

"I appreciate your concern, Sir Roningus, but I assure you I am quite safe here. As you saw when you first tried to enter my study unannounced, Sir Heraclese and Sir Galdren are more than capable of seeing to my security."

Standing at the forefront with Ionnus, Grisbane, and Osric behind him, Roningus bowed his head lowly as he spoke. "Their resolve is unquestionable, your holiness, but with all due respect, I still believe it would be wise to—"

Argos chuckled, bringing Roningus's words to a sudden stop, and shook his head. "The walls of Ascention have kept its high priest safe for nearly a century, Sir Roningus. Have you filed your report yet?"

Pausing for a moment, Roningus lowered his head in defeat as he replied. "No, your holiness."

Argos continued to smile brightly as he spoke, the door opening as a robed acolyte brought in a tray with a steaming hot beverage. "That would be a good place to start, then. As for this letter you've brought me, I'll see to it at once. Ah…here's my tea."

Remaining standing at attention, Roningus glanced over at the acolyte briefly before looking back to Argos, making his final plea as the high priest took a long sip of his tea. "It would do much to put my mind at ease if you would at least have Sir Heraclese and Sir Galdren stand watch here in the room with you."

Setting his cup down, Argos's smile wavered momentarily as he looked down at his cup before looking back up to Roningus. "If the council of arch clerics finds it necessary once they've reviewed your findings, I will indulge their request. In the meantime, however, I…I…" Faltering with his words, sweat began beading upon Argos's brow, the elderly high priest reaching up and wiping at his forehead with his sleeve.

Observing his sudden change in expression, Roningus frowned. "Is something wrong, your holiness?"

Forcing a smile, Argos looked up at Roningus, shrugging helplessly. "Just the strains of old age…it will pass…" Reaching for his cup, Argos's fingers fumbled clumsily with it until knocking it from the desk, the high priest slumping sideways in his seat as his breath grew shallow and rasping.

Roningus's eyes grew wide, racing forward as he called out, "OSRIC!"

The battle cleric lunged forward as well, the two of them bracing Argos as he fell from his chair.

Looking up, Roningus shouted at Grisbane as Osric began tending to the high priest. "STOP THAT ACOLYTE!"

It was just as Grisbane turned towards the doors that the two black caped paladins burst through, simultaneously drawing their longswords.

"What happened?!" the one on the left shouted, Grisbane blowing past them and charging out the door, looking to his left before turning and dashing right.

Dipping his right shoulder down in front of him, Roningus plowed through the two paladins as well and rushed out the door after Grisbane. Looking to his left and seeing a host of bewildered looking clerics and paladins as Grisbane raced in that direction, it was when he looked right that he spotted him: the robed acolyte, calmly weaving his way through the crowds of people who had not yet become aware of the commotion.

"Move!" Roningus shouted, taking off in a full sprint and shoving people out of his way.

When the acolyte turned and spotted him, he immediately took to running as well, knocking several clerics over as he did so.

"STOP THAT MAN!" Roningus shouted, a pair of blue caped paladins near the end of the hallway turning just in time to see the acolyte dashing between them.

But one of them reacted instantly, stepping forward with his left foot and grabbing hold of the acolyte as he planted him hard on the stone floor. As the acolyte's face hit the ground with a loud smack, the paladin wrenched his arm up behind him while simultaneously digging his knee into the small of the man's back, pinning him to the ground.

Looking surprised by his own instantaneous reaction, the paladin looked up as Roningus came jogging over to them, speaking as the two lifted the dazed acolyte from the ground roughly and dragged him towards the penitent's cells. "What has this man done, oathbrother?"

Barely able to contain the fury in his voice, Roningus glared down at the man they carried as he responded. "This *coward* served poison to High Priest Argos."

"He WHAT?!" cried the other paladins, the false acolyte spurting blood from his smashed nose with rasping laughs, speaking in gurgles as reddish-pink saliva began to trickle down his swollen lips.

"Praise be to Necros! Only death awaits those who hide behind the false father's—" But the heretic's words were cut off as Roningus grabbed hold of him by the back of his neck with his left hand, wrenching him from the other paladins' grasp and slamming him face-first into the wall directly to the right.

"Roningus!" one of the paladins yelled, rushing over and wrestling the limp figure of the heretic from Roningus's grasp before he could draw him back and do it again.

As the blue caped paladins dragged the man away, Roningus turned and slammed his fist into the wall, staring at the wet splatter where the heretic's face had made contact with it. Letting out a long, growling sigh, and barely acknowledging that both Ionnus and Grisbane had joined him, Roningus clenched his fist tightly, looking up as a massive crowd began to form outside of the high priest's office.

"How long has he been standing guard?" Ionnus asked, standing next to Grisbane as the two of them watched Roningus stand still as a statue before the coffin in which the high priest's body had been laid to rest.

Standing at perfect attention, dressed in his full plate, Roningus had insisted on taking what many considered to be an unhealthy number of shifts in what would be a constant week-long vigil. The plain wooden casket in which Argos's earthly remains rested was on display for any who wished to pay their respects in the altar room of the cathedral, a pair of iron braziers constantly fed incense by clerics who attended the vigil. Traditionally, it was broken into shifts, numerous paladins taking turns standing guard so that the high priest's remains were never left alone while a new high priest was determined. But Roningus frequently dismissed many of his oathbrothers who came to relieve him, and when he wasn't standing guard, he seldom ate or slept, instead working through his grief by swinging blunted training swords at wooden dummies until he could scarcely lift his arms. Grisbane and Ionnus had even carried him to his bed once when he had exhausted himself to the point of collapse.

"Too long," Grisbane said, sighing and folding his arms.

Nodding for a moment, Ionnus stepped forward as he spoke. "I'll go speak with him."

Once Ionnus was within several feet of him, Roningus shook his head, his narrowed eyes visible through the slit in his visor. "You have my thanks, oathbrother, but I do not require relief just yet."

"Roningus, you need to eat something. Let me stand watch while you and Grisbane go get something to eat."

When Roningus didn't move, Ionnus sighed heavily, and when he spoke again, it was in a pleading tone.

"Roningus, you can't blame yourself for what happened. Let me stand watch so you can—"

"I could have stopped it," Roningus said suddenly, saying the first words he'd said other than turning other paladins away since the high priest's death.

Ionnus blinked, his eyes going wide. "No…there was nothing you could have done…all the arch clerics agreed you did everything you could to—"

Roningus shook his head, cutting Ionnus off. "No, I didn't. I noticed something was off about the acolyte that brought him his tea, but I was in such a hurry, I paid him no mind."

Ionnus paused, contemplating what Roningus had said before responding. "Neither did either one of our oathbrothers in black that stood watch at the door. And if you hadn't reacted so quickly, the heretic might have gotten away, but because of your quick response, he now sits in a penitent's cell awaiting his sentencing."

For several long seconds, Roningus said nothing, until finally he shook his head again. "It wasn't enough."

Ionnus frowned. "You're too hard on yourself. If anything, you should be hailed a hero for all you've done in service to the church in such a short time."

"He's completely out of control! Did you hear Sir Vygmar's account of what he did to that heretic in the hallway?!" Brogam was sitting upright in his seat, his voice growing in volume and indignation.

Vogoth rolled his eyes in response. "Don't be so melodramatic, Brogam. That 'heretic' poisoned the high priest; had I the chance, I'd have throttled him myself. Besides, the only time you seem to worry about the code of conduct is when dealing with Roningus…why is that, I wonder?"

"He's unstable," Brogam said defensively.

"How much longer until the conclave reaches a decision?" one of the arch clerics asked, Vogoth's eyes widening in relief at the change of subject.

"The laws of the church dictate they have until the end of the vigil, at which point food and drink will be relegated to bread and water, and they shall no longer be permitted to retire to a bed to sleep each evening until they have made their decision."

Brogam narrowed his eyes at Vogoth as he spoke again. "I can promise you this: if elected high priest, my first official act will be to reign in that wild horse of yours, Vogoth. Roningus should have never been cloaked in blue, or even anointed for that matter."

Smiling tiredly, Vogoth responded in a weary voice. "Then I pray to Mithos that the conclave sees fit to elect another as high priest. One who is not so quick to dismiss the value of a knight as strong and courageous as Sir Roningus."

It was at that moment, however, that the doors swung open, a young acolyte standing timidly in the doorway.

"What is it, lad?" Vogoth asked, the young boy no older than fifteen glancing nervously around the room before speaking.

"The conclave has made its decision."

Seated in the mess hall, Ionnus and Grisbane both sipped quietly at their mugs, until finally Ionnus broke the silence. "Just a couple more days and Argos will be laid to rest in the tomb of heroes. Roningus will come around once the vigil has ended, and then we can focus on getting back to work."

"Are you sure?" Grisbane asked, quirking a brow.

Ionnus fell silent again as the two returned to staring into their mugs.

Eventually, Grisbane broke the silence again. "Where's Osric?"

Ionnus shook his head and shrugged. "I haven't seen him since the…since High Priest Argos…"

Grisbane closed his eyes, nodding his understanding, until a cleric burst into the mess hall. His eyes wide, he spoke in an elated voice that made both of them sit up and take notice, as did the rest of the clerics and church knights within the mess hall. "The conclave has elected a new high priest!" he cried out, the whole room going silent.

"…well?! Who is it, then?! Speak, boy!" came the impatient voice of a black caped paladin.

"Brogam! Brogam is to succeed Argos as high priest!"

As Roningus approached the high priest's throne, Brogam narrowed his gaze upon him.

Genuflecting, Roningus bowed his head respectfully as he spoke. "I am here to answer your summons, your holiness. What would the church ask of me?"

"Rise, Sir Roningus," came Brogam's response in a flat tone. Roningus rose dutifully, standing at perfect attention in the high priest's presence.

For several seconds, Brogam looked Roningus up and down, as if waiting to see if he would give any indication of displeasure at Brogam's recent appointment. But when his expression remained sincere and his posture refused to falter, Brogam cleared his throat and began to speak, while Vogoth lifted his hand inconspicuously to his mouth to hide his grin.

"Sir Roningus, I have received disturbing reports concerning you conducting yourself in a way that does not adhere to the code of conduct. What do you have to say in your defense?"

Roningus paused for a moment to consider Brogam's words, his eyes never leaving Brogam's. "My apologies, your holiness, but I am afraid I know not what reports you speak of."

Leaning forward, Brogam's impatience broke through, apparent in his voice. "You know exactly of what I speak, church knight! You had a man in captivity who had already submitted to arrest, and yet still saw fit to stain the walls of the church with his blood." As Brogam spoke, he adjusted the robes of the high priest that he wore; they were as yet unfamiliar and uncomfortable to him, and he repeatedly shifted in his seat to reposition them.

"I say nothing in my defense, your holiness. The reports are true; when the heretic began speaking his blasphemy within the walls of the church, I grew outraged, and in my grief over the death of High Priest Argos, my initial reflex was to silence his blasphemous tongue in the swiftest way I was able."

Brogam practically sneered, his voice dubious. "That is your excuse? Rage, fueled by grief?"

Roningus shook his head curtly, keeping his eyes focused on Brogam the entire time. "I make no excuses, your holiness. I only try to explain my actions."

For a long moment, Brogam frowned at Roningus, until finally he looked to the door, signaling to a black caped paladin standing at it. "Sir Roningus…in light of your recent actions, it is by my divine right as the high priest of the church of Mithos that I hereby demote you…"

At his words, Vogoth's eyes grew wide, his hand dropping from his mouth as he turned to regard Brogam as if he were a madman.

"…and strip you of your rank and station. Remain standing, so that your oathbrother may cloak you in brown once more."

"This cannot be done! Such a thing has never been done in the history of the church!" Vogoth shouted in an incredulous voice.

As the black caped paladin approached Roningus, Roningus made no movement, standing statuesque as his oathbrother undid the clasps that held his blue cape to his pauldrons and carefully began to fold it. Throughout the ordeal, Roningus's expression remained unchanged, the same unblinking gaze looking dutifully up to High Priest Brogam.

Rising from his chair, Vogoth swiftly moved towards the paladins, reaching out with his hand as if to stop the one cloaked in black.

"Arch Cleric Vogoth, return to your seat at once or you will be restrained."

When half a dozen church knights began to move in, Vogoth stopped, turning to face Brogam with open contempt etched on his face. "Your petty vendetta against this man has brought shame and disgrace to the church, and to the order of the church knights. I hereby recuse myself from the council of arch clerics, and take my leave with or without your consent." That said, Vogoth turned, shouldering through a pair of purple caped paladins that had begun to move in on him, and disappeared from the council chamber.

Once Vogoth was gone, Brogam looked back to Roningus, who had remained standing at perfect attention throughout the whole ordeal, the black caped paladin fastening the clasps of his former color onto his pauldrons. This done, Brogam waved a dismissive hand. "You are dismissed. Return to your former station and await further orders."

"As the church commands, your holiness." Roningus knelt once more, then turned and strode calmly out of the council chambers.

Brogam let out a heavy sigh once he had left, shaking his head. "Things will return to normal soon enough. I think we can all agree that—"

But when he turned and looked to the rest of the remaining arch clerics, Brogam was met with a host of castigating looks, each set of eyes regarding him disapprovingly and a couple even shaking their heads openly. Silently, they all stood from their seats, their customary bows to take their leave looking forced and not without hesitation, then filed from the council chambers.

Seated on his throne, alone save for the paladins that remained to stand guard, Brogam grumbled quietly, swatting the cup sitting on the small table over next to him in frustration.

As Roningus stepped into the mess hall, it took but a moment for the room to go silent as all eyes fell upon him, the color of his cape in particular. More than a few narrowed their eyes in disapproval, and several even shouted out angrily about what an outrage it was. Yet even with the entire mess hall rallying to his cause, Roningus bore his indignation with unwavering grace, seating himself with Ionnus and Grisbane and accepting a bowl of barley and oat porridge that was slid in front of him.

"He can't do this!" Ionnus shouted, temporarily disinterested in the hard biscuit he had been pulling apart and stuffing into his mouth.

"Brogam is the high priest. He does as he pleases," Roningus said, dipping a wooden spoon into his bowl and calmly taking a bite.

"Why didn't you fight it?" Grisbane asked, taking a sip from his mug afterwards.

Roningus paused with his spoon half-way up to his mouth, his eyes narrowing slightly as he stared at the drops of porridge that fell back into the bowl. "It would have given him the reason he sought to absolve me from knighthood. It was apparent in his eyes he wanted me to react." That said, Roningus took the spoon into his mouth again and continued eating, Grisbane shaking his head.

"It's no matter. He'll have to acknowledge his mistake after our next assignment," Ionnus said, stuffing another piece of biscuit into his mouth.

For a moment, Roningus stared into his bowl, until finally looking up at Ionnus with a puzzled expression. "What assignment?"

Ionnus quirked a brow, chewing and swallowing before speaking again. "You mean to tell me he didn't brief you on our next mission?"

"My orders are to return to my former station and await further orders."

Letting out a loud growl, Ionnus had to bite down on his finger to prevent himself from swearing, leaving Grisbane to the task of informing him. "Heretics are moving against Cynegald, and the church has called for aid. We're riding out first thing tomorrow morning, under the command of Sir Rhygar the Ruinous Hammer."

Roningus blinked. "...the Hammer of Forthos is going to war?"

"Aye, and I'm more than a bit disappointed to see you relegated to guard duty, lad." The voice, deep, booming and thick with a Forthos accent, was unmistakable. Laying his wide gauntleted hand on Roningus's shoulder, Sir Rhygar looked down with an expression of sincere regret.

Standing at an unimposing 5 feet 9 inches, what Sir Rhygar lacked in height he made up for in dense muscle and broadness of shoulder. Unmistakably a son of Forthos, his fiery red hair was cropped short, a grizzly looking beard complete with a rich, full moustache adorning his squarish jaw, and his emerald green eyes gazing down upon Roningus with a look of regret. Clad in a suit of unusually thick plate armor, Sir Rhygar wore a black cape and carried a rounded metal shield instead of the customary kite design, the front of which was studded with black steel. Hanging from his right hip was his fabled weapon Skyhammer, a two-handed warhammer that he'd had shortened for one-handed use. The head was a large block of pitted black steel affixed to a steel haft, the head shaped so that one end was a square face while the other ended in a tapered spike, little in the way of ornament resulting in a simplistic design.

"I'd hoped to bring you along and see that fancy Two Rivers style of yours first hand."

Roningus closed his eyes, sighing disappointedly.

"Can't you bring him with us? It is well within your right to assemble your unit as you see fit." As Grisbane spoke, Ionnus looked up and nodded hopefully; a hope that was swiftly extinguished as they saw the sad smile on Rhygar's face.

"Were it that I could, lads...but Brogam was specific. Sir Roningus is to remain in Ascention, until such time that he learns to conduct himself in a manner 'befitting a paladin of Mithos'. Personally I'd've done the same to the bastard that poisoned Argos, but that's irrelevant now. Brogam's out to get you, lad, so you'd best lay low...for the time being."

Ionnus let out a heavy sigh, tossing what remained of his biscuit aside. "What difference does it make? With Brogam as high priest, Roningus will never receive fair treatment, and will probably spend his entire knighthood cloaked in brown."

Rhygar's sad smile turned to a genuine grin, and as he spoke, he winked. "That may be true...but I have it on good authority that the conclave is already beginning to regret their decision, and Brogam set a new precedent when he stripped Sir Roningus of his rank."

Seated in his room, Vogoth was pouring himself another glass of wine when the knock at his door came.

"Tell the high priest I have no interest in speaking with him, presently," he called out, taking a long sip as the door swung open.

Arch Cleric Rasthmus stood in the doorway, a very young man who had just recently succeeded Arch Cleric Glendorl upon his passing. "My apologies, Vogoth, but I'm afraid I come bearing no such summons."

As he spoke, Rasthmus grinned, to which Vogoth couldn't help but give a half-hearted smile in return. "I already know it was in bad form to storm out the way I did. No doubt the new high priest had several unflattering remarks to make about me once I had cleared the door."

"On the contrary, none of us remained in attendance once Sir Roningus had been dismissed. Whatever High Priest Brogam said is between him and Mithos."

Quirking an eyebrow, Vogoth offered Rasthmus the only other chair in the room; a small, rickety wooden seat that Rasthmus accepted graciously. "Wine?" Vogoth asked, reaching down to retrieve another glass, to which Rasthmus shook his head.

"No, thank you. It's not becoming to drink before one's afternoon meal." Rasthmus smiled, to which Vogoth nodded in consent.

Rasthmus was young, but he was very clever, and his devotion to the church was so great he had almost been ordained a battle cleric. Tall and of a slender, athletic frame, Rasthmus watched the world through deep, brown eyes that didn't miss a single detail. His head, which once grew long waves of light brown hair, was shaven completely bald; an act of piety that Rasthmus carried out willingly. As he nodded, Vogoth took another drink, setting his glass down before speaking.

"Normally I would agree, but after the proceedings of this morning's council gathering, I found myself in need of a glass or two. If you haven't come to deliver a summons, and you haven't come to have a drink with me, then why are you here?"

Rasthmus chuckled silently, reached over, and lifted Vogoth's glass, taking a sip before setting it back down on the desk. "I came to talk to you about Brogam, actually."

Vogoth scoffed, staring at Rasthmus as the younger arch cleric set the glass back down. "What is there to say? The man is high priest. His word is law as far as the church is concerned."

Rasthmus nodded, looking around down at the ground as if contemplating Vogoth's words for a moment, then looked back up. "Yes, but there are many who believe the conclave made a mistake when they appointed Brogam high priest."

Nodding, Vogoth reached over for his wine, but came to an abrupt halt as Rasthmus continued.

"…including many members of the conclave itself. Tell me, Vogoth…are you aware of what the letter addressed to the high priest said?"

Staring at Rasthmus in confusion, Vogoth shook his head as he spoke. "No, none of us were…why do you ask?"

"Simply put, there are many of us who believe we are on the verge of a full-scale war. The conclave appointed Brogam because they believed him to be the most reliable…they thought he would best serve as a defender of the church, and ensuring the safety of Ascention and all of her people. But as we speak, Sir Rhygar is gathering an entire column of church knights, and come dawn tomorrow morning, they ride for Cynegald."

"Did they not call for aid?"

Rasthmus smiled, nodding once as he spoke. "Indeed they did, but we believe Brogam is acting based on information in that letter that Sir Roningus brought back with him. Information he has refused to disclose to the council of arch clerics. I tried to reason with him personally, and when I mentioned that his actions were not garnering confidence in him from the conclave, he had me escorted out of his office without hearing another word. Vogoth…"

Then, leaning in, Rasthmus's voice grew quiet; apprehensive, almost.

"…the conclave is of a mind that they made a mistake."

Chuckling once, Vogoth shook his head and took another sip of wine. "It's a bit late for that, I'm afraid. What is done cannot be undone."

Rasthmus's smile returned, and again he seemed to contemplate Vogoth's words. "Just as a paladin cloaked in blue cannot be cloaked once more in brown?"

Vogoth's eyes narrowed slightly, and he cleared his throat. "What are you implying, Rasthmus?"

Tilting his head, the smile faded from Rasthmus's face. "The conclave's lack of confidence in Brogam grows more and more with each decision he makes. If they had the support of the council of arch clerics, it is possible a new high priest could be appointed… one that would carry on in Argos's footsteps in safeguarding the church against her enemies. We're on the verge of war, Vogoth… and many believe that Brogam's folly will lead us to ruin."

10

Approaching the coastal city of Cynegald, Sir Rhygar brought the column to a halt, lining them up in rows. In the distance, the city was in a state of turmoil; more than a few towers of smoke rose from burning buildings, and the sound of plate-mailed dreadknights on the march mixed with the occasional scream of a woman or the dying throes of a man carried across the field.

Shouting in his loud, booming voice, Sir Rhygar rode back and forth in front of them, maintaining perfect control of his armored warhorse with his left hand. "Our main priority is to reach the church. Once there, we fortify our position, then branch out and ride down as many heretics as possible. Swords!"

On his command, the entire column drew their weapons, Sir Rhygar unholstering Skyhammer from his side. Giving the weapon a few menacing swings with his right hand, Rhygar fell in with the front line of the column and sounded the order.

"FOR THE GLORY OF MITHOS!"

From the second row in, Ionnus and Grisbane shouted loudly, brandishing their swords above their heads and charging forward in unison with their oathbrothers.

As the column descended upon Cynegald, the situation was proven to be as dire as it appeared; patrols of armored dreadknights awaited them eagerly, having barricaded the streets to impede the church knights' horses, and positioned pikemen on the ground to combat the mounted paladins. The only building yet to fall was the church, a small building near the center of town made of stone and with a wooden roof. Churches of Mithos were traditionally built to act as fortresses during times of war, and this one was no exception.

Nevertheless, there were dreadknights positioned all around it, having abandoned their siege and instead starving the church knights out. Rows of dead civilians were lying along the sides of the roads, their bodies carefully lain side by side so close together that their shoulders touched.

Their senses heightened from the rush of adrenaline, the column of paladins rode upon the barricades and pikemen with a righteous fury, trampling the shattered remnants under hoof as they began cutting through pikemen with their swords.

Sir Rhygar held Skyhammer high above his head, and each time it was brought down, it caved in the helmet of a dreadknight and sent him collapsing onto the street. Working in tandem, Ionnus and Grisbane continued to cut their way through the pikemen with their oathbrothers, riding side-by-side so no pikemen could overtake them and lance their horses. It was when they had almost reached the church that the call came out; Sir Rhygar's voice, clear and easily audible even over the tumultuous roar of combat.

"NECROMANCER!" he cried, and in response, every church knight's helm immediately began scanning the battlefield with a frantic sense of urgency.

With a slow, ominous grace, the bodies of the fallen began to rise, as well as those of the townsfolk who had been lined up along the streets. Their vacant eyes stared unblinkingly, and in unison they began shuffling towards the nearest church knight they could find. Dreadknights who had risen dropped their weapons, scraping their metal plated boots along the stone streets with outstretched arms. Horses reared up in a panic when the undead got too close, a few dumping their riders onto the ground, leaving them prone and overwhelmed as the shuffling horde swarmed in on them.

"FIND THAT DAMNED NECROMANCER!" came Rhygar's furious voice, accompanied by a resounding thud as Skyhammer bit into another helmet. "AND YOU! GET INTO THE CHURCH, AND DON'T COME BACK WITHOUT A CLERIC!"

As he yelled, he pointed at Grisbane with Skyhammer. Grisbane nodded once and looking back to the doors of the church.

"On me, oathbrother!" Ionnus cried, pulling his left foot from its stirrup to plant a kick square in the face of a recently risen dreadknight that was trying to pull him from his horse.

Together, the two rode down living and undead alike, slashing and charging through them until they reached the perimeter the church knights had set up around the cathedral. Once at the doors, they quickly dismounted, tying the reins up as Grisbane pounded on the door with the pommel of his longsword.

"I am Sir Grisbane the Herald of Justice! Open the doors, we need a cleric immediately!"

For several seconds nothing happened, but then the bar was lifted and the door creaked open. An old man, dressed in the robes of an acolyte, peered out at them, gawking at them in disbelief. "We have but three clerics, and they are presently tending to the wounded!"

With a frown, Grisbane sheathed his longsword, shouldering his way in through the crack between the doors and striding in. Looking around, it took him several seconds to spot a cleric, his blue and white robes heavily stained with blood.

Striding over swiftly, Grisbane placed a hand on the cleric's shoulder. "You are needed outside immediately."

Glancing at Grisbane over his shoulder, the cleric shook his head. "I cannot leave. There are too many wounded to tend to."

Turning, Grisbane looked back at the door, then swiftly removed his helmet, tossing it aside before doing the same with his gauntlets. "Then I shall take your place. Go now."

Slowly and without any urgency, Sir Roningus walked his patrol route through the church. With an entire column of his oathbrothers gone, the building was eerily quiet and felt almost empty. Clerics shuffled by silently, most of whom nodded their heads in courteous greeting to which Roningus responded in turn. It was as he made his way along one of the western halls, however, that a door swung open and Vogoth stepped out. Dressed in his clerical robes, Vogoth's eyes widened as he almost struck Roningus with the door.

"Oh! My sincerest apologies! I should have been more careful, Sir...Roningus?" As he recognized the Drakmahr family sigil on the front of Roningus's armor, Vogoth quirked an eyebrow. "What brings you to the clerical wing?"

Lowering his arm, which he had instinctively braced forward to shield himself from the door, Roningus bowed his head and waved Vogoth's apology away politely. He reached up and lifted his helmet from his head, tucking it under his left arm and doing his best not to frown as he spoke. "My patrol route."

Rolling his eyes, Vogoth shook his head, turning and heading up the hallway alongside Roningus and matching his leisurely pace. "Were it within my power to restore your station and cloak you in blue once more, I would. Yet for whatever reason, Brogam seems to have singled you out."

Nodding solemnly, Roningus spoke in a cordial tone that hinted at his frustrations. "The high priest acts on behalf of the All Father himself; it is not my place to question his decision."

Looking over to Roningus, Vogoth smiled, sidestepping a cleric as he replied, "Your place is not wandering about these halls, Sir Roningus. Your faith is admirable, and your humility even more so. But you are destined for greatness, that much is certain…and Brogam is a fool if he believes it is the will of Mithos that you should spend your days pacing around the church."

Pondering Vogoth's words for a moment, Roningus looked over as if to speak, but was interrupted when a sudden outcry was heard.

"Ascention is under attack! Dreadknights have breached the walls and are making their way towards the church!"

Immediately, the peaceful church became a swarming beehive of activity, clerics and paladins running every which way as acolytes fought to stay out of the way.

Without a moment's hesitation, Roningus slid his helmet on, taking Vogoth by the arm and escorting him swiftly down the hallway. "With me, Arch Cleric…we must get you to the council chamber to ensure your safety."

As the cleric stepped outside of the church, Ionnus quickly closed the door behind him and pounded on it twice, the bar sliding back into place with a loud thud and making the massive wooden doors quiver momentarily.

"On me, cleric!" Ionnus shouted, bringing his shield up and racing forward towards the line the other church knights were holding.

"What is the meaning of this?!" the cleric cried in confusion, at which point Sir Rhygar came bludgeoning his way through the sea of fighting to where he could be heard.

"WE NEED A CLEANSING!"

Upon hearing Rhygar, the cleric looked around, immediately recognizing the taint of the dead god that was present in the fallen villagers and dreadknights.

"I'll need a moment!" the cleric yelled, reaching down under his robes and retrieving his silver holy symbol.

"Why do you think *we're* here?!" Ionnus shouted back, stepping forward and taking his place in the line, leading with his shield and catching a dreadknight square in the visor.

In perfect tandem with one another, the paladins continued to block, parry, and slash away at any who came near the doors of the church, and subsequently the cleric.

"GET YOUR ARSE MOVING, CLERIC!" came Rhygar's voice, as he slammed his studded shield into an undead villager before planting the face of Skyhammer into the head of another. Each time one of the shuffling undead tried to lay hands on him, he swatted them away with his shield, then followed through with a deadly overhead swing from Skyhammer, spattering bits of skull and flesh on the stone each time.

Meanwhile, the cleric brought his hands up, mouthing his silent prayers to Mithos.

"YOU! HUNT DOWN THAT NECROMANCER AND SEND HIM TO MEET HIS DEAD GOD!" came Rhygar's command, turning his head and shouting at Ionnus.

Glancing around him to make certain Rhygar was in fact speaking to him, Ionnus nodded and pushed forward, his shield brothers at his sides pressing in to close the gap after he had waded out into the middle of the melee.

Inside the church, one of the other clerics came rushing over to Grisbane, looking around in confusion. "Where has Cleric—"

"He was needed outside," Grisbane interrupted, unstrapping the shield from his left arm and letting it fall to the ground. "Tell me what to do."

For a moment, the cleric regarded Grisbane doubtfully, but when it had become clear there was no alternative, he turned and sped off, calling out behind him as he did. "Come with me immediately."

Following closely, Grisbane swept after the cleric, moving diligently through rows of people lying on the ground. Some didn't look all that bad. Others he was almost certain wouldn't make it through the night. But when they finally came to a stop, Grisbane found himself standing over a paladin with a grievous wound to his side, blood oozing slowly through the hinges of his breastplate and pooling onto the ground. His eyes widening, Grisbane froze in place for a moment, the image of Sir Resmeron's face flashing in his mind, until the cleric's shouting snapped him out of it.

"Church knight! Did you hear what I said?!"

Grisbane shook his head to clear it as he spoke. "No, I didn't—"

"We need to get him out of his armor immediately! Help me undo the fastenings of his breastplate, and be ready with those clean bandages to apply direct pressure to the site of the wound."

When the cleric knelt down and began to work, Grisbane's instincts kicked in. Dropping to his knees, his hands swiftly undid the fastenings on the breastplate, pulled it off and immediately applied the bandages as he was instructed.

"Good. Now hold that in place while I get the astringent ready…"

As they reached the council chambers, Roningus reached out and pressed through the door, and was about to pull Vogoth through when he saw the look of horror on the arch cleric's face. It was then that he turned and looked, spotting the cloaked figure seated in the high priest's throne, a familiar voice speaking to him as blue-skinned fingers closed tightly around the ornate quarterstaff they held.

"I was expecting the high priest to arrive first."

Pushing Vogoth back out into the hallway, Roningus barked his order at the arch cleric as if Vogoth were one of his own men. "Bar the door behind me." That said, he slammed the doors shut before Vogoth could protest.

From atop the high priest's throne, Asmodeus chuckled darkly as the sound of Vogoth barricading the doors was heard. "You haven't prevented anything, you know. Today is the day the church of Mithos falls."

With a casual sort of calmness, Roningus slowly approached Asmodeus and drew the longswords from behind his waist. When Asmodeus stood from the throne, he reached up and pulled his cloak off, tossing it aside and spreading his bat-like wings open wide.

"The sun will set, and the church of Mithos will remain standing. As it has, and always will." As Roningus spoke, Asmodeus cracked his knuckles, leaving his quarterstaff standing straight up in the air by itself and approaching Roningus eagerly.

"Come, church knight…come and see how swiftly you fall without the aid of your battle cleric…"

Cleaving his way through the swarm of cold bodies that pressed in on him from every direction, Ionnus looked around frantically. The rotting stench of the undead that began to surround him twisted his stomach in nauseated knots.

Ionnus split the head of an undead cobbler to his right in half with a casual swing and kicked at the knees to bring the shambling corpse crumpling to the ground. He shouted out as he turned to slam shield first into an armored dreadknight that reached for him with outstretched arms. "It's no good! There are too many of them!"

Letting out a furious roar, Rhygar brought Skyhammer down upon the shield of a dreadknight, the man screaming as his arm shattered. "CLERIC, WE NEED THAT CLEANSING NOW! PRAY TO MITHOS FASTER!"

As if in response, the cleric looked up, raising his eyes skyward. He let his holy symbol fall to his chest as he lifted his hands up to beseech the heavens for their blessing. And, as the light of the sun grew brighter, the All Father's blessings poured down upon them, the corpses that walked among them bursting apart as if consumed from within by a divine flame and turning to ash.

The field of battle suddenly much less convoluted, Ionnus glanced around, immediately spotting a small group of dreadknights surrounding the armored necromancer, who was staggering as his control over the dead was wrenched from him forcibly. Taking up a defensive formation, the three dreadknights raised their shields, forming a wall around the necromancer and drawing their weapons back.

"HERE, LAD! BREAK THROUGH THEM AND GET TO THAT NECROMANCER!"

Hearing Rhygar's voice, Ionnus turned just in time to see Skyhammer leave his hand, the burly paladin tossing the hammer in Ionnus's direction and setting the weapon spinning end over end. Rhygar drew his back-up longsword and resumed the melee without missing a beat.

Dropping his longsword in alarm, Ionnus reached out and grasped at the weapon as it drew near, catching it in the middle of the haft. The weight of it caught him off guard, almost causing him to drop it, but when his hand found the grip at the bottom of the haft, his fingers closed around it tightly, the balance and weight of the weapon feeling as natural as if it were an extension of his arm. Turning his gaze on the necromancer once more, Ionnus turned the handle in his grip, raising the head of Skyhammer and approaching the dreadknights ominously.

"Good…now hold these back while I extract the shards of metal from where the tip of the sword broke off…"

As the cleric spoke, Grisbane nodded, wiping at the sweat on his brow with his forearm, the metal vambrace smearing it more than anything and ultimately not doing him much good. As the heavily sedated paladin moaned in pain, Grisbane swallowed hard, looking over at his wounded oathbrother's pale face as his hands began to tremble.

The cleric immediately looked up, speaking in a sharp tone. "Eyes forward, church knight. Never mind the noises he makes; if left in, these shards will work their way inward and take his life one day. Steady your hands."

With a nod, Grisbane reached down, plying the incision open and holding it open while the cleric went to work with his metal instruments, digging out small slivers of steel. Suddenly the man screamed, bucking and arching his back.

"Hold him!" the cleric shouted, pulling his instruments away before the paladin inadvertently harmed himself.

Bracing the paladin's chest with his right forearm, Grisbane pushed him back down onto the table, holding him there as he thrashed for a moment before looking up to the cleric, nodding as he opened the incision with his left hand once more.

Working diligently, the cleric continued to extract small slivers of splintered steel, Grisbane watching intently as he spoke. "How did he come by this wound?"

His eyes narrowed in concentration, the cleric didn't look up as he responded. "A new tactic employed by the dead god's dreadknights. Daggers that break off with a sharp twist, lodging these metal splinters in the victim. They are designed in such a manner that they will continue to work their way inward, and over time dull pain will grow into excruciating agony before finally the internal damage takes the victim's life. Needlessly cruel, but very effective. There we are…"

On his last words, the cleric removed the final shard, letting it drop into a small box before wiping his hands on the front of his apron.

"Can you sew, church knight?"

Grisbane blinked once at the cleric's question, his response in an unsure tone. "I…I've mended small tears in canvas tents, before, but—"

"Good. Use the astringent in the bottle here, and stitch up the man's wound. Leave him a mug of whitewine for the pain in case he awakens, and come find me when you're done. There is much more to do."

"Wait! I don't—"

That said, the cleric was gone, leaving Grisbane alone with his groaning oathbrother, glancing down at the curved bone needle and thread laying on the small stand next to the table.

With the rest of the dreadknights engaged and trying to hold off the fervent onslaught of the church knights, the three dreadknights huddled defensively in front of the necromancer shifted uneasily as they saw Ionnus drawing near, the black steel head of Skyhammer poised to descend upon them.

"You are three against one! Kill him and be done with it!" the necromancer shrieked, shoving the middle dreadknight forward.

Emboldened by the necromancer's words, the remaining two dreadknights broke off, moving forward and spreading out to approach Ionnus from three angles at once.

Immediately recognizing the danger of being surrounded, Ionnus dropped back, keeping his shield in front of him and Skyhammer at the ready. Seeing this, the rightmost dreadknight chose that moment to press his attack, readying his shield as if to lead with a parry that would knock the brutal hammer out of the way and leave an opening. But Ionnus easily recognized the stance, and as the dreadknight tried to rush him and follow through with an overhead bash from the pommel of his sword, Ionnus brought the head of Skyhammer down, catching the dreadknight in the side of his right knee. The dreadknight's legs were nearly swept sideways from the force of the blow, and he screamed loudly as the agony set in.

Seizing on the opportunity, the two remaining dreadknights rushed in, coordinating their attacks. The one to Ionnus's left came in high, leading with a powerful downward stroke of his longsword intended to put Ionnus off balance and leave him open, the other dreadknight positioning himself to deliver what would be a killing stroke.

Spotting the tactic, Ionnus spun right, pressing his left shoulder up against the dreadknight to his left's shield and following through with a horizontal swing from Skyhammer that caught the dreadknight in the back, sending him sprawling forward. Keeping the momentum of Skyhammer going, Ionnus then brought it up above his head, the other dreadknight scrambling to position his shield between himself and the warhammer. But it proved to no avail, for as Ionnus brought the weapon down upon him, there was a loud crash accompanied by a sickening snap. The dreadknight howled in pain as Ionnus planted his foot on the front of the dreadknight's breastplate and sent the heretic tumbling to the ground with a shove.

By the time the third dreadknight had turned around, Ionnus caught his shield with a backhanded swing from Skyhammer, the tapered spike punching through the shield as if it were paper before continuing on into the dreadknight's arm. Ionnus drew back his shield and pulled hard, wrenching the dreadknight towards him and striking with the edge of his shield at the same time, catching the dreadknight square in his visor and instantly knocking him unconscious.

Ionnus pulled Skyhammer loose and turned to face the necromancer.

"You have accomplished nothing, boy…I am not so feeble as the brittle arch clerics of the false father..."

"We shall see," Ionnus said calmly, continuing to close in.

Reaching behind his back, the necromancer brought forth a vicious looking length of spiked chain, the ends fitted with spiked weights. Grasping the slack in his left hand, he set the end spinning in his right, allowing Ionnus to get a few steps closer before lashing out with a powerful swing of the chain.

Bracing his right hand with his left to prevent it from shaking, Grisbane cautiously worked the needle and thread through the incision in the paladin's side, the muscles in his face actually beginning to ache from how narrowed in concentration his eyes were. Each time the needle went in, the man would grunt lightly, but otherwise remained relatively quiet. Finally, with the last stitch, Grisbane let out a tremendous sigh of relief, tying the knot in a hitch fashion commonly used to tie down tent flaps. When it was done, he reached up, wiping the perspiration from his forehead.

"Thank you…" the man said weakly and not without great effort.

Looking up, Grisbane smiled, reached over, and laid a consoling arm on his shoulder. "You're going to be alright. I'll leave some whitewine here for you; drink some if the pain returns."

That said, Grisbane stood, looking around. It wasn't long before the cleric found him, brushing past him to examine Grisbane's work. Looking over the stitches, the cleric nodded, then turned to look at Grisbane and nodded again.

"Nicely done. Are you certain you haven't missed your calling as a cleric?"

Grinning, Grisbane shook his head. "We are all where we are meant to be, so long as we follow the All Father's guidance. What's next?"

As the chain flew out, Ionnus jumped to the side to avoid it, the necromancer yanking it back and taking to spinning it at his side again. As it regained momentum, he brought it above his head, the spiked weight at the end circling above him menacingly until suddenly he made his move. Redirecting the chain's trajectory, the necromancer lashed out with a powerful downward swing that caught Ionnus off guard. Ionnus was barely able to react in time and get his shield up. The weighted end slammed against his shield, staggering him just long enough for the necromancer to draw back and swing again, keeping the heretic just out of Skyhammer's range as he effectively cowed Ionnus under his shield.

Realizing his shield wouldn't hold and that the necromancer would eventually break through, Ionnus seized the first opening he could take; the moment the weighted end hit his shield again, the front already dented to the point where another blow would have punctured it, Ionnus lunged sideways in an effort to create distance once more. But the necromancer pursued aggressively and, with a practiced maneuver, brought the chain around in a wide horizontal sweeping motion that wrapped around Ionnus from behind. One of the spikes caught in the crevice of his breastplate.

With a hard pull, Ionnus was spun around, and the necromancer was swift to follow through with a quick lash from the reserve in his left hand, catching Ionnus across the front of his visor with the chain and ripping the helmet from his head. Ionnus staggered, bringing his shield up instinctively, only to feel the spiked chain wrap around his left calf. But just as the necromancer went to pull, Ionnus pivoted with all his strength, stepping back and effectively pulling the necromancer within reach. With both hands holding the chain, the necromancer watched on in horror as Skyhammer rose into the air, the tapered spike arcing gracefully as Ionnus brought it down in an overhead swing. As the tip of the spike punctured the helmet, it continued on through the necromancer's skull, the armored priest of the dead god's body going completely limp as blood spattered through the slits in his visor and sprayed the front of Ionnus's armor.

Immediately, the weight of the dead god's presence lifted tremendously. As the dreadknights grew visibly demoralized, the paladins pressed on with a renewed sense of vigor, and before long the dead god's heretics were sounding the retreat.

Stopping to pick up his helmet, Ionnus looked over when one of the dreadknights he'd bested began chuckling. Sliding his helmet over his head, he stepped over to where the man lay.

"Perhaps your helm inhibits your vision, heretic, but your unit has abandoned you. Repent now, and perhaps you'll be shown the All Father's mercy."

"You are a fool, church knight…the battle is not lost…it is only just beginning…"

Looking up and glancing around, Ionnus nodded before looking back down. "Your faith is most admirable, heretic."

"Not here…" the dreadknight said, chuckling weakly and coughing.

Pausing for a moment, Ionnus crouched down as a sense of dread slowly began to creep over him. Using the spiked end of Skyhammer, he removed the dreadknight's helm from his head, tossing it aside and stepping onto the dreadknight's breastplate. "What do you mean, 'not here'?"

"Weren't you cloaked in blue, last we met?" Asmodeus asked, slowly beginning to circle Roningus.

Keeping step with the half-fiend, Roningus held his swords at the ready. Asmodeus walked casually in circles, glancing at Roningus over his shoulder as he moved. He frowned slightly when his words failed to elicit a rise out of the paladin.

"Indeed I was," Roningus said calmly.

With a heavy sigh, Asmodeus held his hand out, the quarter staff that had been standing by the throne flying to his hand when summoned. The moment his fingers closed around it, Asmodeus leapt forward, leading with the end of his staff in a flurry of jabs. Expertly, Roningus sidestepped each one, and when the half-fiend tried jabbing at him with the points of his wings in an effort to distract him, Roningus answered by swatting them away with the carefully honed edges of his swords. It only took one connecting hit for Asmodeus to fall back before diving in again, bringing the end of his quarterstaff down in a hard vertical swing aimed for Roningus's helm.

Bringing the flat of his left blade up to block the attack, Roningus followed through with a strong forward thrust with his right. Asmodeus brought the opposing end of his quarterstaff down to swat the thrust aside. Pivoting to his right, the half-fiend lashed out at Roningus's helm with a pointed elbow. Roningus ducking out of the way just in time to see Asmodeus's feet leave the ground. Reacting instantly, he dove forward, tucking and rolling out of the way just as Asmodeus slammed knee-first into the ground.

Spinning around, Roningus lashed out with his swords, more as a way of keeping the half-fiend off of him as he regained his bearings. Dipping backwards and narrowly avoiding the blades, Asmodeus stepped in, pivoting to his right and launching a precision strike with the tip of his right wing aimed to catch Roningus in the visor and knock him off balance. But Roningus took him by surprise, leaning back far enough to allow the tip of the wing to stop inches in front of his face, bringing his crossed swords up and shearing nearly a foot off of the wing's end.

Asmodeus roared in pain and frustration, leaping back from Roningus and tucking his wings up behind him defensively. Flourishing his swords at his sides, Roningus approached Asmodeus with an aggressive demeanor, the half-fiend finding himself on the defensive for once. Roningus lashed out, his swords working in tandem as he spun, sidestepped, and continuously pressed forward, the arrogant, cock-sure expression on the half-fiend's face being replaced with one of grim determination.

For how long they fought on, neither was certain, but when they finally found themselves pausing to catch their breath, Roningus stood with a sword still pointed defensively at Asmodeus while the half-fiend kept his quarterstaff at the ready. Both were breathing heavily.

Asmodeus chuckled, grinning wickedly as he spoke. "Your armor…exhausts you…you cannot continue much longer…"

As if in response, Roningus stood up straighter, and with some effort began to regain control of his breathing. "Your injury screams…for your attention…you are visibly distracted…"

The grin fading from his face, Asmodeus regarded Roningus for a long moment, studying the Drakmahr family sigil on the front of his breastplate. When Roningus drew in a deep breath, it was clear that the church knight would soon be ready to continue.

Asmodeus studied the Drakmahr sigil on the front of Roningus's breastplate as he spoke. "Why…are you…cloaked…in brown, once more…church knight?"

With a single chuckle, Roningus brought his longswords to a ready position. "Admit that you're stalling for time, and perhaps I'll tell you."

When Asmodeus laughed between gasps for breath, Roningus lowered his swords, and Asmodeus stood his quarterstaff on the ground. "So honorable…even when facing one…beyond redemption. Tell me your story…church knight."

Roningus shook his head, gripping his swords in his hands. "I am but an instrument of the church. Capes mean little; it is what lies within oneself that matters most."

Asmodeus smirked, taking another deep breath and beginning to regain his composure. "What if I could offer you more?"

Roningus shook his head. "Spare me your heresy, half-fiend."

"But what defines heresy, church knight?"

"The church—"

"The church. Not man…not reason…not logic…the church. Your demotion…what brought it about?"

Pausing for a moment, Roningus tilted his head. His faith was unquestionable, but his curiosity to see where the half-fiend was going with his line of questions got the best of him. "I mishandled a prisoner who had already yielded himself to the church's fair justice."

"A poisoner."

When Roningus nodded, Asmodeus chuckled silently. "You knew," Roningus said plainly.

Asmodeus nodded as he continued. "It should come as no surprise. Had his efforts failed, it would have fallen on me to carry out the mission. What did you do to the man?"

"I lost my temper and introduced his face to a wall."

His grin widening into a genuine smile, Asmodeus laughed as he spoke. "As well you should have. Not only did the man assassinate the figurehead of your faith, he did so in the most craven way imaginable. Did he not deserve worse?"

"It is not my place to judge," Roningus said, his tone remaining flat.

"Isn't it? Hmm…" As he trailed off, Asmodeus raised his eyebrows thoughtfully.

Shaking his head again, Roningus laughed. "You have me figured wrong, half-fiend. I am not so easily manipulated."

The grin returned to Asmodeus's lips. "Of course you are."

With a casual flourish of his swords, Roningus was poised and ready to go again. "That you believe that does not surprise me, half-fiend. For you know nothing of true faith."

Asmodeus narrowed his eyes, reaching over and lifting his quarterstaff from the ground. "I have stood in the dead god's presence, church knight. Can you say the same of the feeble old man you call All Father?"

"I cannot."

"Then do not deign to lecture me on the meaning of faith."

As Roningus spoke, he drew his weapons back; his left sword went down by his right side, his right sword poised behind his head. "It is not faith that spurs you to action, half-fiend. Pain…fear… anger…these are the tools of the dead god. True faith is feeling the All Father's presence, knowing that your purpose is just and rising to the challenge laid before you, that you may return to the All Father's loving embrace in the afterlife. What has your dead god promised you, half-fiend?"

Asmodeus opened his mouth as if to speak. Faltering when words failed him, he paused, looking to the ground for a moment. Gripping his quarterstaff tightly, he looked back up, his eyes narrowed on Roningus. "I am ready, church knight."

"So you think."

Straining to get the bench he was using to barricade the door in place, Vogoth let out a heavy sigh. Once it was done, he turned and hurried down the hallway, cautiously looking around each corner before proceeding in the event more of the dead god's heretics had breached the church's walls. It was when he had almost reached the hallway that lead to his chambers that he spotted Brogam, surrounded by a dozen paladins cloaked in black, escorting him towards the arch cleric council chambers.

"Vogoth!" Brogam said in alarm, three of the paladins instinctively reaching for their longswords before realizing who it was. "What are you doing?! We must get to the council chambers at once!"

Shaking his head, Vogoth strode forward, the paladins forming a defensive ring around the two as they conversed. "The dead god's heretics are defiling the streets of Ascention with their footsteps, and you keep twelve black cloaked oathbrothers by your side for your own peace of mind?!"

Brogam blinked, taken aback that anyone would question his actions. "The high priest—"

"Is bound to keep the best interests of the holy city of Ascention in mind! Eight of these men could be out defending Ascention's walls!"

His expression turning from surprise to anger, Brogam's voice grew indignant. "How DARE you question my authority as high priest?! In light of recent events, I hardly see the need to justify—"

Shaking his head, Vogoth silenced Brogam with a gesture of his hand. "I haven't the time to argue with you. You four, come with me. Your oathbrother faces one of the dead god's assassins alone in the council chambers and will need your help. You four, escort the high priest to his chambers. Once his position is secure, two of you remain behind to stand guard. The other two will rejoin you four in bolstering the city's defenses."

"You can't do this! You have no authority! I am high priest, not you, Vogoth!"

Rolling his eyes, Vogoth sighed heavily, drew back his fist… and delivered a resounding blow that caught Brogam in the jaw, the high priest going immediately unconscious and falling into the arms of two of the paladins. "Oathbrothers…the high priest has fainted." Vogoth said, shaking his hand painfully. "Carry him to his chambers, if you would. You four, on me. The rest of you, to the walls."

"Yes, arch cleric," the paladins responded, and not without a sense of tremendous relief and enthusiasm, Vogoth noted.

That done, Vogoth turned, rushing back towards the council chamber doors with the four paladins in tow.

As Ionnus pushed through the ring of paladins that had gathered around Sir Rhygar, the fiery haired paladin from Forthos clapped him hard on his pauldron. "Nicely done, lad! You were meant to swing a hammer!"

That said, Ionnus handed Skyhammer over, speaking in a hurried tone. "Sir Rhygar, we've been deceived! Cynegald wasn't the main target; Ascention was!"

His laugh fading quickly as he holstered Skyhammer at his side, Rhygar's bushy red eyebrows furrowed darkly. "What're ye sayin', lad?"

"We must ride for Ascention at once!"

For a long moment, Rhygar studied him. "That's not possible. Our horses are already lathered from battle. The soonest we could leave would be tomorrow morning."

Ionnus shook his head. "We must leave tonight, today even. As we speak, the majority of the dead god's dreadknights and necromancers are launching a full-scale assault on the walls of Ascention."

For several long seconds, Rhygar examined Ionnus closely, leaning forward when he finally spoke. "How did you come about this information, oathbrother?"

Leading with his staff, Asmodeus leapt forward, swinging low and trying to put Roningus off balance before following up with a spinning back heel kick. His feint worked, and as Roningus moved to step out of the way , Asmodeus's heel caught him square in the breastplate, sending him staggering back a step. Following through, Asmodeus spun around, bringing his quarterstaff up above his head, swinging it in a full circle to gain momentum before bringing it down in a horizontal swing that clipped Roningus in the side of his head, nearly knocking him over and snapping one of the angelic wings off of his helmet. But Roningus recovered quickly, and just as Asmodeus spun around again to deliver another crushing blow, Roningus stepped in, slashing out with both swords and leaving a tremendous gash on the half-fiend's wings.

As Asmodeus staggered forward, Roningus seized the opportunity and stepped up, crossing his blades in front of the half-fiend's throat. "Drop your weapon."

For a moment, Asmodeus hesitated, but when he felt the edges of Roningus's longswords pressing against his neck, he complied. It was then, at that moment, that the sound of the doors being unbarred was heard, Vogoth's muffled shout heard from the other side.

"Sir Roningus! Are you alright?! We're coming in!"

"Now is your chance, church knight…you could kill me right now, and if you told them it was in fair combat, they'd believe you. You could bring an end to this war…or, you could let me live, only for me to escape and continue to wreak havoc upon you and your church."

Once, and then twice a shoulder rammed into the doors, and in response Roningus kicked Asmodeus in the back of his knees, bringing him to a kneel. "Hands where I can see them."

Grinning, Asmodeus raised his hands and placed them behind his head. "I hope you live long enough to see what a mistake you've made…"

"Sir Roningus! Oathbrothers, seize that half-fiend! Sir Roningus, are you alright?!"

Nodding, Roningus relinquished Asmodeus to the black caped paladins as they took hold of him, two of them taking hold of his arms while a third kept a sword point pressed into his back, the three of them escorting him from the room. "I am unharmed. Where is the high priest?"

"Resting peaceably in his chambers…the stress of the assault caused him to faint."

When one of the paladins who remained chuckled once, Vogoth shot him a sharp glance. Looking around for a moment, Roningus walked over and retrieved the piece of his helmet that had broken off, turning the wing over in his hand for a moment before tucking it into a belt pouch. That done, he walked over to the window and glanced out; city guards swarmed the streets like an ant hill, while the local militia worked to keep women, children, and the elderly safely secured.

The whole city was at war, and from the arch cleric council chamber's window, one could see it unfold before them.

"Your orders, arch cleric?"

His eyebrows furrowing, Vogoth turned and looked to the window. "Our city is under attack, Sir Roningus. Fall in with your oathbrothers, and do not let the dead god's heretics take her."

Cresting the hills of the grassy plains, it became immediately apparent that the column of paladins had arrived too late. The city of Ascention, her gates normally thrown open wide at the first sighting of a column's return, remained closed.

Well outside the reach of the dead god's archers that patrolled Ascention's walls, citizens that had managed to escape took refuge within the camps of the surviving city guards, a number of paladins and clerics intermingling with them. At the sight of the enormous host of church knights, otherwise weary and downtrodden faces suddenly brightened, invigorated by the hope that their city might yet be saved.

As the column joined with the refugee camp, Sir Rhygar rode forward, Sir Ionnus at his side. "Who has command here?!"

As he shouted, a purple-caped paladin stepped forward. "Sir Belgroth the Lightbringer. Command is yours if you would have it, oathbrother." As he spoke, Belgroth clasped his right fist, beating it against his left breast in the formal salute of the church knights.

Sliding down from his horse, Rhygar reciprocated the gesture as he spoke. "You are relieved, Sir Belgroth. Tell me what's happened here."

Belgroth winced, as if the mere thought of it pained him.

Nodding, Rhygar turned, addressing the column. "CHURCH KNIGHTS! REINFORCE THE REFUGEE CAMP! I WANT MY TENT ERECTED IMMEDIATELY AND A WAR ROOM ESTABLISHED. THE DEAD GOD HAS DESECRATED OUR HOLY CITY WITH THE FILTH OF HIS FOLLOWERS, AND HIS BLASPHEMY SHALL NOT GO UNANSWERED! YOU HAVE YOUR ORDERS!"

Immediately, the entire column of church knights dismounted from their horses, going to work assimilating with the refugee camp and transforming it into a base of operations.

Rhygar pointed a finger at Ionnus. "YOU! With me!"

Ionnus nodded, handing off his horse and hurrying forward as Rhygar lead the purple cape towards the camp.

"Do we have anyone within the walls?" Despite his shortness of stature, Rhygar's stride carried him swiftly, and Belgroth found himself having to almost jog to keep up at times.

"Last we knew, Sir Roningus and his unit still held the church."

Roningus is alive, Ionnus thought, a sudden rush of adrenaline coming over him at the prospect of seeing his friend again. Just as he was about to speak out of turn, however, Rhygar asked his question for him.

"Roningus?! The man was caped in brown when we left for Cynegald! How is it that Brogam put a brown cape in charge of the church's defense?!"

"The high priest has been confined to his quarters. When the heretics first began their assault, the stress proved to be too much, and High Priest Brogam fainted."

"You mean to tell me the man is still out?!" Rhygar asked incredulously.

Belgroth shook his head as he responded. "No, the high priest has awoken, but since his fainting spell it was decided that it would be best for him to remain confined to his room despite his numerous protests, lest he be overcome with another one."

"Who gave these orders?"

"Arch Cleric Vogoth. He was giving orders on behalf of the high priest before we were cut off and driven from the city."

Pausing for a moment, Rhygar laughed boisterously. "Well then, perhaps not all is lost if the high priest has been sequestered for the benefit of his health! The man is an ass!"

Belgroth's eyes went wide and, as he spoke, he bowed his head reverently. "One should not speak of the high priest in such a manner, Sir Rhygar…"

Furrowing his eyebrows and frowning, Rhygar shook his head. "That man follows his own agenda, and spurs the guidance of the All Father. I say again: the man is an ass!"

Doing his best to stifle his chuckling, Ionnus reached out and held back the tent flap as they reached it. After Belgroth stepped through, Rhygar turned to Ionnus, looking down at the longsword belted at his waist.

"There's got to be a blacksmith somewhere in this camp; do something about that. Have it melted down if you have to, but you were meant to swing a hammer, lad. I saw the way you bludgeoned your way through those dreadknights."

Ionnus paused, glancing down at the longsword at his side. When he didn't move at first, Rhygar spoke one last time before disappearing into the tent.

"You have your orders."

Pushing his way through the crowd, Grisbane finally spotted Ionnus. Rushing up to his friend's side, Grisbane tapped him on the shoulder, and when Ionnus recognized him the two immediately clasped hands and engaged in a half-embrace.

"I've not spoken with you the entire trip back! Where have you been?!" Grisbane asked, the two stepping back from each other and grinning.

"Riding alongside the Ruinous Hammer! He wants me re-armed with a warhammer as soon as possible."

Quirking an eyebrow, Grisbane frowned slightly. "A warhammer? So all your time spent in sword training is to be for naught?"

Shaking his head, Ionnus grinned and clapped Grisbane on the shoulder, leading him in to camp as they continued to speak. "It's neither as clumsy nor barbaric as it is made out to be; I had a chance to put one to use against the necromancer back in Cynegald along with his three bodyguards, and—"

"You slew a necromancer?!" Grisbane said excitedly, his eyes growing wide.

Ionnus chuckled quietly, nodding his head. "Indeed I did. I'll be interested to hear what Roningus has been doing to keep himself occupied…though I find it hard to imagine he could top such a story."

"Is he still alive?"

"Last anyone saw him, he was holding the church. Apparently Vogoth acts on behalf of the high priest now, and has charged Roningus with maintaining the church's defenses."

Grisbane blinked, nodding slowly.

After a moment, Ionnus spoke up again. "Where were you, anyway?! Rhygar sends you in to bring a cleric, and you hide behind the doors of the church?!"

Grisbane grinned, shaking his head. "No…nothing like that. I did help save a man's life, though…"

Making their way through the camp, they came upon the blacksmith. Standing over an anvil and hammering away at a farming tool he was repairing, Murik Dregland stood at a squat 5'6", his chiseled torso a wall of corded muscle from working the forge day after day. Looking up as they approached, his emerald green eyes glowed brightly, his mouth turning up in a crooked smile.

"Church knights. To what do I owe the pleasure?"

Looking over the modest forge that Murik had put together, Ionnus had to repress a frown as he spoke. "I'm told you're one of the few blacksmiths that made it out. Can you make weapons?"

Murik quirked an eyebrow, his smile widening as he spoke. "Can I make weapons, he says. What is it you'll be wanting, then?"

"I need a hammer."

Holding out the heavy forge hammer in his right hand, Murik chuckled sarcastically as he spoke. "That'll be 50 gold."

Ionnus rolled his eyes and sighed. "A *war*hammer…"

Pondering the idea for a moment, Murik shrugged. "I suppose I could make one. Have you got the materials? Steel's a bit hard to come by, if you haven't heard…farmers are turning down offers for their farming tools that would normally bring them to their knees, praising Mithos for sending such good fortune their way."

Reaching down, Ionnus withdrew his longsword, inspecting it one last time before offering it handle-first to Murik.

Glancing at it, Murik laughed once silently, dousing the heated metal in the barrel of water beside him and setting his hammer down. Stepping forward, he took the weapon in his right hand, looking it over before testing the weight of it and nodding in approval. "This should do it. Want me to turn the rest into a dagger?"

Ionnus shook his head. "Use it all."

His eyes going wide, Murik chuckled again. "Well alright then…"

Inside the tent, Rhygar paced back and forth as Belgroth recounted what had transpired. "...Roningus held the walls as best he could, but even with the added numbers of the militia, the dreadknights had the advantage of training. Seasoned fighters are no match for merchants and cobblers."

Nodding, Rhygar stopped, glancing down at the map. "How long was he able to hold them?"

"Nearly a fortnight."

"And how long ago was that?"

"Only a few days...from what I've seen of his ability, there's a good possibility the Wrathful Tempest still holds the church."

Pausing, Rhygar glanced over at Belgroth, grinning. "And what is it you saw, Sir Belgroth, that would leave you so openly lauding an oathbrother cloaked in brown?"

Belgroth smiled, as if reassured by his own words. "We expected them to be through the gates within a matter of days. When we finally were forced to sound the retreat and fall back to the church, Sir Roningus remained behind until the last of the militia had retreated, then quite literally fought his way back to the church and secured her doors. He is...a force of sheer destruction on the battlefield, and all who saw him agree that Mithos was with him. Some speculate that...perhaps Retribution will—"

Waving a dismissive hand, Rhygar shook his head. "I won't hear any more talk of that temperamental sword! Faith, determination, and the will to survive win battles, not some glowing weapon! Besides...I don't trust any sword that picks and chooses who gets to swing it..."

A brown cloaked paladin burst through the tent flaps. "Sir Rhygar! About those orders you gave me..."

Looking up from his map, Rhygar gave the paladin a stern look. "Well go on, out with it then! Have you found someone who can get into the city undetected or haven't you?!"

"I believe I have, sir. If you would follow me…"

"WHAT?! You mean to tell me you didn't bring him with you?!"

"I insisted, sir, it's just that…well, he refused…apparently the church of Mithos doesn't hold any sway over him…"

Growling irritably, Rhygar shook his head, stepping out from behind the table and making his way through the flaps, following the brown cloaked paladin. Eventually they came to a merchant's tent, where a shifty young man was set up selling all manners of goods from farming tools to blankets to weapons.

Glancing the items up and down, Rhygar spotted the smithing mark of the church's blacksmith on one of the blades, and glared at the man as he spoke. "Where did ye get this sword, boy?"

The blond haired merchant began to tremble, looking to the brown cloaked paladin for help. "Y-you promised he wouldn't…"

Looking over to Sir Rhygar, the paladin put a hand on his arm before addressing the boy. "We're here to see your boss…is he in the back?"

Glancing around nervously, the blond man looked unsure of whether or not he should answer, until a particularly refined sounding voice drifted from behind a set of curtains.

"Ah, so Sir Rhygar has come to call! Splendid! Percival, do be a good host and fetch something to drink for the good church knights! Please, step in to my office!"

Quirking an eyebrow, Rhygar cautiously pushed through the curtains, and stepped into a back room that was larger than the tent itself. Decked out in the finest one could acquire given the circumstances, a young man looking to be no older than twenty-five reclined on a cushioned sofa, a small table set up with various nuts and dried fruits. Dressed in pristine white fineries with a black silk top hat pulled down over his face, as the two entered the young man sat up. His black hair was carefully styled, and when he smiled pleasantly at them it accentuated the handsome cleft in his chin. Studying Rhygar with his deep brown eyes, the young man stood, bowing in a way that almost seemed patronizing before gesturing to the chairs before him.

"Please, do make yourselves comfortable! I'm afraid this is all I have to offer at the moment, as I was forced to leave a good deal of my possessions inside as we fled."

"Looks like you're still doing alright for yourself, selling stolen weapons and goods…" Rhygar said in an irritable tone as he took a seat.

Without so much as flinching, the young man's smile widened, yet when he spoke he was able to perfectly mimic an innocent tone. "Good and kindly church knight, I'm afraid I know not what you speak of! But, a thousand pardons…it occurs to me that while I know well who both of you are, I haven't introduced myself yet! My name is Ser Roderick. I understand you have a business proposition for me?"

14

"If you're so slick, how'd you end up stuck out here with the rest of these folks?" Sir Rhygar asked, eyeing Roderick suspiciously.

Roderick chuckled as he leaned over, grabbing a handful of the exotic nuts in the dish sitting on the table. "My dear friend… you are working on the assumption that I am, in fact, stuck…an assumption that I'm afraid is entirely untrue. The simple fact of the matter is I am providing supplies for the good citizens of Ascention both outside her walls…and within them as well."

That said, Roderick flicked a nut into the air, catching it in his mouth effortlessly and smiling at Rhygar as he chewed.

"The camp folk say he's the one they come to anytime there's something they need and can't get their hands on…food, soap, blankets, particular items of clothing…he's even established trade with the people on the inside, effectively keeping Ascention's economy running during her occupation."

As the paladin spoke, Rhygar continued to stare at Roderick, while Roderick continued to flip nuts into the air and catch them in his mouth, nodding in agreement with what the brown caped paladin said from time to time.

"So if you can get inside, why don't you just tell us how to do so ourselves so we can put an end to this and get on with our lives?" Sir Rhygar asked, his patience beginning to thin.

"When you have something of value, never accept any less than what it is worth...plus fifty percent." As he spoke, Roderick grinned charmingly, flashing his perfect white teeth.

Rhygar scowled, leaned forward, and reached out, grasping the front of Roderick's garments at his chest and pulling him forward. Leaning in close and nearly pressing his bulbous nose against the perfect point of Roderick's, Rhygar spoke in a slow, dangerous tone. "Now you listen to me, cutpurse...you're going to show us how you're getting in and out, and you're going to do it for the good of the church. This city bled defending your thieving skin, and it's time you repaid her for her valor."

The smile fading from his lips, Roderick narrowed his eyes slightly. His voice, which had been polite and even amiable up until then, grew eerily calm. "I'll say this but once, church knight, so pay close attention; you will unhand me at once, or I shall disappear from this wretched place entirely, and the dreadknights that rape your holy city can have their way with her like a murder of crows, picking clean a freshly laid corpse. And make no mistake...there is nothing you, nor any of your church knights can do to stop me. Do we understand each other?"

Pausing for several seconds, Rhygar's hand slowly released Roderick's garments, though his facial expression remained unchanged.

Leaning back against his sofa, Roderick smoothed out the front of his outfit, looking upon Rhygar with a frown. "For that, the price just went up."

"Spare me your bravado, boy. Just get ready to make a run, and don't think about disappearing or, on my honor as a knight of the church, I'll hunt you down and see you hanged for your heresy."

Smirking at the word "boy," Roderick nodded. "You know where to find me when your message is ready."

"Pews can be replaced. This isn't a suggestion."

"But, Sir Roningus…these pews were hand-carved by master craftsmen from—"

"You have your orders," Roningus said, turning and striding away, the cleric he'd just instructed to dismantle the pews that lined the altar room watching him leave with an expression of dismay etched in his face.

The main door to the cathedral was barred shut by three large wooden beams, the bottom of which had recently started to crack and looked as if it were about to break. Replacements had run out two days ago, and Roningus had been forced to improvise; alternate sources had run out, and so the pews of the church were next in line for repurposing. Even as he passed by the door, the dreadknights outside began battering at it anew, the massive wooden doors groaning against the wooden support braces he'd had set up to prevent the door from splintering.

Moving in swift steps down the western hall towards the stairs to the second floor, it was as he rounded the corner that he came face to face with an unknown intruder.

"You must be—" was all the man managed to get out, as Roningus drew his blades in a flash and lashed out to push the intruder back and put him on the defensive. The man ducked and sidestepped the blades lazily, as if it were a play that he'd grown tired of reenacting.

"Identify yourself!" Roningus shouted, holding his blades at the ready.

Chuckling lightly, the man shook his head. "Calm yourself, Sir Roningus…I come with a message from your fellow church knights."

"How did you get in here?!" Roningus asked, immediately glancing back to the door to make certain it was still barricaded shut.

"Finding ways in to places that try their best to keep people like me out is a speciality of mine… Allow me to introduce myself. I am Ser Roderick, and I come bearing good news." As he spoke, Roderick flashed a charming grin.

Lowering his swords but not putting them away, Roningus spoke in a flat tone. "Let's have it, then."

Nodding, Roderick continued. "Your fellow church knights have returned from Cynegald, and have joined with the refugees camped outside to form a base of operations. They plan to retake Ascention."

Roningus pondered Roderick's words for a moment. "We need supplies. We're running out of clean water, and our food stores will be depleted soon after."

Roderick nodded. "How many of you hold the cathedral?"

"Fifty-three of us, not including the conclave, the council of arch clerics, and the high priest. Two of us are wasted standing outside the high priest's chamber doors, ensuring he remains confined to his room."

Roderick's smile widened as he spoke. "Ah yes…I'd heard of the high priest's fainting spell."

Roningus sheathed his blades, resuming his former stride. "Who holds command outside the walls?"

Turning, Roderick fell in next to him, keeping pace as he replied. "A charming fellow by the name of Sir Rhygar the Ruinous Hammer…" It was then that Roderick blinked, surprised by the sudden realization that he had taken to following Roningus so naturally.

"What are they planning?"

"Ehm…there aren't any plans as of yet…" Roderick said, glancing back and still wondering how he'd ended up reporting to a church knight.

"You can breach the walls and move through the city without being detected?"

Roderick nodded, the thought restoring his confidence. "As often as necessary."

Coming to a halt, Roningus turned to face Roderick, the two seeing eye-to-eye through Roningus's visor. "Then there is much work to be done if we are to reclaim Ascension."

"Ah, there you are! I figured you'd be showing up soon. I suppose you'll be wanting your weapon, then?"

Laughing silently, Ionnus nodded. "If it's ready…"

"I said it would be, didn't I?" Murik retorted, with more than a hint of mock indignation. Still hammering away, he motioned towards a makeshift workbench with a nod of his head. "Go on and give her a swing, then…see how you like the feel of her."

Stepping forward, Ionnus paused to admire the warhammer Murik Dregland had crafted. The haft, made of solid ebony, measured at four feet long with a dark brown leather grip wrapped carefully around it near the base. The head of the hammer was a sinister looking thing to behold; a square head with a concave face left four protruding corners that would prevent the weapon from glancing off of a suit of plate, the opposing end a raven's beak hook that looked as if it could shuck a man from his armor like an oyster. The head was forged in one piece, and extended down the haft in as a sleeve that was bolted tightly to the ebony beneath it.

Marveling at it for several seconds, Ionnus reached out, lifting the weapon in his hand and testing the weight of it.

"I take it you like it, then?" Murik said, having stopped his work to turn and grin at Ionnus.

"It's…it's…"

Murik chuckled, shaking his head. "A fine weapon, for one of the church's finest. I'll trade you a holster for that scabbard you've got on your waist…"

As he spoke, Murik pointed to a studded leather holster mixed in among several other odds and ends, Ionnus nodding eagerly and laying the warhammer on the table before undoing his belt. Once he'd made the exchange, he redid his belt and lifted the warhammer again, sliding it haft-first into the holster and seeing how it felt before drawing the warhammer again to give it a few test swings, nodding in approval.

"What do you want an old scabbard for?" he asked, still admiring the craftsmanship on his new weapon.

"Most church knights fancy the sword over the mace or the warhammer…I'll be able to turn a profit on that by offering a sword to go along with it."

"Ionnus! Sir Rhygar has called a war council!" came Grisbane's voice as he came striding over to the smith's setup.

Nodding, Ionnus turned to Murik and was about to speak before Murik cut him off.

"Let me guess…I'll get paid once the city's been retaken?"

His mouth hanging open, Ionnus stared at Murik for a moment before speaking. "H-how did you…"

Grinning, Murik shook his head and waved him away. "The church has racked up quite a tab the past few days…you aren't the first one to come to me for a new weapon or have a piece of armor repaired."

That said, Murik waved him away and began hammering at what looked like the beginnings of a throwing knife.

Falling in with the other brown capes, Ionnus and Grisbane showed up as Rhygar was giving his briefing. "…walls are patrolled at regular intervals day and night. Our inside source tells us that the city guards hold the palace under Prince Theodric's command, and that Sir Roningus holds the church with roughly fifty men. All citizens within the walls have been cornered in the riverfront district, and the dreadknights utilize the palace district as their base of operations. In essence, they are exercising martial law."

As Rhygar continued to speak, Ionnus looked over, noticing a well-dressed man wearing a top hat and with a clefted chin standing next to Rhygar, a disinterested look on his face as he scanned the gathering of paladins.

"Who is that man?" Ionnus asked, nudging Grisbane with his elbow.

"That's Rhygar's inside source…a man named Roderick."

"He looks questionable," Ionnus said, quickly looking back as Roderick caught his gaze and grinned slightly.

"He is. Apparently when Rhygar found him, he was selling stolen weapons and various other supplies. We couldn't pin anything on him, though, so there wasn't anything we could do. From what I hear, he's found a way to get in and out of Ascention as he pleases, and is even able to relay messages to Roningus."

"So he IS alive?!" Ionnus said, a little too loudly.

"Sir Ionnus," Rhygar said, turning his eyes on the paladin for a moment as if to rebuke him. But then, catching sight of the warhammer holstered at his side, he grinned and nodded approvingly. "That's an excellent weapon you've acquired."

"Thank you, sir," Ionnus said with a nod.

Rhygar continued his briefing. "We're orchestrating a joint assault with our oathbrothers who still hold the church. Our main priority is safeguarding the high priest, the council of arch clerics and the conclave."

"What makes you so certain this inside source is as capable as they claim?"

As if on cue, Roderick grinned and stepped forward. "I thought you might ask that…"

With a wave of his hand, he produced the ornate silver holy symbol carried exclusively by the high priest, holding it up for all of the paladins to inspect before laying it down carefully on the table.

"…so while I was there, I had a look around and brought you a souvenir. Now, if there aren't any more ridiculous questions, I believe we have work to do. Your high priest will have no doubt noticed he's misplaced this by now, and I imagine he'll want it back."

15

As he walked his route atop the walls of Ascention, the dreadknight looked out warily at the camp of refugees. It had doubled in size a week ago, when the paladins they'd lured to Cynegald had returned. Talk among the townsfolk they held within the city's walls suggested the church knights were planning an offensive, and would soon move to reclaim the city. More disturbing, however, was the thought that news was being spread from outside the walls to within and, as a precaution, trade had become severely restricted.

Glancing over the side of the wall, the dreadknight looked at the cooking fires that dotted the landscape in the distance, the sun setting on the horizon bathing the scene in hues of pink and purple. It was just as he finished admiring the view and was about to turn around that he felt a sudden prick, as if something had bitten him on his back, followed by the sensation of metal sliding between his ribs and then an agonizing pain. His breath failed him before he could scream out and, as he collapsed to the ground, the last thing he saw was a young man, clad in white fineries, casually wiping blood from the slender blade of a rapier as he stood over him.

That done, Roderick sheathed his sword, crouching down over top of the dreadknight as the man gasped his dying breaths.

Sliding his fingers under the collar of the dreadknight's breastplate, Roderick pulled out the symbol of Necros the man wore around his neck, and snapped the cord as he plucked it from him like a flower from the soil.

"Pardon me, but the church pays good money for these so they can be destroyed…you don't mind, do you?"

As the man's fingers fumbled weakly at Roderick's sleeve, his life swiftly draining away from him, Roderick smiled, nimbly handling the symbol before making it disappear with a simple palming trick. He reached down and patted the dreadknight consolingly on the side of his face.

"There's a good lad."

His bounty secured, Roderick stood and made his way over to the mechanism that opened the gates at a leisurely saunter, quietly humming a festive tune as he pulled back the release lever for the counterweight. The gears within rumbled loudly as they turned, and the gates of Ascention were almost fully opened before the dreadknights sounded their alarm, the paladins of Mithos charging forth from where they'd concealed their formation.

Now to hold the gate… Roderick thought, carefully removing his white overcoat. Underneath, he wore a bandoleer holstering no less than a dozen masterfully forged throwing knives that slung over his left shoulder and under his right arm, and a long sleeved white shirt under that.

Reaching back behind his waist and producing a pair of tightly fitting calf skin gloves, he pulled them on just as the first of the dreadknights to respond to the open gates was making his way around to where the gate mechanism was. Turning, Roderick smiled handsomely and drew his rapier, to which the dreadknight responded by leveling his crossbow on him and loosing the bolt. Casually stepping to the side and allowing the bolt to fly past him, Roderick turned, grinning wickedly as he advanced upon the dreadknight, who in his panic to reload his weapon had dropped the winch and was fumbling with the bolt.

"How unfortunate that they only saw fit to issue you a crossbow...and that you missed..."

As the gates swung open, Rhygar chuckled and shook his head. "I'll be damned."

That said, he unholstered Skyhammer, brandishing the weapon high above his head.

"FOR THE GLORY OF MITHOS!" he cried, and all at once the sound of a column of church knights hell bent on reclaiming their beloved holy city was heard thundering across the plains.

They had used the refugee camp and its occupants to their advantage, drawing attention away from their position by lighting an overabundance of cooking fires each night so that when the time had come nothing looked out of the ordinary. Now, racing across the plains at full speed, the column of paladins reached the gates within moments. Sir Rhygar led the charge, the first to smash through the wooden barricades on his armored warhorse.

Dreadknights poured out of occupied homes serving as barracks, and within moments the streets of Ascention were filled as church knights and dreadknights clashed in fervent combat. Sir Rhygar continued to press the charge, battering dreadknights about the heads with Skyhammer until the paladins had gained a foothold at the entrance. Once the dreadknights had fallen back to further within the city, and the paladins went to work setting up their base within the walls, Rhygar turned and pointed at Ionnus.

"YOU!"

Startled momentarily, Ionnus turned. "Yes, sir?!"

"FIND RODERICK! I WANT A STATUS REPORT FROM THE CHURCH!"

Standing alone in the bell tower, Roningus smiled as he watched the gates of Ascention open in the distance. Sliding his helmet on his head as the alarm was raised, Roningus continued to watch as the paladins poured through and began making headway through the sea of dreadknights that separated them from the church. After several minutes he turned, swiftly descending the steps and pushing through the door, nearly knocking over a blue caped paladin as he did so.

"Sir Roningus! A man in white has—"

"I already know. Where is he?"

"In the alter room...he said he has a message for you. How did he…"

Roningus chuckled once. "That is not for you or I to know, oathbrother. Only that he is on our side for as long as we can afford him."

Striding purposefully through the halls, Roningus reached the altar room to find Roderick pacing back and forth in the open space where a row of pews used to be. As he entered, Roderick looked up, his eyes widening as his charming smile returned.

"Ah, Sir Roningus! There you are!"

Glancing down and inspecting Roderick, Roningus spotted the empty bandoleer slung over his chest. "You've been busy."

Looking down at his emptied arsenal, Roderick chuckled. "Quite. Unfortunately, there is little time for exchanging pleasantries…your comrade Sir Rhygar has established a foothold inside of the city's gates, and he wishes for you and Prince Theodric to flush the dreadknights out of their bases while he continues to advance further into the city. He's quite literally attempting to crush them between two walls of paladins. An aggressive and rather brutal tactic, but from what I've seen of him, he knows little in the ways of subtlety."

Roningus nodded as he spoke. "I could only take ten men with me and leave the church safely guarded. How does Sir Rhygar propose I make such a push with so few men?"

Roderick pointed at Roningus with his index finger, bowing his head as if to acknowledge his concern as he spoke. "An excellent question, and one I'm not unprepared for. As it turns out, Prince Theodric and his father, King Theroric, are more than happy to grant the majority of their personal guard to the reclaiming of Ascension. Leaving behind a token force to ensure the safety of the palace servants and non-combatants, they'll essentially be sacrificing a good portion of the palace to the destruction of the dreadknights in order to give you the men you need. Prince Theodric has proclaimed he will personally assist you in the matter, and that you may leave all of the remaining church knights behind to safeguard the church."

Roningus grinned, shaking his head. "I should have known..."

Tilting his head, Roderick grinned. "Mmm...quite. Now then, if you'll kindly come with me, we shall hurry to the palace at once and meet up with Prince Theodric."

Nodding, Roningus turned, shouting in a commanding tone that one couldn't help but respect. "Sir Drogan!"

A purple caped paladin came hurrying forward, standing at full attention before the brown-caped Roningus. "Yes, Sir Roningus?!"

"You have command now. Continue to follow the plans as I've outlined them, and make certain the high priest remains confined to his chambers. I'll not have him fainting again. You have your orders."

"Yes, Sir Roningus!"

That said, Roningus and Drogan exchanged the formal salute before Drogan strode off. Turning to Roderick, Roningus nodded. "I am ready now."

Chuckling once silently, Roderick nodded. "Why am I not surprised?"

As they reached the palace, they found Prince Theodric awaiting them anxiously. Standing at just under five and a half feet, Prince Theodric's black hair grew thick and unruly like the mane of a lion, complete with wide, long sideburns that nearly reached his chin. His eyes were a bright shade of light blue, and what he lacked in stature he made up for in physique; his thick arms bulged with heavily corded muscle, his square-ish torso looking to be built from brick with a powerful pair of legs beneath him.

A squire was helping him into his armor, a combination of chain mail and plate mail pieces. He wore an exquisite yet modest breastplate with a chain shirt underneath, and a pair of plate gauntlets. A pair of studded leather leggings reinforced with iron rings were tucked neatly into a pair of plated boots, his helm fashioned in a fearsome visage with a pair of horns mounted on the sides like those of a bull. As Roderick and Roningus approached, Theodric's eyes lit up, a smile forming upon his lips.

"There they are! The church knight and his escort, and just in time! I'll be suited up and ready to go in but a moment… Pierce! Help me get this damned buckle done! There's a good lad. Go and bring me my ranseur then, won't you?"

Chuckling, Roningus stepped forward and fell to one knee. "Your High—"

"Don't start with that already! Last time I checked, my father was still king, so you can save your 'your highnesses' for him."

That said, Theodric's grin widened, and Roningus couldn't help but laugh as he rose. Turning his attention on Roderick, Theodric looked him up and down once.

"And who is this who kneels to no man?"

With an artificially apologetic smile, Roderick shrugged his shoulders. "No one of importance, your highness. Just a man, doing his civic duty."

"Hah! The hell you are!" Theodric said as he inspected the buckle his squire had done for him. When Theodric nodded his approval, the boy ran off to retrieve his weapon before Theodric leveled his gaze on Roderick once more. "I've heard of the exorbitant fee you're leveling on the church for your services! You listen to me, cutpurse...I don't want so much as a single bill crossing the church's threshold. When this is over, you come see me, and we'll settle any monetary issues. Understood?"

Roningus bowed his head reverently. "That is most generous of you, your highness..."

Roderick laughed lightly, and gave a half-hearted bow as he spoke. "As you command, your highness."

Frowning, Theodric quirked a brow at Roderick briefly before turning to take his ranseur from the squire. An illustrious weapon fit for a warrior prince, Theodric's ranseur stood over six feet tall. Wrapped near the bottom and again near the top with black leather grips, the haft was carved from a single branch of a tree from the Greatwood, the resulting product being flexible yet strong enough to support all of Theodric's weight while in his armor if necessary. The three-pronged head of the weapon was forged from adamantine, and extended a full foot down the haft in a metal sleeve that was meticulously secured through the wood with four bolts. In the center of the head, where the three prongs connected, a sparkling blue sapphire had been worked into the metal and made visible from both sides.

Taking the weapon in his hand, Theodric flourished the polearm with an ease of effort that came from years of practice, practicing a few jabs with it before turning and pointing it at Roningus, grinning wickedly. "Let the bastards come! Hah hah!"

"If you two are ready, then, I shall make my way back to Sir Rhygar and inform him that the plan shall commence." As Roderick spoke, he half-bowed again, then turned and strode off, disappearing around a corner.

Watching him as he left, Theodric rested the butt of his ranseur on the ground, waiting until Roderick was out of earshot before he spoke. "What do you make of that man, church knight?"

For several seconds, Roningus said nothing, until finally he spoke up. "That one is very dangerous. Following his lead, we made it from the church to the palace without so much as alerting a single dreadknight, though several fell to the point of his rapier. I've never seen a man so able to move in total silence, and he strikes with the surest hand I've seen and without the slightest hesitation. Whatever he asks when this is over, I suggest we pay it to him."

Nodding, Theodric took up his ranseur once more before sliding his helmet on. "Something about him is strangely familiar... it would be impossible for him to be that man, though, considering at the time I would have been just a boy, barely older than five."

Pausing for a moment, Roningus turned, and the two looked at each other for a long moment before bursting out laughing at the absurdity of the notion.

The attack came swiftly and from seemingly nowhere. The dreadknights who had been assigned to maintaining surveillance of the palace stood not a chance; Theodric's royal guardsmen descended upon them in an instant and without mercy. Numbering at less than one hundred, but trained extensively in combat styles suited for close quarters and an urban setting, the royal guardsmen were not quite as heavily armored as the church knights but came close. Round metal shields with vicious spikes mounted on the front were put to deadly use, their curved hook-shaped swords designed for slashing and ripping armor open, an actual hook on the back designed for catching spears and disarming weapons. Their helms bore large red plumes and no visors, instead consisting of one solid piece with holes in the front for their eyes that opened into a slit that extended down the center of the front, a thin strip protruding downward to protect the bridge of the nose. Wearing the same breastplate and chain shirt combination as Theodric, they took their armor a step further by wearing plated greaves, their shins and the tops of their boots studded with small spikes that they used to their advantage in combat.

As they fell upon the dreadknights outside the palace, it was Roningus who called for the charge, leading with Prince Theodric as the two rushed forward at the front of the line. Slashing through wooden pikes, Roningus unleashed all of his fury upon the dreadknights, swinging his carefully honed blades with such force that on several occasions he clove straight through a dreadknight's helm, and in one such instance his sword was buried in a dreadknight's head down to his neck. Delivering a powerful front kick and pulling hard, Roningus would unlodge the weapon and continue to fight, and it wasn't long before he found himself having to chase down heretics as they fled from him.

Theodric, on the other hand, sounded less like he was in the middle of a melee and more like he was at a particularly lively party. His booming laughter resounded through the streets as the tip of his ranseur danced between dreadknights, pushing shields out of the way with ease and always seeming to find the gaps between the plates of a suit of dreadknight armor. Hooking the front of a visor with the right point of his ranseur, Theodric pulled a dreadknight to the ground before taking his weapon firmly in both hands and punching through the slits in the visor, howling with laughter as he rounded on the next one.

As the fighting came to an end, the last of the dreadknights proved to be one of true faith by refusing to renounce his evil ways before being summarily executed. Theodric found Roningus performing the execution, having sheathed the sword in his left hand and holding the other with both, the point of which rested on the back of the dreadknight's neck and pointed downwards towards his torso.

"...the crime of unrepentant heresy in the holy city of Ascension, you are hereby found guilty. May the All Father have mercy on your soul."

When the dreadknight spat on the ground, Roningus did not hesitate, driving the point of his longsword down with a powerful thrust then twisting hard, the dreadknight spasming violently before going limp as blood began to spill out of his mouth. It wasn't until Roningus withdrew his blade that the man slumped over onto the ground.

"Was it wise to execute that man, Sir Roningus? Had he talked, he might have told us something of value," Theodric said, nudging the fallen dreadknight's limp body with the butt of his ranseur.

Shaking his head, Roningus retrieved a rag from one of the pouches that lined his belt and began wiping the blood from his blade. "His was a powerful heresy; his firm beliefs in the dead god's lies would have stayed his tongue."

Theodric laughed once loudly, taking his ranseur in his left hand and removing his helm by one of the horns with his right. Handing it to one of the royal guardsmen, he took a water skin and drank from it, offering it to Roningus as he spoke. "So where do we go next, then?"

Glancing at the water skin and shaking his head, Roningus continued attending to his weapon. "The riverfront district. Most of Ascension will be safe within their homes, but many of those that live near the river have no such luxury. Besides…it's high time the thieves guild repaid Ascension for the protection her walls have given them."

Nodding his approval, Theodric watched Roningus for a moment before speaking again. "How much longer are you going to be? I've just had my first taste of combat, and now you pause to wipe your sword like it were the runny nose of a child?"

Without so much as giving Theodric a sidelong glance, Roningus held up his sword, inspecting his work. "A good weapon will only remain a good weapon with proper care, and I refuse to use anything less than a good weapon."

"Sir Rhygar! The thief Roderick has returned!"

"Well?! Bring him here!" Rhygar boomed, sending the purple caped church knight scrambling.

When he returned, Roderick was at his side, his left hand holding his miraculously unstained white overcoat slung casually over his shoulder, his hat looking slightly askew atop his head. Glancing around, Roderick grinned as he looked back to Rhygar.

"For the life of me, I can't understand what you church knights have against comfortable accommodations…"

Scowling, Rhygar looked back down at the map on the table surrounded by torches in sconce stands that served as his base of operations. "Just tell me what you've come to say."

His eyebrows widening, Roderick nodded. "Very well, then. I was able to successfully unite your Sir Roningus with the good Prince Theodric, and the two of them have begun causing quite a stir among the remaining dreadknight forces. I personally witnessed an entire platoon on the move, with orders to set up a barricade to prevent them from reaching the riverfront district."

Rhygar paused, looking up from his map. "The riverfront district… so he means to…heh heh, Roningus, you clever bastard! Ionnus!"

"Sir!" came Ionnus's reply as he rushed forward.

"Take a half-column of brown capes and meet up with Roningus in the riverfront district. Make sure Grisbane is among them. It's time the three of you were reunited and working together again. Once there, inform Sir Roningus he is to double back and begin flushing out dreadknights along the main road, where we shall rejoin with him. You have your orders."

"Yes, sir," Ionnus said, his clenched right fist beating his left breast with a clank before he turned and strode off.

"What about you, cutpurse? You've proven you're more than capable with that rapier. How'd you like to join the reclaiming of Ascention?"

With a light chuckle, Roderick shook his head. "Thank you for your generous offer, but I'm afraid I must politely decline…it seems as if my task is finished, and so I shall leave the bulk of the fighting to those more capable than I. As such, I shall retire to the comfort of my quarters outside the city walls. Oh, and I do believe you owe me for these, as well."

Reaching up, Roderick undid the buckle of the bandoleer that was slung across his chest and set it down on the table. A number of unholy symbols of Necros were strung through each empty sheath, and after he'd set the bandoleer down he reached behind his back, retrieving a large cluster of them that had been bound together and hung from the back of his belt. More still he produced for the next minute or so, from various pockets both hidden and plain, as well as from inside the sleeves of his shirt. Some were simple, carved from wood, whereas others were ornate works of silver or gold, encrusted with precious gems, and had very obviously been taken from high-ranking officers.

Rhygar watched on in an astounded sort of fascination, and when Roderick had finally finished, the total of them all numbered at well over a hundred.

"You…you slew over a hundred men, just walking through town?" Rhygar asked, sifting through the unholy symbols that now covered his table and trying to get an accurate count of them.

Quirking an eyebrow, Roderick laughed, and responded in an amused tone. "How delightfully absurd! No, good church knight, I would say that fewer than thirty fell to my blade. A good number of them now roam the streets without the symbol of their faith, however. Some of them may have even noticed by now, I'd dare say. Whatever the going rate is on symbols of the dead god will suffice…just include it in my payment, when this is over. I'm sure I can trust the church to be fair in the counting and recompense for each of them, yes? Very good, then."

That said, Roderick turned and strode off, waving over his shoulder as he called out one last time.

"Farewell, church knights! Do me a kindness and be sure to succeed, lest I not be paid for my services rendered!"

Leading the push down the southern road to the riverfront district, Ionnus beat his way through dreadknights with his new warhammer, the weapon performing better than he'd hoped. The concave surface of the head with the pointed corners kept it from simply grazing off of angled surfaces, and the raven's beak proved a valuable tool for punching holes and ripping through chain mail. Ever at his side was Grisbane, working in tandem and taking down the ones that managed to escape Ionnus's warhammer, his classic style of swordsmanship cutting through dreadknights with steady precision.

As a dreadknight deflected what would have been a crushing blow from Ionnus, Grisbane stepped in, his sword finding the gap underneath the dreadknight's shield arm. When Ionnus's hammer came down again, the dreadknight's shield did not rise, and his screams were brief before the crumpling of his helm silenced them.

"How much further until we reach the riverfront district?!" Grisbane shouted, another platoon of dreadknights pouring out of an alleyway to reinforce the failing barricade they had set up.

"Shouldn't be much further! That smoke should be coming from the chimney of the Vulgar Cleric!" As he shouted, he turned and looked about him at the church knights that remained. "How many oathbrothers have fallen?"

"Seven, so far, and Sir Kysgar continues to fight with a broken shield arm!"

Ionnus laughed, shouting out as he swung his hammer at another dreadknight. "Kysgar!"

"Yes, sir!" came Kysgar's voice from further down the line, the brown caped paladin deflecting blows with his sword as his shield bearing arm hung limp at his side.

"Fall back and let Grisbane set your broken arm!"

"Yes sir! As soon as we reach the riverfront!"

Even as Ionnus was about to protest, Kysgar found his opening, a well-placed horizontal slice opening the dreadknight's throat and bringing him sputtering to the ground.

When finally they reached the riverfront, however, their welcome was not the warm and happy one they had hoped for. The royal guards had formed a perimeter, and as Ionnus approached, the guardsman greeted him stiffly.

"Identify yourself, church knight."

Pausing, Ionnus looked over to Grisbane in disbelief. When Grisbane shrugged, Ionnus looked back, taking an equally rigid tone.

"Sir Ionnus the Righteous Shield. Who has command here?"

At that, the guardsman laughed. "That depends."

"...on?" Ionnus asked, growing increasingly impatient.

"On who you ask."

When Ionnus sighed, Grisbane stepped forward. "Let us through. We need to speak with Sir Roningus."

"Roningus is busy."

"I've had enough of this," Ionnus said bluntly, pivoting and trying to shoulder his way through the royal guardsmen.

"Hold!" the guardsman shouted, unsheathing his weapon, along with several others that moved up to support him, the remaining church knights doing the same.

"WHAT'S THE MEANING OF THIS?!" came Theodric's voice, preceding his appearance.

In an instant, all weapons were sheathed, and all heads turned on him as the sound of over half a hundred armored men went to their knees.

"Oh, get up damnit! What in the abyss is all this squabbling about?!"

"Your highness! These church knights arrived, and are demanding to speak with Sir Roningus. We held the perimeter, just as you instructed."

With a nod, Theodric patted the guardsman on the shoulder. "Well done, Percival."

"Begging your pardon, your highness, but…what exactly is going on here?" Ionnus asked.

Rolling his eyes, Theodric reached up and ran his fingers through his hair, then motioned for Ionnus and his company to follow him. "Your oathbrother is trying to negotiate the help of the thieves guild with their leader."

Ionnus and Grisbane glanced at each other for a moment, Grisbane asking the question on both of their minds. "So? What's the hold up?"

With a sigh, Theodric shook his head. "It isn't going well."

"Where is Roningus now?" Ionnus asked as Theodric led them through the perimeter and along the winding streets of the riverfront district.

"The Vulgar Cleric. Sir Roningus and the halfling have come to a bit of an impasse, it would seem."

"Halfling?" Grisbane said, tilting his head questioningly. "Did you say halfling?"

Theodric nodded. "Apparently the leader of the thieves' guild was a halfling this whole time. Goes by the name of 'Slade'. He's a shady little bastard."

Upon reaching the doors of The Vulgar Cleric, Theodric paused and turned to Ionnus and Grisbane.

"Now I know it's difficult, but you have to promise you'll behave yourselves…Slade's already warned he'll up and disappear if Roningus threatens to imprison him one more time."

Glancing at each other, Grisbane and Ionnus turned and nodded to Theodric, the three of them pushing through the doors.

Looking to be no taller than three feet, Slade leaned back in a chair with his feet up on the table that stood between him and Roningus. Clad in a loose fitting white tunic and a pair of leather trousers that tucked into a supple pair of knee-high calfskin boots, his spikey brown hair was held back by a pair of goggles that he wore upon his forehead. A pair of leather bandoleers crossed over his chest holding a plethora of throwing knives sized for his small hands, and a belt with numerous pouches was buckled around his waist. A gold chained necklace that hung from his neck was tucked into his tunic, the sleeves of which had been rolled up to reveal a number of intricate tattoos along his forearms and wrists. Clenching a slim-stemmed pipe in his teeth, the acrid smelling smoke produced by an opiate known on the streets as "angel's breath" lingered in a heavy cloud above him.

As the three of them entered the tavern, Slade looked up with a wholly unimpressed expression before returning his attention to Roningus. He took another drag on his pipe before speaking, his deep voice sounding mismatched with his child-like stature.

"I've already told you, Roningus. You want our help? You pay us what you would have paid Roderick. It's as simple as that."

Sitting across from the halfling, his helmet laying on the table, Roningus stared at Slade with a stoic expression, his voice flat. "And I've already told you I'm not here to bargain with criminals."

With a sigh, Slade tapped the ash in his pipe out onto the floor, then reached into a belt pouch and began filling it again. "Then I don't understand why we're still having this conversation."

"Because if the dead god's heretics take the city, you'll be hanging by your neck from Ascension's walls within the month," Ionnus said, pushing his way past Theodric and approaching the table.

Without so much as looking up to acknowledge him, Slade took the thin stem of his pipe in his teeth, motioning to a thug standing near the hearth who lit a splint of wood and brought it to him. Using it to light his pipe casually, it wasn't until Slade had exhaled heavily into the air that he finally spoke.

"Governing bodies come and go, but the guild endures. Truth be told, it would not affect us all that greatly were the dead god's dreadknights to retain their hold on this city…business has been conducted much the same as usual during the city's occupation."

"Ascention has been your home! How can you stand by and let her be ransacked and taken over while you smoke your pipe and do nothing?!"

As he listened, Slade wearily blew smoke rings into the air, and once Ionnus had finished, he turned his head. "Aren't you the same people that have been looking for me so you could throw me in one of your cells for the rest of my life?"

It was as Ionnus was about to speak, however, that Roningus held up his hand, cutting him off. In utter silence they sat, Slade continuing to blow smoke rings into the air until finally the lack of conversation got his attention. The halfling looked over to find Roningus staring through him with an unsettling placid expression.

"Have you ever been to a city enthralled by the dead god, halfling?"

For a moment, Slade looked at Roningus, glancing up at Ionnus as if expecting an explanation, then looking back to Roningus when none came. "As a matter of fact, I haven't. Business here keeps me rather busy."

Roningus nodded slowly. "I have. I was only a boy when I saw it…a choking, oppressive place, where the citizens were treated like livestock, only as useful as what they could produce. And it wasn't a place for criminals, I assure you. Most people think the dead god's followers are a cult of lawless killers, moving from city to city to spread crime and corruption."

Quirking an eyebrow, Slade took his pipe in his hand, and for the first time seemed to be really paying attention to what Roningus said.

After a moment, Roningus continued. "Crime…corruption… these are merely the means to an end, tools used by the dead god to gradually subvert everyone to his will. Destroying the foundations of a civilized society so it can be rebuilt in a twisted mockery of equality. Everyone is expected to work, young and old alike, and everyone is given their daily 'standard'. Just enough food to watch your children go hungry while you gradually starve to death, falling asleep each night to the sound of high ranking dreadknights toasting their good fortunes, echoing through the streets. If you're caught stealing, you're dragged to the town square and executed, your body left for the crows as a warning for others. If you turn on your neighbor when they transgress the law, you're given additional food as a reward for your civil service. The entire city becomes a riverfront district…and the people you now think are your allies would claw you to death if they thought it would earn them a loaf of bread."

As Roningus's words sank in, Slade's eyes fell to the table, his laidback expression showing the first signs of genuine concern.

"They are not without law, Halfling," Roningus continued, his tone as flat as it had been when he began. "Quite the opposite, they have many laws. None of them are meant to protect you or your freedom."

That said, Roningus folded his arms across his chest, continuing to stare at Slade in silence. The room had gone completely quiet, the only sounds heard being the faint idle chatter of the royal guards and church knights outside the tavern.

Staring at the table, Slade took another long pull from his pipe, sighing heavily before looking back up to Roningus. "We cannot simply ignore that you aligned yourselves with Roderick. He is an adversary of the guild."

Roningus nodded once slowly. "Remember this conversation, then, when the dreadknights loop a noose around your neck and fling you from the walls of Ascension."

That said, Roningus reached for his helmet, tucking it under his left arm as he stood and turned to walk away from the table. Ionnus, Grisbane and Theodric fell in behind him as he did so.

"Wait…" came Slade's voice from behind them, his tone regretful.

"I've waited long enough while you sit and disrespect me by openly smoking an illegal substance in front of me as if the law no longer applied. If you have a change of heart, you'll gather your men and have them prepared for battle within the half hour."

As he finished speaking, Roningus pushed through the doors of The Vulgar Cleric, the four of them stepping outside.

"What was that?!" Ionnus said excitedly once they were out of earshot of The Vulgar Cleric.

Turning to both of them, Roningus quirked an eyebrow, grinning slightly. "It's good to see both of you, too."

Laughing, Ionnus stepped in, clasping hands with him as the two engaged in a half-embrace, Roningus doing the same with Grisbane once they were done.

"So what do you think will happen now that the halfling has a fire lit under him?" Grisbane said, his grin reaching from ear to ear.

"Slade is easy to understand. To be honest, most of what I was doing was getting a feel for him to see what his true motivations are. Fortunately, for as crafty as he is, his motivations are rather base. His pride will crumble before his greed."

Chuckling, Ionnus clapped Roningus on the shoulder. "Nicely done! Now what's this I hear about you taking command in the church?"

Smiling, Roningus nodded. "After we were forced to abandon the walls, Arch Cleric Vogoth charged me with defending the church. He acted on behalf of High Priest Brogam, who it seems is prone to fainting spells."

"Hmm. Odd that they should manifest so late in his life," Grisbane said, rubbing his chin thoughtfully.

"I wouldn't dwell on it too much, oathbrother. Now is not the time." As he spoke, Roningus gave Grisbane a meaningful glance, and Grisbane nodded slightly in recognition.

"So what's the plan now?" Ionnus asked, looking around anxiously.

"We make a push towards the gates, and crush any that stand between us and the stronghold there. Who has command?"

"Sir Rhygar the Ruinous Hammer," Ionnus said, looking over as Theodric approached them.

"Well?! Are we doing this or not?! I'm tired of sitting around on my arse!" As Theodric spoke, he donned his bull-horned helm and tapped the butt of his ranseur on the ground impatiently.

Roningus nodded, donning his helm as well. "Have your men get ready. Dawn will be upon us soon, and I'd rather not have the sun in my eyes when we make the push." That said, Roningus turned to Ionnus. "How many oathbrothers are with you?"

"Forty-three remain, and Sir Kysgar has suffered a broken shield arm."

"Who has command here, then?"

"Command is yours if you would have it, Sir Roningus." As he spoke, Ionnus bowed his head, Roningus's nodding slightly in response.

"You are relieved. Sir Kysgar!"

Moments after shouting, Kysgar appeared, his newly set arm hanging from his neck in a sling made from a long strip torn from his cape. Looking first to Ionnus, who nodded his head in Roningus's direction indicating the change of command, Kysgar turned to Roningus immediately.

"Yes, Sir Roningus?"

"How is your shield arm?"

Pausing as if suddenly remembering there was anything wrong with it, Kysgar looked down, wiggling his elbow back and forth in the sling that hung around his neck. "Strong as ever."

With a chuckle, Roningus nodded. "Go easy on it for now, and fall back if your sword arm grows weary."

"Yes, sir."

"FORM UP!" Theodric shouted, laughing joyously as the guardsmen scrambled to obey.

It was just as final preparations were being made that Slade reappeared...followed by just over thirty men, all dressed in a combination of loose fitting clothes and mixed pieces of leather armor. Many had bows slung over their shoulders, quivers bulging with arrows hanging from each hip, while others looked to be covered entirely in throwing knives. Tilting his head as Roningus approached, Slade glanced back at the men and women he'd brought with him before looking back to Roningus.

"I don't want any of my people getting hurt. We'll take to the roofs to provide support from above, and take down any crossbowmen we encounter."

Nodding, Roningus looked at the gathered entourage that Slade had brought with him.

"Oh, and one more thing...they answer to me, not you." As Slade spoke, each man and woman nodded their heads, a look of firm resolve in their eyes.

Undaunted, Roningus continued to look them over, nodding his approval as he looked down to Slade. "And you will answer to me."

Slade's eyes flashed with anger, shaking his head as he jabbed a finger into the stomach of Roningus's breastplate. "These aren't your oathbrothers, church knight. These people are risking their lives—"

"Really? Tell me...what's that like?"

When Roningus spoke, he tilted his head, Slade's mouth hanging open mid-sentence. Roningus looked up to the gathering of thieves, as if opening the question to all of them as well. None of them would meet his gaze, and when he looked back down, Slade nodded once begrudgingly, his eyes fixed on the ground.

Roningus nodded slowly as he spoke. "Glad we understand each other. Take to the roofs if you wish, and verify your targets before you loose your arrows. I don't want any accidents to happen. Advance with us, and if you run in to any problems, you let us know right away. You have your orders."

With a sigh, Slade motioned with a nod of his head, and the gang of thieves dispersed, swiftly ascending the sides of buildings with a practiced ease of motion.

"Good call on the halfling. I have to admit, having archers on the roofs will make this a great deal easier," Ionnus said, watching as Slade scrambled up the front of a shop building as if it were a ladder.

Nodding slowly, Roningus turned and began moving towards the front of the lines. "Ascention is their city, too. Now come…let us crush the heretics between two walls of steel."

No sound was given to indicate their charge. Roningus and his church knights fell upon the dreadknights and their barricade with a righteous fury, Roningus in the front lines alongside Ionnus and Grisbane. Advancing through the streets and slaying all who stood in their way, whenever the dreadknights tried to reform their lines, Roningus would call to the thieves on the roof tops, and a volley of arrows and crossbow bolts would rain down upon the dreadknights.

"Sir Roningus, we're almost to the gate! Sir Rhygar's men have them flanked!" Theodric cried, sweeping the legs of a dreadknight with his ranseur and bringing it above his head with a spin before driving the point through the visor of the dreadknight's helm.

Glancing to both sides, Roningus spotted Kysgar as he disarmed a dreadknight and knocked him to the ground with a powerful front kick to his shield. "Kysgar! Fall back! The rest of you form up! We're making the push!"

On his command, the church knights formed a tight wall with their shields, longswords drawn back and poised to thrust out at the remaining dreadknights. Steadily they continued to push the dreadknights, until just after dawn when they spotted Sir Rhygar's column near the main gates.

"HOLD STEADY, OATHBROTHERS! DON'T LET THE BASTARDS THROUGH!" came Rhygar's voice, the church knights digging their feet in and pushing back against the frantic dreadknights.

Once it had become apparent that their position had been taken, the dreadknights broke and took to the side streets, scattering among the houses to regroup later. Roningus called for the thieves to open fire, and arrows and bolts fell upon the heretics as they fled. It was as the church knights and royal guards were giving up their cheer of victory that Roningus found Rhygar, the two clasping hands and engaging in a half embrace.

"Roningus! You look like hell! Why did you abandon the city to these filthy heretics?!" As he spoke, Rhygar laughed, Roningus chuckling as he responded.

"Command is yours if you would have it."

Pausing, Rhygar looked Roningus over for a moment before shaking his head. "No...I don't believe I shall. Your unit will continue to answer to you for the time being. Come with me, we have much to discuss. There's a long road between us and the church, and the dead god's heretics will be eager to avenge their fallen..."

Standing on opposite sides of the table, Roningus and Rhygar looked over the map, their helms laying off to the side. Roningus's hair was plastered to the side of his face, and when a church knight brought him a water skin, he promptly upended it over top of him, leaning his head back and emptying its contents onto his face and drinking what he could catch in his mouth. Handing it off when he was done, he tossed his hair back, sending droplets spraying behind him before leaning back over the table, water dripping from his nose and chin onto the map.

"Watch it, now!" Rhygar shouted, pulling the map away.

"They've taken to the smaller streets and alleys, and are likely using civilian homes as cover."

"Cowards…" Rhygar muttered.

Roningus nodded in agreement. "We need to clear the main road and make our way to the church. Now that they're trapped inside the city, they'll likely try to take the church and hold it hostage." As Roningus spoke, Theodric made his way over to the table, his ranseur slung on his back and holding his helmet by one of the horns.

"Then let's plow our way through the bastards!" he cried, slamming his fist on the table impatiently.

Shaking his head, Roningus pointed at the labyrinth of side streets and alleyways that led off of the main road. "They've got us flanked from both sides this way, and from what Roderick was able to tell us, the bulk of their forces are holed up here…at the Vagrant Bard. They could easily mobilize and bring down the entirety of their forces upon us that way. What we need…is a unit to strike at their base to draw their attention, while the majority of our forces secure the main road to the church."

"Let's get to it, then!" Theodric shouted.

"PRINCE Theodric! Please calm yourself! None are as eager to cleanse this city of these repulsive heretics as we, but planning these things takes time. If we wander in thrashing about, we'll be cut down or pushed back before we even begin." As he spoke, Rhygar jabbed his finger into the map, as if to emphasize his point.

"Bah! Fine, make your damned plans, but be quick about it! I didn't put this armor on so I could stand around and look handsome!" As he spoke, Theodric turned and stormed off, nearly knocking over a church knight who was hurrying over to them.

"Sir Rhygar! One of the dreadknights that survived the reclaiming of the southern road has agreed to repent his sins and offer up what little he knows, that his life may be spared."

Glancing over to the church knight, Rhygar furrowed his eyebrows in thought for a moment before looking back to Roningus. "What do ye think? Should we hear what the craven has to say?"

Shrugging, Roningus scooped up his helmet, tucking it under his left arm and leading Rhygar as he did the same. "I see no reason why not. We're always looking for converts, after all."

When they arrived, it was easy to see why the dreadknight had been taken; a bolt had caught him in his left calf just below his knee, making escape impossible. Most of his armor had been stripped off, save the greaves on his left leg where the bolt still protruded. Seated on a cot with his leg propped up, the pale man with light blond hair and green, serpent-like eyes looked up as Roningus approached, smiling exhaustedly as he spoke.

"The Wrathful Tempest. Word has it that you show less restraint than we do in combat."

"You would know had your back not been turned as you fled," Roningus replied, walking over and inspecting the bolt in the man's leg.

"Remind me to thank your archers when I meet them," the man said as he leaned over and spat on the ground.

"You'd better have something worthwhile for us, heretic," Rhygar said calmly, gripping the handle of Skyhammer and eyeing the bolt still protruding from the man's leg.

"Oh, I imagine I do…but first, I'd like this bolt removed if it isn't too much to ask."

"We'll have it removed when you prove to us you're worth keeping around. Our clerics are busy tending to the men your fellow heretics wounded, and I'll not pull one of them away to save the life of a craven who seeks only to save his own wretched life under the false pretense of having valuable information." As he spoke, Rhygar's temper began to flare audibly, and by the time he was finished speaking, Roningus had to put an arm out and hold him back.

For several long seconds no one said anything more, until finally Roningus spoke up. "What shall I call you, heretic?"

Narrowing his eyes slightly, the blond haired man hesitated a moment in his response. "...Barton."

Nodding, Roningus stepped forward, extending his hand to Barton. In response, Barton reached up and took it, the two shaking briefly before Roningus continued. "A pleasure to meet you. Now, here is where you're at, in case you've forgotten. You are presently sitting in the middle of our encampment at the front gates with a crossbow bolt through your leg. In less than two days' time that wound will begin to fester, and in all likelihood you will lose your leg. From there, your chances of survival will plummet as the infection continues to spread throughout your entire body. So here is my proposition. I am going to stop talking, and you are going to start." That said, Roningus went silent.

Barton stared at the bolt in his leg, weighing his options, until finally he let out a resigned sigh, his head sinking down. "Bring me your map..."

"Listen up! New information has come to light recently, and we now have reason to believe the dreadknights have been purposely withholding their necromancers!" Standing before the entire assembly of church knights and royal guards, Sir Rhygar spoke as loudly as he could, his voice nearly staggering those in the front row.

"They have no power here within Ascension's walls!" came a shout from one of the church knights.

"What harm can they do on hallowed ground?!" came another.

"IF THEY TAKE THE CHURCH, THEY CAN UNLEASHE A HORDE THE LIKES OF WHICH YOU'VE NEVER SEEN!" Rhygar shouted, silencing the murmurs that had begun to rise. When the crowd stayed silent for a moment, Rhygar cleared his throat and continued. "Now, as I was saying before I was interrupted… reaching the church has become our main priority. Our newly updated map shows that the bulk of their forces are indeed holding out here, at the Vagrant Bard. A direct assault, however, would be folly…as it seems they have a dreadnought with them…"

Even as Rhygar spoke the words, he faltered with them, as if it disturbed him simply by saying them. The silence of the church knights was absolute, and for several long moments no one said anything until a random church knight spoke up.

"Why have they withheld it thus far?"

"More than likely, they haven't finished putting it together yet, but our informant tells us they more than likely started the moment we took the gates."

At first, no one spoke, but then a droning chatter gradually rose from within the paladins' ranks, Rhygar speaking solemnly over the noise.

"Sir Roningus has volunteered to take as many men as are willing to go with him. To be perfectly honest, there is little chance any of you will survive, but in keeping the dreadnought off of the main force you will buy us the time we need to establish our foothold within the church. Do I have any volunteers?"

Immediately, several hands shot up, more and more slowly but surely raising in the air until eventually there were nearly two score church knights, Ionnus and Grisbane among the first to raise their hands.

Rhygar nodded his approval as he continued. "Those of you that have volunteered are to report to Sir Roningus immediately. He has command of your unit, now. You have your orders."

As the assembled paladins broke apart, Theodric came up to Ionnus, placing his hand on the church knight's pauldron. "Hold on just a moment, church knight! I'm coming with you!"

Turning around, Ionnus smiled sadly at Theodric, shaking his head as he spoke. "I am afraid we cannot allow that, your highness. The risk is too great."

"To hell with the risk! Ascention is my city as well, and I'll not sit idly by while the task of defending her falls squarely upon the shoulders of the church!"

Grisbane sighed, frowning as he spoke. "That simply isn't an option this time, your highness. Did you not hear? They have a dreadnought with them, and it will be operational by the time we reach them."

Furrowing his brow, Theodric looked back and forth between the two of them. "So? What's a dreadnought, and why should I be so afraid of one?"

Pausing, Ionnus looked over to Grisbane, who after a moment gave a consenting nod. That done, Ionnus looked back to Theodric. "Imagine, if you can…a giant, wrought from flesh and steel…infused with false life by a high priest of the dead god. Stitched together from the corpses of a score of men, bound in shards of metal armor and driven only by its desire to consume mortal souls. Weapons have little to no effect on it, and somehow it is able to resist the cleansing powers of even the highest ranking battle clerics. Simply put, they are indestructible instruments of the dead god's will."

"Listen, church knight...I don't know what sort of mess you're trying to get yourself into, but we—"

"You'll be perfectly safe from the roofs," Roningus said, interrupting the halfling in mid-sentence.

Shaking his head, Slade folded his arms across his chest. "My men saw them hauling the pieces of that thing in. Most of them are of the opinion we should abandon this altogether and return to our hideout."

With a sigh, Roningus nodded his consent. "Very well. Report to Sir Rhygar. At the very least you can provide cover fire for the drive down the main road."

With a scoff, Slade turned and strode away. Ionnus watched the halfling leave as he approached Roningus slowly, Grisbane right behind him.

Once the halfling was out of earshot, Ionnus spoke. "So, commander...what's your plan?"

Shaking his head, Roningus drew in a deep breath, holding it for a moment before exhaling, and finally answering. "My plan is to slay a dreadnought."

For a moment, Ionnus and Grisbane looked at each other, then back to Roningus as Grisbane spoke. "You're not serious, are you?"

Hesitating a moment, Roningus looked to Grisbane, the faint hint of a smile on his lips. "I didn't say it was likely to succeed."

19

"Our plan is a relatively simple one," Roningus said, addressing his unit.

Just shy of eighty had volunteered, Ionnus and Grisbane among them. More than a few of them were of higher rank, yet stood in perfect formation, listening attentively as Roningus spoke.

"We make our way through the side streets, two-by-two. If they form up and block your path, fall back and draw them into the alleys, then regroup with Rhygar's men on the main road so that Slade and his archers can pick them off. They don't know the layout of the city as we do, and in that sense we have an advantage."

"What happens when they unleash the dreadnought?" The question was spoken in earnest, all of the assembled church knights glancing over at their oathbrother who had spoken it before looking back to Roningus for the answer.

Nodding silently for a moment, Roningus looked away as he replied. "I'm not yet certain. For now, your standing orders are to fall back if the dreadnought is sighted. None will question your bravery, nor will it be considered a violation of the code of conduct. In the meantime, pray that Mithos presents us with an answer."

With a solemn nod, Roningus dismissed them, the church knights falling in to their formations as one readied a horn.

On his command, the sound was given, and the church knights began their assault. Pouring through the side streets off of the main road, the paladins swarmed over the random patrols of dreadknights, falling upon them like locusts and bringing them down swiftly. Roningus lead a group of six, Ionnus and Grisbane among them, and more than once when the dreadknights would form up he would call for the retreat, luring them towards the main road where Rhygar's men were making their push towards the church and calling down a rain of arrows from Slade's archers before returning to the alleys once more. It was when they reached the Vagrant Bard, however, that Roningus called them to a halt, the paladins surrounding the inn from nearly all sides. Quietly Roningus stepped forward, his longswords bloodied from use and down at his sides.

Normally quite loud and boisterous, the Vagrant Bard was eerily silent...no sound could be heard coming from within, and when the other paladins moved to advance with him, Roningus signaled for them to hold their position. It was when he was almost to the door that it came, the massive, heavy oaken door flying open with such force that it burst off its hinges, tumbling forward with such momentum that Roningus had to dive to avoid it. Landing on his shoulder and tucking into a roll, Roningus came up from the roll into a kneeling position, his eyes snapping towards the door.

It was then that he saw the dreadnought...standing at a dizzying eight feet tall, the abomination of flesh and steel had to duck to get through the door. Moving with a cocksure deliberation, the dreadnought slowly rose up to its full imposing height and surveyed the gathered church knights. Its muscular limbs were stitched together from carefully matched strips of cold, lifeless flesh, large sections of plate mail infused directly in to them and adorned with jagged spikes. Its head, if it could be considered as such, looked to consist mostly of a torturous-looking greathelm attached directly to its shoulders with scarcely a neck to speak of, its vacant gray eyes glaring unblinking at the church knights as it lumbered forward. Large, powerful legs carried it in thunderous steps, its legs infused with the same armored plating as its torso. It carried no weapons, for it had no need; the knuckles of its right hand were studded with black steel spikes and its left hand had been replaced with a double headed warhammer larger than the skull of a horse.

Immediately, six church knights rushed forward, assaulting the dreadnought all at once.

"For the glory of Mithos!" they cried, brandishing their weapons and leading with their shields.

"NO!" Roningus cried, but too late did his order come…in an instant, the dreadnought grabbed the nearest church knight's entire head in its hand, crushing it as easily as if it were simply closing its fist.

Ignoring four of the others that hacked at the seams that bound its limbs together in vain, the dreadnought put its foot on the shield of the next, stepping forward and knocking the church knight to the ground, delivering a swift stomp to his chest while he was dazed with such force that his breastplate was nearly flattened even with him still inside it. Seeing their oathbrothers fall in such a manner, the remaining four concentrated their efforts, seeking to bring down the monster's left leg. But the dreadnought swung wide with its warhammer and caught one in his shield, knocking him clear away to slam against a wall before following up with a vicious overhand blow from its right hand, ripping the church knight's shield away when he tried to block. It followed up with a downward stroke, and the church knight raised his shieldless arm in vain as the warhammer connected with the top of his helm and crumpled his spine, slaying him where he stood.

The two that remained broke, and as they retreated, the dreadnought gave chase, catching one by the arm and flinging him effortlessly into the other. They landed in a pile, and it advanced on them, stomping one out before reaching down and dragging the other several steps, all while the church knight hacked frantically at the dreadnought's wrist before it finally swung him against a wall until his blood smeared the stone work. Turning, the dreadnought tossed the church knight's lifeless body aside, and as it leveled its sights on the remaining paladins, Roningus shouted, "HOLD POSITIONS!"

Glancing at each other briefly, the paladins brought up their shields, forming up and watching as the dreadnought slowly began lumbering towards the nearest grouping.

"Halt!" came a sudden voice from within the inn, the dreadnought going completely still as the command was issued.

For a long moment, nothing happened, but then a dreadknight appeared in the doorway. Clad in black armor with the dead god's emblem displayed prominently on his breastplate, a crimson red cape hung from the man's pauldrons and billowed gently with each step. Reaching up, he grasped his ram-horned helm and lifted it from his head, his cold blue eyes falling upon Roningus as he tucked the helmet under his left arm. He ran his right hand over his bald-shaven head, twisting his neck in either direction until it cracked, giving Roningus a condescending smirk before he spoke.

"The Wrathful Tempest, cowed before the might of the dead god. You've been a thorn in my side ever since we arrived to liberate this wretched city from the false father's grasp."

Roningus stood calmly, wiping the blood from his right-hand sword.. "Identify yourself, heretic."

With a sneer, the bald dreadknight shook his head, his ghastly complexion glowing in the prc-dawn light. "I think not. You will come to know my name before I put you to the sword. For now, simply knowing that I am the harbinger of your false father's demise is enough."

Finished cleaning his right sword, and moving on to his left, Roningus glanced casually over at the dreadnought. The hulking monstrosity stood still as a statue and continued to stare at the paladins who stood bravely before it, their shields raised and their swords at the ready. "You place far too much faith in the boon of your dead god. Even as we speak, the heretics along the main road are being overrun by my oathbrothers, and once we reach the church and call upon our battle clerics, the war is as good as won."

The dreadknight's lips widened into a smile. "Is that a fact?"

Finished cleaning his swords, Roningus returned the cloth to his belt pouch, giving his blades a flourish before facing the dreadknight with a ready stance. "Come, let us settle this in single combat. Your men need not die in vain this morning."

His smile widening, the bald dreadknight turned to gaze upon the idle dreadnought, the monster turning to face him as he addressed it. "Dreadnought...go and lay waste to the church."

The dreadknight's words drew a gasp from Roningus as the monstrosity turned, shambling off in the direction of the church without so much as a word.

"NO!" Roningus cried, the dreadknight laughing amusedly as he donned his helmet once more.

It was as the paladins started forward, however, that dreadknights began pouring out of the inn and from the side alleys behind it, rushing forward to engage the church knights.

Turning, Roningus bellowed to be heard over the sound of clashing steel as paladins met dreadknights head on with a renewed sense of vigor. "IONNUS! GRISBANE! GET TO THE CHURCH AND WARN RHYGAR! YOU'VE GOT TO STOP THAT DREADNOUGHT SOMEHOW!"

With a nod, Ionnus took off, Grisbane close behind him as he shouted back, "What are you going to do?!"

"I've got a pact of Necromancers to slay!" came his response, Roningus rushing forward towards the door and cutting down dreadknights as he went.

But the bald dreadknight stepped in front of him, and the other dreadknights parted around them, leaving him to deal with the Wrathful Tempest as he drew a spiked flail and spun it above his head. "You'll not enter this inn, church knight…not so long as I draw breath."

"That, heretic," Roningus replied, "is easily rectified."

"How do we stop this thing?!" Grisbane cried, ducking under a dreadknight's sword and stopping to plant his foot in front of the heretic's legs. A swift elbow to the back sent the dreadknight sprawling to the ground before Grisbane continued to rush forward.

"I don't know, but we must warn Sir Rhygar!" Ionnus replied, bringing his warhammer down on top of a dreadknight's shield. He utilized the opening left to deliver a powerful front kick that knocked the heretic prone, allowing Ionnus to trample him as he kept pace with Grisbane.

The dreadnought continued on in a steady path for the church, trudging down side alleys and streets, completely ignoring Ionnus as he ran up and buried the raven's beak hook of his warhammer into its back. Ionnus found himself being lifted from the ground and dragged along, until finally he pulled the weapon free and tried for the blunt end instead. The concave square head of the hammer slammed against the meaty muscle of the dreadnought's back, soliciting not even so much as a sideways glance from the dead god's monster. Each time the hammer hit, the flesh split open, only to reseal the moment the hammer was removed. Taking the warhammer to the side of the dreadnought's right knee didn't merit the creature's attention either, and after beating on it several more times in frustration, Ionnus looked to Grisbane helplessly.

"Well…that was my idea! What's yours?!"

Looking around frantically, Grisbane turned his gaze upward, spotting archers on the rooftops in the distance. "Come with me!"

Leading Ionnus, Grisbane headed left down a side street, then abruptly cut right and headed back towards the main road, the two running as fast as their legs could carry them to get ahead of the dreadnought. When they came out upon the main road, they were a short distance behind Rhygar's men, and Grisbane immediately waved his arms at Slade.

"Halfling! Redirect your arrows on the dreadnought, approaching from the west along Forte's Pass! We must stop it before it reaches the church!"

Nodding, Slade turned, barking orders at the thieves that lined the rooftops.

Within seconds, Sir Rhygar had fallen back, storming over and grasping Grisbane roughly by the front of his breastplate. "WHAT'S THE MEANING OF THIS?! Those archers were providing necessary cover fire to keep—"

"Dreadnought! Coming this way! Headed for the church!" came Grisbane's hurried response, the dreadnought lurching into sight down the side street he pointed at.

Looking down the road, Rhygar's eyes went wide, releasing Grisbane and looking up at Slade. "OPEN FIRE! SLOW THE DAMNED THING DOWN SO WE CAN SECURE THE CHURCH!" Then, turning back to Grisbane, Rhygar pointed Skyhammer in the direction of the Vagrant Bard. "DAMNIT! Where is Sir Roningus?!"

Looking over, Grisbane watched as a swarm of arrows fell upon the dreadnought, the dreadnought continuing on through them as if they were nothing more than a cloud of bothersome gnats. Those that hit plated metal bounced off, and the ones that managed to pierce the dreadnought's flesh were swiftly pushed out and fell to the ground as the creature's body closed up and mended its own wounds.

"He stayed behind to root out the pact of necromancers that give it life! Concentrate on the head!" Grisbane shouted. Slade nodded and barked orders at the thieves.

"Well he'd best hurry, or the church won't be standing before long!" Even as Rhygar spoke, the second volley of arrows clattered off of the dreadnought's greathelm of a head, one stray bolt managing to find its way through a slit in the visor.

Reaching up, the dreadnought plucked the bolt from its eye without so much as slowing down, discarding it as it reached the road. From there, it continued its advance.

Rhygar called out to the paladins in the rear of the line. "DREADNOUGHT FLANKING!"

Immediately several paladins turned, and within moments, they all had eyes on the dreadnought approaching them.

"What do we do?!" Ionnus said, his voice frantic as the dreadnought began wading through paladins and dreadknights alike, swatting any aside who were unfortunate enough to be in its way.

"There's nothing we can do, lad…" came Rhygar's response, watching helplessly as the dreadnought continued its unstoppable march towards the church.

20

"Half-fiend! Wake up! Breakfast!"

The paladin fumbled to unlock the cell door with his left hand while holding the bowl of oat porridge in his right. There, seated cross-legged in the middle of the floor was Asmodeus, his eyes closed in quiet meditation. His wrists were shackled, the chains that held them fastened securely to the wall behind him. Stepping towards him carefully, the brown caped church knight spoke as he slowly knelt down to lay the bowl before him.

"Here you are, half-fiend."

Without opening his eyes, Asmodeus inhaled lightly through his nose. "Porridge again?"

Shrugging, the church knight turned, speaking as he closed the cell door and locked it. "If it's any consolation, we've all eaten it just as often as you have."

Smiling slightly, Asmodeus nodded slowly as he opened his eyes, taking the bowl in his hands. "And the high priest as well?"

Chuckling, the church knight shook his head. "You never give up, do you?"

With a sigh, Asmodeus took the spoon in his hand, speaking as he lifted it to his mouth. "Not when the price of failure is so great."

Suddenly, there was a loud crash heard from above, rumbling the very foundations of the church and knocking crumbled bits of debris from the ceiling. At the same moment, both of them looked up, the church knight speaking in a confused tone. "What was that?"

Asmodeus grinned, setting his bowl down. "It would seem my liberation is at hand."

"NO!" Ionnus cried, standing next to Grisbane and watching on in horror as the dreadnought began smashing its way through the front doors of the church with the warhammer that served as its left hand.

Again and again it raised the warhammer and brought it down, each time the doors splintering more and more until finally they gave way, the dreadnought grabbing hold of the door on the right where the hole had been made and ripping it off its hinges. Tossing it over its shoulder as if it were a scrap of paper, the dreadnought brought down the door on the left with another casual swing from its warhammer, only having to duck its head slightly to step under the enormous doorframe. Immediately, chaos erupted in the streets as dreadknights and church knights alike rushed towards the doors, tripping and stumbling over each other all while swinging their swords wildly and fighting each other off. Soon the fighting that had occupied the streets had spilled into the church, the clashing sound of steel echoing while the dreadnought waded through a sea of bodies, swatting any aside who stood in its path as it laid ruinous waste to the structures within the altar room.

Reacting swiftly, Rhygar turned and bellowed orders at Slade. "FIND RONINGUS AND HIS UNIT! SUPPORT HIM IN

ANY WAY YOU CAN! THAT PACT NEEDS TO BE BROKEN IF WE'RE TO STAND ANY CHANCE OF SAVING THE CATHEDRAL!"

From the rooftops, Slade watched on in awe amongst his gang of thieves, Rhygar's shouting catching his attention. Nodding energetically, Slade gave the orders and the thieves were on the move, skittering nimbly across the rooftops towards the Vagrant Bard.

That done, Rhygar turned, pointing to Ionnus and Grisbane. "You two, come with me! We're getting the hell in there and making sure those filthy heretics don't make it to the high priest!"

Stepping forward, the bald headed dreadknight swung out at Roningus with his flail, Roningus dipping to the side to avoid it and swatting at his arm with the sword in his left hand. But the dreadknight continued the motion, bringing his left arm around in a wide shield bash that caught Roningus off guard, square in the chest, knocking him back and putting him off balance. Seizing his opportunity, the dreadknight followed up with a powerful downward stroke that caught Roningus on his left pauldron, staggering him and nearly bringing him to his knees. Gritting his teeth at the pain, Roningus was barely able to sidestep the next vertical swing, cursing silently when the dreadknight spun around to put his shield between himself and Roningus's sword. Roningus began to circle him, as the dreadknight kept himself between Roningus and the door of the inn, bringing the flail up above his head, swinging it in circles.

"Tired already, Wrathful Tempest?"

In response, Roningus leapt forward, swatting the dreadknight's flail away with the sword in his right hand and delivering a forceful forward kick to the dreadknight's shield, sending him reeling back a few steps.

"You'll not cut through me so easily, boy."

"I'll cut through you all the same," Roningus replied, giving the swords in his hands a flourish. Glancing up at the flail circling above the dreadknight's head like a buzzard waiting to descend upon him, Roningus found himself wishing for a brief moment that he had a shield, but quickly dismissed the notion.

"I think not. Reports tell me you were the one who held the church...tell me, what chance do you think your oathbrothers stand now that the dreadnought comes for them?"

"Enough talk," Roningus said and, with the same ferocity as before, he went on the offensive, slashing at the dreadknight's hand, his swords dancing in perfect tandem as he fought to create an opening.

But the dreadknight's words proved not to be a simple boast, and Roningus found himself evenly matched. Each time one of his swords left an opening for the other, the dreadknight's shield would rise up to meet it, or a swing of the flail would force Roningus to forgo the attack for a position outside of the flail's arc.

Growling in frustration, Roningus pressed a rapid assault in an effort to cow the dreadknight. Upon gaining his first few steps, his vigor was renewed at the prospect of pushing the dreadknight back to the inn. But as if sensing his motives, the dreadknight drove his shield into Roningus's breastplate, shoving him backwards. He followed with a series of wide-swinging horizontal strokes from his flail, forcing Roningus to duck. It was then that Roningus realized what had to be done.

Stepping forward once more, Roningus led with a low swing from his left sword. Doing as Roningus anticipated, the dreadknight spun around and brought his shield down low, continuing the movement in order to bring his flail around in a horizontal sweep.

But as the dreadknight deflected his blades, Roningus brought his arms up, allowing the spiked head of the flail to strike him in the ribs, catching it with his left arm and pinning it to his side.

As the wicked metal spikes on the flail's head punched through his breastplate and pierced Roningus just below his ribs, he brought the sword in his right hand above his head. With a swift twirl, he grasped it upside down, driving the point into one of the small links of chain that held the flail's head to the handle. So forceful was his thrust that it sheared through the link almost instantly, and he let the flail head fall to the ground, wincing painfully as one of the curved blades caught on his ribs momentarily.

Slumping down to one knee from the sudden onslaught of fatigue, Roningus was forced to drop his weapons. The dreadknight planted his foot on Roningus's chest, looking to push him over in his weakened state. But Roningus persevered, and as the dreadknight's foot met his chest, he reached up, grabbing hold of it with both hands and wrenching it hard to the right. The dreadknight's ankle shattered with a cracking sound, and he was flung to the ground.

With great effort Roningus stood, grasping his sword handles weakly and sheathing the one in his left hand that his arm might hold his side. Staggering over to where the dreadknight lay on the ground, Roningus used the tip of his sword to lift back the bald man's visor. The dreadknight's teeth clenched in agony as he looked down in dismay at his right foot which rested at an unnatural hundred and twenty degrees from its normal position. Holding the point of his sword just above the dreadknight's eye, Roningus breathed heavily as he spoke.

"I will hear your last confession if you'd have one, heretic."

Laughing, the bald dreadknight turned his head and spat. "I believe I shall…starting with when I was but a boy, when I slew my own father after praying to Mithos didn't stop the beatings… and, perhaps when I'm done, there may yet be a stone left standing of your false father's cathedral worth defending."

Frowning, Roningus removed the point of the sword from the dreadknight's face. To execute an enemy, even a dreadknight, without offering a final confession if possible was considered an unrighteous kill. Turning, Roningus strode towards the inn.

"A church knight will be along momentarily to accept your surrender…and to tend to this," he said, nudging the dreadknight's broken ankle forcefully with his foot.

Pushing their way along the outside of the swarm of combat that was taking place, Rhygar, Ionnus, and Grisbane helped each other scale the wall and entered the church through a broken stained glass window. As Grisbane reached down to give Ionnus a hand up, Rhygar bore down upon a dreadknight, rushing forward with Skyhammer, the massive head of the weapon battering the dreadknight's shield until its insignia became unrecognizable. Once through, Ionnus and Grisbane stepped forward to flank, and within moments, the dreadknight was dispatched.

"This way!" Rhygar said, leading them towards the hall that led to the high priest's chambers.

Looking over, both Ionnus and Grisbane watched in dismay as the dreadnought continued to wreck everything in its path, sundering the altar with a heavy handed chop from its right hand before taking hold of a dreadknight by his leg and using him to beat a paladin to death. The beast then moved on to the golden relief of the symbol of Mithos that stood at the back of the top tier of the dais.

"There's nothing we can do! We have to trust Roningus to deal with the necromancer pact that keeps it going! Come on!" Rhygar shouted again, jarring Ionnus and Grisbane from their momentary stupor.

Pushing forward, the three of them fought their way through dreadknights, offering aid to any of their oathbrothers they came across, until finally they reached the hallway that lead to the high priest's chambers. It was as they came upon the hallway, however, that they saw him; standing in the doorway, with several of their fallen oathbrothers near his feet, Asmodeus stood...holding the high priest's right arm wrenched up behind his back.

"Step aside, church knights, or the old man dies."

Snorting derisively, Rhygar gripped Skyhammer tightly in his right hand, crouching down as if to advance.

"Do as he says!" Brogam shouted in a terrified voice.

"Coward!" Rhygar roared, making no attempt to conceal his disgust. "You know what awaits you in the afterlife, and yet you'd have us let the half-fiend go free in order to save your own skin?!"

"Do as I say! Stand aside at once, or face excommunication!" Brogam replied, and with an angry growl Rhygar complied, Ionnus and Grisbane following his lead.

"There's a good sheep," Asmodeus said, grinning wickedly.

"How did you escape?!" Ionnus cried, backing away slow.

"You are a fool if you truly believe your mundane shackles and iron bars were detaining me, church knight," came Asmodeus's chiding retort, pointing the tip of his quarterstaff at Rhygar as he carefully passed through the paladins. Once he had gotten past them, he spun around and began backing away carefully, being sure to keep Brogam between himself and the three of them.

It was as they were watching on helplessly, however, that one of their oathbrothers approached silently from behind. His arm still wrapped in a sling, Sir Kysgar came up swiftly, bringing his sword above his head for a downward slice that would have rent the half-fiend's back open. But when Ionnus looked over at Kysgar's approach, Asmodeus saw the shift in his gaze, and instinctively brought his quarterstaff behind him to block the impending attack.

In that instant Grisbane lunged forward, grabbing hold of Brogam and wrenching him from Asmodeus's grasp. Snarling at the loss of his valuable prisoner, Asmodeus spun around, jabbing Kysgar hard in the stomach with the end of his quarterstaff and leaving it hanging in midair. He grabbed hold of Kysgar's head as the paladin hunched over from the blow. With a fluid motion that came naturally to the half-fiend, there was a loud snap, Kysgar's body going limp as a rag doll and collapsing on the floor.

"NO!" Rhygar screamed, rushing forward with Ionnus as the two brandished their warhammers and pushed Grisbane and the high priest behind them. But Asmodeus was too swift for them, snatching his quarterstaff out of the air and taking off in a sprint towards the front doors of the church.

"I'LL HUNT YOU TO THE DEPTHS OF THE ABYSS, HALF-FIEND! DO YOU HEAR ME?!" Ionnus bellowed, throwing his warhammer at the half-fiend's heels in frustration and letting out a wordless howl as his rage overtook him.

Pushing the high priest aside, Grisbane rushed over to Kysgar, removing his helm with a hopeful sense of urgency only to be met with the blank stare of Kysgar's lifeless eyes. Looking up to Rhygar, Grisbane shook his head.

Rhygar snarled as he rounded on Brogam. "Your cowardice cost us Sir Kysgar's life!"

Trembling, Brogam looked between the three of them, and when he didn't receive the reassuring look he was seeking, his fear turned to defiance. "I am the high priest of Mithos! My continued existence is essential to the ongoing—"

"YOUR LIFE! Is worth LESS than the puddle of PISS you left on the floor when the half-fiend had you in his grasp!" Rhygar roared, bringing his face so close to Brogam's that the spittle from his mouth spattered on the high priest's face.

That said, Brogam went silent, and it wasn't until several seconds later that Grisbane finally spoke up. "What do we do now?"

Glaring at Brogam, Rhygar spoke in an infuriated tone. "We guard the high priest. Kysgar sacrificed his life to save him; I won't let that sacrifice be in vain. In the meantime, Roningus had better get off his arse and stop that damned dreadnought before there's nothing left of this cathedral."

21

His swords clenched tightly in his hands and still favoring his left side with his arm, Roningus marched towards the inn without hesitation. As he passed through the open doorway, a pair of dreadknights spotted him and drew their weapons.

"The commander promised a bounty of one thousand gold to the man who slays the Wrathful Tempest."

Nodding slowly, Roningus gave the blades in his hands a flourish, bringing them to rest in a readied position, noting with slight dismay that the two dreadknights began swinging heavy flails in a circular motion above their heads as they moved in. The one to his left reached him first, coming in low with a horizontal swing aimed at the side that he'd been favoring. Knowing he couldn't sustain another blow to his ribs, Roningus stepped back out of the way only to find himself lined up for the dreadknight on the right as he brought his flail down in a forceful vertical stroke. Moving swiftly to sidestep the swing, Roningus waited until the dreadknight had fully extended before moving in on him. Reacting instantly, the dreadknight brought his shield up between them, pushing hard to knock Roningus back. But Roningus anticipated the maneuver, grabbing hold of the edges of the shield and holding firm.

When the first dreadknight swung again with a powerful diagonal stroke, Roningus brought the dreadknight's shield arm up above him, sending the head of the flail glancing off to the side. The dreadknight he had a hold of drew his flail back, preparing for another attack. Roningus reacted by delivering a front kick with his right foot that caught the dreadknight in the stomach. As the dreadknight doubled over, Roningus held on to his shield arm, looking up just as the other dreadknight brought his flail swooping down upon him.

When Roningus forced the man's shield arm into position again, a loud snap was heard as the arm shattered. After he'd blocked the next swing, Roningus gave the arm a twist, bringing the dreadknight to his knees as the man howled in agony. With another twist of his arm, Roningus had the man lying on his back. He let go of the shield as the man fell and sidestepped another swing from the other dreadknight before delivering a strong kick to the fallen dreadknight's head, the man's grip on his weapon and shield going lax as he went unconscious.

Now facing a single opponent, Roningus moved as if to circle around into the room, but the dreadknight kept footing with him, keeping himself between Roningus and the hallway that lead from the taproom to the inn. With room to spread out, Roningus carefully backed away, winding his way through the empty tables that were normally filled with laughing patrons. Once they had a table between them, the dreadknight laughed.

"Why do you shy away, church knight? Have you lost your faith?"

Chuckling once in response, Roningus suddenly kicked the table hard, shoving its edge into the dreadknight's stomach. As the dreadknight staggered backwards, Roningus rushed forward, planting his left foot on top of the table and launching himself into the air, leading with his right knee and connecting with the front of the dreadknight's helm. As the helm fell from the dreadknight's face, blood gushed from his nose, now positioned to the side of his face.

Landing on his feet, Roningus immediately pressed his advantage, swatting away a clumsy swing of the dreadknight's flail and knocking it from his hand before taking his left sword to the side of the dreadknight's right knee, catching him in the unprotected hinge and bringing the dreadknight to the ground. As the dreadknight looked up, coughing as blood drained rapidly into his throat, Roningus stood over him, leveling the point of one of his swords on the back of the dreadknight's neck and positioning for the kill stroke.

"M-mercy…" the dreadknight sputtered, hocking up a large clot of blood as he bowed his head.

Standing over him, Roningus spoke in a solemn tone without moving the sword. "Cast your weapon aside." Once the dreadknight had done so, Roningus bade him remove his shield, gauntlets, and breastplate, all of which the dreadknight did.

Once he was done, the dreadknight looked back up, his eyes hopeful. "Will you spare me?"

"Indeed I will, heretic," Roningus replied, sheathing the sword in his left hand. Grabbing hold of the dreadknight's right wrist, with one fluid motion Roningus drew the edge of his blade across the back of the dreadknight's hand, leaving a long gash that extended from the outer edge almost to just past his middle finger.

When he released him, the dreadknight quickly withdrew, looking down upon his hand in horror as he discovered his thumb and index finger were the only two that still functioned. "What have you done to me?!" the dreadknight cried, shaking his hand vigorously and frantically trying to coax movement from his other fingers.

"That hand will never raise a weapon against myself nor my oathbrothers again. Consider yourself fortunate, for I've left you the use of your thumb and first finger that you still might steer a plow or till a field. A life of hard labor shall be your penance for your sins against the church."

"You've left me a cripple!" the dreadknight wailed, looking up to Roningus with eyes full of despair.

"Even so, you are still more capable than many, and you'll be spared the fate of your companion who lies on the ground over there. Count your blessings, heretic, and go forth with the All Father's forgiveness." That done, Roningus reached in to one of the pouches on his belt, producing a long strip of linen and handing it to the dreadknight. "See to your wounds."

For a moment, the dreadknight looked as if hopelessness would consume him, but then gradually he nodded, taking the bandage and wrapping his hand in it as best he could. Leaning in, Roningus grabbed hold of the leather cord around the man's neck, and with a hard tug, pulled the silver symbol of Necros from him, tossing it into the hearth before turning and heading towards the hall.

As the dreadnought smashed through the doorway leading beyond the altar room where civilians typically weren't allowed, Grisbane shook his head and sighed. "Any time now, Roningus…"

Returning to the group with his warhammer in hand once more, Ionnus looked back momentarily before looking to Rhygar. "There must be something we can do."

"NO!" Brogam wailed, his voice sounding desperate. "You can't leave me! I forbid it!"

His eyes narrowing, Rhygar turned and paced over to the high priest, and when he spoke, his voice sounded gravely offended and bordering on outraged. "Your holiness…are you implying that your faith in the All Father has wavered to the extent that you no longer trust one of his most dedicated soldiers to keep you safe?"

Brogam's eyes went wide, and as he shook his head, his words came out in a stammer. "That…that isn't what I…what I meant was, you see, is…"

"Then surely you would not object to these two doing anything they can in an attempt to bring an end to the dead god's abomination laying waste to this sacred cathedral?"

Finding himself beaten with reason once again, Brogam shook his head. "No…no, I suppose not…go, with my blessing, church knights…"

Nodding, Rhygar turned to Grisbane and Ionnus. "Find a way to slow it down. Buy as much time as you can, but whatever you do, don't get yourselves killed. The church will have much need of you both when this is over."

Nodding, Grisbane and Ionnus brought their clenched fists up, beating against their left breasts in the formal salute of the church knights with a clank. Rhygar swiftly returned the gesture. That done, the two slipped off, making their way around the edge of the melee towards the dreadnought.

As they drew nearer, Ionnus groaned. "Somehow, I'd forgotten how big this thing really is."

"Never mind that…how are we going to slow this thing down? Our weapons don't even get its attention," Grisbane said, the two ducking as the dreadnought ripped a stone bench from the ground with its right hand and tossed it behind it, sending it sailing over their heads and crashing loudly into the ground.

"…what about its head?" Ionnus said, his tone ponderous.

Thinking on the matter for a moment, Grisbane nodded. "It's worth a try…now how do we reach it?"

Gripping his warhammer tightly in his hand, Ionnus approached the dreadnought cautiously, motioning for Grisbane to follow. "*You* are going to climb it…" he said, coming to an abrupt halt as the dreadnought began pushing over a stone effigy of Mithos.

Laughing incredulously, Grisbane turned and looked to Ionnus as the two stood amidst a sea of clerics and acolytes fleeing the area and trying to get away from the dreadnought without getting caught up in the melee going on in the altar room. "Of course I am. Alright, then…help me get a foot up," Grisbane said, sheathing his sword and unbuckling his shield.

Looking to Grisbane and frowning slightly, when Ionnus spoke he took on a tone of mock indignation. "Fine, I'll just do everything."

That said, Ionnus ran forward, gripping the haft of his warhammer in both hands and coming up behind the dreadnought from the left. Grisbane followed closely behind him. Putting all of his strength into both his arms, Ionnus swung from his hip, catching the dreadnought in the back of its left knee. A crunching sound was heard, and the monster paused as it was briefly brought to a kneeling position, the bones already visibly realigning themselves and beginning to mend underneath the skin.

"NOW!" Ionnus shouted, ducking down behind the dreadnought and holding his shield up with both hands to provide a platform for Grisbane to jump from.

Planting his right foot on the shield, Grisbane leapt into the air towards the dreadnought, wrapping his arms around the monster's neck and clinging for dear life as his feet struggled to find a foothold.

"Don't let go!" Ionnus yelled, swatting at the dreadnought's hand with his warhammer as it groped around at its back, trying to grab hold of Grisbane.

"Don't let it grab me!" Grisbane shouted back.

Ionnus circled around in front of the beast and swung his warhammer at it frantically to get its attention. At first, the dreadnought seemed intent on getting hold of Grisbane, but eventually, when Ionnus turned the head of his warhammer around and began punching holes in the dreadnought's chest with the raven's beak, it turned its focus on him. When the monster reached out towards him, Ionnus swung his shield at its hand, trying to knock it away. In response the dreadnought simply grabbed hold of the shield, crushing it with a simple closing of its fingers and holding on, lifting Ionnus off the ground by his shield arm.

Dropping his warhammer, Ionnus frantically undid the buckles of his shield, his arm sliding out and allowing him to drop to the ground just as the dreadnought's warhammer sailed right through where he had previously been hanging but a moment ago.

"Make something happen up there!" Ionnus roared, fumbling to retrieve his warhammer as he watched the dreadnought crumple up his shield like a wad of paper and toss it aside.

"Not as easy as I'm making this look!" Grisbane replied, clamoring up the spiked plates that had been fused into the dreadnought's back.

Reaching from behind the monster's head, he grabbed hold of the front of its helm by the slits for its eyes with his left hand, planting his right foot on its shoulder and drawing his sword from its sheath. Immediately the dreadnought reached up, grasping at him and swinging with its warhammer in a frenzy. Grisbane ducked the warhammer and, in the process, lost his footing. As he fell, he held on tightly to the helm, wrenching the dreadnought's head back and forcing it to plant its right foot behind it to keep from falling over backwards, leaving Grisbane dangling one-handed from its head as the dreadnought flailed its arms wildly at him.

"Good! You're doing good! Keep it up!" Ionnus called, swinging the point of the raven's beak into the back of the dreadnought's hand and pulling with both hands to prevent the beast from grabbing hold of Grisbane.

"Your approval isn't helping!" Grisbane called back, hammering at the side of the dreadnought's head with the pommel of his longsword.

"Just keep it up! Roningus will come through soon, I know it!"

With a well-placed heel kick, Roningus busted the door open to reveal the pact of necromancers; a circle of seven of them, all garbed in ceremonial robes, were gathered around a hastily constructed altar. Painted in the center if its chest with the ram-horned skull of Necros, the bloody, mutilated body of their sacrifice to the dead god lay between them, surrounded by lit candles. As Roningus stepped in, the seven of them looked up, their chanting coming to a halt as a look of general terror began to spread over their faces.

Slowly, Roningus stepped forward, faltering slightly as the pain in his side swelled up then began to fade again.

"Impossible..." one of the necromancers said, the pact tightening their grips on each other's hands.

"None of you shall leave this room, heretics...I come bearing the All Father's justice, and each of you shall answer for bringing your dead god's abomination inside the walls of his holy city."

That said, Roningus gave his swords a brief flourish, and with a righteous fury swung out at the servant of the dead god that stood nearest him, his screams and soon those of the others echoing throughout the very streets of Ascension as the Wrathful Tempest fell upon them with all the might of the All Father behind him.

As Grisbane hung from the dreadnought by one hand, he swung wildly at the monster's hand with his longsword to keep it from grabbing hold of his leg and snapping it between its thumb and index finger. The dreadnought suddenly lurched forward as if something had pierced it through its abdomen. So sudden and forceful was the motion that Grisbane was catapulted forward, sailing a full ten yards through the air before landing with a painful sounding crash on the ground.

What in the name of Mithos just happened? Grisbane thought, just as the excruciating pain of a pair of broken ribs overtook him. Gasping for breath, he struggled to roll over and failed, and was beginning to grow frantic until Ionnus rushed over and assisted him.

"Grisbane, are you alright?!"

Reaching up and pulling his helmet off, Grisbane closed his eyes and sucked in air, his hair stuck to his face in a sheen of perspiration. The cool stone floor felt heavenly on the back of his head, and when he spoke, his voice shook as the effort wracked him with pain.

"Is it over?"

Ionnus pointed back toward the dreadnought, his voice brimming with excitement. "Yes, he's done it! Roningus broke the pact!"

Turning his head to the side, Grisbane glanced over and saw the motionless body of the dreadnought lying on the ground, its limbs twisted and bent in awkward positions from where it had crumpled. Smiling weakly, Grisbane laid his head back again.

Good, Grisbane thought, his eyelids growing heavy. *Mithos won't mind if I just lay here a moment and close my eyes…*

As a pair of clerics carefully lifted the unconscious Grisbane from the ground onto a litter, Ionnus and Rhygar watched as a team of black caped paladins went to work dismembering the dreadnought with axes.

"How soon after did the dreadknights retreat?" Ionnus asked, wincing as one of his oathbrothers wrenched the helm head from the dreadnought's shoulders, its contents spilling out onto the ground in a puddle of viscous fluids and cranial organs.

"Almost immediately. Once word of the necromancer pact being broken got around, not to mention the fall of their commander, the bastards killed themselves overrunning our fortified position at the gate to get out of the city. Slade and his archers picked off a good number of them as they fled, but the majority of them made it out alive."

Sighing, Ionnus crossed his arms, the two standing in silence for several minutes as the team of paladins continued to haul pieces of the dreadnought away. Then, a sudden realization crept over Ionnus, causing him to look over to Rhygar with great alarm. "Roningus! Where is he?!"

Glancing over at Ionnus, Rhygar chuckled as he looked back upon the spectacle before them. "They found him at the Vagrant Bard, cleaning his damned swords like he hadn't just massacred a room full of necromancers. Took a nasty wound from the dreadknight commander, and even managed to convert a heretic. Had to cripple the man's right hand to do it, but still…"

Taking a drink from a water skin offered to him by a passing cleric, Ionnus spoke as he handed it back. "Where is he now?"

"In the infirmary wing, no doubt. Go ahead and check on him, then report back to me. We need to get this city cleaned up before we start bringing people back in, and I'll need your help directing our recently drafted volunteers."

That said, Rhygar grinned, to which Ionnus replied with a smile of his own.

Making his way into the infirmary wing, Ionnus was met with a sea of injured church knights, clerics, and more than a handful of civilians. Wading his way through the frantic network of clerics that were rushing about trying to tend to the wounded, Ionnus reached out and grabbed hold of the shoulder of one, a pretty young blonde woman with a slender figure and sky blue eyes. Stitched in red onto the left breast of her clerical robe was what appeared to be an open hand reaching out as if in a gesture of assistance, the badge of office worn by the sacred sisters that ran the infirmary.

"Excuse me, cleric…where would I find the Wrathful Tempest?"

At first, the woman looked down at the hand upon her shoulder, then looked up to Ionnus. Eyeing him warily, she quirked an eyebrow and spoke in an almost reprimanding tone. "I'm not entirely certain I want you getting him all riled up. We had a hard enough time convincing him to take a bed."

Immediately removing his hand from her shoulder, Ionnus held it up as if he were swearing an oath. "On my honor."

Regarding him for several more seconds, the woman finally conceded, motioning towards a back corner with a nod of her head. "Over there, next to the one with the broken ribs."

With a nod, Ionnus went to turn and head in that direction, until he found the woman's finger pointed right in his face.

"On your honor, no trouble in my infirmary. Understood?"

Taken aback, Ionnus nodded, and it was only then that she moved on, allowing him to pass.

Approaching the bed, Ionnus saw Roningus sitting up in bed, his back leaned up against a wall. With a blanket pulled up around his waist, Roningus was the only soldier in the infirmary whose armor wasn't laid out next to him. His bare torso was wrapped in a wide layer of bandages with a faint red spot on his left side where the bleeding had been stopped.

Coming to a halt at the foot of his bed, Ionnus shot Roningus a quizzical look.

Roningus sighed, closing his eyes as he spoke. "They took my clothes. Ishana says if I try to get up again, she'll take the blanket next."

Ionnus laughed, looking over his shoulder. "Where is she?"

Leaning his head back against the wall, Roningus spoke without opening his eyes. "Always watching me, apparently. Blonde hair, a hundred and ten pounds soaking wet, and runs this place like a prison."

Scanning the room, Ionnus spotted the blonde woman he'd spoken to on his way in just as she looked over at them, her gaze meeting his and shooting him a dangerous look. His eyes going wide as if he'd been caught doing something he shouldn't be, Ionnus quickly turned back around to Roningus.

"Oh, her...yes, we've met."

Looking over at the bed to Roningus's right, Ionnus saw Grisbane. Lying flat on his back, his gear stacked neatly next to him, Grisbane snored softly. His torso was wrapped in snug, thick bandages, and even as Ionnus looked at him, he stirred briefly before rolling over and turning his back to them.

Chuckling quietly, Ionnus looked back to Roningus. "How long has he been out?"

"Not long. We were actually talking for quite a while before you showed up. He told me about the dreadnought…I'm sorry I couldn't—"

Ionnus shook his head vigorously. "Don't be absurd. If it weren't for you, that thing could very well still be tearing up the church. You're a hero, as far as all of us are concerned."

Smiling slightly, Roningus opened his eyes, meeting Ionnus's gaze. "I wonder if high priest Brogam will agree."

"I wouldn't be too concerned with that…" came a voice, Arch Cleric Rasthmus appearing suddenly and as if from nowhere.

"Arch Cleric…" Ionnus said reverently, bowing his head. Roningus did the same, sitting up straighter as he did so.

Rasthmus smiled, shaking his head lightly. "That won't be necessary, church knights…you and your oathbrothers have saved the church, and have driven the dead god's filth from the city. The church, and the city of Ascension itself, owe you all a tremendous debt of gratitude. You in particular, Sir Roningus…the conclave remembers how valiantly you held the walls for as long as possible, and then safeguarded all of us once the heretics had breached the gates. Your loyal service to the church is above and beyond that which Mithos asks of us all."

With his head still bowed, Roningus spoke. "I would not have succeeded had it not been for the guidance of the All Father and the support of the church and my oathbrothers."

His smile widening, Rasthmus bowed his head in acknowledgement. "So humble, even in victory. Alas, I am afraid there are many pressing issues that require my attention, but I wished to stop in and express my gratitude as well as ensure you that we all pray for your swift recovery. Convey my sentiments to your oathbrother when he awakens, won't you?"

When both Ionnus and Roningus nodded, Rasthmus bowed politely one last time before turning and dissipating into the tumult of clerics rushing from bed to bed. It wasn't until several seconds after he was gone that Ionnus broke the silence.

"What was all that about?"

"What do you mean?" Roningus asked, nodding his head as a cleric came up and offered him water.

Waiting until the cleric had gone, Ionnus spoke as Roningus took a long drink. "That bit about not worrying about whether the high priest agrees or not…you don't suppose the rumors are true, do you?"

Finishing the mug of water and setting it aside, Roningus raised a confused eyebrow at Ionnus. "What do you mean?"

Glancing around to ensure no one was listening, Ionnus leaned in and spoke quietly with an incredulous expression on his face. "You mean you really don't know? Word has it they're looking to revoke Brogam's anointment as high priest, and put Vogoth in his place…especially considering Brogam's state of mind after Asmodeus broke free and held him hostage—"

"ASMODEUS ESCAPED?!" Roningus shouted, his eyes lighting up.

"WHAT DID I SAY?!" came Ishana's voice, roaring above all the others.

Before Ionnus could even turn around, the small blonde woman was upon him, her fingers grabbing hold of Ionnus by the collar of his breastplate and dragging him away from Roningus's bed.

"But I didn't…he was—" Ionnus stammered, looking back to Roningus for help.

"I warned you! Don't go riling him up!" Then, pausing, Ishana rounded on Roningus, who already had his legs swung over the side of the bed. "Should I take that blanket with me now?!"

Immediately Roningus came to a halt, clutching the blanket around his waist defensively.

Eyeing him for a moment, Ishana gave a curt nod. "Back in bed."

As Roningus nodded and resettled himself, she rounded her gaze on Ionnus.

"You. Let's go."

That said, Ionnus barely had but a moment to look back at Roningus helplessly before Ishana dragged him from the infirmary by his armor.

"The damages will take the better part of a year to repair. The dreadnought did major structural damage to the load bearing archway in the main entrance, and we'll have to bring in a team of masons to repair the interior wall behind the main altar." As Rhygar spoke to Vogoth, Vogoth let out a sigh, reaching up and rubbing his temples with the thumb and index finger of his right hand.

"And what of the dreadknight commander?"

"Escaped after his defeat by Roningus, as it turns out, with the aid of his dreadknights. We've enlisted help from the Journeyman's guild in tracking them down."

Nodding, Vogoth looked up, folding his arms. Standing side by side, the two of them looked at the broken stone altar that the dreadnought had smashed in half. Several seconds went by, until finally Vogoth broke the silence.

"How is Sir Roningus?"

"Recovering. Ishana had to take his clothes away to keep him in bed."

Chuckling once, Vogoth nodded. "That's good. He'll need that enthusiasm in the days to come. This transgression cannot go unanswered."

Grinning, Rhygar nodded. "A good number of my oathbrothers have expressed a concern…that Brogam's dislike of the Wrathful Tempest will prevent him from being given the necessary honors that he has unquestionably earned."

Looking over to Rhygar, Vogoth smiled. "I will do everything within my power to ensure that Sir Roningus is raised to a station more befitting one of his ability. Be sure to let your oathbrothers know, as well."

"Glad we understand each other," Rhygar replied, the two exchanging a knowing look.

It was at that moment that a young acolyte, robed in white and blue, came hurrying forward. "Arch Cleric Vogoth! The council of arch clerics is gathering immediately! They told me to summon you, and to inform you that it is concerning a grave matter in regards to the well-being of the church."

Quirking an eyebrow, Rhygar looked over to Vogoth. "What's this all about?"

Chuckling lightly, Vogoth patted Rhygar's right pauldron. "If it's what I think it is, you may get your wish sooner than you had hoped."

Rain continued to pour down, the sky dismal and overcast even at midday with a chilling wind coming in from the north. The lone traveler slogged his way through the muddy wet grass towards Ascention. Tightly gripping the gnarled wooden staff in his hand, he stepped up to the gates, surprised to find them closed. When the gate guard noticed him, he leaned out from the shelter of his watch post to look down upon him.

"Who goes there?" the guard shouted, cupping his hands over his mouth.

In response, the traveler looked up, his steel blue eyes squinting as they leveled on the guardsman. Clenched tightly in his teeth, his long stemmed pipe was lit, and thick clouds of heavy smoke billowed up from beneath the brim of his hat.

Squinting down at the man for several seconds, the guard's eyes suddenly grew wide. Turning, he stumbled over himself as he hurried over to the winch, releasing the mechanism and opening the city gates.

"What's going on?!" the guard captain cried, rousing from his place in the guard post nearby and nearly knocking the brazier containing a roaring fire over as he stood abruptly.

Striding out through the rain and ready to sound the call at a moment's notice, he was just about to grab hold of the gate watchman when he spotted the pointed end of the traveler's hat. He immediately forgot the open gates, and rushed over to watch. The figure cloaked in dark brown oilskins, grasping the wooden branch fashioned into a staff, leisurely made his way down the main road of Ascention. With a nod of approval, he turned back around to the gate watchman.

"Go ahead and close the gate back up, he's through."

With a formal nod, the gate guard turned the winch, and the enormous wooden gates slowly closed back in to place with a loud creak that echoed through the streets.

Unimpeded, the cloaked traveler continued on, his already wrinkled face crinkling up in a contented smile as he continued to smoke his pipe and made his way towards the church.

"It simply cannot be done," a fat, balding cleric of the conclave said, shaking his head so vigorously the wattles beneath his neck shook. "There is no precedent for it. The rules of the church are very clear: a high priest serves until death or failing health prevents him from doing so."

"We all agree that electing Brogam was a mistake! How do you think precedents come to be in the first place?! The first clerical conclave had nothing to go on but the guidance of the All Father, and it was their decisions that set the precedents you cling to so dearly!" came the retort of a thin, boney cleric, his energetic blue eyes seeming mismatched with his fragile elderly frame.

"What you're suggesting goes against centuries of tradition! There's also our image to consider. What will the people think of the church if we evict our own high priest from the throne and anoint another? The conclave has always acted on the guidance of Mithos, and if we do as you would have us it would be the same as accusing the All Father of being wrong!"

"Are you accusing me of heresy?!"

"Call it what you will!"

Back and forth the two sides went, neither one conceding any points to the other. Finally, when it seemed as if the entire conclave were about to erupt into chaos and the acolytes near the entrance were about to call for assistance in returning order to the room, the doors swung open. In walked the traveler, reaching up to remove his hat as he strode past the acolytes and ignored their protests.

Immediately, a reverent silence fell upon the room, the uninvited stranger coming to a stop in the center of the circle of seats where the conclave had gathered. His wild, unkempt gray hair lay in disarray upon his shoulders, his full beard hanging down past his chest. Looking around at the gathered clerics, he stood his wooden staff next to him, and when released, it remained standing as if it were still held. Hanging his hat from it, the man then turned and looked around at the gathered clerics, until finally one spoke up, his voice timid.

"Our apologies, master wizard, but this is a private gathering of the conclave..."

Nodding, the man removed the pipe from between his teeth, grasping the bowl between his right thumb and index finger. "Not just wizard...I am Loremaster, and I know full well what goes on within these walls. I have been observing your struggles as of late, and I come now to offer you counsel in these dark times. For all its inconsistencies, the church of Mithos is at its core of good intention, and I do not wish to see the stain of the dead god become permanent."

Glancing around at each other, a general murmur rose up among the clerics, until finally another spoke out, his tone much more bold than the last. "Loremaster?! The Loremasters disappeared from the world centuries ago! Your trick with your staff would be amusing to a child perhaps, magician, but perhaps you should read up on your history when concocting your lies!"

Smiling, the intruder nodded his head slowly. Taking the stem of his pipe in his mouth, he casually stepped forward, reaching up and removing his cloak as he did so. When he released it, it walked itself over to his staff and hung itself from it below his hat. Underneath, he wore a very faded set of arch mage robes worn by the highest order of the magus, the dark blue inlaid with the runic signet of the arcane university embroidered into the front in golden thread. A brown leather satchel slung over his left shoulder, and as he took the stem of his pipe between his teeth once more, he lifted the flap to open it, rifling through its contents with his right hand.

The clerics watched on in a stunned silence, the one who had spoken against him showing signs of increasing discomfort as the intruder continued to say nothing, until finally he produced a small golden coin. Taking it between his thumb and index finger, he flipped it to the cleric, the cleric fumbling to catch it as it hit him in the chest. After turning it over and inspecting it for several seconds, the cleric looked back up, confused.

"Is this supposed to be a bribe? What is the purpose of this coin?"

Motioning to the coin with a nod of his head, the intruder spoke in a patient tone. "What can you tell me about that coin?"

Looking down at it more closely, the cleric held it up in front of his face for a closer inspection. Stamped in the center with a somewhat familiar design, it was no bigger than an Ascention standard press coin, but had not been carefully shaped and sculpted for optimal aesthetics the way Ascention's were.

Looking it over, the cleric frowned, tossing it back to the intruder as he spoke. "The branding looks familiar, but I can't be certain as to exactly where it came from without consulting the archives."

Chuckling, the intruder caught the coin, holding it up and glancing over it as he replied. "Interesting. I thought for certain a cleric of the church would have recognized one of Ascention's own coins. You certainly collect enough of them in donations."

Frowning, the cleric shook his head. "If that were a piece of Ascention gold, I would indeed have recognized the standard."

Nodding, the intruder took on a solemn expression. "I am certain of it as well. To be fair, I may have asked too difficult a question…this standard hasn't been pressed into Ascention's gold for centuries. You said the design looked familiar to you?"

As he spoke, the intruder widened his eyes, and the cleric nodded his begrudging admittance.

"That's because this particular piece dates back to the draconic era, before the church in Forthos had been established. As such, the influence of the Dragon Knights has not yet been incorporated into this design. See? You can see it right here…" Leaning over the waist-high divider that stood in front of the first row of seats, the intruder showed it to the nearest cleric, who nodded his head in approval.

"If your story were true," the indignant cleric chimed in, with the same flippant tone as before, "then how come none of these coins are around any longer?"

"An excellent question," the intruder said, pointing to the cleric with the stem of his pipe as a teacher would a student who had reached the conclusion he'd been guided towards. "This coin is one of very few left, as the rest have likely been destroyed or melted down. I got this one on my most recent trip to your holy city."

"But you said yourself this type of coin hasn't been used for centuries!" the cleric cried out in defiance.

In response, the intruder looked up at him, his eyes gleaming as he smiled patiently at the frowning cleric.

Realizing the implications, the cleric scoffed, waving a dismissive hand. "The beggar has stumbled upon a piece of history and would have us believe him a Loremaster!" he shouted. A few of the clerics seemed to nod their agreement whereas the rest maintained an uncertain silence.

With a light chuckle, the intruder turned, flipping the coin into the air towards the center of the circle around which the conclave's seating was arranged.

When the coin hit the ground, a loud crack and boom was heard as if a massive explosion had gone off. The clerics watched on in sheer terror as the floor crumbled away to reveal an enormous gaping chasm that led to a pit of molten lava below. A massive, scaled reptilian hand reached up, grabbing hold of the edge of the chasm, and a dragon seeming to have coalesced from pure magma pulled itself up from the pit. So large was it that though it barely came up high enough to rest its elbows on the ground, the fearsome creature's head nearly touched the highly vaulted ceiling. When it leaned forward to level its gaze upon the dissenting cleric, the entire section in which he sat could feel the heat of its breath as it exhaled slowly through its nose. Rivulets of glowing hot magma streamed down its back and sides, a pair of burning orange eyes staring darkly at the dissenting cleric as a pair of long whiskers that served as eyebrows twitched in contemplation.

Paralyzed with fear, the cleric maintained a death grip on his seat, until with a casual snap of his fingers the intruder dismissed the entire apparition in a puff of smoke that filled the entire room. As the clerics waved their hands frantically in front of their faces to clear the smoke, the intruder gradually made his way to the center of the room, picking up the coin once more and inspecting it as if enamored with its magical capabilities.

Seeming satisfied, he turned back around, grinning mischievously at the dissenter as he spoke in a tone of genuine inquiry. "What do you think? Will my parlor tricks serve me well as a street magician?"

When the dissenting cleric was unable to respond, the intruder chuckled once more, returning the coin to his leather satchel.

"Loremaster...what shall we call you?" came the voice of one of the younger members of the conclave, his eyes wide in a mixture of fear and awe.

Turning, the Loremaster smiled warmly, tilting his head as he spoke. "My name is Garadain, and as I said before, I have come to offer you counsel in these dark times."

As the young cleric nodded another spoke up, his tone curious like that of a child's though the man was easily well into his thirties. "What would you have us do?"

Taking a series of drags from his pipe, Garadain observed the cleric who had asked the question for a moment before answering. "It is not my place to tell you what to do. What I can tell you, however, is this...the decision you make today will determine the fate of your establishment. I urge all of you to consider very carefully what you wish for your city; will you adapt, allowing the winds of change to drive the sails of this church along the gently flowing river which is time...or will you remain stoic like the rock, gradually eroding away until all is forgotten and nothing remains?"

"The conclave has renounced their decision! Brogam's anointment as high priest has been absolved!" the young acolyte shouted, bursting through the doors into the mess hall.

Immediately, Ionnus and Grisbane glanced up from their meals, looking at each other as if to confirm that they'd heard correctly before looking over to the boy along with every other church knight and cleric in the room.

"That's impossible! The high priest serves until death, thus it is written in the laws of the church," came the dismissive voice of a nearby cleric, quirking his eyebrows at the boy as if he were spouting gibberish.

"A Loremaster has arrived, and in taking his counsel they decided to proceed without precedent!" the boy said, looking around to everyone and no one in particular.

Immediately a crowd began to form around him, asking him questions and demanding answers as the boy tried his best to respond to them all at once. After several seconds, Ionnus and Grisbane looked back across the table at each other, each one giving the other the same hopeful look.

"…do you think…?" Ionnus started, sounding as if even afraid to hope.

Grinning slightly, Grisbane's eyes lit up, nodding his head as he spoke. "It's happening. The rumors were true, it would seem."

Contemplating his words, Ionnus looked down into the contents of his bowl for a minute, looking back up with the same hopeful look in his eyes as Grisbane. "We should tell Roningus… he'll want to know."

Nodding, Grisbane lifted his spoon, swallowing down a mouthful of the oat and barley porridge they'd been served. "After we eat. Thanks to Ishana, we can be certain he's not going anywhere."

Nodding once, Ionnus looked back down to his bowl distractedly, looking up yet again as he posed his question. "Who do you suppose will be anointed as the next high priest?"

It was just then that Rhygar appeared, setting his bowl down next to Ionnus's and taking a seat. "Mornin', oathbrothers."

"Sir Rhygar," they both replied, bowing their heads respectfully.

Grisbane spoke up as soon as they were done. "Who are the likely candidates for anointment? Is there any word?"

Grinning and chuckling silently, Rhygar nodded his head as he took a bite of his porridge, waiting until he'd swallowed before speaking. "There is one name that keeps coming up…has a lot of supporters among the arch clerics and the church knights alike."

"Who is it?" Ionnus asked, both him and Grisbane practically on the edge of their seats.

With a smile derived from openly enjoying the suspense he held the two in, Rhygar looked between them before leaning in, lowering his voice as he spoke. "If rumors and hearsay are to be believed…Arch Cleric Vogoth will sit the high priest's throne on the morrow."

Standing at the wooden table containing the ballot boxes, the bleary eyed cleric gazed down at the count he'd taken on his ledger. The room was awkwardly silent and uncomfortably warm, the entire conclave having gathered in the rather sparse room reserved for the electoral process of choosing their new high priest. The chairs were ornately carved from wood, carefully stained to a beautiful mahogany finish and very purposely left without any sort of cushioning.

"The tally thus far…Arch Cleric Rasthmus seven, Arch Cleric Lyras four…Arch Cleric Vogoth forty-three…who has not yet cast their vote, brethren?"

"Six votes aren't going to change anything! Just make the declaration so we can get on with it!" cried a bearded, rotund cleric of the conclave, shifting uncomfortably in his chair as it dug into his plump sides.

Screwing his face up in genuine indignation, the cleric tasked with maintaining the voting ledger was about to open his mouth until Garadain cleared his throat. When the cleric looked over, the Loremaster gave him a nod, the cleric stifling his irritation and looking back down to the ledger.

"Then, it would seem we have reached a majority. Bring forth the candidate."

Turning, one of the black caped paladins at the door opened it and stepped out, returning with Vogoth a few minutes later. Stepping forward, Vogoth glanced over at Garadain, the Loremaster smiling subtly and giving a slight nod.

"Arch Cleric Vogoth…you have been chosen by the conclave to bear the mantle of high priest, that you may guide and protect the church in times of peace and war. Will you sit on the All Father's throne, and speak on his behalf?"

Pausing for a moment, Vogoth looked down, his brow furrowing in thought for a moment before looking back up. "I will."

Seated on the edge of his bed, armored from the waist down and with a layer of clean white bandages still wrapped around his torso, Roningus carefully rubbed oil into the glossy black leather that covered the breastplate of his suit of armor. It wasn't until the sound of clanking metal signaled the approach of two paladins that he looked up, still working oils into the leather as they spoke with him.

"Sir Roningus."

"Oathbrothers," Roningus replied, and all at once the three of them gave the traditional salute, Roningus pressing his clenched fist against his bare chest.

"We are to escort you to the council of arch clerics at once. Will you require assistance donning your armor?"

As the one to his right spoke, Roningus looked up. It was one of the church knights who had followed his command while they'd held the wall, and again once when they had fallen back and held the church. His cape, which had been blue at the time, was now a resplendent purple, and hung neatly from his pauldrons.

Shaking his head, Roningus put the rag away with which he had been working on his armor, pulling a thick long sleeved tunic on before reaching for the padded clothing worn under his plate. "That will not be necessary."

Once he had at last buckled his scabbards behind his waist and sheathed his longswords, Roningus carefully buckled his brown cape to his pauldrons. Once he'd tucked his helmet under his left arm, he reached into a pouch on his belt to ensure the wing that had been broken off in his encounter with the half-fiend was still there, then nodded to his oathbrothers.

As they led him out of the infirmary, he stopped before Ishana, offering her the traditional salute as he spoke. "You have my sincerest thanks, sister. I apologize for any trouble I may have caused you."

Sternly quirking an eyebrow at first, as Roningus spoke Ishana's harsh gaze melted, the hint of a smile creeping up on the corners of her lips. "You're quite welcome. Mithos's blessings be upon you."

"And you as well," Roningus replied, bowing his head respectfully before turning and following his oathbrothers.

It wasn't until they were a ways down the hallway that the church knight cloaked in purple spoke again. "I'd like to personally thank you, oathbrother. It was because of your guidance and direction that I was promoted. They've been rounding up those that served under you and promoting them all day…we've all been wondering when you would receive your summons. I personally volunteered to bring you to the council chambers."

Glancing over, Roningus smiled slightly and nodded, remaining silent.

The paladin to his left, cloaked in blue, spoke up after they'd walked several more steps. "It is said that you brought down the dreadknight commander in single combat…is this true?"

When Roningus looked over to the blue caped paladin, the church knight turned his gaze forward, snapping to attention as if he'd made the mistake of casually addressing a superior despite the rank he held over Roningus.

"My apologies, Sir Roningus…"

Roningus shook his head, looking forward as he spoke. "No apology is necessary, oathbrother. It is as you have heard, though the battle cost me a great deal."

As they reached the council chamber, the two church knights that accompanied Roningus hurried ahead to open the doors, holding them for him as he passed through. Upon entering the chambers, Roningus dutifully paced over in front of the throne of the high priest, dropping to his knee in genuflect, bowing his head, and clasping his right fist against his left breast.

Smiling, Vogoth stood from the high priest's throne, garbed in the robes of the high priest and wearing the anointed crown atop his head. Descending the steps, as he reached Roningus, he reached down, grasping him by his vambrace and pulling him to his feet. As Roningus stood, Vogoth met his gaze, and when the high priest spoke, his voice bordered on reverent.

"Such a devoted servant of the All Father kneels before no man. Rise, Sir Roningus."

Nodding his head, it was then that Roningus noticed all of the arch clerics were standing, including Brogam who had a rather abashed look on his face. Then, slowly and with great emphasis, Vogoth bowed lowly to him, and as he did, the arch clerics followed in his example. Looking around, it was then that Roningus heard a multitude of metallic sounds, each paladin in the room beating their right fist against their left breast and saluting in unison.

After a moment of stunned silence, Roningus was able to find his voice. "The council honors me, as do my oathbrothers."

Smiling warmly, Vogoth clasped his hands behind his back. "This church and the city of Ascension owe you a debt which can never be repaid. Remove your cape, Sir Roningus."

As Roningus undid the clasps of his cape, Vogoth continued to speak even as he carefully folded the brown cape up neatly.

"My predecessor has openly admitted to misjudging you, both in character and devotion." That said, Vogoth took the brown cape from Roningus and handed it off to a young acolyte that rushed forward. Then, circling slowly around behind him, Roningus listened as the unfurling of cloth was heard, keeping his eyes forward and doing Brogam the courtesy of not looking in his direction at the mention of "predecessor."

It was then that Roningus felt Vogoth's hands upon his shoulders, and by the time he looked down, Vogoth was already making his way back around in front of him. Roningus could make out the golden embroidery on the corners of his new cape, which was unmistakably black.

"I hereby rise you to the highest rank of church knight, and cloak you in black as is the custom of the high priest. The sword Retribution remains silent, even in these troubled times, but the slight against our holy city must not go unanswered, lest the dead god's corruption continue to spread. It is thus, as is my right as high priest, that I send you forth on a crusade to cleanse the dead god's blasphemies from these lands, and to restore the true faith to the western kingdoms. Will you accept this holy calling, Sir Roningus?"

Without so much as a second's hesitation, Roningus gave his response. "As Mithos calls, I am bound to obey, for I am but an instrument of the All Father's will."

"Then kneel, Sir Roningus, and be anointed."

As the doors of the council chamber closed behind him, Roningus slowed his pace, taking a moment to allow the gravity of the situation to sink in. It was then that he heard a voice calling his name.

"Congratulations, Sir Roningus! I suspected they would elevate you in rank, but truth be told I did not realize it would be to such an extent."

To his right, an old man huddled in robes wearing a pointed wide brimmed hat stood, leaning on a gnarled wooden staff and carrying a bundle wrapped in brown cloth.

Smiling uncertainly, Roningus tilted his head, coming to a halt as the old man approached. "Many thanks…my apologies, but I'm afraid you have me at a disadvantage."

Slowly making his way up to Roningus, Garadain grinned at him from under the brim of his hat, shifting the bundle under his left arm restlessly. "Do an old man a kindness and hold these, would you?"

Before Roningus could reply, Garadain carefully laid the bundle in his arms, letting out a sigh of relief. Surprisingly light despite how heavy the old man made it look, Roningus balanced the bundle as best he could while still trying to hold on to his helmet. Garadain casually produced a long stemmed pipe from his satchel and began to fill it with a pungent dried herb from a brown leather pouch.

"My name is Garadain…and I've come to offer your church my counsel, for what it's worth."

Mulling his words over for a moment, Roningus's eyes went wide as he suddenly realized the implications. "You are the Loremaster!"

Chuckling, Garadain shook his head, produced a small wooden splint, and lit it on a nearby votive candle before taking it to his pipe. Within seconds, thick white smoke began pouring out from underneath the brim of his hat, Garadain waving the splint in the air to extinguish the flame before speaking again. "I am not 'the' Loremaster, simply 'a' Loremaster. There are more than one of us, you know."

Grinning, Roningus nodded. "How long will you be staying with us?"

"As long as necessary, I suppose…the high priest has asked me to oversee the record hall in the meantime, but I wanted to come congratulate you before I made my way there. The black suits you nicely, I think."

Glancing over his shoulder at the majestic black cape that hung behind him, Roningus spoke as he turned his head forward once more. "I am to become the embodiment of the All Father's retribution, though the sword remains silent."

His smile widening, Garadain nodded. "So I have heard. The church seems to put a great deal of their trust in this weapon… perhaps it is teaching them a lesson?"

Furrowing his eyebrows, Roningus pondered Garadain's words for a moment, looking back up with a hopeful expression as he spoke. "Patience?"

"Strength. When Mithos chooses a champion, the importance of his calling will likely decide the fate of this world. For now, the church must prove it has the strength to endure. Do you know what brought about the church's first crusade?"

"We journeyed to the four corners of the western kingdoms, spreading the word of Mithos."

Garadain nodded, taking a long pull from his pipe before replying. "You established yourselves. You gained a foothold in Forthos and made an alliance with the elves of the Greatwood. You found yourselves unwelcome on the sands of Alazrahdin, and were unable to convert the barbarians of the northern plains. Yet you've never truly faced any real opposition. The gods are letting fate unfold, and the strength of man's faith will determine the outcome. This is why the sword remains silent."

Roningus nodded silently, contemplating Garadain's words. Just then, a familiar voice was heard crying out from down the hallway.

"Roningus!" came Ionnus's excited shout. Both he and Grisbane hurried towards him with royal blue capes hanging from their pauldrons. As they drew near, Garadain smiled to them, turning to Roningus one last time.

"I'll leave you to celebrate with your friends. Consider my words carefully, for yours is a heavy burden to bear." That said, the Loremaster turned and walked off slowly, nodding to Ionnus and Grisbane as he passed them who both bowed their heads respectfully in turn.

"Cloaked in black! Look how high the savior of Ascention has risen, Grisbane!" Ionnus said, grinning and reaching out to grab Roningus's cape between his fingers.

Standing next to him, Grisbane grinned, clapping Roningus on the shoulder. "Congratulations are in order, it would seem. Shall we celebrate, or does your new rank prevent you from mingling with the lower members of the order?"

Chuckling, Roningus shook his head. "By all means. Loan me some coin and I'd be happy to treat you both to a drink."

As they all laughed, Ionnus glanced down at the bundle in Roningus's arms, furrowing his eyebrows and still grinning as he spoke. "Hey, what have you got there?"

Looking down, Roningus realized suddenly he was still holding Garadain's belongings. "Oh! These belong to the Loremaster! I was just…"

But as he looked up, Garadain was nowhere to be seen.

"What is it?" Grisbane asked, looking down at the bundle curiously.

Shifting it in his arms, Roningus handed off his helmet to Grisbane, carefully taking the swaddled items in his arms and pulling back the cloth. Underneath, an exquisite pair of matching longswords in ebony scabbards laid side by side, a uniquely fashioned cross-shaped holster to hold them lying on top. As all three of their eyes went wide, Roningus carefully removed one before handing the other along with the holster off to Ionnus, drawing the blade from its scabbard.

Forged from black steel, the handle was intricately wrapped in dark brown leather, a simple round pommel perfectly balancing out the weapon. In the flat of the blade near the hilt, a pair of arcane runes glowed in luminescent blue, pulsating with a mysterious energy. As Roningus held the sword upside down out in front of him, the three of them inspected it for a good long while before Ionnus finally broke the silence.

"I think it's safe to assume he meant for you to have these."

"Black steel never loses its edge...I wonder what the runes are?" Grisbane said, reaching out and flicking the blade to hear its vibrating hum.

Seated in his chair, the bald headed dreadknight commander knocked the mug of white wine away. "Just set it."

That said, the black robed necromancer nodded, taking the horribly mangled ankle in his hands. With a sudden motion, the necromancer twisted the ankle back into place, the bald dreadknight letting out a ferocious growl and grasping at the arm rests on his chair.

Watching on, Asmodeus smiled amusedly. "So. Even the mighty Xaphan is no match for the Wrathful Tempest. Suddenly being bested by him doesn't feel like such an insult...I mean, surely if he was so skilled as to defeat you, then what chance did any of—"

"ENOUGH! I will not tolerate mockery from the dead god's lap dog! Do you hear me?!"

Asmodeus laughed wickedly. "Your hubris has likely cost you the use of that ankle. At best, you will be able to hobble about I suspect, and that's once it has fully healed."

Practically growling, Xaphan grabbed hold of the pitcher of white wine and threw it at Asmodeus, the half-fiend dodging it casually and folding his arms across his chest.

"Careful, now. You might hurt someone."

"GET OUT!" Xaphan howled, to which Asmodeus shrugged and turned, stepping out of the dreadknight commander's quarters.

A few seconds later, another robed necromancer appeared, his hands folded within his sleeves. "Losing Ascention cost us a great deal. You assured us all that we would be able to hold the false father's city."

With a scowl, Xaphan shook his head and looked away.

After several moments of silence, the necromancer spoke again. "What is our next move?"

Looking up, Xaphan narrowed his eyes at the necromancer. "We invaded their city, slaughtered their church knights, and wrought havoc on their church. What is our next move, you ask? We dig in, fortify our walls, and prepare for war."

As a loud knock at the door broke the pre-dawn silence, a pale man of a thin frame with scraggly black hair looked up from his modest breakfast with a start. With watery porridge dribbling down the left side of his face, he cautiously made his way towards the door. Reaching up to rub the back of his neck beneath the high collar of his shirt, he ran his fingers up through his unkempt hair. Several days' worth of stubble on his face added to his slovenly appearance. Upon reaching the door, he pressed his ear against it, listening carefully for several seconds until a stern sounding voice came from the other side.

"We know you're in there. Open the door."

Silently mouthing obscenities for a moment, the man looked around worriedly as he contemplated his response. Finally he cracked the door slightly. Peering out from behind the door, his suspicions were confirmed: the man who stood in front of the door was a church knight, the visor of his angel-winged helm glancing down at him through the crack. On the front of his breastplate was a crest the man did not recognize, a seraphic looking woman clenching a sword to her body standing in the middle of an asymmetric sunburst. A black cape billowed gently behind him as a slight breeze picked up. Two blue caped paladins stood at either side of him and at the ready, one a full head taller than the other two and somewhat broader of shoulder with a warhammer holstered at his right side.

"What do you want?" the man asked, doing his best to sound threatening but ending up sounding more intimidated than anything, a mistake that almost made him cringe immediately.

But the church knight gave no response, and after several seconds of uncomfortable silence, the man spoke again.

"I do not wish to be disturbed, so unless you've something to say then piss—"

"You know why we're here. I can see it in your eyes," the black caped paladin said in a cold voice, his cape catching on the handle of one of the swords sheathed at the back of his waist.

Now backed against a wall, in his desperation the man found his courage, resorting to bravado as his last resort. "I know what you church knights are about! You see what you want to see, whether it's there or not! Well you're not coming in here, and I'm not coming out there!"

Putting emphasis on the last of his words, it was then that the black caped church knight was spurred into action. With a swift, powerful front kick, he burst through the door, knocking the man backwards onto the ground and stepping in through the doorway, the two blue caped paladins following closely behind him.

"Ionnus, close the door," the black caped paladin said, the tall broad shouldered one nodding and pushing the wooden door closed behind him. That done, the black caped church knight moved over top of the man, bending over and grabbing hold of him by the front of his shirt as he scrambled backwards in a vain attempt to get away.

Lifting the man up onto his feet roughly, the church knight reached out and grabbed hold of the left side of his collar, pulling it aside. Underneath, a pair of puncture wounds that looked as if they had healed over and been reopened were plainly visible, and after looking down at them for a moment, the church knight looked the man in the eyes through his visor.

"You were right, Roningus. He's our guy," said the other blue caped paladin, standing off to the side while the broad shouldered one moved to stand in front of the door.

Staring hard at the man through his visor, the black caped church knight let the man wriggle in his grasp for a moment before he spoke again. "Where is their den?"

His expression turning horrified, the man shook his head helplessly. "I…I don't know what you're talking—"

"THEIR DEN. WHERE IS IT?" the church knight demanded, leaning in closer this time.

Paralyzed with fear, all the man could do was shake his head.

"Just tell us where it is, friend. We're here to help," one of the others said, though which one the man couldn't be certain.

His gaze was transfixed on the pair of dark brown eyes that glared at him through the visor of the angel winged helm, as if the black caped church knight could see the sins of his past and was passing his final judgment on him. Shaking his head, the man tried to speak but found that his voice had left him.

"How long have you been letting them feed from you?" the black caped church knight asked, and when the man still would not speak, the church knight dragged him over and sat him down forcibly in a chair, then turned and dragged another chair over to sit directly across from him.

Sitting upright with his hands resting on his knees, the black caped church knight continued. "We've tracked them here. We know they're nearby. And when we found out they were slipping in and out through the palisade gates at night, we knew we'd find someone like you. We're going to find them, one way or another. And we're going to drag them out into the sun, kicking and screaming. Whether or not you're tried for willingly associating with abominations of the dead god depends entirely on whether or not you help us now."

For a moment, the man said nothing, and it was just as the black caped paladin was about to stand up and leave in disgust that the man made the briefest of motions: a downward glance at the wooden floor beneath them.

The church knight paused, looking the man in the eyes, until he did it again, more deliberately this time, glancing down at the floor for a moment then back up to the paladin, pleading with the look in his eyes. Nodding, the black caped paladin signaled silently to the other two, the broad shouldered one opening the door as the smaller one took the man by his shoulders, guiding him outside.

It was then that the man saw them: seated atop their armored war horses, the column of paladins were accompanied by a score of battle clerics, a sea of brown, blue, purple, and black capes mixed with the unarmored devout, all of them watching the house intently. As the man was handed off to a cleric, he looked back towards the house as the cleric began to speak to him.

"Come…I'll hear your confession now."

Removing his helm, Roningus paced about the room, studying the floor intently. After several seconds, Ionnus glanced around in confusion. "What are you looking for, exactly?"

His eyes narrowed in concentration, Roningus shook his head. "I'm not sure yet, but I'll know it when I see it."

With a chuckle, Ionnus glanced back out the door towards where Grisbane was handing the pale man off to Osric. "You don't actually think he was telling the truth, do you?"

Roningus remained silent, until after a moment, something caught his attention. Kneeling down, he reached out and ran the tips of his gauntleted fingers over a portion of the floor, speaking quietly. "Bring your warhammer over here."

Quirking an eyebrow, Ionnus unholstered his warhammer and approached Roningus slowly.

Once there, Roningus pointed to a spot in the floor. "Put the raven's beak in there, and pull."

Without question, Ionnus lifted his warhammer above his head, driving the sharp point of the raven's beak end of his hammer into the wooden floor. Then, grasping it in both hands and planting his feet firmly, Ionnus pulled hard, and when he did, a large section of the floor swung up, revealing a hidden crawl space beneath the floor. Roughly four feet were between the dirt ground and where the floor of the house actually began, Roningus immediately dropping down onto the ground and leaning down in through the trap door to investigate.

Ionnus, who still held the section of the floor with the end of his hammer, pushed it aside as he moved towards Roningus. "Hey, be careful! You don't know what's down there!"

His head submerged in the hole in the floor, Roningus motioned for Ionnus to be silent. For a long moment Roningus held him in dead silence, until finally he slowly began to crawl away from the hole on his stomach, pushing himself up off the ground as quietly as he could. As he dusted himself off, he spoke to Ionnus in a quieted tone. "Carefully lay that down, without making any noise. I think I heard one of them stirring."

Striding outside with his helm tucked under his left arm, Roningus stopped as Grisbane turned to greet him. "Find anything?"

Responding with a silent chuckle and a slight grin, Roningus motioned for the church knights to form up, which they did summarily. Once they had gathered, Roningus addressed them in his commanding tone. "Five of them. One of which I believe to be the one we've been searching for. I need fifteen volunteers."

One-hundred and twenty-five hands immediately went up in the air, Roningus silently pointing at random church knights and even a few clerics. The ones he pointed to moved off to the side of the group, segregating themselves as he continued speaking.

"We have a chance to do this quickly and quietly, without upsetting the townsfolk and without anyone getting hurt. They've gone underground for the day, and we're going to haul them up into the sunlight in their coffins. Six of you will be responsible for hauling them over to the trap door in the floor, and then the rest of you will help get them up above ground and carry them outside. We need to do this as carefully as possible; we don't want them waking up and starting an incident. The rest of you will form a defensive wall around the house; I don't want villagers seeing what happens and going into a panic. Grisbane and Ionnus, the two of you will oversee the operations out here. Once the coffins are outside, bust them open and keep them pinned to the ground while the sun does its job. I'll oversee the extraction team. You have your orders."

One-hundred and twenty-five heads nodded in unison, and immediately they all went to work. Those church knights that had been called upon undid the buckles on their shields, removing their helmets as well and stacking them neatly in an organized sort of pile. The battle clerics carefully laid their studded wooden clubs aside, and together they moved silently into the house. The remainder of them formed a wall of shields around the house, obscuring the view as the sun continued to rise and the first villagers began to appear from their homes.

The process was slow and gradual, and made all the more difficult given the lack of clearance inside the crawl space. Working on their hands and knees, six of them carefully moved the coffins towards the trap door, lifting it up through the opening and handing it off to six others with the help of the three who were stationed at the opening to make sure the transition went smoothly.

Once outside, the six laid the first coffin down, three of them retrieving pry bars from the saddle bags of one of the pack mules they'd brought along. Lining up along one side, the three of them got their leverage, and on Ionnus's silent three-count they forced the lid open abruptly, revealing the ghastly looking creature within. The moment the sun first touched its skin, the vampire's flesh seared and split open as if it were being cooked from the inside, its milky white eyes opening wide as it was violently awakened from its daytime torpor.

As its hands shot out to grasp the sides of its coffin and lift itself out, however, Ionnus stepped in, planting his plated foot on the creature's stomach and shattering its hands with a casual swing of his warhammer any time it tried to grab hold of his leg. Grisbane stood with his longsword at the ready, but in a matter of mere moments, the creature was reduced to a smoldering pile of charred flesh and scorched bones, with barely a chance to let out a single horrified scream. Once it was done, Ionnus and Grisbane stepped away, allowing a team of battle clerics to clear away the remains while the hauling team brought out the next one.

One by one, the coffins were brought out and their occupants summarily executed, save for one that Roningus specifically had held back. The markings on it were subtle, but with a trained eye Roningus spotted them immediately; a small pair of infernal runes that signified the leader of the den's coffin, which was in every other way identical to the others.

Bringing it out just through the front doors to where the sunlight met the shade of the house, Roningus signaled for the three with pry bars and called them over. Prying it open with the same sudden force, the vampire had but a moment to open its eyes, groggily at first but then widening in fear as Roningus reached in and grabbed hold of it by the front of its tunic.

Garbed in tattered rags and with long, greasy black hair, the sickly looking male bared its fangs at Roningus, hissing threateningly. In response, Roningus drew back his right fist, delivering a powerful closed-fist strike to the vampire's mouth with a full follow-through that broke the point off of the vampire's left fang. Momentarily dazed, the vampire blinked as Roningus dragged it out of its coffin, holding its head out in the sunlight for a few seconds; just long enough to scorch its head before pulling it back into the shade and letting its blisters quickly begin to heal over. Just when its skin had returned to a raw pink in color, Roningus thrust it out into the sunlight again, waiting only a small bit longer this time before pulling it back, the vampire letting out an ear-splitting screech as it was hauled into the shade again.

As its face finished regenerating once more, Roningus was just about to drag it back out a third time when the creature cried out in a shrill voice. "Stop! What are you doing?! What do you want?!"

In response, Roningus pushed it back out into the sun for the third time, letting its face start to blister before pulling it back in and speaking in a tone colder than death itself. "The bald headed dreadknight commander. What is his name?"

Blinking as its face scabbed over and healed up again, the vampire shook its head. "I can't—"

Without hesitation, Roningus pushed it out into the sun again, and again the vampire hissed and squealed as the flesh of its face immediately began to bake, and when Roningus pulled it back into the shade, it was still sizzling and smoking. "His name."

Snarling, the vampire shook its head as its hair began to grow back. "You threaten me with death, when in truth I would welcome the dead god's embrace! I'll say nothing!"

His caustic glare unflinching, Roningus thrust the vampire back out into the sun, once again waiting until smoke began to rise from its skin before pulling it back, speaking as it began to regenerate once more. "This can continue all day. I have a hundred oathbrothers who would happily line up to take my place should I grow tired." That said, Roningus thrust the vampire out into the sun once more, speaking as the flesh on his face began to blister. "HIS NAME."

That said, he pulled the vampire back, giving him a moment to regenerate again before moving to push him back out for the seventh time, the vampire grabbing hold of his vambrace in desperation as he gasped his response.

"Xaphan! His name...is Xaphan!"

Nodding, Roningus pushed the vampire back out into the sun, pulling him back just as his skin began to catch fire this time. "And where does Xaphan make camp?"

Wincing as a layer of crisped black skin flaked and fell from his raw face, the vampire spoke in a submissive tone. "There is a city...hidden within the southern mountains...where the dead god reigns..."

"A city called...?" Roningus replied, and this time the vampire didn't hesitate.

"Demhora! The city of Demhora pays homage to the dead god, and seats one of his cathedrals! Xaphan made camp there last I knew!"

With a long sigh, Roningus tightened his grip, lifting the vampire up and dragging him out fully into the sun, holding it firmly in his grasp as the creature flailed and screamed as it was set ablaze. When its body had gone limp, Roningus let it fall to the ground, turning as one of the battle clerics brought him his helmet.

"Oathbrothers, get this cleaned up. Clerics, I want this house cleansed and sanctified. You have your orders."

As the paladins and clerics set about their work, Grisbane and Ionnus made their way over to Roningus.

"Demhora. Never heard of it," Ionnus said, Grisbane nodding in agreement.

"I suspect there's a reason for that," Roningus replied, the three of them going silent as they watched the remnants of the coffins get broken up and used as firewood to burn the remains.

26

"A den of no more than five vampires, and you required an entire column of church knights and twenty-five battle clerics?" Brogam asked, glancing down at Roningus incredulously.

When Roningus shot him a glance, Brogam shifted uneasily in his seat, and after a moment, Roningus looked back to the high priest. "Tracking down that single den required nearly a month of scouring the countryside, and yielded us two valuable pieces of information. First and foremost, we have the name and approximate location of the dead god's main cathedral. Second...they are afraid of us...and they know we're coming for them."

Raising his eyebrows interestedly, Vogoth looked over at Brogam as he spoke. "Where is this main cathedral of the dead god you speak of?"

Realizing Vogoth's implications by looking at Brogam, a slight grin crept along the corners of Roningus's mouth as he replied, his gaze still trained on the high priest. "Demhora, a city hidden in the Slagspire Mountains to the south. Its exact location has yet to be confirmed, but I've sent two of my men to consult the Loremaster."

"How did you come about this knowledge?" Brogam asked, screwing his face up suspiciously.

Vogoth stared irritably at Brogam as Roningus responded.

"I was able to detain the leader of the den and press him for information."

Brogam snorted a derisive laugh. "Pressed! More like tortured, I'm willing to bet. Did you at least dispose of the creature appropriately?"

Having grown fed up with Brogam, Vogoth interjected. "I've had quite enough out of you, Bro—"

"I dragged him out into the sun, and held him kicking and screaming as the sunlight scorched the flesh from his bones…I couldn't possibly begin to accurately reproduce the inhuman noises he made as I held him in place, the light of the All Father cleansing his stain from this world. Afterwards, the villagers came out in throngs to thank us and praise the church of Mithos for the service it had done them, and the crying mother of a child the den had slaughtered had her first peaceful night's rest without waking up screaming from night terrors. Are you satisfied with my conduct, Arch Cleric…?" And even as he spoke, Roningus turned, leveling his caustic glare upon Brogam and sending the arch cleric cowering back into his chair with the steel in his voice. "Or…would you have preferred I had brought him back to Ascention for a fair trial?"

As the prospect of a vampire within the walls of the church dawned on Brogam, he shook his head timidly. With a nod, Roningus turned to face Vogoth again, who glared at Brogam another moment longer before turning back to Roningus.

"Have you learned anything else?"

"I'm afraid that is all we know at this time. As I said, I've sent two of my men to consult with the Loremaster. We're hoping he can provide us with more information on the whereabouts of this city 'Demhora'."

Nodding, Vogoth gave Roningus leave with a wave of his hand, Roningus genuflecting before turning and striding out of the council chambers. Once he was gone, Vogoth closed his eyes, speaking in a stern tone. "Everyone out."

After a momentary silent pause, the other arch clerics all stood from their seats, beginning to shuffle towards the door before Vogoth spoke up again, pointing at Brogam.

"You stay."

Taking on an affronted expression, Brogam looked about him, only to find the other arch clerics avoiding his gaze and hurrying to exit the council chambers. Once they were all gone and Vogoth and Brogam were alone, Vogoth motioned to the two black caped paladins to close the door. Once they had done so, Vogoth turned his glare upon Brogam once more, Brogam narrowing his eyes in response.

"Do you mean to assault me again? You and I both know I'm not prone to fainting spells, yet you still have most of the church in on your ridiculous—"

"What I did…saved this city from imminent destruction. I'm going to be blunt with you, Brogam…I know not what you have against the Wrathful Tempest, nor does it concern me. But like him or not, that man saved not only this church but this entire city, and you WILL show him a modicum of respect!"

For a long moment, the two men stared at each other, until suddenly Brogam let out an indignant huff. Standing from his seat, he moved to descend the steps.

"I did not dismiss you, Arch Cleric," Vogoth said flatly.

Brogam paused a moment, glancing over his shoulder, then made his way towards the door.

"Church knights, seize Arch Cleric Brogam."

Immediately, the pair of black caped paladins descended upon Brogam and took him by his arms. Brogam shrieked and struggled wildly in vain, the two heavily armored paladins holding him fast where he stood and scarcely reacting as the arch cleric writhed within their grasp. Slowly and with a great sense of deliberation, Vogoth made his way down to where Brogam was held, making his way around in front of him.

Giving Vogoth an icy stare, Brogam's voice was dripping with venom when he spoke. "I demand that I am unhanded at once! This is no way for an arch cleric of the church and a devoted servant of Mithos to be treated!"

With a heavy sigh, Vogoth shook his head. "I'm afraid that won't be happening, Brogam. I've tried to be civil, and I've tried a stern approach, and yet still you care for naught but your own well-being and station. My patience with you grows thin, Brogam, but fortunately I am not the man you are. As such, I intend to recondition you…remind you of what it means to serve. Church knights?"

"Yes, High Priest?" the two answered in unison, forcing Brogam to stand at attention with them even as they restrained him.

"You are to escort Arch Cleric Brogam to the penitent cells. Once there, he is to be supplied with a bucket, clean water, a stiff bristled brush, and a set of plain spare robes should he not wish to dirty his arch clerical garments. Each day, he is to scrub out all of the penitent's cells and empty their night soil pails. At night, he shall sleep on a bed of straw in an empty cell, just as the penitents do."

As Vogoth spoke, Brogam's eyes went wide, his outraged expression growing red with anger. "I am an arch cleric of Mithos, not some lowly servant!"

His stoic voice matching the look on his face, Vogoth continued. "If he refuses his daily penance, the arch cleric shall fast instead and take only water. I will check in with him in one week's time, and once every week thereafter, until Mithos has imparted you with the wisdom of what it is to truly serve. Mithos's blessings upon you, Arch Cleric, and may you find enlightenment as you purge yourself of your hubris."

That said, Vogoth nodded, and the black caped paladins pushed through the council chamber doors, dragging Brogam along with them, Brogam's cries of protest echoing through the hallways all the way to the penitent's cells.

Pushing several books aside, Garadain spread the large map out on the table. Taking his hat off, he set it atop his staff, which stood straight up and down on its own next to the table. "I know the city of which you speak…though last I visited they declared for Othron, god of the harvest, and knew nothing of either Mithos or Necros. Tell me, what is so important that you would chance to pass through the Slagspire Mountains and risk the wrath of the stone giants?"

Looking over the map, Grisbane and Ionnus said nothing at first, until finally Grisbane looked up and responded. "A vampire confided the location of the dead god's main cathedral to Roningus before he was given the true death, and the city of Demhora is the location he gave. How large a force do you reckon we can expect?"

"That depends…" Garadain said, holding a wooden splint over a lit candle until it took the flame, then using it to light his pipe. "I imagine they've expanded considerably, and taking into account what I project would be their average annual growth… they could likely host a sizeable force."

Looking up from the map, Ionnus turned to Grisbane with a puzzled expression. "Does any of this seem odd to you? Why would they make their stronghold in a remote city seated within the Slagspire?"

Nodding, Garadain pointed to the map with the long stem of his pipe as he spoke. "It would be an ideal place to hole up. Easily defensible, and to approach from the north would mean losing a sizeable number of your forces to stone giant attacks."

Sighing, Ionnus shook his head.

"…what about from the south?" Grisbane asked, still studying the map.

"Hmm…that could work…" Garadain said, pausing to puff at his pipe before continuing, "…but to do so would require travel by sea, and I fear a landlocked city such as Ascention will find its naval prowess…lacking."

Undaunted, Grisbane continued looking around, until finally he pointed his finger at a city on the map. In response, Ionnus chuckled. Garadain raised his eyebrows, nodding approvingly.

"Fine," Ionnus said, scooping up his helmet. "But you're pitching the idea to him."

"Forthos?" Roningus said, his tone rendering the word as much of a question as it was a statement.

Grinning, Grisbane nodded. "We approach from the south, by sea. It's common sense, really, and even the Loremaster said it was a good idea."

Nodding, Roningus's expression remained unchanged. "It is indeed, except for one thing. The Dragonknights hold the city of Forthos, and I don't believe they would take kindly to an entire column of church knights and twenty-some battle clerics marching into their city with the excuse of 'we're just passing through'. While it is true we've established a small cathedral in Forthos, that doesn't exactly give us free reign to come and go as we please, and such a large number of church knights passing through could cause an unwanted stir among the townsfolk."

Furrowing his brow as he contemplated the flaw in his plan, Grisbane shrugged and looked back up. "Let Ionnus and me take a small unit and ride down to speak with the head of the Dragonknights."

When Ionnus nodded in agreement, Roningus turned back to Grisbane, standing from his chair as he spoke. "Take ten brown capes and five blue with you. You've a long journey ahead of you, so be sure to provision yourselves accordingly. Send word of the Dragonknights' response with seven of the brown capes if it is favorable; otherwise, you all return as a unit. You have your orders."

"Yes, Sir Roningus," the two of them said at once, beating their clenched fists against their left breasts as they stood, bowing ceremoniously. When Roningus returned the gesture, the two of them turned and exited, a robed acolyte appearing as they exited the war room.

"Sir Roningus? Loremaster Garadain wishes to speak with you."

Roningus found Garadain seated behind his desk, hunched over his large map of the western kingdoms. As he approached, Garadain looked up, smiling amiably with the long stem of his pipe clenched between his teeth.

"Sir Roningus. Thank you for coming; I hope I was not out of line asking one of the church's acolytes to deliver my message?"

Shaking his head, Roningus sat his helmet on the edge of the table, leaning over the table and looking at the map. "Not at all. What have you found?"

Grinning, Garadain nodded. "Right to the point, eh? Just as well, I suppose. If I am right, it's probably best if you depart as soon as possible."

Furrowing his eyebrows, Roningus looked up from the map at the Loremaster. "What do you mean?"

"Well…I've cross-referenced my own maps and star charts with the accounts of what little information your church was able to pry from the dreadknights you took captive before they bit out their own tongues…and I believe I've located several smaller cities that have fallen into the dead god's grasp. What with your two companions riding for Forthos, I thought now might be a good time to start tying up some loose ends before you begin positioning for your final assault."

Nodding slowly, Roningus looked back down at the map that was laid out before them. "Show me."

Staring at the marked map that now lay upon his desk, High Priest Vogoth tented his fingers together. "I've already granted you command of a column of your oathbrothers in addition to as many as twenty-five battle clerics…I don't understand what it is exactly that you're asking of me? If it is my blessing, you already have it, Sir Roningus."

Roningus bowed his head respectfully. "Your support is not misplaced, your holiness. What I ask of the church is a guarantee."

Quirking an eyebrow, Vogoth tilted his head. "What kind of guarantee?"

As he spoke, Roningus looked up. "It is my desire that as we liberate each city, we leave behind a number of our order to repurpose any place of worship they may have already established should the townsfolk wish it, allowing them to declare for Mithos and affording them our protection."

Frowning slightly, Vogoth remained silent for several moments as he contemplated Roningus's proposal. "That column represents a sizeable portion of our forces, and if my memory serves me correctly, you are already planning a move against their main cathedral in a city called…"

"Demhora. Yes, your holiness, but I believe in doing so we can ensure that the dead god's influence does not spread across the western kingdoms again. You have charged me with stamping out necromancy from these lands, and that is what I intend to do."

With a heavy sigh, Vogoth regarded Roningus a while longer until he spoke again. "And what of Demhora? Your oathbrothers and those clerics will be sorely missed when at last you make your final move against the dreadknight commander, Xaphan."

Grinning slightly, Roningus nodded. "That they will, your holiness. But I've given Sir Grisbane and Sir Ionnus new orders, and if Mithos should will it, we may soon have new allies in our war against the dead god's heretics."

"What do you make of the town?" Roningus asked. Having brought the column to a halt at the bottom of the large hill their path wound around, Roningus used the overlooking hill to conceal the column from view. He lay on his stomach atop of it, staring down at the settlement below.

Looking through a spyglass, the purple caped paladin that lay next to him carefully surveyed the town and surrounding area, speaking as he did so. "Heavily vested in livestock, judging by all the fencing that's been put up...looks like they have a cathedral...not a very big one..."

"What's it made of?"

"Wood," the purple caped paladin said, looking over to Roningus and grinning knowingly before putting his eye back to the spyglass.

"Walls?"

"Hmm..." the church knight muttered, looking carefully before snapping the spyglass shut and shaking his head. "None. Should we form up and prepare for the charge?"

For a long moment, Roningus simply stared at the settlement nestled in the middle of the open plains below. Roningus watched the minute silhouette of the townsfolk going about their day to day lives as one would observe an ant hill. "No. Go tell Sir Rhygar to round the men up for briefing. You have your orders."

"Yes, Sir Roningus," the purple caped church knight replied, crawling backwards down the hill until it was safe to stand. Then he turned and strode down the side of the hill towards camp.

Several minutes later, the entire assembled column and battle clerics were standing in an orderly fashion, Sir Rhygar nearby.

"So…what's the plan? We ride the bastards down and set fire to that wooden blasphemy of theirs?" As Rhygar spoke, he couldn't hide his grin, already anticipating the event.

Chuckling once, Roningus shook his head, smiling slightly at first as he spoke. "Not yet. As far as we know, they don't know we're here yet, so we have a chance to learn all they know about us. I need three volunteers."

As always, every hand present shot up, some even raising both thinking to double their chances. Roningus carefully scanned the assembly and settled on two black capes and Osric.

"Hey! I've more experience than either of those two! Why aren't I good enough?!" Rhygar exclaimed, his face rapidly turning red with indignation.

Glancing over at Rhygar, Roningus's expression remained indifferent as he spoke in a flat tone. "This will require a certain amount of subterfuge, and your face is too recognizable, oathbrother. Your renown would blow our cover."

The red anger immediately beginning to fade from his face, Rhygar begrudgingly nodded his head. "Well…I suppose that's true…"

Turning, Roningus addressed the three who were already separating themselves from the crowd. "We'll be leaving our armor behind."

The two church knights gave each other uncertain looks while Osric merely nodded his head.

"What about our shields?" one of the church knights asked, the two of them visibly concerned.

Roningus shook his head as he responded. "Staying behind. Weapons as well. Arms will be procured on site as needed."

Despite their apprehensions, the two church knights nodded without hesitation. That done, Roningus turned to Osric.

"Though it pains you, I'll need you to leave the symbol of your faith behind, cleric."

For the first time, Osric flinched like the church knights had, but gave a consenting nod of his head.

"As for the rest of you, make camp and get settled in. Sir Rhygar will hold command of the column until I return. You have your orders."

On his command, the column began to disperse, the three he had selected going about making their necessary preparations. Rhygar held back, waiting until the others had gotten to work making camp before taking Roningus aside.

"Are you sure this is wise, Roningus? This seems rather dangerous, considering the likelihood that the payout will be marginal at best…"

Contemplating Rhygar's words a moment, Roningus nodded his head as he spoke. "Mithos watches over us, oathbrother. Our cause is just, and I trust the All Father will not guide me in error."

It was before the sun began rising that the four of them set off, Roningus giving Rhygar some final commands before they left. "Be prepared to ride hard for town if you see a black smoke signal. If we haven't returned in one week's time, come find us and prepare for the worst."

That said, Rhygar nodded, and the two of them clasped hands and engaged in a half-embrace. Then, turning to the other three, Roningus stepped forward and set off taking the lead. Dressed in tattered rags and mismatched clothes, Roningus had made them smear themselves with filth from the horses.

When one of the paladins had grimaced and wrinkled his nose in disgust, Roningus had simply continued to rub handfuls up and down his garb, speaking plainly. "You'll get used to it. It is meant to keep guards from getting too close to us, and may very well save your life."

Now, as they crested the top of the hill and began making their way down the other side with the village in sight, Roningus addressed the three of them while they walked.

"What is my name?"

"Morden," one of the church knights replied, to which Roningus nodded as he continued.

"And yours?"

"Elias," Osric responded, his tone serious.

"Lar."

"Bram."

The other church knights chimed in, Roningus nodding his approval.

"Where are we coming from?"

"Pysmouth."

"Why did we leave?"

"Osric—"

"Who?!" Roningus interrupted, the church knight immediately realizing his mistake and correcting himself.

"Elias heard that the sailors in Cynegald were looking for able-bodied laborers to work the docks, and we're passing through on our way there."

"Who did Osric hear that from?" Roningus prodded, the church knight responding immediately with a facial expression to perfectly match his confused tone of voice.

"Who's Osric?"

Roningus nodded again. "Very good. Who did Elias hear that from?"

"I can't recall, though he had a strong smell of the sea about him, so we took him on his word," answered the other church knight.

As they drew closer to the town, Roningus motioned silently to the three of them, and immediately they all adjusted their gaits, their demeanors changing drastically. No longer the proud, marching paladins in service to the church of Mithos in the holy city of Ascension, the beggars Morden, Elias, Lar, and Bram timidly shuffled their way towards the town, struggling to carry on what with how malnourished they were. Once or twice, Lar stumbled and Bram had to help him to his feet, Morden cursing at them both to keep moving.

Reaching the edge of town shortly before mid-day, Garadain's suspicions were quickly confirmed. Wary, downtrodden looking townsfolk shuffled about their day-to-day activities, most of them afraid to make eye contact even with a group of beggars. When Lar approached one with open hands pleading for alms, the man reeled back from him as if he were a leper, shaking his head and hurrying away.

The city itself looked rather plain; most of the buildings were heavily dilapidated except for a few sanctioned for what Elias guessed to be the governing body that controlled the town. As they passed by a tavern, a brief look inside revealed no townsfolk, though plenty of off-duty guardsmen could be heard laughing and telling stories as they downed tankards of ale, and they even heard the faint sound of music coming from somewhere within. But they had no sooner begun to approach the doors that one of the guards inside spotted them, cursing and shooing them away while informing them the tavern was for city guards and officers only.

The streets were wide enough for a horse-drawn cart, yet everywhere they looked they saw people carrying loads on their backs or pulling small carts on foot, despite all of the livestock closed up in fences. The main roads were cobbled with stone, though a number of side streets were simple dirt roads with a bit of gravel thrown down for traction. Everywhere they went, people avoided looking at each other, plodding along their routes as if they were trained horses, and not once did they see a single child playing anywhere. Passing by an alley, they caught a glimpse of two guards arguing over a dead body lying on the ground, and it was just as they realized that the two men were arguing over the corpse's possessions that one of them looked up and swore at them to keep their mouths shut and get moving.

All routes seemed to lead to the center of town, where a massive platform had been constructed. Making their way towards it, a closer inspection revealed the creaking wooden construction to be heavily bloodstained, a chopping block set up in the middle of it with a sharpening wheel off in one corner. It was as they were examining the construction that a man on a horse dressed in guardsman attire rode up, reining in his animal and not bothering to correct it when it tried to bite Elias.

"What are you doing?" the man demanded, looking directly at Bram.

Wearing a chainmail shirt over top of a black boiled leather jerkin, the man's pale green eyes leveled on the beggars with resentment, wrinkles from age forming at their corners. His hair, thick, shaggy and rust colored, was beginning to thin on top, leaving him with a horse-shoe patterned baldness that he tried to rectify by letting what little was left on top grow longer than the sides. A full moustache grew on his upper lip, the rest of his brutish face clean shaven, and his growling voice bordered on threatening.

"We were just passing through, on our way to Cynegald…what is this?" Bram asked, tapping the wooden platform with his hand.

The man scowled, shaking his head. "Visitors are not welcome at this time. Ugh…what is that smell?" Even as he spoke, the man's face wrinkled up in disgust, and he brought his gloved hand up to cover his nose.

"Please, sir…we've been on the road for days, and we only mean to stay in town long enough to find a bit of hospitality…" Moving closer towards the guard as he spoke, Morden held his hands out in a pleading gesture, the guard rearing his horse back and turning sideways.

Removing his right foot from the stirrup, he kicked out with the heel of his boot, catching Morden in the chest and sending him staggering to the ground. "Get away from me! Go find charity somewhere else, or I'll have you chained to a wall in the prison."

Slowly climbing back up to his feet, Morden brushed himself off, while Lar stepped in to plead their case anew. "Not charity, sir… we're willing to work, if anyone would have us on, but we can't travel any further without a few days rest...Elias, he—"

Without so much as a word of warning, the guardsman reached down and pulled loose a spiked flail, brandishing it high above his head at Lar who cringed and fell over backwards trying to get out of the way. Laughing, the guardsman spat on him before speaking again. "This is your last warning. Get out of town and keep moving, or I'll have you all hauled off to rot in prison."

"Come now…there's no reason for such hostility, sir. All we ask is a chance to rest in town for a few days and regain our strength before we continue on. What harm is there in that?"

With a growl, the guardsman turned his attention on Elias, lifting the flail above his head and giving it a few circular swings before bringing it down low for a wide horizontal swing that would have caught Elias in the jaw. But Morden reacted instantly, and in a flash he had a hold of the guardsman's arm and had unseated him from his horse, pulling him to the ground with a crash. It was then that the four beggars became very aware of the crowd of gaping onlookers that had begun to surround them, the doe-eyed townsfolk watching on in a mixture of fascination and fear, many of them constantly looking over their shoulders as if someone might come up and cuff them on the back of the neck.

Looking up at the four beggars from the ground with an astonished expression, the guardsman's eyes lingered on Morden for a moment, the intensity of Morden's gaze leaving him paralyzed with fear for several seconds before he was able to find his courage again.

"GUARDSMEN, TO ARMS!" he cried, and almost instantaneously there was a stir from the gathered crowd as a number of similarly dressed officers began to appear, all of them brandishing spears.

Still gazing upon the unseated guard on the ground with smoldering eyes, the grounded officer watched as Morden's expression suddenly shifted from aggressive to startled, his eyes going wide and turning about to hold his hands up in surrender as he spoke in a frantic tone. "I'm sorry, it was an accident! I only meant to step in the way of my companion, and when I raised my arm to shield myself I panicked! I didn't mean to pull him from his horse!"

Moving in unison, the guards surrounded the four beggars, leveling the heads of their spears on them, Lar, Bram, and Elias following Morden's lead and holding their hands up in a gesture of surrender. Rising up off the ground, the guardsman holstered his flail and climbed back up on his horse, dusting himself off and bringing his mount around to where he could get a better look at the four men's faces.

"What should we do with them, Captain Torvald?"

Glaring hard at Morden, Torvald wrapped the reins of his horse tight in his hand. "Throw them in prison. Tie that one to a stake and flog him first, then shackle him to a wall."

"NO!" cried Lar, lunging forward in a desperate plea.

In response, one of the guards turned their spears around, striking him with the butt of the haft in the back of the head and knocking him to the ground. In that instant, the rest of the guards descended on the beggars, two to each one, taking them by their arms and dragging them off with a few left over to keep their spears pointed at them.

Turning around, Torvald shouted menacingly at the assembled crowd. "BACK TO WORK! ALL OF YOU! Half rations this evening for any who stay behind to gawk!"

Lowering their heads, the townsfolk resumed shuffling along to their destinations. Once Torvald was satisfied they had dispersed, he turned back around to watch as the guardsmen continued to haul the four beggars off.

And it was in that moment that his eyes met with Morden's again; the beggar's eyes burned through him with a fiery conviction, like a predator eyeing its prey. And for the first time in a very long time, Torvald felt a shiver run down his spine as a sense of genuine fear washed over him. The notion took more than several seconds to pass until he scoffed, laughing it off uncertainly, and steered his horse down one of the city's side streets.

Seated on a cold, damp floor, Elias, Lar, and Bram were shackled together at their ankles with a long chain that was bound to an iron ring protruding from the solid stone wall. The cell they'd been thrown into ran the length of the hallway, and was designed to hold a number of unfortunate occupants in a line. There were several doors along the wide iron bars that kept the inmates penned in, and guards routinely walked through and jabbed the ends of their spears at prisoners that clamored against the bars begging for water. The sounds of starving moans and agonizing whimpers were frequent, and the smell of soiled garments and festering wounds was enough to make one sick.

Yet despite all the unpleasantness, the beggars seemed not to notice it nearly as much, for coming further down the hallway the unmistakable sound of braided leather lashing into bare flesh was heard, followed by a hoarse yet familiar voice screaming out. Each time, the three of them would wince, Elias closing his eyes and silently mouthing a prayer. Sometime later, the lashings finally came to a stop, and a pair of guards came dragging Morden down the hallway by his arms. His body was limp, and the ragged clothes he'd worn on his torso had been ripped open, leaving him bare from the waist up. His muscular torso was covered in long, swollen bruises, some of which were split open and bleeding, and his wrists were chaffed raw from where they'd bound and hung him from the ceiling.

When the guards reached the cell doors where the other three were, the one with the keys opened it up so the others could bring him in, and when they let go of him, he fell to the ground without moving. Crouching down, the other guard clamped a shackle around Morden's ankle, binding him to the same chain as the others, before the two of them exited the cell and locked the door behind them.

Immediately, Elias and Lar moved to roll Morden over, but just as they were about to lay their hands on him, Morden pushed himself up, crawling over to the wall and leaning against it as he sat up. Glancing down at his stomach, Morden prodded one of the swollen lacerations there, gritting his teeth when it bled readily. Looking upon him with horrified expressions, it was Lar who finally broke the silence.

"Are you going to be alright?"

Glancing over, Morden shook his head and waved him off. "I'm fine."

"But…when they hauled you in…"

Letting out a grunting sigh, Morden laid his head back against the wall and closed his eyes. "They weren't going to stop until I blacked out, and the idea of letting that continue any longer than it had to did not appeal to me."

"So…the screams…"

Morden grinned slightly as he spoke. "Oh, those were real, but stifling them would have only encouraged them to try harder."

Blinking, Lar and Bram shook their heads in wonder, while Elias laid a comforting hand on Morden's shoulder. But then, the sound of approaching feet sent them scurrying back into position, the four of them hanging their heads dejectedly.

"Feeding time, maggots!" one of the guards shouted. The prisoners that were able to move clamored against the bars and stretched their arms out as the three guardsmen handed out scraps for them to fight over.

As the second day passed, Morden's bruises turned dark purple with light green outlines, and for the most part the four beggars were ignored by the guards. The other prisoners were able to tell them little other than the petty crimes for which they'd been imprisoned, one man having been given a one year sentence for being overheard voicing his dislike of the way the guards were treating people. The general census from the other prisoners was that the four of them would likely be turned loose and thrown out of town when more room was needed. When food came, they fought with the other inmates for scraps, then handed them off to those that were crippled or lacked the strength to get to the iron bars, standing watch over them while they ate so that other prisoners didn't simply take it from them.

It was on the fifth day, however, when the four were beginning to think that their excursion would be in vain that the approach of an irregular number of guards caught their attention. Eight of them total, all bearing spears and walking with a formality they hadn't seen since they'd been dragged in.

"On your feet, beggars," one said, as he unlocked the door nearest the four of them. Pulling it open, the guards began to swarm in, undoing the shackles around their ankles as a few of the others beat back the other prisoners with the hafts of their spears.

Once they'd been unchained, Morden and the others were pulled roughly to their feet and shoved out into the hallway, one of the guards making a point to kick over a waste pail, sending a stream of human waste spilling out towards the other prisoners and chuckling as they struggled against their chains to get away from it.

The guards lined them up and searched them first, then shackled their wrists together, marching them back up the hallway and through a series of corridors until they were taken into a plain room with a long wooden table in the middle of it. On one side of it four wooden stools were set out, a single chair sitting across the table from them. That done, four of the guards exited the room, leaving four behind to watch over them while they waited.

For how long they sat waiting, none of them could be sure, taking in their surroundings and studying the gash marks in the table encrusted with dried blood, until finally the door swung open again. Slowly, a hooded figure made its way through the door, and as it did the guards closed the door behind whoever it was. Morden, who was furthest to the left, kept his head down and stared at the table, though Lar, Bram, and Elias all looked up and watched as the figure shrouded in oilskins came around and took a seat at the other side of the table. It was then that Morden heard a familiar voice, and as he did...*Roningus* looked up.

"The beggar disguise was fairly clever, I'll give you that. You certainly had Torvald fooled, and truth be told I might not have thought anything strange about it had I not seen your column hiding on the other side of the hill as I flew over."

It was then that Asmodeus reached up with his hands, bound in rope gloves stained with fresh blood, and pulled back his hood. Starting at his left and working his way right, it was when he reached Roningus that he stopped, tilting his head as if he were unsure at first until his eyes gradually widened...a wicked grin forming at the corners of his mouth.

"The Wrathful Tempest...how convenient. And here I thought you'd be safe and sound back at your column's encampment, waiting for scouts that wouldn't return."

"Half-fiend," Roningus said flatly, eyeing Asmodeus with a cold expression.

Narrowing his eyes a bit, Asmodeus tilted his head. "Tell me…why would the savior of Ascention risk his life coming into hostile territory…COMPLETELY unarmed…unless he had some sort of contingency plan in place?"

In response, Roningus tilted his head to match the angle at which Asmodeus had, his gaze meeting the half fiend's. "I couldn't help but notice a distinct lack of any new decoration. Did the dead god not commend you for fleeing from battle so valiantly?"

Asmodeus chuckled, shaking his head, and as he spoke, he folded his hands on the table. "Of course…because a church knight of the false father would have stood his ground and been cut down as the mob overtook him, and his oathbrothers would later call it courage instead of what it really is…asinine."

"Death in service to the All Father is never wasted, half-fiend. Such love and devotion are concepts your dead god could never begin to grasp. Speak not on such matters as if you had insight to offer, when in truth you only make apparent your ignorance." As Osric spoke, his eyes almost seemed to glow, the steadfast conviction in his voice like a rock amidst a raging sea.

Leaning his head back and laughing, Asmodeus turned his attention on Osric and was still chuckling when he replied. "My, you're certainly well-practiced when it comes to reciting your creed, aren't you?! What else have they trained you to say?!"

"Don't feed in to him, Osric. Your words are wasted on this one," Roningus said, Osric narrowing his eyes and frowning slightly.

With a sigh, Asmodeus reached up and rubbed his right temple, shifting and slouching down into a relaxed position in his chair as he looked the four of them over. For several long moments, Asmodeus said nothing, until finally he stood from his chair, addressing the four guards in the room. "Get four more guards, and get these men on their feet."

Opening the door, the guard nearest the exit leaned out and called for others, and within moments four more came marching in, the eight of them grabbing the church knights and cleric by each arm and lifting them from their stools.

"On me," Asmodeus said, turning and striding out the door. Heading down a vaguely familiar set of hallways, Asmodeus led them out the front doors of the prison, passing through a number of check points and locked gates with ease as he was immediately recognized by all.

Once they stepped out into the light of the sun, Torvald came riding up on his horse, immediately dismounting and falling in next to Asmodeus.

"What are you doing with my prisoners?!"

Turning, Asmodeus abruptly drew back his fist and struck Torvald square in the bridge of his nose, knocking him to the ground and sending blood streaming down into his moustache from his now broken nose. Moving to stand over him, Asmodeus drew his fist back again, kneeling down and grabbing hold of the front of Torvald's uniform and pulling him up off the ground.

"YOUR PRISONERS…are CHURCH KNIGHTS! Perhaps if you'd taken the time to QUESTION THEM instead of just throwing them in the DUNGEON so you could get back to STUFFING YOUR FACE, you might have RECOGNIZED the FACE of the WRATHFUL TEMPEST!" Each time Asmodeus raised his voice, Torvald winced, putting his hands up to protect his face. "DULLARD!" Asmodeus shouted one last time, shoving Torvald away before continuing on.

Torvald stumbled, struggling to regain his footing and looking up just in time to meet Roningus's gaze, his eyes immediately narrowing in an intense hatred as if he blamed the church knight for not being forthcoming about his identity and sparing Torvald this embarrassment. In response, Roningus shot

Torvald a caustic glare, though this time the guard captain did not back down.

Once they reached the platform in the center of town, Asmodeus motioned to a guard, and had him bring forth a length of chain. Taking it in hand, Asmodeus looped it through the shackles of Roningus, Osric, and one of the church knights before bringing the ends together at one of the support beams, chaining them to the platform with a heavy padlock. Turning to Roningus, Asmodeus took the remaining church knight by the back of his shirt, his tone more of a threat than a statement.

"Last chance, Tempest. What are your column's standing orders?"

"Tell him nothing, Sir Roningus!" the church knight cried, to which Asmodeus responded by reaching up and dislocating the man's jaw with an effortless twitch of his hand, the church knight letting out a wordless howl of pain.

Grimacing, Roningus stared down the half-fiend, until finally Asmodeus shrugged. "So be it." Then, grabbing the church knight by his shackles, Asmodeus dragged him up the wooden steps onto the central platform, ignoring the small crowd of guards and civilians that had begun to gather.

Unceremoniously, Asmodeus brought the church knight to his knees with a strong kick to the side of his leg that shattered the joint, and while the church knight knelt prostate, the half-fiend reached down, grabbing hold of his throat with his right hand. A tight, sudden grip followed by a powerful jerking motion and the church knight's throat was ripped free, the man slumping over and sputtering loudly, blood pooling rapidly on the wooden stage around him. Tossing the hunk of dead flesh in his hand aside, Asmodeus kicked the gurgling church knight over onto the platform, descending the steps calmly as if nothing had happened.

"Leave the body for the crows," he called as two guards rushed towards the steps. The two of them nodded and backed away to let him step down.

Roningus's anger overcame him, and as it did he fought wildly against his chains, shouting and cursing the half-fiend with such force that his face grew a deep shade of crimson. Osric closed his eyes, mouthing silent prayers for the departed. When Asmodeus approached, Roningus lunged at him, Asmodeus responding by casually shoving him back towards the thick wooden beam they were chained to, taking a step back just out of reach when Roningus came at him again.

As the blood of their fallen oathbrother continued to spill, the gurgling noise went silent, and blood began to drip down upon them from on top of the platform, fueling Roningus's rage further and sending him into a frenzy as he pulled at his chains until the shackles dug into his wrists.

Folding his arms calmly across his chest, Asmodeus turned to the other church knight that still remained, speaking with an eerie sort of cadence to his voice. "You can spend the night out here, trying to sleep standing up with nothing to lean against while freezing from exposure, and tomorrow you can meet the same fate as your oathbrother up above you. Or, you can tell me right now what your column's standing orders are…your life will be spared…and I'll see that you are released unharmed. The choice is yours."

For a long moment, the church knight looked down at the ground, breathing heavily from having overexerted himself against his restraints, and when he first looked up, the expression on his face led Asmodeus to believe he might have gotten him to crack. "Your offer…is a tempting one, half-fiend…I must admit… however…temptation is one of many tools the dead god uses to lure the righteous from their path…and while I'd like to believe your lies, that does not change that they are, in fact, lies. You have nothing to offer me, half-fiend…so take your false promises and go."

Nodding slowly, Asmodeus turned, speaking as he walked off. "See you tomorrow, then."

After several moments, the crowd began to disperse, and the three were left alone to stand at the foot of the platform, chained together and unable to sit or lean, their arms held above their heads as blood continued to drip down on them.

"Oathbrother…cleric…I am sorry for bringing this upon you…and for endangering your lives so recklessly…it was foolish not to take the Ruinous Hammer's council to heart…" Roningus said, his grief showing in his voice.

Turning, the church knight shook his head, grinning weakly. "Do not be sorry, Sir Roningus. Even if I die here, I know what awaits me in the afterlife, and the potential gains were well worth the risk. Things don't always go as we would like them to."

As the man spoke, Osric nodded, weighing in once the church knight was done. "We knew full well that death was a very real possibility coming along with you. It is a reality we are prepared to face. We will tell them nothing, Wrathful Tempest. Besides, our efforts have not been in vain; we now know beyond a shadow of a doubt just how deeply rooted the dead god's followers are in Western soil."

Nodding, Roningus shifted out of the way of the continual dripping of blood, clenching his fists tightly and unclenching them to keep the circulation going. "Small reward for such a high price."

29

As the midday sun rose into the sky, Asmodeus stood in the shade of a building. He folded his arms across his chest, watching the three remaining prisoners standing defiantly with their arms shackled to chains above their heads. The cleric and the unknown church knight both had their eyes closed, their faces smeared with dried blood from where they'd tried to wipe it off with their shoulders and forearms. It was Roningus who stood, straight and defiant, his eyes fixed on the half-fiend from the moment he'd emerged from the building and never leaving him. Roningus had made no effort, letting the streaks of crimson run down the side of his face onto his neck, giving him an almost feral appearance.

Narrowing his eyes, it occurred to Asmodeus what he had to do, calling for a nearby guardsman without looking away from Roningus's gaze. "You there. Bring me Torvald."

"Right away, sir." Turning, the guard hurried off.

Still, Roningus continued to stare through the half-fiend.

Asmodeus grinned slightly and spoke quietly to himself. "You *will* break, Wrathful Tempest. And I will be the one to break you."

A few minutes later, the guardsman returned, Torvald trotting up behind him on his horse. His nose was bandaged and stuffed with red stained gauze, deep purple and green bruises swelling up around his eyes. As he reined up his horse to look down on the half-fiend, he did his best to scowl but ended up wincing in pain instead.

"What's this? The half-fiend thinks to give me orders now? I'll have you know I've reported you to Xaphan for your conduct yesterday."

Asmodeus responded without looking up. "Did you send a request for additional units while you were at it?"

Furrowing his eyebrows, Torvald looked down at the ground for a moment, and was about to speak when he looked back up before Asmodeus cut him off.

"I didn't think so. That would require forethought, and you've already more than demonstrated your inability as such. It matters not, however. This city is soon to be lost, but I intend to see the Wrathful Tempest taken out of the war before it happens. I want him unshackled, taken to a private cell, and fed well. He is not to be disturbed or harassed by any of your lackeys; I want him well-rested and at his best come tomorrow."

"And what makes you think I'm about to take orders from the likes of you?" Torvald said indignantly.

Slowly, Asmodeus turned, looking Torvald in the eyes and speaking in a deathly calm tone of voice. "Question me…one more time, dreadknight…and find out."

Gripping the reins of his horse nervously, Torvald backed his horse away a few steps, turning and riding off at a brisk trot towards the execution platform, motioning for a handful of guardsmen to follow him.

As the first guardsman drew near to unbind him, Roningus waited until the man was upon him before lifting his legs up, hanging from his shackles and locking his ankles around the back of the guardsman's neck in a swift motion. With a hard twist, the guard was brought to the ground, his neck letting out a muffled pop as it was shattered. Immediately, the other guardsmen went to move in, preparing to beat Roningus into submission with the hafts of their spears, until Torvald shouted out.

"NO! The half-fiend wants him unharmed. You three, restrain him. Take him to one of the single cells in the holding area."

Nodding in response, three guards moved in, grabbing hold of Roningus as he struggled wildly against them while another undid the shackles that bound him to the chain. Yet still, the four men struggled to maintain their hold on him, and it wasn't until the help of an additional two guardsmen was enlisted that they were able to carry him to the prison. Once they'd shoved him into his cell, the door was quickly slammed shut, Roningus throwing himself against it and screaming wildly at the guards, the three nearest the door backing away in a hurry.

Seated on floor, Roningus leaned against the wall. His left leg extended out before him, his right leg bent up at the knee with his right arm resting upon it at the wrist. Looking up as a guard approached, he saw a wide rectangular wooden plate laden with more food than the other prisoners saw in an entire day in his right hand and a wooden mug in his left.

Roningus closed his eyes, speaking plainly. "Take it away. I'll not feast while others beneath me starve."

Stopping at the cell door, the guard sighed heavily. "The half-fiend wants you well-nourished for tomorrow. Has something big planned for you, apparently."

Roningus shook his head, keeping his eyes shut as he replied. "I'll have none of it."

The guard nodded quietly for a moment, looking down at the plate before looking back up to Roningus. "He thought you might say that. And if you did, he told me to inform you that none of the prisoners will be fed until you eat everything on this plate."

Slowly, Roningus opened his eyes. "Then have it for yourself, and say nothing to him about it, but make certain the others are fed."

Grinning slightly, the guard shook his head. "Sorry, but I've seen what the half-fiend does to people who don't obey his orders. Captain Torvald's eyes have nearly swollen shut, and he'll be lucky if he ever breathes through his nose again. Either you're eating this, or the entire ward goes hungry."

Narrowing his eyes, Roningus tilted his head. "Why do you serve the dead god's abomination? Why do you follow the orders of a self-serving man like Torvald?"

The guard shrugged casually, opening a slot near the bottom of the door and sliding the wooden tray and mug through onto the floor, before pulling up a chair and taking a seat in front of the cell. "I follow orders because it's them that run this town right now. Not all of us buy into this dead god nonsense. A few even still pray to Eormic."

"Eormic? The benevolent one? And what do they ask of him?"

Frowning and looking at the ground for a moment, the guard shrugged again as he looked back up. "Probably for protection. When they're found out, they usually end up disappearing or dying conveniently in an accident. Eat up; I'm supposed to watch you to make sure you finish it all, and none of the others get fed until you do."

Gritting his teeth, Roningus sat forward, bringing his right knee underneath him and reaching out. Grabbing hold of the plate and mug, he sat back carefully, crossing his legs and laying the plate in his lap before taking a sip from the mug and laying it next to him. "What is the general opinion of Mithos, then?" Roningus asked, lifting a strip of seared beef from the plate and taking a bite from it.

"Resentment, for the most part. A lot of folk don't understand why a war that isn't theirs is spilling over into their village, and they aren't too happy about it. Only one they like less is probably Necros."

Sighing, Roningus shook his head. "This is exactly what we're fighting. I would hope they'd understand that."

"That may be so. But you have to remember that these folks had barely heard of your god Mithos or the dead god Necros until Xaphan's men took over. It isn't hard to press unarmed farmers into service when you've got armed men to back you up."

"They why do you back them?!' Roningus asked again, his voice rising as the guard's words caused his temper to flare.

"This isn't about right or wrong, church knight. This is about making sure my family is safe. If that means bringing you a plate of food and some water and making sure you eat it, then so be it."

"These men have slaughtered your fellow townsfolk. Do you not grieve their loss?" Roningus asked, staring long and hard at the guard.

In response, the guard gave Roningus a tired look. "Grieving grows easier over time. You'd be surprised how well fear and the will to survive can motivate a person."

After finishing his meal in silence, Roningus handed the plate and mug over to the guard, getting his personal assurance that the other prisoners would be fed. Clean water was made available to him, and for the remainder of the evening Roningus occupied his time as best he could with exercise. When another guard brought him a plate of food for his evening meal, he ate it without question, once more ascertaining the assurance that in doing so none would be denied their meals.

It was as he was lying on the floor doing some sit-ups by candlelight that Asmodeus came to him, grinning as he saw Roningus working out. Sitting forward with such force that it carried him up on to his feet, Roningus pressed against the bars of the cell, wrapping his hands around the bars and staring through them at the half-fiend.

In response, Asmodeus grinned, folding his arms across his chest and tucking his wings behind his back. "Very good. Hold on to that hatred. You'll need it for tomorrow."

"Where are my companions?" Roningus demanded, ignoring the half-fiend's remark.

"Which one?"

When Roningus narrowed his eyes, Asmodeus sighed, shrugging his shoulders.

"The cleric is where you last saw him. The church knight chose to defy me once more…so I sent him to join his oathbrother at the side of his god."

Instantly, Roningus's arm shot through the bars, grabbing hold of the front of Asmodeus's clothes and pulling him forward. But Asmodeus reacted with a speed to match Roningus, and in an instant he had broken free of Roningus's grasp and stepped back out of reach as Roningus fought against the iron bars, the rage welling up in his voice.

"THE DEAD GOD WON'T RECOGNIZE YOU WHEN I'M FINISHED WITH YOU, HALF-FIEND!"

Asmodeus chuckled, beginning to pace back and forth in front of the cell as he continued. "Did you enjoy your meal? Your fellow inmates on the floors below you had to go without so that you could be afforded such extravagance."

His eyes going wide in horror as he realized the half-fiend's implications, Roningus slowly turned from the iron bars. Walking to the back of the cell and planting his hands against the wall, he hung his head, standing in silence for several moments while Asmodeus continued to pace.

Coming to a stop, Asmodeus approached the bars once more, reaching up and placing one hand flat against them as he spoke again. "Get your rest, church knight. Come tomorrow, the entire village will watch on as the savior of Ascension is brought to his knees by the champion of the dead god."

Calmly, Roningus turned and walked towards the bars again, and it was then that Asmodeus noticed that his expression had gone unsettlingly placid, the rage having fled from him and replaced with one of tranquility.

Upon reaching the bars, Roningus simply stood, his hands gently wrapping around the iron bars that separated him from Asmodeus. "I made the mistake of granting you mercy once, half-fiend. Know that it will not happen a second time."

Smirking, Asmodeus shook his head, taking his hand down and turning to leave. "You assume you will live to be given a second chance."

At midday, they hauled Roningus out onto the central platform in shackles, a guard taking the haft of his spear to the back of Roningus's knees and dropping him to the ground while they waited. Several minutes later, Asmodeus appeared as the crowd was beginning to gather, his hands wrapped in the same bloodstained rope gloves he'd worn when he slew the church knights. The bodies had been cleared away, and though Roningus had looked about to see if they'd been put on display, he was unable to find them. As the half-fiend ascended the steps, the guards pulled Roningus to his feet, who stood motionless with his wrists bound in front of him.

"Key," Asmodeus said, the guard nodding and handing it to him. "Leave," came the half-fiend's next command, and the guards nodded in response. As Asmodeus stepped up and began to unlock the shackles, Roningus looked down and noticed Osric peering up at him from under the edge of the platform, his face alight with a hopeful expression.

Glancing up a bit, Roningus saw Torvald, barking orders at the guards to form a ring around the platform. His eyes were nearly swollen shut, and his nose was healing crooked. When he saw Roningus looking at him, Roningus grinned, causing Torvald to glare at him as best he could through his bruises.

Just then, the lock that held his shackles closed clicked open, the manacles falling from his wrists. Reaching up, Roningus rubbed the place on his wrists where they had rested, Asmodeus tossing the key aside and kicking the manacles away. Then, stepping back, Asmodeus folded his hands in front of him, bowing slightly while maintaining his gaze upon his opponent. Then he dropped back into a crouching stance with the front of his fists up in front of him at face-height, his arms bent at the elbows.

Looking up, Roningus tilted his head. "Am I to fight without longswords?"

In response, Asmodeus grinned, shaking his head. "Hand to hand combat is the great equalizer. It is the only way to ensure that opportunity is equal."

Smirking, Roningus nodded slowly. "Equal. Despite your years of training."

With a heavy sigh, Roningus bent his knees slightly, clenching his fists tightly. Holding his right fist with the back of it facing the ground and close to his chest, he presented his left forearm and the back of his left fist to the half-fiend in the Western boxing style practiced by the church knights of Ascension. Rocking forward on the balls of his feet, it was just as Asmodeus was about to leap forward that they heard it; a thunderous sound, as over a hundred war horses were seen pouring down from the hilltop, the column of church knights galloping at a full charge towards the village.

Glancing over at the sight of the approaching column, when Asmodeus looked back to Roningus, he was grinning.

"Just in time," Roningus said.

It was when Asmodeus smiled in return that Roningus stopped, the half-fiend speaking in an amused tone. "I knew the city was lost the moment I saw the column hiding behind the hill, church knight. All I wanted was the opportunity to break you myself before they arrived to rescue you. Killing your oathbrothers was an added bonus."

Turning his head to one side and cracking his neck, Roningus braced himself as he spoke. "A slight I intend to repay ten-fold. Come, half-fiend. Before my oathbrothers arrive and deprive me of my satisfaction."

30

Bolting forward, Asmodeus lashed out at Roningus with a flurry of vicious jabs and elbows, keeping Roningus's arms busy protecting his head while the half-fiend landed knees in the church knight's side. Roningus found himself hard pressed to gain the offensive, shrugging off the blows to his torso relatively painlessly while trying to duck out of the way of the half-fiend's punches. Just when Roningus would think a pattern was emerging, Asmodeus would switch his style, or bring his wings into the melee and use them with surprising efficiency, sweeping at the church knight's legs or occupying his arms to allow the half-fiend to catch Roningus with a swift backfist to the side of his jaw.

Realizing he was losing rapidly, Roningus growled angrily and lunged forward, catching Asmodeus in the stomach as he tackled the half-fiend with his shoulder. Wrapping his arms around the half-fiend's waist, Roningus lifted him off the ground, twisting and slamming him down onto his back. He quickly moved in and dropped down to pin the half-fiend's arms to the ground with his knees. It was when Roningus drew back his fist and had time to look Asmodeus in the eyes that it dawned on him.

I am stronger than him.

Realizing this, Roningus brought his fist down in a right hook, catching Asmodeus in the side of the jaw with such force that it turned the half-fiend's head to the side. Reacting immediately, Asmodeus brought his legs up, wrapping them around Roningus's neck and pulling him backwards onto the ground with enough force to knock the church knight's head against the wooden platform. The half-fiend rolled into a backwards somersault and came up in a standing position. Roningus grinned, pushing himself up off the ground as he rubbed the back of his head.

As he stood watching the church knight, Asmodeus cracked his jaw. His eyes narrowed as he resumed his former stance, spreading his wings out wide.

"GUARDS! Line up! Prepare to defend against the charge! Officers, to your stations! Half-fiend! Now is not the time! We have a city to defend!" Torvald shouted, reaching down and unholstering the flail at his waist.

Immediately, guards and dreadknight officers alike began to scatter, but Asmodeus remained where he stood. Roningus resumed his western style boxing stance.

"Your city is lost, dreadknight," Asmodeus responded, his eyes never leaving Roningus. "Feel free to stand your ground and show your devotion to the dead god, but I intend to finish what I've started."

This time, it was the church knight who launched the offensive, swinging out with powerful blows that knocked the half-fiend off balance even though he deflected them. When Asmodeus countered with rapid fists and elbows, Roningus would harden the muscles along his sides and grit through them, making the half-fiend pay for each blow by punishing him with another in turn.

By then, the population had begun to grow restless, torn between watching the half-fiend battling Roningus, and watching the rapidly advancing column of church knights. Soon, the guards were forced to divide their attention between keeping the increasingly agitated townsfolk in line and preparing their defenses, and it wasn't long before they abandoned the former for the latter. The townsfolk broke and ran for their homes.

Glancing over at the spectacle as he cowed the half-fiend with a powerful overhand swing, Roningus smiled. The sight of the column's impending arrival bolstered his spirits. Stepping forward, Roningus brought his knee up, and when the half-fiend predictably brought his hands down to block, he extended his leg the rest of the way, planting his foot on Asmodeus's chest and shoving him backwards.

Again, the half-fiend was quick to regain his footing, snarling loudly and swearing in the abyssal tongue; a gnashing, hissing language with prolonged consonants and a spastic cadence to it.

Years of training in heavy plate has left his body built of brick, the half-fiend thought to himself, calmly moving his open hands around in opposing circular motions in front of him as he re-centered his mind.

In response, Roningus made a brushing motion on his chest, as if sweeping away the half-fiend's blows, before slowly raising his fists again, a grin on the corner of his mouth.

"RIDE THE BASTARDS DOWN!" Rhygar screamed, with Skyhammer raised high above his head.

The city guards were lined up three men deep, many of which held pikes whereas others stood on phalanxes to brace them. As he fell upon them, Rhygar swatted a phalanx away with Skyhammer and caught the man with a vicious backswing that knocked him to the ground to be trampled.

Further back from the initial line, Torvald sat atop his horse along with his fifty dreadknights, all of whom were mounted as well. "HOLD!" Torvald shouted, as the guards began to break their line and flee from the church knights.

"SPARE THE CIVILIANS! FOCUS ON THE DREADKNIGHTS!" Rhygar bellowed, his booming voice carrying over the resounding pitch of battle that had begun to fill the streets.

Some guards stayed behind, mostly those who had succumbed to the promises of the dreadknights and held the dead god in revere. The paladins swarmed over them, their trained warhorses shouldering past their phalanxes and pikes to afford their riders the opportunity to cut through them with their longswords, and their misplaced faith was the end of them.

As Rhygar continued to lead the charge, Torvald rode out to meet him, the two of them taking a pass at each other. When Torvald swung out with his flail, Rhygar brought Skyhammer up to parry, deflecting the head of the flail away and catching Torvald with a backswing between his shoulder blades, sending him sprawling forward on his horse but still remaining seated. As the two men reined their horses in and brought them around to face off once more, paladins and dreadknights alike formed a ring around them, a wall of horses encircling the two as they clashed weapons again.

"Throw down your weapons, church knights! You have no authority here!" Torvald shouted, swinging his flail in circles above his head to gain momentum.

"YOU! Get Roningus his weapons and see to Osric!" Rhygar bellowed, pointing to a battle cleric carrying the pair of bundled weapons.

In response, the cleric nodded, steering his horse towards the platform and riding hard for it.

Seeking to take advantage of the moment when Rhygar looked away, Torvald spurred his horse towards the church knight, leveling a horizontal swing of his flail at the other man's chest that caught him full in the center of his breastplate, nearly unseating the Ruinous Hammer.

Swearing so loudly that he was heard over the disapproving calls of the paladins, Rhygar righted himself in his saddle, turned around, and charged Torvald. He brought Skyhammer down on the dreadknight with such force that Torvald fell backwards from his horse. Rhygar kicked his left leg over the back of his mount and stepped down to engage Torvald on the ground. Torvald scampered away on all fours, Rhygar and the church knights laughing as he did.

"Fear not, heretic…I am not so craven as you. Ready yourself, that we may continue."

Torvald stood, brushing himself off and scowling at Rhygar. "Do not mistake a tactical mind for cowardice, church knight!"

Smirking, Rhygar shook his head, clanging Skyhammer against his shield as he advanced. Bringing his flail up above his head to circle about like a vulture once more, Torvald met him, going on the offensive with a series of overhand strokes. With each one, Rhygar casually raised his shield to meet it, the head of the flail glancing off to the side. Torvald's frustrations mounted, until finally, Rhygar pressed forward with a shield bash, knocking the head of the flail away, then followed up with the spiked end of Skyhammer. The metal point punched through Torvald's breastplate, the dreadknight letting out a sudden bursting cough and spattering the front of Rhygar's plate mail with flecks of blood. His eyes grew wide, and when he looked down at his chest, Rhygar pulled the hammer out, a loud sucking noise heard coming from the hole with each breath he drew.

As Torvald fell to his knees, Rhygar stepped up, calmly reached down, and took the flail from his hand. The ring of paladins and dreadknights watched on in solemn silence amidst the otherwise general turmoil engulfing the entire city.

"This can't be…I hold the dead god's favor…" Torvald said between pained breaths, his voice full of disbelief.

"The dead god favors only himself, lad," Rhygar replied, his voice stern but not without compassion.

"I…I would speak with a cleric…" Even as he spoke the words, Torvald collapsed over onto his side, his breathing growing increasingly shallow.

Rhygar nodded, and with a motion of his hand, a cleric pressed through the wall of mounted paladins.

Going from a complete standstill to a full sprint in the blink of an eye, Asmodeus leapt into the air, his right foot extending out in a jumping kick aimed to catch Roningus in the head. Roningus reacted just in time, dipping out of the way to his left and bringing his right arm up, where he hooked it under Asmodeus's left knee and tangled the half-fiend up in mid-air. He brought the half-fiend crashing to the ground, and caught him in the bridge of the nose with a forward punch delivered from the shoulder. In response, Asmodeus got his foot up under Roningus, kicking the church knight in the chin with enough force to send him staggering backwards with a crash to the ground. Bringing his knees up to his chest, Asmodeus hopped up from the ground and threw himself on top of Roningus, his rage carrying him forward as he wrapped his fingers around the church knight's throat, spreading his wings out wide behind him.

Though his face began to swell with red, Roningus remained calm, reaching up and grasping at the rope gloves that wound up the half-fiend's forearms. Unable to pull the half-fiend's hands away or pry them from his throat, Roningus stretched his fingers out, stiffening them as best he could despite how badly they shook. With as much strength as he could muster, he drove the points of his fingers into the pits of the half-fiend's arms. Instantly, Asmodeus felt his grip go lax as he lost all feeling, recoiling from Roningus in horror. He backed away swiftly, fighting with his arms which refused to move.

"NO!" Asmodeus screamed, watching on helplessly as Roningus rolled over and coughed forcibly, regaining his breath.

Forcing himself to his feet, Roningus turned as a cleric came running up to the platform, speaking in an urgent tone. "Roningus! Your blades!"

Before he'd even gotten the words out, the cleric unfurled the sheet they'd been bundled in, tossing the swords into the air as he did so. Watching as the cross-scabbard containing the blades drifted towards him, when Roningus reached out, his hands felt the familiar leather of their handles, and in a fluid motion he had them drawn as the scabbards clattered to the ground.

Feeling the final push at hand, Roningus turned, brandishing the blades in perfect unison with graceful sweeping flourishes as the twin longswords seemed to chase each other. Roningus went so far as to turn one about in his hand twice in a dazzling display of handling before bringing them down to his sides, tilting his head as he returned his focus to the half-fiend and holding his arms out as if to grant him the first move.

Asmodeus smirked, shaking his arms as the feeling returned to them. "You dishonor our match with your weapons, church knight."

"You know nothing of honor, half-fiend."

"Your faith in your weapons will be your downfall."

"Your faith in your dead god will be yours."

With a snarl, Asmodeus held out his left hand, and a faint whistling sound was heard as his quarterstaff came spinning through the air towards him. Asmodeus caught it without so much as glancing in its direction.

Slowly, Roningus lifted the sword in his right hand, cutting an "X" into the air in front of him and pointing the tip of the blade at the half-fiend. In response, Asmodeus smirked, giving his metal staff a spin and grasping it in both hands, bringing one end of it down near his feet, the other kept up in front of him for turning swords aside.

And then Roningus advanced upon him.

Unhindered by his plate armor, Roningus found the motions of his Two River style came almost effortlessly, though in truth he'd have preferred the protection his armor afforded him. Still, as his longswords danced in his hands, he pressed the half-fiend back to the edge of the platform, pirouetting with his swords crossed above his head as Asmodeus charged past him, then turning and driving the half-fiend back across the platform again.

Each time Asmodeus thought he'd found an opening, his staff was swatted away with the flat of a longsword, and the half-fiend would have an instant to react lest the other one catch him with its counter strike. It was as they were nearing the other edge of the platform that it happened; as Roningus feinted, Asmodeus took the bait, leaving himself open wide.

With no time to reposition, Asmodeus brought his staff up above him, Roningus cleaving through it with a downward stroke of the sword in his right hand. Discarding the pieces as the enchantment fled them, Asmodeus tumbled past Roningus in a forward somersault and took off in a run, leaping into the air as his wings flapped furiously, taking to flight. All in the same motion, Roningus turned around, hurling the longsword in his left hand end-over-end at his fleeing opponent, then following up with another strong throw from the right. The second longsword tumbled after its counterpart one second behind, Roningus following through with the motion and watching as the swords chased after Asmodeus.

The first one caught him in the back of his right shoulder, the point of the blade easily lodging itself in his torso and spinning him around from the sheer force with which it had been thrown... positioning the half-fiend to watch as the second blade followed up, catching him square in the chest. The fluttering of his wings came to a sudden halt as his red eyes looked down in shock, his blue lips parting as his mouth fell open. To Asmodeus, it was as if it were all in slow motion...he looked down and saw Roningus, watching him with his narrowed gaze as the half-fiend fell from the air like he'd been dropped.

And then, there was the crash. Everything he'd heard about black steel proved to be true...even with all of his weight on top of it, the black steel blade lodged in his back bent without breaking, carving through the flesh of his torso as if it were water. Laying on his back, staring up at the sun in the sky, it seemed like hours before Roningus came to stand over him, kneeling down and taking the half-fiend's hand in his own.

When Asmodeus chuckled, a spurt of red erupted from behind his teeth, staining them. "It would seem your god was with you this day...church knight." His voice was barely a whisper, and when Asmodeus spoke, Roningus had to lean in to hear him.

"My god is always with me, half-fiend. He is with us all, even those who reject him."

Letting out a weak chuckle, Asmodeus shook his head. "Spare me your sermons...there is no hope for me. My place is at the foot of the dead god's throne. It is where I belong."

"No one is beyond forgiveness. Not even you."

Asmodeus closed his eyes, his lips turning up in a faint smile.

Roningus reached down, lifting his head up to help him breathe in his last moments.

"Are you so certain? You have seen the blood that stains my hands...still, I must commend you...you were like none I have ever faced before..."

Roningus nodded, and held the half-fiend until his chest went still. Once it had, his body gradually phased out of the material plane, leaving Roningus's longswords to clatter to the ground in its wake. Taking them by their handles, Roningus knelt a moment longer, leaning upon them as he prayed silently. Then, finishing up, he spoke as he blessed himself with a gesture.

"Be at peace, half-fiend, and may you come to know the All Father's mercy."

As they came within sight of the city of Forthos, Ionnus and Grisbane's small company of church knights lined up. They did their best to look as formal as possible, surrounded by lush, rolling hills of the healthiest green grass they'd ever seen. The countryside that surrounded Forthos was frequently subjected to light rains that would last for days at a time, followed by brief intermissions of the clearest azure skies and golden sun in the western kingdoms. Presently, the rains had just begun, the clouds not yet fully formed, casting a wide rainbow over the city's ancient stone walls. Small homes dotted the open fields, bent-back farming folk looking up from tending their crops as the church knights passed.

Pale-skinned and broad shouldered, fiery red hair was predominant among the people of Forthos, their eyes typically of an emerald green shade to match the landscape. Many men grew a full beard, but here and there a pair of thick, shaggy sideburns or a well-groomed moustache could be found, and the hair on their heads was cut to an almost uniform shortness. The women preferred to let their hair grow in cascading waves or wild curls down past their waists. Dressed in attire not dissimilar to that of the farming folk on the outskirts of Ascension, they stopped and looked up as the small group of church knights rode by, some even turning to make japes and laugh with their comrades.

"I've never felt so out of place in my life..." Ionnus said, leaning over and speaking quietly to Grisbane.

"Keep your head up. Sit tall and proud. We represent the church of Ascension."

The city of Forthos itself looked almost as a rock that had become rooted in mud; large, round, heavy stones pitted from centuries of rain stood atop a grass mountain, a mingling of new stones visible from where time and the elements had necessitated the replacement of parts of the wall. Even from such a distance, a stone dragon statue could be spotted looming over the city, its wings curled protectively around what laid beneath it. Whereas Ascension was more or less rectangular, designed in straight lines for ease of road construction and city planning, Forthos was a misshapen circle, with a confusing road pattern that seemed to defy logic just for the sake of it. Several large battlements lined the top of the walls, continuously patrolled by the city guards, with arrow slits and trap doors for boiling pitch above the main entrance gates.

Upon reaching the front gates, a guardsman sporting a full red moustache and a wisp of a goatee on his chin stepped forward, his green eyes looking upon the church knights with great amusement. Garbed in a ring mail shirt worn over a boiled leather jerkin, a long sleeved white tunic underneath came down to his knees, and a simple iron helm sat atop his head. Bearing a round wooden shield reinforced with studded iron bands and a longspear, the guardsman smiled affably.

"Greetings, lads! Looks like ye've come an awful long way, but it pains me to inform ye that ye won't be getting' in today, I'm afraid."

Grisbane and Ionnus turned to each other in disbelief, before Ionnus finally looked back to the guardsman. "Sir, we are emissaries from the church of Mithos in Ascention! We have a cathedral here within your very walls!"

Frowning, the guardsman shook his head. "Never heard of it."

Ionnus glanced back at Grisbane to see if he were imagining what he had heard, then turned back to the guardsman, his tone growing increasingly exacerbated. "I know for a FACT that we have…what…are you laughing?"

And indeed, the guardsman had dropped any and all pretense of sincerity, and laughed openly at Ionnus as the church knight sat bristling in his saddle. "Ah hah hah! Oh, I wish ye could see yer face right now! Knows for a fact, this one does! Hey Charlie, open the gate! This one knows for a fact where he's going!"

More laughter was heard from above the gate accompanied by the sound of a winch beginning to turn. As the gate slowly creaked open, the guardsman reached up, wiping a tear of laughter away from the corner of his right eye, still chuckling as he spoke.

"Welcome to Forthos, lads! Aw, spare me yer sad faces, now. C'mon, give us a smile."

Still frowning, Ionnus looked over to Grisbane, who despite his best efforts was shaking so hard with stifled silent laughter that he had to lean forward and brace himself on the back of his horse's neck.

"See? There we go," the guardsman called after them as they rode past, Ionnus leading the group through the gates.

Once inside, Ionnus waited until they were out of earshot before he spoke. "Hopefully they aren't all like that."

Still chuckling, Grisbane shook his head. "We're in, at least. Now we just need to find the cathedral so we can report."

Coming to a halt, the semi-circular area in which they stood opened up with roads in several directions, like spokes extending out from the central hub of a wheel. Looking around for several moments, Grisbane leaned over and flagged down a young boy wearing naught but a pair of dirty leggings and a leather vest, his orange red hair a tangled mess.

"Excuse me, young man…we're looking for the church of Mithos. Can you direct us there?"

Nodding silently, the boy held out his open palm, and it only took Grisbane a moment to discern his meaning. Digging into one of his belt pouches, Grisbane produced a pair of silver pieces, stamped with the standard of Ascension. Turning them over in his hand, the boy turned and pointed down one of the roads.

"Head down that way, take the first right, go down to where the white door is and turn left, then make your way up the steps and keep going past the ivy wall then turn right at the stump. Ye can't miss it."

That said, the boy smiled brightly before turning and trotting off, skipping a few times before breaking into a full-blown sprint when Grisbane called after him.

"Hey, wait! That doesn't do us any good!"

"Save your breath, he's gone," Ionnus said, sighing heavily afterwards.

"Well, we may as well start exploring then…how hard can it be to find?"

For several hours the church knights made their way through the winding stone roads of Forthos, at one point getting their hopes up high when they thought they'd discovered the stump the boy had mentioned only to find themselves lost again a few minutes later. The city itself possessed a rustic sort of beauty vastly different from that of Ascention. The cobblestone walls crawled with thick, leafy vines lining every road, and gave the entire city a connectivity unparalleled by any other of the major cities in the western kingdoms, as if the entire place were marbled with a walking path that grew wider or narrower as necessity saw fit. Elaborate aqueducts carrying naturally flowing spring water ran through the city, powering enormous mills and providing fresh drinking water at nearly every corner. Everywhere one looked there was green of some kind to be found, be it in vegetation, architecture, or the eyes of the people that inhabited the town.

The townsfolk were kind enough, yet each time the church knights tried to ask for directions, they wound up getting themselves even more lost, until finally one man out for a walk with his daughter took pity on them and offered to lead them to the cathedral. Holding the little girl's small hand in his own, the man spoke of the city's history and architecture proudly, pointing out landmarks as they passed them and giving names to the streets they traversed, which did nothing in the way of orienting the church knights. One building in particular stood out to them, however.

"There it is, lads…the hall of the Dragonknights. Pride of Forthos, she is…"

Built into the base of the stone dragon relief they'd spotted when they first approached, the pathway leading to the front doors of the hall went through the ribcage of a dragon, the points of the ribs buried in the ground and over twenty-four feet in height where they connected to the spine. Worn smooth as ivory and slightly yellowed from age, the rib bones were wide enough apart that one could easily pass through them with their arms fully extended to either side. The dragon statue itself was a fearsome thing to behold, curling its wings around the enclosure protectively and turning its head towards those who would approach the walkway, its teeth bared and jaw opened wide as if to breathe down molten flames upon those with ill intentions. The base it sat upon was three stories tall, nearly twice as large as the main cathedral of Mithos back in Ascension.

The familiar sounds of a training yard in use could be heard from behind the building, and a pair of Dragonknights stood guard outside the wooden doors. Clad in their customary steel blue ring mail, they were armed with vicious barbed longspears and large scale-shaped shields. Their helms were forged in the likeness of a dragon's head, their gazes peering out through where the dragon's eyes would be with elaborate reptilian wings extending back from the sides of the helm.

"Are those real dragon bones?" Grisbane asked, the church knights looking upon the ribcage in a mixture of fear and fascination, contemplating a creature of such monstrous proportions.

"Aye, lads…remains from back when the Dragonknights ruled the skies atop the majestic creatures they're named after. 'Course, no one's seen a dragon for hundreds of years…"

As they passed by the structure, the pair of Dragonknights spotted them, offering up the formal salute of the church knights, to which the paladins responded in kind.

Finally, they reached the cathedral of Mithos within the city; small, square-ish and rather out of place. The building looked as if it could barely hold half a column of church knights, with stables for half as many horses. With scarcely a training yard to speak of, one needed only look upon the building to realize it did not see much use.

Dismounting their horses, the church knights thanked the man, his little girl smiling and waving goodbye as they went their separate ways. Making their way to the stables, the seventeen church knights found no stable boys, instead having to care for the horses themselves. Aside from a few stalls occupied by neglected old garrons, they had the run of the stable, unsaddling and brushing down their horses before seeing them fed and watered. That done, they made their way to the front doors of the church to formally present themselves, thinking it odd that no one had come to welcome them yet.

Knocking loudly on the large wooden doors, when no one answered for several minutes, they let themselves in. The interior of the building was eerily quiet, and not a single candle was lit, leaving the church knights to fumble their way through the dark hallway into the altar room. There, a single beam of sunlight provided dim illumination, allowing them just enough light to get a better look at their surroundings. The pews were covered with a thick layer of dust, and the only candles that looked recently lit were the ones at the altar.

"Where is everyone?" one of the brown caped church knights asked, to which another shrugged his shoulders.

"I expected a warmer reception than this…" Grisbane said, removing his helm and dropping down to one knee to genuflect before the altar, blessing himself.

Just then, a noise was heard, and all sets of eyes turned to a darkened hallway near the back of the altar room. An old man garbed in clerical robes emerged, feeling his way with a thin stick that he clacked about in front of him, his sightless eyes turned slightly skyward as he listened carefully to how the clacks resonated. His voice was warm and amiable, but the hesitation in his stride suggested each step was an exertion for him.

"Greetings, and Mithos's blessings be upon you! I was beginning to wonder if I would ever have another visitor! I've already said mass once today, but I would be happy to do so again if you'd like."

Looking to each other for a moment, Grisbane gave Ionnus a puzzled expression before turning and walking over to the elderly cleric, taking the old man's hand in his own as he spoke. "Greetings, cleric. I am Sir Grisbane, the Herald of Justice. My oathbrothers and I have come from Ascension to speak with the head of the Dragonknights. Is there room enough for us to stay here?"

His lips forming a sad smile at Grisbane's words, the blind cleric nodded, a single tear welling up at the corner of his eye and falling down the side of his face. "Praise Mithos…I was beginning to think I would die here alone."

"Alone? What are you talking about?" Ionnus asked, stepping forward.

Turning in the direction of Ionnus's voice, the cleric's smile grew sadder and wider. "I am the only one who kept the faith, I am afraid. The few clerics who served under me and the church knights that kept us safe abandoned their vows, claiming that the seeds of the true faith were not taking root here in Forthos. I must admit, things have been bleak, but to abandon their vows?" Even as he spoke the last words, he recoiled from them, as if the thought repulsed him.

Grisbane narrowed his eyes. "Abandoned their vows? How do you mean?"

Taking Grisbane's hand tightly as if worried he too might run off, the blind cleric continued. "Your oathbrothers that guarded this church joined up with the city guards, I believe, whereas the clerics that maintained the cathedral left to take up lives amongst the townsfolk. Even the stable boys are gone, and so it falls upon me to feed the few horses that were too old to be worth taking."

"And they just left you here?" one of the other blue caped paladins said, his voice equal parts outrage and disbelief.

In response, the blind cleric nodded, another tear falling from his chin.

"Why didn't you send word of what had happened?"

"At first I thought I'd be able to bring in new followers, but by the time it became apparent I could not, the All Father had taken what was left of my sight."

With a heavy sigh, Grisbane looked back to Ionnus, and Ionnus nodded in response.

"Come, cleric…I'll assist you in saying mass," Grisbane said. "We have been on the road a long time, and are in need of prayer."

Afterwards, they supped on coarse bread and dried strips of salted beef stewed in hot water with carrots and onions, washing it down with water from a fountain out in the churchyard. Over supper, the cleric told them of the decline of the church over the past several months, and they learned that he had been living there alone for the past three. Local food vendors from the market would bring him food from time to time, though they themselves did not adhere to the faith of the All Father, but rather were simply taking pity on a blind old man.

Once they had eaten, they helped the elderly cleric back to his quarters, making certain he was comfortable before taking stock of the church. Ionnus left one of the brown capes to stay with the old man for reassurance that he wouldn't be left alone again.

"Deserters…" Grisbane said, his lips curling up as if the word had left a bad taste in his mouth.

Nodding, Ionnus went over the notes he'd been taking. "We'll have to make a point to thank the townsfolk that kept him fed. By my count, it looks as if most things of value were taken when they left; the armory is barren save a few rusted longswords and a badly battered shield, and the coffers are completely empty."

Scoffing, Grisbane lit candles in the altar room and went to work dusting off the pews. "It is fortunate we came along when we did, then. Should we take two of the blue capes with us and meet with the Dragonknights tomorrow?"

Nodding, Ionnus looked up from his notes. "Yes, I believe we shall. And while we're at it, I want to inquire about these deserters. They left this old man to die blind and alone in this church, and I intend to see that they're branded for the criminals they are."

In response, Grisbane's mouth turned up in a smile, and he slowly nodded his agreement.

Accompanied by two of their blue caped oathbrothers and passing underneath the draconic ribcage that covered the pathway leading to the Hall of the Dragonknights, Ionnus and Grisbane did their best to sit atop their horses proudly and with an air of dignity. But, in the end, their curiosity won out and they gawked openly at the wonder that surrounded them. Grisbane still looked back at it as Ionnus addressed the Dragonknights guarding the front doors.

Clad in metallic blue scale mail, they wore the ferocious dragonhead helms of their order with great pride, their shoulders thrust back as they stood up straight. They grasped the hafts of their longspears with forearm-length leather gloves reinforced with plated steel to match the color of their armor. The heater shields they had strapped to their left arms were pointed at the bottom and had a crescent shaped notch at the top for bracing their spears. The hafts of their longspears were wrapped in leather along the middle and at the butt; the head of the spears an asymmetrical bident with a shorter prong that curled slightly upwards towards the longer one, which sloped gradually so that its point was centered with the haft, the edges honed sharp.

Coming to a halt before the Dragonknights, Ionnus pondered how quickly the spear could wreak havoc on a breastplate or shear the leather straps of a shield as he spoke. "Greetings, friend. My name is Sir Ionnus the Righteous Shield. Might we seek an audience with your commander?"

Looking Ionnus up and down with a stern set of emerald green eyes, the Dragonknight seemed to measure him for a moment before posing his question. "The last of the church knights broke their vows and deserted. Have you any proof to support your claim to knighthood?"

Reaching up, Ionnus removed his helm, tucking it under his left arm. Reaching down underneath his breastplate, he produced the symbol of his faith he wore around his neck, holding it out for the Dragonknight to inspect. For several moments the Dragonknight looked it over, until the other standing next to him spoke up.

"Seems to me as though there would likely be a few of those floating around, if you catch my meaning."

Grisbane and Ionnus turned to glance at each other, trying to decide whether to be shocked or insulted that their faith had been called into question. It was then that the doors swung open, a Dragonknight garbed in silver scale but otherwise looking identical to the others addressing the two of them.

"Come with me, church knights. Commander Caydan would have a word with you."

Immediately, the guards at the door stepped aside, and the silver Dragonknight beckoned them through. As the doors shut behind them, the silver Dragonknight addressed them once more.

"This way, church knights."

Ionnus nodded, speaking in a polite tone. "I appreciate you vouching for us in regards to our faith, dr—"

"Save your thanks, church knight. I vouched for nothing; the commander heard of your arrival in Forthos and wishes to inspect the supposed church knights of Ascention for himself."

"Supposed?!" Grisbane said, his voice incredulous.

Without so much as glancing backwards, the silver Dragonknight chuckled. "Church knights are a rare sight in Forthos, and even more so recently. Forgive us if your blue capes and suits of armor do not adequately satisfy our suspicion. The Dragonknights have not forgotten our alliance with the church of Mithos, but that does not mean we are willing to believe any who show up at our doors waving about a symbol of the church knights' faith."

Leading them down a long stone hallway lined with a crimson red carpet, they ascended a wide flight of stairs onto a landing where the hallway opened up into a hub, a number of hallways branching out from where they stood.

"What have you people got against grid patterns?" Ionnus asked, watching as metallic blue and black Dragonknights moved about freely, many of whom stared openly at the small group of church knights.

Each of them carried crescent-notched heaters and wore bident spears on their backs in custom holsters specifically designed to draw weapons easily.

As they continued to walk, Ionnus spoke as he looked around him. "How long has Commander Caydan held command?"

Without so much as slowing down, the silver Dragonknight took a sharp right, the church knights hurrying to keep up as he replied. "Commander Caydan has held command for going on seven years. He is a direct descendant of Commander Donovan, the last of our order to mount a dragon and ride the skies."

His eyes widening slightly, Ionnus looked over to Grisbane momentarily before looking back. "How long has it been since the Dragonknights mounted dragons?"

For once, the silver Dragonknight glanced over his shoulder, and when he answered, his voice had taken a pensive tone. "It has been nearly three centuries, but we remain hopeful that one day we shall be reunited."

The doors to the commander's audience chambers were made of polished silver, a pair of dragons in flight engaged in aerial combat etched into the front of them and leafed in gold. As the silver Dragonknight approached them, he came to a stop, knocking thrice before an authoritative voice sounded from the other side.

"Enter."

Pushing through the doors, the silver Dragonknight held them open and allowed the church knights through. Inside, standing before a table, was the commander. Standing at a domineering six and a half feet, the commander wore a resplendent suit of golden scale mail, the texture of the scales made to look like that of an actual dragon. His dark brown leather gloves came up nearly to his elbow, a layer of golden scale affixed to the back of his fist and forearm, a pair of thick buckles beneath his wrists. A magnificent pair of lobstered metal pauldrons adorned his shoulders, the one on his left shoulder with a guard affixed to it shaped like the wing of a dragon that protected his neck. His helm, which lay on the table, was in the likeness of a regal gold dragon, complete with decorative whiskers and a pair of long curved horns that extended half a foot behind his head. The spear at his back bore a sinister looking bident spear head looking to be forged from a pair of dragon's teeth, one longer than the other.

"That thing looks like it could punch clean through a breastplate..." Grisbane muttered, speaking softly enough that only Ionnus could hear.

Looking up from the documents he was presently looking over, Commander Caydan had long, fiery red hair that fell wildly around his shoulder in waves, his eyes a pair of glowing green emeralds, and his complexion fair even by local standards. A full, thick, neatly groomed moustache of the same color as his hair ran along the top of his lip down to his jawline, where it came to a point before running up along his jawline until it connected with the hair on his head, a lone tuft of hair adorning his chin just beneath his bottom lip.

Broad of shoulder and square of chin, if ever there were a true son of Forthos, Caydan looked the part.

When he stood to his full height, he was eye to eye with even the burly Ionnus, and he grinned with a casual confidence as the church knights gave him their formal salute. Returning it with a polite bow of his head, he spoke in a baritone voice with no hint of urgency.

"So these are the church knights, come all the way from Ascension. I hear you even wear the sign of the All Father around your necks as proof."

"Commander Caydan…were it that we could prove our faith, we happily would," Ionnus said, bristling slightly at the commander's laid back attitude.

Noticing this and chuckling silently, Caydan shook his head. "Settle down, lads, I'm not here to take the piss out of you."

Opening his mouth as if to speak, Ionnus suddenly fell silent, his mouth closing as he glanced over to Grisbane with a look of uncertainty before looking back to Caydan with a quirked eyebrow. "I'm sorry…take the…what, now?"

Laughing, Caydan shook his head. "Well you either aren't from around here or you're a damn good actor, for sure. Anyways, normally we wouldn't have given it any thought until one of these turned up in the hands of Flavicius Vyrwen, an old thrifter who'll buy just about anything if he thinks he can turn a profit on it." That said, Caydan grabbed something on the table, and tossed it towards Ionnus, who caught it in front of his face.

When he opened his hand, the glint of a silver holy symbol of Mithos was unmistakable. Closing his hand around it tightly, Ionnus closed his eyes, gritting his teeth and sighing heavily.

"They…they traded the symbols of their faith for coin…as if they were common finery?" Grisbane asked, his voice and expression equally mortified.

In response, Ionnus nodded silently.

"How could they do such a thing?" one of the other church knights asked, the four of them showing increased signs of agitation.

Chuckling once, Caydan shook his head as he spoke. "Because you're in Forthos, lads…and that there bit o' metal you're holding that's so precious to you is made of silver. Nothing against your religion, but it hasn't exactly taken well with the locals if you catch my meaning. They mostly ignore it, truth be told."

"They said our brothers who broke their vows fell in with the city guards…is there any way of finding them?" Grisbane asked. Ionnus looked over as Grisbane spoke, and then turned to face Caydan with the same hopeful expression.

In response, Caydan laughed once more, motioning to a blue Dragonknight behind him. "I'm way ahead of you, lads…you didn't think the Dragonknights would forget their alliance with the church, no matter how broken down and decrepit it's become? Who do you think has been feeding the old man and keeping an eye on him this whole time?"

As he finished speaking, six Dragonknights dragged in three men. They took the butts of their spears to the backs of the men's knees and brought them to the ground.

When Ionnus walked over to look down upon them, the one in the middle stared up through a pair of gray-blue eyes, but only for a moment before turning back to the ground in shame. Shaking his head in disgust, Ionnus turned and walked back over to his spot at the end of the table across from Caydan, who stood with his arms folded across his chest and his head tilted to the side.

"They're your deserters, lad. What would you have done with them?"

"They abandoned an old man who could barely see, sold off the church's few possessions, and left him to die alone," Grisbane said. "Brand them and cut them loose to beg for a living for the rest of their days."

"Please, have mercy, oathbrother! Surely you must—"

With an alarming speed and ferocity, Grisbane rounded on the one who had spoken, grasping him by the hair and pulling his head up before drawing back a threatening fist. "You do NOT call me oathbrother, do you hear me, deserter?! You gave up that right when you traded the symbol of your faith for…what?! A handful of coin?!"

His eyes wincing in pain from how tightly Grisbane held him, the man breathed through gritted teeth and struggled to find his voice. "We never abandoned the faith, even when we discarded our capes and joined the city guard…" he said, to which Grisbane responded by shoving his head back down roughly and standing, brushing his hands off on one another as if touching the man had left grime on his gauntlets.

"We'll hold them for a while longer until you've had a chance to cool down a bit, get your wits about you again before you decide." As he spoke, Caydan gave an upward nod to the six Dragonknights, who pulled the deserters roughly to their feet and hauled them out of the room again.

"There were clerics as well…we're told they took up jobs as merchants here in town," Ionnus said, Grisbane returning to stand at his side.

Nodding, Caydan leaned over his map. "Gone. Fled the city when we brought in those three, more'n likely. Holy men aren't meant for battle like a knight, though. Their cowardice is more easily forgiven, or at least the way I see it."

Frowning, Ionnus let out a sigh, Grisbane taking up the conversation. "We appreciate you taking the time to bring them in for us, Commander, but I'm afraid that wasn't the purpose of our visit."

"Oh, it wasn't?" Caydan said, turning to the silver Dragonknight and giving him an amused smile.

Undaunted, Grisbane continued. "We've been charged with a diplomatic mission by our commanding officer, Sir Roningus the Wrath—"

"Roningus?!" Caydan said, his eyes going wide. In an instant, every Dragonknight in the room had their gaze fixed on the group of church knights, the hollow eyes of their dragon's head helms seeming to stare at them as well.

"The four of you are under orders from the church knight known as the Wrathful Tempest?" the silver Dragonknight asked, Caydan's amused, dismissive attitude suddenly turning greatly interested.

"Yes…we've been sent to entreat the Dragonknights and seek your assistance…we aim to assault the city of Demhora and crush the dead god's main cathedral once and for all, eliminating the stain of necromancy from the western kingdoms."

"Well now…that's very interesting…" Caydan replied, reaching up to stroke his chin thoughtfully.

"How do you know the name Roningus?" Ionnus asked, tilting his head inquisitively.

His smile returning, Caydan chuckled as he spoke. "Your boy Roningus has been a very busy man. Word's coming down from up north that he's moving from town to town like a swarm of locusts, wiping out your dead god's followers and leaving churches to your All Father in his wake. The people have come to herald him as a sort of hero, really. If the rumors are to be believed, he slew a blue skinned demon in single combat with a pair of enchanted longswords. Would've given just about anything to see that, truth be told. Must have been one hell of a fight…" He turned to the silver Dragonknight as he spoke his last sentence, and the silver Dragonknight nodded enthusiastically in agreement. Caydan looked back to Ionnus and smiled.

"So will you help us?" Grisbane asked, his voice apprehensive of what the commander might say.

With a sigh, Caydan stared long and hard at Grisbane first, then Ionnus. The two church knights that had accompanied them stood at attention, while Grisbane and Ionnus stood proudly and met his gaze with their own. At long last, Caydan leaned forward, bracing himself on the table as he spoke.

"The Dragonknights have no vested interest in the church knights' feuds with the dead god's men…"

As he spoke, Grisbane closed his eyes, Ionnus letting out a quiet, disappointed sigh…until Caydan started speaking once more.

"…but I'll be damned if I go down in history as the commander that let the honor of the Dragonknights falter in the face of adversity. The Dragonknights shall honor our alliance with the paladins of Mithos, church knights. So long as you can promise me I'll get to see your boy Roningus in action. Lad's got the dragon's fire in him, if the stories are to be believed."

Their eyes opening wide, Grisbane and Ionnus looked as if they were on the verge of sudden celebration when Caydan cut them off.

"There's still one small matter though, lads…you haven't proven you are who you say you are."

Pausing, it was Grisbane who spoke up. "How can we prove to you we've sworn our oaths?"

Grinning, Caydan glanced over at the silver Dragonknight momentarily who gave him a returning grin and a nod, before looking back to them. "Word has it Mithos himself follows the church knights into battle…I should like to see that put to the test in our practice yard. Square off with one of my Dragonknights and live, and that should more than satisfy the doubts of my men."

Making their way through carpet-lined hallways, the Dragonknights led the paladins in a sort of formal procession, surrounding them on all sides. They didn't seem as awe-struck as the church knights' were accustomed to. Commander Caydan led them, and as he approached a large set of wooden double doors, a pair of Dragonknights in blue scale pushed them open, held them as the procession passed them by, and closed them once they were through.

Outside, the sight of an enormous green yard full of sparring Dragonknights came into view, what looked like a handful of silver scaled captains drilling a multitude of knights grouped together by the color of their mail. Along with the metallic blue they had seen before, there was also a large contingent of onyx black and blood red, each group formed up in platoons and practicing with blunted spears. Numbering in the hundreds, each group focused intently on their sparring, none of them giving the church knights so much as a glance as they passed by. The silver captains continued to shout criticisms or give lessons as if the paladins weren't even there.

As they made their way down the field, Ionnus turned to address the commander. "Among the church knights, the color of one's cloak is an indication of their rank. What significance does the color of a Dragonknight's mail hold?"

Glancing over at Ionnus, Caydan gave his amused smile, speaking as he did so. "The Dragonknights don't have ranks below the commander and the captains. A Dragonknight chooses his colors when he is knighted based on the style of combat he has dedicated himself to. Each captain wore black, blue, or red at one time in their career."

"What's the difference?" Grisbane asked, watching as a pair in blue scale squared off to their right with shields out in front of them, their spears resting on top of their shoulder blades with the tips pointed at each other, preparing to strike.

"The azure legion focuses largely on defense, employing tactics that heavily rely on unit-based movement and forming shield walls that allow them to advance, while using their spears to pierce through enemy defenses. When it comes to holding ground or defending a structure, the azure legion are without question the best of us. The crimson legion is the opposite; focusing heavily on offense, the crimson legion foregoes the use of a shield for greater maneuverability with their weapon. Theirs is an aggressive style, focusing on using the entire weapon instead of just the spear point, some even going so far as to having a head affixed to both ends."

Even as he spoke, two crimson Dragonknights to their left had at each other ferociously, grasping the hafts of their weapons in both hands and delivering swift, accurate jabs as well as carefully executed parrying maneuvers, utilizing the end of the haft for leg sweeps and blunt strikes meant to put their opponent in position for delivering another forceful thrust of their spearhead.

"I think I can guess where this is heading..." Ionnus said as they walked the length of the yard, Caydan chuckling in response.

"Don't go getting ahead of us now, lad."

Eventually they reached the back of the yard, and there they found the onyx legion. Their numbers were significantly less than their counterparts, yet they had the end of the sparring yard to themselves. Grasping their spears near the end of the hafts, they practiced in groups of five against one, the five focusing on providing attacks for the one to cope with while working in offensive maneuvers from time to time.

"And here we have the onyx legion…" Caydan continued, coming to a halt. "Perfect harmony of shield and spear is the style of the onyx legion. Capable of engaging a group of opponents at once, the onyx legion represent total balance of offense and defense, engaging the philosophy of using false openings and sweeping motions while maintaining a complete awareness of your surroundings. Not all are suited for the ranks of the onyx legion, and not all who attempt to join are granted entry. I've lost count of how many I've had to defer to the azure or crimson legions because they were too aggressive, or weren't aggressive enough."

As they stood watching, the one that stood against five brought his spear up above his head, spinning it in a wide sweeping circle that pushed the five back before lunging forward at the one in front of him, his shield coming up behind his head to deflect an incoming spear point.

Smiling, Caydan turned, folding his arms across his chest. "So…which legion would you like your challengers to come from?"

Frowning, Ionnus let out a sigh. "Is this really necessary?"

"Honestly?" Caydan said, chuckling as he spoke. "Not really. But it's good clean fun, innit? And I want to have a look at you swinging that hammer of yours around."

After Caydan had gathered the various legions on the sparring field, each line of Dragonknights grouped by their respective colors, one of the blue caped paladins that had accompanied Ionnus and Grisbane chose one from the onyx legion to be his challenger. Caydan grinned and nodded approvingly.

Stepping forward, the onyx Dragonknight gave a formal salute, to which the church knight replied with one of his own. The Dragonknight spoke in a respectful tone. "With no offense meant to the church knights, I would formally request an additional combatant. It would be an honor to test myself against a pair of Ascention's finest."

Quirking a brow, Caydan smiled and bowed his head in assent. In response, the other blue caped church knight that had accompanied them stepped forward, beating his clenched right fist against his left breast in salute as well.

The Dragonknight returned the gesture as he spoke. "Church knights. It is an honor." That said, he crouched down slightly, bringing his shield up in front of him. Grasping the end of his spear haft, he rested it atop his shoulder blades behind his neck, signaling with a nod of his head that he was ready.

Brandishing the wooden training swords that had been recently procured from town for the occasion, the church knights raised their shields, and the bout began.

Immediately spreading out, the church knights held their shields before them, the Dragonknight calmly keeping footing with them as they moved to surround him. Moving with blinding speed, the Dragonknight lashed out, whipping his longspear around above his head to gain momentum before bringing it down in a low sweep. The church knight to his right took a swift step backwards out of the spear's reach. Seeking to take advantage of the opening, the church knight to the left leapt forward, bringing his sword down in a powerful vertical stroke. But with a grace to his movement as if it were all one motion, the Dragonknight's shield came up between himself and the church knight's sword, his right arm crossed in front of him, grasping the spear with its head pointed behind him.

Loosening his grip, the Dragonknight spun around, letting his hand slide along the haft to the center, keeping his shield up above his head between himself and the sword. When the church knight brought his wooden sword in for a low horizontal swing, the Dragonknight met it with his shield once more, pivoting in the same movement and thrusting at the other church knight to ward off his advance.

Laughing, Caydan cheered as the three continued to do battle, the Dragonknights forming a large ring around them to watch. Each time the onyx Dragonknight turned a swing of a sword or delivered a dangerously close thrust of his practice spear, the Dragonknights would let out a boisterous cheer. Just as often they would roar in approval whenever the church knights began to press the advantage.

Before long, the combatants had begun to get a feel for each other, but eventually one of the church knights let his guard down at the wrong moment and found the tip of a spear pointed right at the gap between his helm and breastplate. Immediately, the church knight raised his sword and shield up in yield, the crowd of Dragonknights letting out another howl of approval. As the defeated church knight backed away, one of the azure legion reached out, placing a hand on his pauldron and offering up words of encouragement.

Now squaring off with the onyx Dragonknight alone, the remaining church knight gave the wooden sword in his hand a flourish. The Dragonknight brought his longspear up above his head, spinning it in the palm of his hand and catching it in the middle of the haft before holding it poised above him like the tail of a scorpion. Then, it was the onyx Dragonknight who went on the offensive, rushing forward with a flurry of jabs that pressed the church knight back, pulling his spear out of the way each time the church knight swatted at it.

Unable to find a way past the church knight's shield, the Dragonknight dropped back, readjusting his grip further towards the butt of the spear's haft and resorting to wide swings. When one landed against the side of the church knight's shield, the Dragonknight followed through, driving it forward to find the church knight behind it. But the church knight pivoted, swatting the spear away with his sword. It was as the Dragonknight withdrew and prepared to lunge again that Caydan's voice was heard above all the noise.

"STOP!"

Immediately, the onyx Dragonknight brought up his spear, standing at full attention. Looking around in confusion, the church knight lowered his wooden weapon respectfully, giving the commander his full attention. Pacing out into the middle of the ring, Caydan came to stand in front of the Dragonknight, glancing at the training spear in his hand as he spoke.

"He'd have sundered your weapon just then. Yeah?"

In response, the onyx Dragonknight nodded. "Yes, commander."

"Yeah?" Caydan continued, quirking a brow. "So why'd you continue using it as if he hadn't? Not very honorable, is it? In a real fight, he'd have had you, yeah?"

The onyx Dragonknight nodded again. "Apologies, commander. In the heat of the moment, I forgot myself."

"Aye. So you know what to do, then," Caydan said, gesturing towards the church knight with a backwards nod of his head before turning and exiting the ring.

The onyx Dragonknight brought his spear and shield up in a gesture of yield as he spoke. "Apologies, church knight. The match is yours. Well fought, both of you."

Overwhelming cheers broke out around them, Dragonknights congratulating the two of them from every direction as the one they had faced made a point to clasp hands with them respectfully and thank them for the match. More than a little confused, the church knights accepted and reciprocated the gesture all the same.

"Alright then, bring on the next one!" Caydan bellowed, his excited grin returning.

"Well…you or me next?" Grisbane said, turning to Ionnus next to him.

Letting out a sigh, Ionnus stepped forward even as he spoke. "I'll go. Let's see what the blue ones are all about."

"Here comes the big one, lads!" Caydan hollered, the Dragonknights meeting him with their resounding approval.

One of the silver captains stepped forward, offering him a slender wooden club with a leather-bound handle. "Closest thing we have to a hammer, I'm afraid," the captain said, offering a slightly apologetic smile.

Waving away the apology and taking the club, Ionnus gave it a few test swings, measuring the weight of it in his hand and nodding his approval before moving to the center of the ring that had been formed. "Who among the azure legion will face me in fair contest?!" he cried, the Dragonknights going wild.

"Show off…" Grisbane muttered, chuckling and shaking his head.

When a blue Dragonknight stepped forward, the noise grew so loud that he could scarcely be heard even as he yelled. "I would be honored to test myself against one of Ascention's finest!"

That said, the two saluted respectfully, and the match began.

Almost immediately, Ionnus realized he had a difficult time ahead of him. Keeping the scale shaped heater up in front of him defensively, the blue Dragonknight held the haft of his spear resting in the notch on top of it, poking defensively at Ionnus each time he so much as moved to advance. Falling back proved to be of little use, as the blue Dragonknight seemed perfectly content to advance upon Ionnus like a wall and provoke him with jabs, his shield always managing to stay between the Dragonknight and Ionnus's club.

When Ionnus sidestepped, the Dragonknight would keep him squarely in his sights, and any time Ionnus tried to charge in shield first, the Dragonknight would meet him head on, slamming into him and driving him back while the point of his spear slithered around his shield, looking for an opening and forcing Ionnus to fall back. Keeping his center of gravity low, Ionnus found overrunning the Dragonknight impossible, and each attempt at a simple flurry of blows from his club resulted in the Dragonknight turning them all with his shield until eventually he would put Ionnus on the defensive with his spear. The gathered Dragonknights burst out in an uproar each time one of them pressed an advantage. For several minutes the two men continued on in this way, Ionnus moving in strong while the Dragonknight refused to yield any ground.

Realizing he was getting nowhere, Ionnus firmly gripped the club in his hand, pausing a moment to take a deep breath.

How would Roningus go about this? he thought to himself, watching as the blue Dragonknight readied himself for Ionnus's next advance.

Then, it occurred to him, and Ionnus found himself grinning. The next time, when Ionnus stepped in, he awaited the inevitable thrust of the spear…anticipated the movement…and promptly dropped his club, grabbing hold of the haft of the spear with his now empty right hand. Looking through the eyes of the Dragonknight's helm, the pair of emerald eyes that suddenly grew wide told Ionnus he had the Dragonknight off-guard as he'd hoped. Ionnus capitalized on his sudden momentum by bringing his shield around to his left in a powerful bash. As their shields collided, Ionnus hooked his left foot behind the Dragonknight's left leg, and with a simple trip, planted him on the ground, yanking the spear from the Dragonknight's hand as the surprise of falling momentarily weakened his grip.

Spinning about, Ionnus quickly planted his foot on the Dragonknight's shield arm, pointing the head of the spear at his right eye. "Do you yield, sir?" Ionnus asked, to which the Dragonknight laughed.

"I do!"

That said, Ionnus stepped back, dropping the training spear and offering a hand down to help him up. After accepting it, the Dragonknight stepped forward, grasping hands with him energetically and roughly colliding into him in a playful manner as he did so.

"This one's got a pair of balls on him! Well met, church knight!" the blue Dragonknight shouted, the ring of Dragonknights rising up in another delighted roar. Picking up their weapons, the blue Dragonknight returned to the ring, Ionnus heading back over to Grisbane.

"You're up," Ionnus said with a grin.

"Hey, thanks," Grisbane said, laughing and shaking his head.

By then, the atmosphere had become quite lively and energetic, the good sportsmanship of the Dragonknights making for truly good-natured competition. Accepting a wooden sword from one of the silver Dragonknights, Grisbane waited until the crowd went silent, shrugging as he spoke.

"Well, we've seen the others...let's have one of the crimson legion, then."

At first, Grisbane wondered if perhaps he'd said something wrong, for no lively cheers accompanied his challenge. Instead, all eyes turned to Commander Caydan, who smiled proudly as he calmly strode out into the center of the ring. Handing off his dragon toothed bident, Caydan accepted one of the training spears from one of his captains, leaning his head to either side to crack his neck as he spoke.

"You're in luck, lad…crimson just so happened to be my colors when I first started out. Let's see if we can't get a win for the Dragonknights before the day's done, eh?"

Blinking, Grisbane looked back to Ionnus, his friend offering an enthusiastic nod and a thumbs up. "Oh hell…" Grisbane muttered, the roar of the Dragonknights drowning him out as their commander held his training spear pointed at the ground at his side, motioning for Grisbane to advance with an inward wave of his hand and grinning from ear to ear.

Tilting his head to the left then right and stretching his neck out, Caydan slung his arms over the haft of the spear as it rested on top of his shoulder blades. His left eyebrow shot up as his right narrowed, and a grin formed on his lips.

"Well come on, then, let's get on with it," he said, standing in a lax, casual stance.

Sighing, Grisbane shook his head, clanging his right gauntlet against his shield to indicate that he was ready. In response, Caydan lifted his left arm from the spear, using the back of his neck as a fulcrum and sending the spear swinging around behind him. He caught it in his right hand and tapped the blunt wooden point against his scale mail in response.

"Wonderful…" Grisbane muttered to himself, keeping his shield up and holding his sword back at the ready. The ring had gone somewhat quiet in comparison to the last two bouts, what little dull chatter there was being that of odds given and wagers made. It came as no surprise to Grisbane when he overheard the odds being against him.

At first, he began to circle around, thinking that forcing the commander to concentrate on his footing might distract him enough to launch an offensive. In response, Caydan easily kept pace with Grisbane, holding his spear lazily in his right hand and still grinning slightly. It was when Grisbane was about to strike that Caydan moved first, lashing out with what appeared to be a casual thrust of his spear. Grisbane swung his sword in an effort to swat at the haft. At the last moment, Caydan pulled back, and in the blink of an eye had both hands on his weapon, falling upon Grisbane with a flurry of precisely positioned jabs that became increasingly difficult to get his shield in front of.

Caydan handled his spear with unparalleled speed and grace; each time Grisbane raised his sword to swing it, Caydan would either knock the weapon away with the head of his spear or jab at Grisbane's sword-wielding hand, knocking him off balance and forcing him to put his shield up and fall back. At one point, Caydan hooked the top of Grisbane's shield with the head of his spear, pulling it down and leaving Grisbane wide open to a thrust that caught him square in the visor. It knocked him backwards and sent him staggering, much to the delight of the on-looking crowd.

Turning, Caydan raised his arms, roaring and smiling happily as the Dragonknights cheered him on before leveling his gaze on Grisbane once more, settling in to make an end of it. Bringing the spear up to spin above his head in the palm of his hand several times, Caydan caught the weapon in both hands and held it above his head, the spear head pointed at Grisbane and poised above him like the tail of a scorpion. Shaking his head from where Caydan had rung him, Grisbane gave the weapon in his hand a flourish before raising his shield once again.

The end to the match came quickly after that. Hoping to gain some momentum, Grisbane led with his shield, stepping in and planting himself before leading with a powerful shield bash that, had it connected, would have staggered Caydan and allowed for a follow-through. Instead, the commander stepped back, allowing the shield to swing harmlessly before him, using his left hand as a point of leverage and swatting the wooden sword away. From there Caydan moved in, turning about and bringing the spear down with a spinning motion that put the point of it behind him, thrusting backwards into Grisbane's breastplate. The impact knocked Grisbane backwards, and as he struggled to regain his footing, Caydan spun back around to face him. He brought the butt of the haft down and caught Grisbane behind his left knee, bringing the church knight to the ground. Then, without a moment's hesitation, Caydan leapt into the air, bringing the wooden spear above his head in both hands, and when he landed, his feet straddled Grisbane, bringing the point of the spear down with such force that Grisbane flinched and turned his head.

When he opened his eyes and looked up, Caydan was standing over him, grinning wildly, with the point of the wooden spear hovering less than an inch away from his throat. Grisbane blinked, and slowly held up his hands to yield the match.

The gathered crowd burst into a deafening uproar, Caydan laughing heartily as he turned and tossed the wooden spear to a nearby silver captain, offering down a hand to help Grisbane up. As the two clasped hands, Caydan pulled Grisbane to his feet and caught him in a half embrace, nodding approvingly.

"You've got stones, lad, I'll give you that! Well fought!"

Chuckling, Grisbane shook his head in disbelief, "You didn't do so bad yourself…"

"Didn't do so bad myself, he says! You heard him, right boys?! The church knight says I'm decent with a spear!" Still laughing, Caydan slung his arm around Grisbane's neck, gesturing to Ionnus and the other church knights to follow him as he dragged Grisbane along with him, taking his dragon-toothed weapon from another captain and holstering it at his back as they walked.

"So does this mean you believe us now?" Grisbane asked, looking up and allowing himself to be dragged along.

"I believed you from the beginning, truth be told. When I found out the boys at the door were having a bit of fun with you, I just decided to join in, is all."

"What?!" Ionnus cried, keeping pace with them.

Caydan laughed, shaking his head. "You church knights are a stiff lot, aren't you? Relax a bit! You're in Forthos!"

Seated around the large wooden table that Caydan had been standing over when they first arrived, the church knights unbuckled their shields and laid them on the table next to their helms.

"So what's this plan of yours, then?" Caydan asked as food and drink were brought in for them. He waved away a platter and leaned his chin on his right fist.

Grisbane spoke up as Ionnus sipped at the mug set before him. "With the blessing and cooperation of the Dragonknights, we would bring our column and score of battle clerics through Forthos to approach Demhora from the south, booking passage on a number of galleys to convey us along the southern shore. We had hoped to gain the assistance of the Dragonknights in this matter, as…well…a sizeable number of our forces had to remain behind to hold Ascension, and our cathedral in Darlisheld has yet to establish itself firmly enough to offer support. Even as Roningus sweeps across the western kingdoms, he leaves men behind to help rebuild and convert those left in the wake of the fall of the dead god, if your reports are true, and if such is the case, we may well have need of more direct assistance from you as well."

Nodding, Caydan lifted a mug and took a long drink. When he lowered it, he noticed Ionnus staring uncertainly at his own mug, and let out a chuckle as he spoke. "What's wrong?"

Looking up, Ionnus shook his head. "Oh, nothing, it's just… isn't it a bit early for ale?"

Caydan smirked, but when Ionnus gave no expression to indicate he was joking, the commander gave him a puzzled look.

"So as I said, any help in the matter would be greatly appreciated," Grisbane continued.

Caydan took another drink and shot another disbelieving glance at Ionnus over the top of his mug before returning his attention to Grisbane. Nodding his head, he swallowed and sat his mug down, wiping his mouth and smoothing out his moustache in one smooth motion.

"I reckon we could work something out. Some of the boys have been spoiling for a fight, anyways…and I think our little bouts out in the training yard lit a fire under their arses. What kind of numbers do you expect to encounter on this incursion of yours?"

"Well, that's the thing…we aren't entirely certain. His knowledge of the area was admittedly a bit outdated, but Loremaster Garadain estimated they could host a sizeable force in Demhora, not to mention approaching Slagspire Pass from the south would yield the dreadknights a golden opportunity to thin our numbers with garrisons and ambushes." As Grisbane spoke, he sat forward in his chair, and when he was done, he took a drink from the mug that had been set before him, looking down and nodding in approval at its contents.

Furrowing his eyebrows, Caydan contemplated Grisbane's words for a moment before responding. "Show me how you mean. Bring us a map, yeah?" he said, motioning to a nearby captain.

Within moments, the captain returned with a large roll of thin, lightly-colored leather. As they all moved the mugs and plates out of the way, the captain sprawled the map out on the table. Caydan used his mug to hold down an unruly corner as Grisbane began pointing and speaking.

"The city of Demhora would be right here, see? So I figure we come along the southern shore…disembark here, and press our way through Slagspire Pass. Chances are, if we've thought of it, they have as well, but when the alternative is marching through stone giant territory…"

Making a sour face, Caydan turned to one of his captains. "Who builds a city in the middle of the mountains, anyways? Seems downright stupid to me."

Tilting his head, Grisbane gave a nod of consent. "At one point, it was likely a peaceful, self-sufficient, remote community. The dreadknights undoubtedly saw the strategic advantage in taking over and erecting their main cathedral there."

Nodding, Caydan looked the map over for a while, finally turning to his captain. "What do you think? Should we rouse the boys at the docks and tell them to get the galleys ready?"

Looking down at the map, the captain gave a casual shrug. "I see no reason why not. They'd have likely turned up at our door sooner or later, anyways. Might as well bring the fight to their home instead of ours."

Grinning, Caydan turned and looked back to Grisbane. "Alright, church knight. Let's get on with this, yeah?"

Grisbane looked over to Ionnus with an accomplished smile. Ionnus nodded his head approvingly, giving him a grin and thumbs up.

Inching forward on all fours, Brogam let out a sigh. Reaching up, the arch cleric wiped at the perspiration on his forehead with his right hand, the skin pink and raw from repeating the motion so often. Dressed in simple linen clothes, he dunked the stiff bristled brush into the water and went to work on the stone floor again. There was a loud clanking noise as the door to the penitent cells area was opened.

Looking up with a hopeful expression, when the high priest stepped through, Brogam immediately frowned, going back to his duties. "Come to gloat, have you?"

Frowning, Vogoth shook his head, gesturing to the brown caped paladin that stood guard near the door. Disappearing for a moment, when the paladin returned, he had a plain wooden chair in each hand, and when the high priest beckoned, he sat them down. As Vogoth took a seat, Brogam braced himself on the chair to stand, accepting the paladin's assistance and seating himself across from Vogoth. For several moments, neither one said anything, until finally Brogam spoke up.

"If you've not come to bask in my humility, then what brings you here?" As he spoke, Brogam slouched down in his seat, exhausted from the work he'd done and not looking forward to that which wasn't yet finished.

"You know why I'm here, Brogam. Each week I've come, and each week you continue to show me that you've yet to grasp the lessons I seek to impart on you. Do you really believe I take pleasure in watching you scrub floors?"

Narrowing his eyes, Brogam spoke in a spiteful tone. "As a matter of fact, I do."

Frowning and meeting Brogam's scowl unabashedly, Vogoth tilted his head as he replied. "Not so. Help me understand, Brogam. Help me understand your reasoning. What has Roningus done to earn such contempt from you?"

For a long time, Brogam said nothing, but it was just as Vogoth was about to leave him for another week that the arch cleric spoke up. "The boy is rash, and too aggressive. I do not believe that he exemplifies the code of conduct, and the more other people heap their praises upon him, the more irksome I find him."

Giving Brogam a disbelieving look, when Vogoth spoke, his tone bordered on confusion. "Is that truly it? He acts his age, and you don't like being disagreed with? Why can't you just admit that you really have no good reason to be so avidly against him?!"

At first, Vogoth wasn't sure if he'd gotten through or not, but then Brogam sighed, his expression relaxing a big as she shook his head. "I don't know. I've prayed to the All Father for guidance and patience. Mithos knows I have. I just can't stomach him."

"And for that you were willing to be openly defiant to the point where it cost you the throne of the high priest, and ended up with you in a penitent cell scrubbing floors?"

Staring at the ground, Brogam looked up at Vogoth as he answered. "Ask any of the clerical conclave and they'll tell you: my election was a mistake. What do you hope to achieve from rubbing salt in my wounds?"

His eyes going wide, the irritation showed in Vogoth's voice as it began to rise. "Again, you imagine slights that simply aren't there! No one is working against you, Brogam! But when your voice of dissent is the only one in the room, perhaps you should take a moment to consider that maybe you need to rethink your stance on the issue! These are trying times, Brogam…we all must work together, or we are doomed to crumble and erode in the stream of time."

Once more, Brogam went silent, but this time Vogoth waited patiently for the arch cleric to process what he had said. Eventually, with another heavy sigh, Brogam nodded slowly. "Perhaps…you arc right. I was convinced that the All Father guided my actions…it might be I was too set in my own mindset that I couldn't hear him calling to me."

Nodding, Vogoth let out a sigh of relief, and as he stood, he held out a hand for Brogam. Taking it, the two clasped hands, and Brogam stood to engage the high priest in a half-embrace.

"Now finish your floors, Arch Cleric. The council has need of your wisdom."

Brogam stared blankly at Vogoth for a moment, his mouth hanging slightly open. "You can't be serious?"

Grinning, Vogoth reached out, clapping Brogam on the shoulder. "I am, actually. No sense leaving a task half finished. When you're done, clean up and don your arch clerical robes, then come up to the council chamber. Sir Christmond will accompany you when you are ready."

Closing his eyes, Brogam nodded silently for a moment, until suddenly they snapped open as he called out to Vogoth. "How goes the Wrathful Tempest's crusade? I've not heard word of him for the past few weeks."

Coming to a halt, Vogoth turned around, smiling from ear to ear. "He's proved you quite wrong, actually, and has shown himself very capable; reports are flooding in of the column of church knights that sweeps across the western kingdoms, eradicating the dead god's influence and leaving behind the seeds of the All Father's forgiveness in his wake. Witnesses who claim to have seen him slay the half-fiend in single combat are all but certain he will be chosen to bear Retribution."

Chuckling once, Brogam shrugged, climbing back down on to his hands and knees to resume his scrubbing. "From the sounds of it, he doesn't need it."

Forty-four church knights, not including the brown capes from Grisbane and Ionnus's regiment that had shown up to bring them the news, and seven battle clerics. This was the entourage that followed the Wrathful Tempest as he made his way along the road to Forthos. Leading them at the head of the pack, Roningus sat on his war horse proudly, holding his head up high and prominently displaying the angel-winged helm he wore upon it. Behind him, the men followed his example, sitting on their horses straight and tall, and riding with a sense of divine purpose.

As the farmers laboring in their fields looked up, they told no jokes this time. Their irreverent grins were replaced with looks of awe, their eyes lingering on the black caped paladin at the forefront who led his men so valiantly. Once they reached the gates, the guard posted at them looked up at Roningus, motioning towards the column of church knights with a nod of his head as he spoke.

"Quite a following you've got there, yeah? Might make a guy nervous, so many armored men on horses come marching up to the gate he's standing in front of like they're expected or something."

When met with an unrelenting stare from behind the slits in Roningus's visor, the guardsman cracked a grin, his voice almost apologetic.

"What? I was only having a bit of fun, yeah? Open the gate, Charlie, the church knights have returned, and their friends are full of piss and vinegar!"

As the gate winch groaned to life, Roningus kicked his left leg over the back of his horse and slid down gracefully. Stepping up to the guardsman, he slowly reached up and lifted the helm from his head, his dark brown eyes boring into the emerald-eyed Forthian. The guardsman shifted nervously, glancing over his shoulder to make sure his comrades were still present, and started when he looked back to find Roningus standing nearly toe-to-toe with him.

It wasn't until the guardsman opened his mouth as if to stammer something out that Roningus's lips parted in a thin smile, his cool voice showing a slight hint of amusement.

"Good one. You almost had me for a moment." That said, Roningus reached out, clapping the guardsman heavily on the shoulder before turning about, returning his helm to his head and spurring his horse through the gates even as he was climbing back on top of it.

Immediately, the entire group of church knights and clerics behind him followed suit, each of them looking down to the gate guard as they passed, the guardsman observing them with a newfound sense of respect. Once they were through, the winch operator let loose a hooting laugh, calling down to the guardsman.

"He got you with that one, didn't he, Liam?! You looked like you'd shat yourself when you turned around!"

"Oh piss off, Charlie!" the guardsman shouted irritably, shaking his head and settling back in to his post.

Inside the gates, a silver Dragonknight captain stood in the entrance hub, accompanied by six of the azure legion. As the church knights dismounted from their horses, he smiled, extending his hand out towards Roningus as he approached.

"Greetings. Are you the one called the Wrathful Tempest?"

Nodding his head, Roningus took the captain's hand, the two shaking firmly as he replied. "I am indeed. Who do I have the honor of addressing?"

"Captain Finn. We're here to escort you to the hall of the Dragonknights, if you would accompany us."

"We would. But first, we would report to the church of Mithos."

The Dragonknight captain shook his head as he spoke. "My orders are to escort you directly to the hall of the Dragonknights. Commander Caydan was very specific in wanting to have a word with you immediately upon your arrival."

Narrowing his eyes slightly, Roningus tilted his head. "Then why didn't your commander meet me at the gate?"

Smiling, the silver captain tilted his head slightly. "You can ask him yourself. He's waiting for you with your 'oathbrothers,' as they call themselves."

As the enormous wooden doors swung open, Caydan looked up from his map, his hands planted on the edges of the wooden table. Immediately, the corners of his mouth turned up in a grin, his burning green eyes looking Roningus up and down and showing a marked increase in the respect they held. Roningus crossed the room with purposeful strides, his black cape billowing behind him as he marched, his hands reaching up to lift the helm from his head as he approached the commander.

"Commander Caydan," Roningus said, looking up into the commander's eyes fearlessly.

Caydan reached out a hand as he spoke. "Wrathful Tempest. If half the stories are to be believed, it is truly an honor, yeah?"

When Roningus reached out, the two of them clasped hands at the wrists. Roningus gave a stern nod while Caydan continued to grin. "With all due respect, what was so pressing that it could not wait until I had reported in at the church?" As Roningus spoke he tilted his head.

A silver captain nearby frowned as he spoke in a reprimanding voice. "Who are you to question the commander?"

Immediately, Roningus leveled his eyes on the captain, his icy stare cowing the man into silence and forcing him to avert his gaze. It wasn't until Caydan chuckled lightly that Roningus looked back. Caydan nodded once in approval.

"I wanted a chance to warn you of the situation before you saw it for yourself. Your oathbrother Ionnus said to let you deal with the deserters as you saw fit."

Narrowing his eyes, Roningus pondered the commander's words in silence for a moment. "…Deserters?"

Caydan nodded, his grin fading as he continued. "Three of them. They pawned off anything they could and fell in with the city guards. Easy enough to sniff out on account of their accents… it's easy to tell who's from around here and who isn't, yeah?" That said, Caydan gestured to a nearby captain, the silver Dragonknight nodding and hurrying off.

"How many remained behind?" Roningus asked, laying his helm down on the table.

"Just a blind old cleric. We kept him fed and made sure nobody troubled him, and a few townsfolk would even visit him from time to time, but otherwise he tended that church by himself."

Drawing in a deep breath, Roningus sighed heavily and said nothing. For several minutes they sat in silence, until finally the deserters were dragged up before them once more and forced to their knees. Still shackled together at their wrists and ankles, when the three of them spotted Roningus's black cape, their eyes went wide.

Still standing at the table, Roningus waited several seconds, letting them writhe uncomfortably in the shame of their actions before addressing them. "Identify yourselves."

"Sir Ulf—"

"NO," Roningus interjected, his furious voice cutting the deserter off. "Your names, not the titles you deserted."

"…Orson," said the one in the middle who had spoken up initially.

"Clayton," answered the one on the left.

"Brindur," concluded the one on the right.

With slow, deliberate steps, Roningus casually approached them, his fists clenched tightly. "Do any of you have the slightest clue who I am?"

Looking to each other for a moment, when they all shook their heads at each other, Orson looked up. "N-no, but we know enough to recognize the significance of a black cape when we see one."

Coming to a halt, Roningus knelt down on his right knee in front of Orson, resting his left hand on his other knee and tilting his head to regard the man as he spoke once more. "I am Sir Roningus, the Wrathful Tempest. Whether or not you've heard of me, I could not care less. Where are the symbols of your faith?"

"We sold them, and traded in our plate to a local blacksmith for chain shirts and boiled leather as the guardsmen wear," Clayton offered, looking up as he spoke but quickly looking back down when Roningus turned to look at him.

"So you are no longer in possession of them? Is that correct?"

"We've managed to round up one of them. Still keeping our eyes open for the other two," Caydan called out from behind the table, his arms folded across his chest and watching the scene play out with great interest.

Without looking back, Roningus nodded, standing as he spoke. "The city guard is aware these men are deserters, then?"

Caydan's grin crept back as he answered. "Whole city's aware at this point, I'd imagine."

Nodding in approval, Roningus looked up to the azure Dragonknights. When he spoke, his tone and expression were that of utter disinterest with the three men that knelt before him. "Unshackle them and turn them loose."

Looking up suddenly, the surprise was evident on the three men's faces, the azure Dragonknights looking to Caydan for approval, the commander giving them a shrug of consent.

"What…what's the meaning of this?" Orson asked, as one of the Dragonknights began opening the manacles that bound him.

Roningus had already turned and was walking away when he replied. "The church has no need for deserters among her ranks, and the city guard will have nothing to do with you now that you've been named as such. Once word gets back to Ascention, you'll be lucky to find work guarding a farmstead for copper pennies. I suggest you apprentice yourself to a tradesman, although as old as you are it is unlikely any will have you."

Looking to each other in panic, Orson shambled forward on his knees, reaching out for Roningus's cape. "Please, Sir Roningus, have mercy on us! Let us atone for our sins and regain our honor by fighting alongside the knights of the church of Mithos!"

Rounding about on Orson as he felt a tug on his cape, Roningus regarded the man contemptuously. "Regain your honor? You wish to regain your honor…and atone? And yet even as we speak, a pair of the symbols of my faith, YOUR FORMER faith… are being passed about for common bits of silver. No…I would not sully our reputation, nor the reputation of the Dragonknights by allowing men wholly lacking in conviction such as yourself even to march behind us into battle. As for your atonement, a life of disgrace shall be sufficient. Consider yourselves fortunate I don't have you branded."

"Sir Roningus, I never abandoned the faith! Times grew trying, and in my weakness I sinned against the All Father! Have mercy, I beg you!" Brindur called out, rising to his feet and pleading with the look in his eyes.

Turning his gaze to Brindur, Roningus shook his head as he spoke. "The path I walk will be more trying than you could ever imagine. If you couldn't handle guarding a blind old man, how could you be trusted to hold your line in the face of an oncoming charge of dreadknights?" Then, turning to the azure Dragonknights, Roningus took a more polite tone. "If you would please, remove them from my sight. I am finished with them."

Nodding, the six Dragonknights took the three men, one on each arm, and dragged them from the hall of the Dragonknights, all three of them looking as if they'd just taken an unexpected blow to the stomach.

"We've got the ships ready," Caydan said, looking up with Roningus as the doors swung open once more.

When Ionnus and Grisbane came walking in, Roningus grinned, and they smiled brightly as Ionnus called out in a cheerful voice.

"Roningus!"

Stepping up to the table, Roningus reached out, clasping hands with Ionnus and Grisbane in turn, engaging them in a half embrace and addressing them both as Ionnus clapped him on his right pauldron. "You both look well. How is the church? I haven't had a chance to report in yet."

Ionnus laughed, pulling his helmet off and setting it down next to Roningus's. "I know I look well, at least! The church is better now with church knights in it. The old man seems overjoyed to have people moving around in it once more, and when I told him you were bringing more, I think he about cried again."

Roningus smiled in return, and Grisbane sighed before speaking up. "So...the final push, huh? Are we ready for this?"

"My boys are certainly ready," Caydan said, grinning.

"We couldn't do this without your assistance, commander," Roningus said. "I'm sure it's been said before, but if the church can ever be of assistance to the Dragonknights of Forthos, never hesitate to ask."

Shaking his head, Caydan waved a dismissive hand. "It's like I told them, yeah? Evil men doing wrong in the world...exactly the kind of thing the Dragonknights are meant to stand against, yeah? Besides, I want to see what you can do with those swords at your back. Heard you gave a half-fiend one hell of an arse kicking."

Smiling sadly, Roningus nodded, letting his gaze fall to the floor as he spoke. "His name was Asmodeus...and...he was an honorable and worthy opponent, if there ever was one. It was unfortunate...that things had to end the way they did. In another life, he would have made an invaluable ally. His devotion, misplaced as it was, was admirable. He followed his orders without hesitation, and strange as it may sound, in the end I came to respect him despite his evil ways."

Nodding, Caydan's grin grew into a genuine smile, the pride and honor of the Dragonknights granting him an insight into Roningus's words that might have been lost on another.

Clearing his throat, Ionnus looked to the map on the table, speaking up in an awkward attempt to change the subject. "So, erm...when do we set sail, then?"

Looking down with him, Caydan sighed. "Like I was telling your boy here, the ships are ready whenever the church knights are. I've booked enough galleys to convey us along the southern shore, and they're all willing to cast anchor and bring those of us that make it home back for the return trip. We just need to give them a couple days' notice to get things sorted out, yeah?"

Nodding, Roningus steeled himself again, glancing over at the map. "Send word to the ships. My oathbrothers are spread thin holding the smaller cities up north, and they're counting on us to wipe the stain of necromancy from these lands once and for all."

Caydan made a tilting nod with his head. "I'll have the boys begin preparations immediately."

Kicking over the body of the fallen sentry man, Caydan casually retrieved his spear from between the man's shoulder blades, his face frozen in a horrified expression as he'd watched the spear soaring through the air with pinpoint accuracy in his direction. The vicious dragon's teeth that served as the spear's head had passed effortlessly through his breastplate, ripping holes in the thick metal like a dagger through paper.

"Almost made it to his horse, didn't he? Looks like your friend was right in guessing they wouldn't expect an approach from the south," Caydan mused as he came to stand next to Roningus. The Dragonknight and the church knight looked upon the city of Demhora from a safe distance. The winding southern pass did well to conceal their formations from enemy sight, the two of them keeping near the mouth of it to avoid being spotted by guardsmen patrolling the wall.

Narrowing his eyes, Roningus stood with his hands resting on his hips, a sudden breeze catching his cape and sending it flapping wildly behind him. After several moments of contemplation, he spoke while continuing to size up the city. "When the dreadknights laid siege to Ascention, they took civilians as hostage and took up residence in their homes, eating from their stores of food and in some instances forcing them into servitude. It is my intent to do this swiftly while minimizing the impact on innocent townsfolk. Dreadknights may hold this city, but if there are any inside who have not taken the dead god's faith then I would see them given the opportunity to rebuild when this is all said and done. Let us show them why ours is the just and righteous cause."

Caydan grinned, turning to glance at Roningus before looking back at the city that lay before them. "So let's kick the bastards' doors in, yeah?"

Chuckling silently for a moment, Roningus nodded and spoke placidly. "Let the history books be written thusly; that the church knights and Dragonknights fell upon the home of the dreadknights with a divine fury, burning them from the face of the earth like a cleansing light."

His grin widening, Caydan looked over to Roningus, his eyes gleaming with excitement. "I like the sound of that."

Seated atop a watchtower along the fortified wooden palisades that surrounded the city, the guardsman on duty let out a long yawn. Reaching up and rubbing his eye, it was just as he was dealing with a troublesome eyelash that a deafening, thunderous sound came echoing from the southern pass. Within moments, the clearing was overrun as church knights and soldiers the guardsman didn't recognize flying dragon banners swarmed out of the southern pass, pressing their horses to a full charge for the southern gates.

At first the guardsman blinked. The city had been on high alert, though the dreadknights wouldn't say exactly why. Furthermore, the bulk of their forces had been used to garrison the northern wall, large wooden ballistas and complex catapults that operated on counter-weights all poised and precisely aimed to rain down upon the church knights should they ride into Demhora. As such, it came as a tremendous surprise that not only had the church knights found a way to navigate the treacherous rocky waters along the southern coast, but had slipped up the southern pass without letting so much as a single lookout make it back to warn them.

The guardsman had heard stories of such brutal efficiency from one church knight in particular, and often the dreadknights would mutter his name with disgust. What it was they called him, the guardsman couldn't recall, as his mind was presently coming to the realization that he should sound the alarm and inform his superior. It wasn't until he was on his feet that the full impact dawned on him, bringing a panic to his voice as he cupped a hand to his mouth and called out.

It took precious minutes before everyone was aware of what was going on, and in that time the massive army was already at the southern gate, forming up in a wall of shields held tightly together so that arrows skittered uselessly across the top of them. It was just as the guard captain reached the southern gate that they had managed to haul forward their massive battering ram. He barely had time to turn and shout out the orders to brace the doors before the first hit came, rocking the palisade back and forth, eliciting groans and creaks from the gates. By the time enough guardsmen had gathered to get the beams in place, the ram punched its way through, splintering the wooden doors reinforced in iron bands and knocking back the throng of guards that desperately tried to hold it shut.

Minutes later, Roningus strode through the gates of Demhora, longswords clenched tightly in his hands, pointing forward with the sword in his right as church knights and Dragonknights swarmed through the shattered remains of the southern gate. His cape fluttered off to his left as rolling thunder was heard above, black clouds blowing in with the eastern winds and darkening the sky.

Moving as quickly as he could through the hallways of the cathedral, the black robed necromancer shoved people out of the way without stopping to make apologies. Upon reaching the doors to the dreadknight commander's chambers, the necromancer pressed through them immediately without knocking. Seated in a wide cushioned chair, Xaphan looked up from the half-naked serving girl who was doing up the straps to a restrictive metal bracing contraption that supported his right ankle. Clad in a simple black tunic over a faded red undershirt with long sleeves and a pair of red leggings, the bald dreadknight tilted his head and leveled his cold gaze on the necromancer.

"An acolyte sees fit to intrude upon my chambers of his own volition, and I find myself wondering what could be so urgent that he would risk his own life in doing so." As he spoke, the young girl fastening the buckles turned to look up at the necromancer, her wincing left eye swollen and bruised.

Glancing down at her momentarily, the necromancer spoke in an urgent tone. "Church knights of Mithos have breached the city! Reports from one of the city guards claims they came up through one of the lesser-known southern routes. We didn't know they were coming until they were practically at the southern gates."

His eyes igniting in a blaze of fury, Xaphan shoved the serving girl aside as he stood, heavily favoring his right ankle. "When did this happen?!" he shouted. The serving girl cowered and scampered out of the way.

"Minutes ago. The city guards mostly have held formation, though a number who apparently never held the faith have fallen in with the church knights. At the rate they're going, they will be through the city and at our doors by this evening."

His pale face flushing red with rage, Xaphan staggered forward, the cumbersome brace on his right ankle making his steps awkward and uncertain. Shouldering past the necromancer, he continued out the door and into the hallway, giving orders without stopping. "I want all men presently not on duty rounded up immediately. I want the number of dreadknights safeguarding the cathedral doubled, and any who are left over will be sent out to take control of those among the city guards who kept the faith. Any who are caught so much as THINKING about defecting to the other side are to be executed as a traitor IMMEDIATELY, no questions asked. Send word to my squire this instant, tell him to have my armor ready by the time I reach the armory."

"Yes, commander," the necromancer replied, hurrying off ahead of him. Within moments, the entire cathedral was in a state of organized chaos, dreadknights and necromancers practically sprinting to get to their stations or fulfill assignments from their superiors.

Moving from one place to another was a struggle for Xaphan, and as he plodded along with each grimacing step, the scene in which he had been maimed played out in his head. The Wrathful Tempest, kneeling down and seemingly at his mercy…and when he'd planted his foot on the church knight's chest to push him over, Roningus had revealed his exhaustion to be a bluff, grabbing hold of Xaphan's foot and shattering his ankle with an aggressive efficiency.

By the time he reached the armory, Xaphan was scowling, passing through a group of dreadknights who were exiting with their gear and weapons. Racks of assorted sinister weapons and suits of plate mail fashioned in a skeletal likeness sat in disarray, as most of the armory had been picked over. Near the back, however, was a curtained side room where Xaphan kept his personal gear, and standing just outside of it was his squire. A small boy no older than ten, the blond haired youth held back the curtain for Xaphan, waiting patiently as the dreadknight commander made his way through.

"Is my armor ready?" Xaphan asked in an irritated voice.

The boy nodded eagerly, and the two entered the room. Once inside, the process of donning his armor was somewhat hampered, as he would often have to sit down in times when he could normally shift his weight to the right instead. By the time it was all said and done, Xaphan had cursed the boy's ineptitude more times than he could count.

Stepping out of the armory, garbed in his full plate and red cape, a pair of dreadknights immediately stepped up to Xaphan, genuflecting before him and bowing their heads.

"Commander, there's been more news…"

"Well? Out with it," Xaphan growled, pulling his helmet on and adjusting the belt at his waist that held his flail.

"We've identified banners that indicate the Dragonknights of Forthos fight alongside the church knights. They've established a foothold in the slums, and with each push they gain control of more and more of the city."

Snarling angrily, Xaphan stepped past the two of them, barking orders as they rose quickly to fall in behind him. "You, bring me the guard that was on watch when they took the southern gate. I want to know why they were able to breach the southern wall as if we'd left it opcn for thcm."

"Yes, commander," the dreadknight to his left said, breaking off and moving swiftly down another hallway.

"And you…" Xaphan said, the dreadknight to his right hurrying up to his side.

"Commander?"

"Rally the necromancers…tell them to release the dreadnought."

"…c-commander?"

Stopping in his tracks, Xaphan rounded on the dreadknight, grabbing hold of the front of his breastplate roughly. "YOU HAVE YOUR ORDERS, DREADKNIGHT! Why do you see fit to question them?!"

Hesitating for a moment, the dreadknight looked away as if carefully choosing his words, looking back only as he began to speak. "…the last dreadnought…it didn't seem to discern between dreadknight and church knight…some of the men think it best if… well…"

Shoving the dreadknight back with such force that he slammed into the wall behind him, Xaphan turned and continued down the hallway. "I don't recall asking what the men think is best. Mine is to tell you what to do, and yours is to obey."

"The main doors to the cathedral are here…but there are side and back entrances here…and here." As he spoke, the city guard captain pointed to the crudely drawn map, pointing out the locations he spoke of to Roningus.

Roningus nodded in response, taking in the information he was being given and mulling it over.

Standing nearby and leaning on the table with his hands grasping the edges, Caydan looked up from the map. "How many of the city guard have kept the dead god's faith, then?"

"Nearly two-thirds, and I suspect the influx of those who reject the dead god is dying off. Xaphan has never been one to tolerate the 'unfaithful,' and many will likely maintain their farce until they are certain they will be safe."

Looking up from the map, Caydan shrugged at Roningus. "It's better than nothing."

Narrowing his eyes, Roningus spoke without looking away from the drawing of the cathedral. "How well manned is this cathedral?"

The guard captain shook his head, sighing. "If I had to guess, I'd say scarcely more than two hundred."

"Hah! The crimson legion's broken lines numbering in the thousands! That cathedral will be ours before sunset!" Caydan proclaimed, smiling proudly.

Roningus shook his head slightly as he spoke. "Two hundred that have the advantage of defending their own cathedral from the safety of stone walls, on unhallowed ground with the full support of their necromancers."

Frowning slightly, Caydan looked back down at the map. "Well when you put it like that…"

It was at that moment that another voice was heard, calling out above the general chatter of their encampment. "Sir Roningus! They're falling back!"

As he came running up to the table, the city guardsman was panting, and when he stopped, he hunched over and braced himself on his knees. Looking away from the map for the first time, Roningus tilted his head in confusion.

"Pulling back? From where?"

"Everywhere! It's as if they're abandoning the city, and falling back to the cathedral!"

Looking over to Caydan, Roningus quirked his left brow. "That can't be right."

Narrowing his eyes, Caydan stepped forward, looking down upon the guardsman that he towered over by at least a foot. "If you're not being honest with us, right now…"

Turning, the guardsman pointed as he replied. "Look for yourself!"

And indeed, as they looked up from their encampment, the sight of church knights and Dragonknights alike chasing after those who had kept the faith and their commanding dreadknights played out before them in the distance.

Turning to Roningus, Caydan grabbed his helmet from the table as he spoke. "Let's go see what this is all about, yeah?"

Nodding solemnly, Roningus reached for his own helmet, the two of them moving swiftly with the guardsman right behind them.

"What's happening?" Roningus asked, returning their salute as Ionnus and Grisbane turned and greeted him with one.

"We're not sure," Grisbane said. "One minute we were fighting for every inch of ground we took, the next they were sounding the retreat and falling back to their cathedral. A wise strategy on their part, actually…catching them unaware and denying them the opportunity to thin our numbers with their war machines, they were losing ground as quickly as we could take it."

Looking around at the now empty city, Roningus clapped Grisbane on his pauldron. "Prepare the men for the final push, then. It would seem the dreadknight commander is eager to meet his end as soon as possible."

When the four of them arrived, the azure legion had already formed a perimeter around the cathedral, staring down the defensive battalions of the city guards commanded by a handful of dreadknights. Stepping up to the front line, Roningus stood behind a pair of Dragonknights, their sideways stance allowing them to form a wall of tightly packed shields with their spears poised in the top notch.

The cathedral itself was a gruesome thing to behold; enormous red banners bearing a ram-horned human skull embroidered in black hung from the parapets, the large wooden doors at the main entrance stained black and reinforced with studded iron bands. Looking less like a cathedral and more like a military installation, the structure was purposely built in sharp, oppressive angles designed to loom over the surrounding area. With each step he took towards the building, Roningus felt the presence of the dead god swell and throb like the dull heartbeat of a wounded animal.

The dead god fears my arrival… Roningus thought to himself, allowing a faint smile of satisfaction. It was then that a door leading out onto a balcony opened up on the third floor, Xaphan stepping out and looking down. Immediately, the two recognized each other. Roningus lifted a finger at the dreadknight commander as he called out in the authoritative tone that had won him the respect and devotion of his men:

"Surrender, heretic, and repent your ways. Yours is the last stain of the dead god upon this land, and I stand here with the Dragonknights of Forthos as my allies, poised to eradicate your blasphemy from the world once and for all."

"You are a fool, Wrathful Tempest! In your arrogance, you've failed to learn one important lesson: never back an animal into a corner, for that is when they prove to be most dangerous!"

"I'm not here to exchange threats, heretic. Surrender or we're coming in." As Roningus spoke, Caydan moved up to stand along the front lines not far off from him, unholstering the spear at his back and eyeing Xaphan hungrily through the eyes of his dragon's head helm.

Xaphan shook his head. "You haven't won, church knight. You only think you have." That said, he gave a dismissive gesture, and the dreadknights ordered the attack.

At first, the attack went as both sides had planned. When the guardsmen fell upon the azure legion, they found the reputation of the Dragonknights to be accurate. The blue-scaled Dragonknights yielded no ground and even managed to drive the guardsmen back over time. As they continued to press their attack, the azure legion would open up and let several members of the Onyx legion pass through. The black knights spread out, wreaking havoc amidst the guardsmen's carefully formed squadrons of soldiers until eventually their entire formation was a sea of turmoil. The azure legion kept the situation contained while the onyx legion drove them into the blue wall to be slaughtered.

It was when the dreadknights began pouring forth from the main doors that the church knights entered the battle, the two factions squaring off almost exclusively amidst the melee that now surrounded the cathedral. When the church knights began to close in on the main doors of the cathedral, a voice was heard crying out above the roar of battle.

"DREADNOUGHT!"

Immediately, Roningus turned, watching the lumbering monstrosity ducking under the doorframe and stepping out into the yard. Glancing over, he spotted Caydan just as the Dragonknight commander saw it as well. They nodded and moved towards the creature in tandem.

"How do we bring it down?!" Caydan shouted, skewering a dreadknight behind Roningus just in time to duck beneath Roningus's blades as they clipped the head off of a guardsman aiming at the back of Caydan's head.

"They're controlled by a pact of necromancers, but they're going to be heavily guarded within the walls of the cathedral! We have to come up with another way!" Roningus yelled back. The two of them turned to face the dreadnought as it stepped on a guardsman, sending a church knight flying with a swing from the heavy maul that served as its left hand. Immediately, dreadknights and guardsmen alike began to fall back, the dreadnought swatting aside those that were unfortunate enough to get shoved into its path amidst the commotion.

Nodding, Caydan spun his spear around in his hand, bringing it to rest behind him. "Right! Let's bring the bastard down, yeah?!" And before Roningus could object, Caydan took off in a full sprint towards the dreadnought.

"Mithos bless us…" Roningus muttered, giving his swords a flourish and falling in behind Caydan.

Once the dreadnought spotted Roningus, it ceased its general mayhem and seemed to focus its lifeless gray eyes on him exclusively, granting everyone around it the chance to fall back to a safe distance. Once the dreadknights were all inside the cathedral, they pulled the doors closed, abandoning any guardsmen who hadn't yet made it in. Without hesitation, the dreadnought lunged for Roningus, leading with a downward swing of its warhammer that would have split his helm and skull.

Jumping swiftly to the side, Roningus followed up with a downward swing that caught the dreadnought just above its left forearm. The rune etched into the black steel glowed brightly as it sliced into the dreadnought's flesh. The dreadnought let out an inhuman howl, pulling its wounded arm back and reaching for Roningus with its right hand, sending him diving off to his left and tucking into a forward roll that brought him up to a kneeling position. Rising its warhammer above its head, the dreadnought swung hard in another downward stroke. Roningus waited until the last second before diving between its legs. The warhammer missing him narrowly, Roningus was just beginning to push himself up from the ground when he looked up and saw Caydan, spear in hand and looking eager.

"Give me a lift!" Caydan cried, racing forward.

"Oh hell..." Roningus muttered, scrambling up into a kneeling position.

Dropping his swords, he clasped his fingers together, holding out his hands and offering a place for Caydan's foot. He lifted up with all of his strength as the Dragonknight commander stepped up and launched himself into the air. Raising his spear above his head, Caydan let out a bestial roar as he drove the dragon-toothed spearhead into the back of the dreadnought's neck, sending the creature stumbling and lurching forward. Planting his feet on its shoulders, Caydan gave the spear a twist, turning the spear head so that the sharpened length of the longer of the two teeth faced downward, pulling down hard on the haft of his spear as he dismounted. The head of the spear rippled through the sick, pasty flesh on the dreadnought's back, laying it open from neck to waist.

Lifting his swords from the ground, Roningus turned, pressing their advantage and going to work on the back of the dreadnought's left knee. Flaying into the soft flesh and tendons of the joint with a flurry of vicious slices, the dreadnought was soon brought down to one knee. Roningus ducked out of the way as it swung its hammer around behind it, bringing the sword in his right hand down upon the joint in a repeated hacking motion while Caydan slashed and stabbed at its right hand to keep it from grabbing him. Eventually, the bottom half of the leg separated from the top, and when it did, Roningus quickly kicked it out of the way before it could heal back up. No longer supported by its left leg, the dreadnought tumbled backwards, landing on its back and screaming in mindless frustration. But Roningus and Caydan had already gone to work quickly, Caydan driving the point of his spear through the palm on the dreadnought's hand and pinning it to the ground.

"Get rid of that hammer already, yeah?!" Caydan said, straining against the strength of the dreadnought to keep the arm pinned to the ground.

Swooping in, Roningus waited until the dreadnought drew the hammer back to swing at Caydan before he reacted, bringing both swords up above his head and bringing them down into its left elbow, forcibly cleaving his way through the ever-regenerating flesh of the dreadnought's left arm. Swing after swing Roningus landed, abandoning form for brute strength as he chopped through the arm until finally it separated at the elbow. One final severing slice finished the job so that he could kick it away as well. Its anger swelling to new heights, the dreadnought wrenched its right arm free, forcing Caydan to duck the haft of his own spear as it flailed about wildly.

"How do you normally go about this?" Caydan shouted, reaching for his spear and missing as it sailed by him again.

"Normally they've already stopped moving when we butcher them!" Roningus replied, stepping around the dreadnought's head as it tried to roll over onto its stomach.

"Well it has my spear!" Caydan yelled back, using the dreadnought's helmeted head as a stepping stone and launching himself at its right hand, his hands closing around the haft of his spear. As the blade dug painfully into the dreadnought's hand, the creature flailed its arm furiously. Caydan hung on as tightly as he could while the creature tried to shake him off.

"That's good! Just keep doing that!" Roningus yelled, coming up next to the dreadnought's head. Bringing his right sword up, he brought it down just below the helmet, ducking out of the way as the dreadnought used Caydan to swipe at him.

"Right! I've got this!" Caydan hollered back, locking his legs around the dreadnought's wrist and pulling hard on the spear to try and direct the hand away from Roningus.

Free from distraction, Roningus went back to work, hacking bit by bit through the thick collarbone that the helmet rested on. It was just as Caydan's spear came free and the Dragonknight commander was thrown clear from the dreadnought that Roningus delivered the final blow, looking up just as the hand was reaching for his head and thrusting both swords through its palm before reaching down and grabbing hold of the helmet. Reaching deep within the reserves of his strength, Roningus planted his feet and pulled with all the resolve he could muster, wrenching the helmet away from the dreadnought's shoulders. As it separated, the contents of the helmet spilled out onto the ground, a nauseating odor pervading the immediate area as blood, brain matter, and other cranial contents pooled around the dreadnought's shoulders. In an instant, the creature went completely limp, its enormous right arm falling lifelessly to the ground. Standing over top of the fallen dreadnought, Roningus paused, looking over and watching as Caydan pushed himself up off the ground with his spear in hand and began to brush himself off.

"Fucking hell!" one of the azure Dragonknights exclaimed, his voice shattering the stunned silence that the entire gathered crowd had stood in.

Caydan laughed loudly, then leaned back his head and let out a victorious cry, brandishing his spear above his head, Dragonknights and church knights alike joining in.

Suddenly and without warning, the seven necromancers that maintained the pack let out blood curdling screams. A wave of unseen energy followed, washing over the entire room, knocking back everyone who stood in attendance and pushing Xaphan down into his seat. In unison, the seven members of the pact collapsed to the ground, unmoving. Uncertainty fueling his anger, Xaphan shouted out his command in a voice to match his temper.

"WHAT'S HAPPENED?!"

Rushing forward, a black robed acolyte knelt down, shaking one of the necromancers by the shoulder momentarily before holding two fingers to the side of his neck. After several seconds the acolyte looked up, his face an expression of confusion and horror.

"They're...dead..."

His eyes narrowing, Xaphan stood from his chair and hobbled over to where they lay. He glared down at the dead necromancer at his feet, who was bleeding profusely from his eyes, ears, and mouth. The other bodies looked much the same, each one's face contorted in their final moments of unbearable agony. Stepping over the corpse, Xaphan proceeded through the circle, and was heading for the door when a dreadknight came bursting through.

"Commander, the dreadnought is dead! The Wrathful Tempest and the golden Dragonknight slew it in single combat! What are your orders?!"

For several long moments, Xaphan stood, unsure of what to do, until finally he spoke in a chillingly calm tone. "Brace the front doors. Do not let them in. Your life depends on it."

Kneeling upon the steps leading up the dais in the altar room, Xaphan held his hands clasped in front of him. Six of the highest ranking dreadknights guarded the door; his personally appointed body guards. Praying silently, it was here that he waited, listening to the thundering sound of the ram battering at the front doors of the church, until the inevitable crash as they were brought down. Judging by how rapidly the sounds of battle approached, Xaphan judged that the church knights had fought their way to the side and back entrances and were gradually closing in on the altar room.

When the clash of steel was heard just outside his door, he knew the time had come. Lifting his helmet from the ground, he slid it over his head, then stood. "Ready yourselves, men. The false father's dogs are at our door."

Immediately the six dreadknights drew their flails, forming up around the altar room door and readying themselves for the approaching battle. Suddenly, the world went silent outside the doors, and for several seconds nothing seemed to be happening. As his men looked to each other in confusion, Xaphan spoke calmly.

"Keep steady. They seek to unnerve us by making us wait."

Redoubling their concentration, the six dreadknights faced the door, weapons held back and poised to strike. Then…slowly, it creaked open, and in the doorway stood Roningus.

His breastplate spattered with streaks of blood, his gold-embroidered black cape ripped and slashed full of holes, Roningus stepped into the altar room, followed by Caydan, Ionnus, Grisbane, and Osric. What appeared to be the entire crimson legion waited in the hallway. Coming to a halt as the six dreadknights fanned out around him, Roningus tilted his head, pointing the sword in his right hand at Xaphan.

"This is between you and me, heretic. These men need not die."

In response, one of the dreadknights rushed forward, lashing at Roningus with the flail in his hand. Reacting instantly, Osric stepped forward, his burning blue eyes engulfed in a holy flame. He brought his studded two-handed club above his head and shattered the dreadknight's weapon hand with a powerful downward swing, then caught the dreadknight in the side of the head with a horizontal swing, carrying him off his feet and knocking him sideways to the ground.

Roningus casually walked forward and lowered his swords to his sides. As the next dreadknight came at him it was Caydan who intercepted, catching the chain that connected the head of his flail to the handle and severing it with a twist of his spear's haft. Then he drove the point of the spear clean through the front of the dreadknight's visor until it came out the back of his head. Ionnus and Grisbane stepped up, occupying the other four as they were joined by Caydan and Osric, while Roningus continued forward.

"What do you hope to achieve here, church knight? Do you truly believe that in slaying me, the dead god will disappear forever?"

Still, Roningus continued forward, his predatory eyes trained on Xaphan. When Roningus said nothing, Xaphan snarled and continued.

"You're wrong if you think this is the end! There will be others, church knight! So long as there is light in this world, the shadows shall always harbor the darkness! The dead god shall rise to power once more, and when he does your precious holy city will crumble!"

That said, Xaphan reached down to unholster the weapon at his side, but was stopped short when Roningus spun around, hurling the sword in his left hand at him. The black steel blade hummed as it soared through the air end over end, Xaphan barely having time to bring his shield up. Yet when the point of the sword met the dreadknight's shield, it pierced through wood and metal, lodging itself in Xaphan's forearm and knocking him backwards. Xaphan cursed in dismay.

Holding out his left hand, Roningus called to the blade, the sword flying from Xaphan's arm and returning to the church knight's empty hand as it was bidden. Watching on in a mixture of bewilderment and fright, the dreadknight struggled to bring his shield up again as Roningus stepped in and hurled the one in his right hand. The blade once again carved through the dreadknight's shield and vambrace alike as it punctured another hole in his forearm. Searing pain shot up Xaphan's arm; the dreadknight fumbled with the straps of his shield and unbuckled them before letting it clatter down the stairs. It was just as he looked up that he saw the sword returning to its owner, its twin sailing towards him with the same speed and accuracy as before. Instinctively Xaphan raised his right hand, realizing his mistake all too late as the edge of the blade cleaved into his wrist, clattering to the ground momentarily before returning dutifully to Roningus as he reached for it.

Time seemed to slow around Xaphan. To his left, he saw the two blue caped church knights as they made an end to their battle with two of his dreadknight bodyguards. When he looked right, he caught the briefest glimpse of the golden scaled Dragonknight sweeping the legs out from underneath another, the point of his spear driving into the dreadknight's breastplate before he'd even hit the ground.

Meanwhile, the battle cleric in naught but his tabard stepped in. What looked like it should have been a solid hit from the swing of a flail missed the cleric completely at the last second, as he brought his two-handed club down on the dreadknight's head. Droplets of blood sprayed out from the dreadknight's visor and splattered the battle cleric's face.

It wasn't until Xaphan looked forward that he spotted one of Roningus's sword again just as it reached him, catching him square in the chest. Xaphan coughed, and as he did he tasted blood in his mouth. Letting his body go limp, he collapsed back against the steps, looking up at the sword protruding from his breastplate.

What seemed like an eternity later, Roningus came to stand over him, reaching up and pushing Xaphan's helmet off with the tip of the sword in his right hand.

"So…you'd slaughter me like the half-fiend…rather than face me in fair combat? Your honor is lacking…church knight…" As Xaphan spoke, the breaths he drew grew increasingly less effective, and he found himself having to pant to keep from feeling as if he were suffocating.

Looking down upon him, Roningus shook his head. "You are not an honorable man, heretic, and are unworthy of the glory of dying in battle. Do not speak to me of honor."

Laughing, Xaphan turned and spat, leaving a streak of red from the corner of his mouth extending out onto the steps. "Go on then…finish what you've come to do…"

But when Roningus grasped the handle of his sword, and Xaphan braced himself for the twist that would end his life…he instead suffered the steel sliding from his chest as Roningus withdrew the sword, wiping the blood from it with a red stained cloth.

"Wh-what are you doing?!" Xaphan gurgled, struggling to breathe as the back of his throat began to fill with blood.

Calmly, Roningus continued about the task of wiping his sword clean, speaking as if he were instructing a squire. "A good weapon will only remain a good weapon with proper care, and I refuse to use anything less than a good weapon."

Scowling, Xaphan leaned his head over to the side and spat again, clearing his throat of the building phlegm and blood before speaking again. "Enough of your talk...kill me and be done with it!"

Finishing up with the first sword, Roningus sheathed it and began to work on the other. "Your death will come soon enough, heretic. Your suffering in this world will seem a trifling matter to that which awaits you in the next."

Feeling himself growing faint from blood loss, the sharp pain that wracked his body increasing, Xaphan forced the corners of his lips up into an ugly smile. "Letting a wounded enemy bleed out? Heh heh...I'll see you in hell, church knight..."

Slowly, Roningus turned his head, his dark brown eyes boring into Xaphan and causing the dreadknight commander to shift uneasily. "And if your dead god is foolish enough to let me in, I'll take over hell in the name of heaven as well."

"You're sure I can't convince you to stay on as an honorary Dragonknight?" Caydan asked, clasping hands with Roningus.

Smiling, Roningus shook his head, gesturing towards the remainder of the column that awaited him with a nod of his head. "You honor me with your offer, but my place is with them. The threat of the dead god may be removed, but the church will always need her sword, even in these times of prosperity."

Grinning, Caydan leaned in, engaging Roningus in a half embrace. When they broke apart, he reached up, clapping Roningus on his pauldron as he spoke. "Come back if you do something fun again, yeah?"

Smiling, Roningus nodded. "Of course. And it goes without saying that should the Dragonknights ever have need of assistance, the church of Mithos stands ready to honor our alliance."

Smiling, Caydan waved as Roningus mounted his horse, riding past the others to the head of the column and leading them away from the city.

As they reached the gates of Ascention, the guard working the winch looked down, his eyes growing wide with excitement as the column approached.

"It's Roningus! The Wrathful Tempest has returned!"

Moving as quickly as he could, the guard grabbed hold of one of the cog's handles and began to turn, the intricate weight and chain system opening wide the city's gates to allow Roningus and the remainder of his column through. Proceeding up the main road of Ascention that led from the gate to the steps of the church, Roningus looked down to his sides as people gathered to wave and cheer. Grisbane rode up next to him and leaned in to be heard over the noise.

"They're here to see you, you know…the least you could do is wave!" That said, Grisbane smiled, rapping Roningus on his pauldron and falling back in line.

Looking around, Roningus slowly held up a hand, waving uncertainly as the crowd roared their approval. It was thus that they proceeded up the road, Roningus dismounting as he reached the steps.

Smiling brightly, Vogoth leaned over to Brogam, who stood at his side along with the other arch clerics who had come out to greet the returning church knights. "What do you think, Arch Cleric? Should we let him continue to wear black for the time being?"

Chuckling, Brogam shook his head. "He's no chosen champion, but he'll do for now I suppose."

"High priest…arch clerics…" Roningus said as he approached the steps, dropping to one knee in genuflect. Every church knight behind him did the same, repeating the ceremonial gesture upon return that had been enacted for as long as anyone could remember.

"Wrathful Tempest…you return with good news, I take it?"

Grinning, Roningus removed his helmet, handing it off to a brown caped paladin and reaching back, taking Xaphan's helmet and holding it out before him as proof of his conquest. "The dead god's stain has been washed from the western kingdoms. In her second crusade, the church was victorious."

But for how long… Vogoth wondered, his silent smile widening as he looked proudly upon the church knights who had returned.

EPILOGUE

Darkness…fear…agony…these were the all too familiar companions that rose up to greet Asmodeus as he was cast into the abyss. The grotesque servants of the dead god marched forward to retrieve him. Landing flat on his back from where he had fallen, the half-fiend looked around him, the green glow of the smoldering necrotic flames and the sounds of thousands of tortured souls wailing in despair welcoming him home.

One of the demons that served the dead god personally leaned down, the oversized jet black spheres that were its eyes glaring down at him while it grinned with a sadistic sort of satisfaction, speaking in an inhuman sounding multi-tone voice as if three talked in unison.

"Welcome home, half-breed." That said, the demon drew back its enormous fist, delivering a powerful blow to the bridge of Asmodeus's nose that slammed his head back against the floor. Immediately blood began to gush from his nostrils, a dizzy feeling overcoming him.

The demon nodded to the companion at his other side and the two grabbed Asmodeus roughly by his arms, pulling him to his feet and dragging him along the floor to where the dead god sat atop his sinister throne. The unmoving corpse stared unblinkingly forward, the flesh having rotted away from its bones in most places. A skeletal hand grasped the sword known as Lifereaver and held it across its lap.

"*You...have failed...*" came the voice of Necros, the cold whisper filling the dead god's hall and resounding off the walls.

Still hanging limply from the grasp of the demons, Asmodeus lifted his head, looking up to the corpse and struggling to focus his blurring vision. "The Wrathful Tempest proved to be too great an adversary...I was unable to—"

"YOU WERE A DISGRACE," came a sudden shout, the enraged sounding snarl heralding the approach of a massive eight foot tall demon.

His sinuous skin a deep shade of purple, his eyes were a crimson red in color, a pair of ivory horns jutting out from just above his forehead before curling upwards, each one coming to a point. Powerful, bat-like wings flexed behind his back, originating from his shoulders with a small pair of claw-like appendages at the end of each one. Like the two demons that held Asmodeus, his sex hung heavy between his knees, grossly oversized in a hedonistic display. His muscular legs bent backwards at the knee as opposed to forwards, his calloused feet ending with a vicious looking set of claws on his toes.

Stepping out from the shadows, the demon made his way around the others, coming to stand directly in front of Asmodeus, staring down at him with the utmost disapproval.

"Father," Asmodeus said plainly, turning his head to spit blood from his mouth.

In response, the demon known as Merrek the Fallen One reached out, grabbing hold of Asmodeus by the throat. The two that held him let go. Merrek lifted him from the ground, grinning in satisfaction when Asmodeus reached up and grasped at Merrek's forearms in a panic.

"I should make a permanent end of you, and feast upon your soul."

In response, all Asmodeus could do was cough and sputter, prying at Merrek's fingers until finally the demon tossed him aside.

Holding out his hand, a flaming scourge materialized in Merrek's hand as he summoned it, holding the nine-tailed whip dangerously at his side as he approached Asmodeus where he lay.

"There was nothing I could do...by the time I had arrived in town, the Wrathful Tempest already had his column poised to strike..." Asmodeus said, fighting to push himself up off the ground.

In response, Merrek drew back his flaming scourge, and with a powerful swing sent the tips of it lashing across the half-fiend's back. Instantly splitting skin and leaving searing burn marks wherever it touched, Asmodeus cried out in pain and fell to the floor again.

"Consider yourself fortunate, for the dead god has decided to show you mercy." Following his words, Merrek drew back the scourge again, and when he struck, Asmodeus cried out once more, the half-fiend collapsing with exhaustion as the fiery weapon leeched the very life force from him.

Mustering all the strength that he could, Asmodeus rolled himself over onto his back, lying motionless with his eyes closed and breathing heavily. A meaningless gesture in the abyss, but one he'd grown accustomed to from his time on the prime plane.

"*Remove him...from my sight...*" came the dead god's command, the demonic servants grabbing hold of Asmodeus by his arms once more and dragging his limp body back down the hall from whence they had come and down the steps into the dungeons of the dead god's fortress.

Upon reaching his cell, the demons heaved Asmodeus in, letting him fall to the ground face first and laughing when he lacked the strength to push himself up. After the loud slam of the cell door,

Asmodeus listened as the two disappeared, laughing and making japes at his expense in the abyssal tongue as they left.

Then, Asmodeus was alone.

For how long he lay on his stomach unable to move, he didn't know, but by the time he found himself able to push himself up onto an elbow, his joints and muscles ached. Every so often, an ear-splitting scream would rise up above the clamor of anguished souls, the only sounds to accompany him; memories of such noises lulling him to sleep in the days of his youth flooded back to him.

Glancing around, Asmodeus blinked, his eyes gradually readjusting as he recalled just how dark a place the abyss truly was. To say his cell was sparse was a drastic understatement; without even so much as a soft bit of something to wad up and rest his head upon, the only item within his cell was the disfigured remains of its previous occupant. By the time he was able to sit up, his eyes had almost fully readjusted to the darkness, and in glancing through the bars of his cell he could see that his was at the very end of the hallway.

Wincing in pain as he carefully repositioned himself with his back against the wall, Asmodeus drew in a deep breath and sighed, Roningus's words echoing in his mind.

No one is beyond forgiveness. Not even you.

Laughing silently to himself at the notion, Asmodeus leaned his head back against the wall, shaking his head and speaking out loud to himself. "Empty words from an idealistic fool."

Yet still, Asmodeus found himself dwelling on how the church knight had spoken with such conviction, as if he truly believed them. Was it possible? Recalling all the times he had stained his hands with innocent blood, Asmodeus dismissed the notion and sank into a troubled sleep.

When he dreamed, he dreamt of the church knights he had slain back in the nameless town where Roningus had defeated him and sent him back to the abyss. He found himself atop the execution platform, kneeling and holding the body of the black caped church knight in his arms, his hands still wet from where he'd ripped the man's throat out. Looking down upon the church knight's pale face, when the dying youth looked up at him it was not with a condemning gaze as he expected, but one of great sorrow.

"I forgive you…" the church knight whispered, even as his life blood flowed from the hole in his throat where Asmodeus had rent him open.

Suddenly overwhelmed with a sense of tremendous guilt, it was when Asmodeus looked up that he saw them…the nameless faces of the people whose lives he'd taken, all in the name of the dead god. Each of them stared up at him wordlessly, crying tears of blood and giving him the same look as the dying church knight he held in his arms.

His heart pounding rapidly in his chest, Asmodeus glanced around frantically, until suddenly he heard the voice of Roningus once more.

"Here…take my hand…"

Looking to his right, he saw the Wrathful Tempest standing above him. The stern brown eyes of Roningus looked upon him with a sense of compassion the half-fiend had never been shown.

"No one is beyond forgiveness. Not even you," Roningus said, extending his hand down further, urging the half-fiend to take it.

Reaching out slowly, Asmodeus began to close his fingers around the church knight's hand when…

He awoke with a start, his heart beating so loudly he could almost hear it over the wailing souls lost in the blackness of the abyss. Realizing he was laying on his side with his head resting on his arm, Asmodeus pushed himself up, looking around him. Curling his knees up to his chest, he sat with his arms drawn around his legs until the sound of approaching footsteps broke his meditations. The familiar sight of the two demons from the dead god's hall filled him with a sense of dread.

One of the two opened the cell door and spoke in an eerie tone that made one's flesh crawl. "The dead god has summoned you."

Pausing for a moment, Asmodeus slowly stood, his distrust beginning to rise once he saw the eager look in their eyes. Walking with one on either side of him, he returned to the throne room of Necros, the corpse of the dead god still seated as it always was.

"*Kneel…*" came the whispered command.

Asmodeus fell to his knees immediately. Standing at the foot of the stairs leading up to the dead god's throne was Merrek the Fallen One grinning wickedly at Asmodeus.

"*For your failure…you must be punished…*" came the whisper of the dead god once more, upon which the demons near him grabbed hold of his arms and stretched them out to his sides.

Looking to each one in turn, Asmodeus looked back up to the dead god just as Merrek summoned a vile looking saw-bladed sword into his right hand. His fear turning to desperation and ultimately to anger, Asmodeus fought in vain against the relentless grasp of the demons that held him, shouting his pleas at the dead god in a mixture of terror and anger.

"There was nothing I could do! The price of failure is not mine to bear; it was your dreadknights who allowed the Wrathful Tempest to sweep across the western kingdoms with such a minimal effort! THEY are the ones who should be punished! I did everything that I could!"

Stepping around one of the demons that held him, Merrek spoke in a rebuking tone. "Your whimpering falls upon deaf ears, half-breed. The dead god has decided the price of your failure." That said, he reached out, grabbing hold of the wing that sprouted from Asmodeus's left shoulder. Leveling the jagged blade of the sword on top of the joint where it originated from, Merrek spoke in a grunt. "Hold him tight."

The demons tightened their grip, and Asmodeus's screams filled the dead god's hall as Merrek began to saw.

Once it was done, Merrek tossed the lifeless wing aside, the demons releasing their grip on Asmodeus's arms and letting him fall to the ground. Blood gushed freely from the open wound where his left wing had once sprouted from. Merrek summoned a tongue of flame in his left hand and held the flat of the blade over the top of it. It was when the blade glowed red hot that he placed his foot on Asmodeus's back, putting enough weight on him to hold him down while simultaneously pressing the flat of the blade against the open wound. A loud hissing sound was heard accompanied by the smell of searing flesh, and Asmodeus let out a wordless, excruciating howl, too exhausted from his struggle to move as the scorching metal cauterized the wound.

When it was done, Merrek stepped away from him, motioning towards him with a nod. The two demons lifted him from the ground, the one on the right grabbing hold of his face by his jaw and lifting his head up, forcing his gaze upon the dead god once more.

"*Consider this...your penance...take this time...to contemplate... how you will redeem yourself...*" came the voice of Necros, the dreadful whisper filling the halls as the lifeless skeleton sat motionless on its throne. That said, the demons dragged Asmodeus back to his cell, tossing him in and slamming the doors shut behind him.

Pain like Asmodeus had never known ravaged his torso, and for quite a while he found himself unable to move his left arm lest he be wracked with sharp pangs that rendered him immobile. Hours turned into days, and days into weeks before the sensation left him entirely, yet all of it seemed like an eternity to him as he sat in the darkness of his cell. It was as he sat cross-legged in the middle of the floor, furling and unfurling his remaining wing to familiarize himself with how the loss of its counterpart felt that the thought occurred to him.

Why do I kneel?

An entirely alien idea to him, at first Asmodeus was surprised it had even occurred to him. But the more he meditated on the question, the more he found himself wondering why it hadn't occurred to him sooner.

"Why do I kneel?" he said aloud to himself, furrowing his eyebrows in confusion. What purpose did it serve? Surely if the dead god was omnipresent as he claimed to be, even he could see that the fall of the dreadknights was not his fault. Why, then, would Necros see fit to take his wing, to allow Merrek to scourge him mercilessly?

At first he found his thoughts dangerous, pushing them from his mind as if the dead god would hear them and send his demons to torture him for his insolence. But when the demons did not come, Asmodeus found his mind returning to them more and more frequently, until finally it dawned on him.

"He is not a god worth serving." Saying the words out loud, even as he spoke them, Asmodeus felt emboldened by them, a sudden weight beginning to lift from his shoulders as his enthrallment to the dead god fled him. In that moment, he knew what he had to do, and so began his training.

Relentless and with little rest Asmodeus trained, honing his body and regaining his strength. Physical strength had been his downfall in his fight with the Wrathful Tempest, and each time he pushed himself off the ground and felt the burn in his arms he could almost envision Roningus giving him an approving nod, the church knight's words becoming his mantra.

No one is beyond forgiveness. Not even myself.

Time passed unnoticed by Asmodeus, the half-fiend continuing a strict regimen that focused on building his strength while at the same time utilizing what limited space he had to maintain his dexterity. Practicing vaults on the floor, hanging by his ankles from the holes in the cell door to do sit-ups, Asmodeus found himself wholly driven by his new purpose for existence, devoting all of his energy to improving his body and meditating to focus his mind when he rested.

By the time the demons returned for him, more time than he could have hoped to keep track of had passed. One of the demons scowled as they came upon him meditating peaceably instead of wallowing in despair as they had hoped. Wrenching open the cell door, the demon spoke with an irritable inflection.

"The dead god summons you, half-breed."

His eyes opening, Asmodeus stood without saying a word, casting a glare upon the demon as he stepped to the cell door. Glancing down and noticing the marked increase in his strength and definition, the demon took a measured step back, giving him room to exit before the two of them fell in behind him, trailing a few steps back.

Upon reaching the throne room, Asmodeus found Merrek waiting for him once more, the Fallen One standing at the foot of the steps with his arms crossed in front of him. When Asmodeus remained standing, Merrek frowned.

"The dead god has a task for you, that you might redeem yourself. Kneel before him."

Slowly, Asmodeus tilted his head, looking first to Merrck before turning his gaze up at the skeleton that sat on the throne. "I will not."

"*Kneel...*" came the dead god's command, and at once Asmodeus felt a tremendous weight upon him, pressing him down towards the ground.

Despite all of his newfound strength, Asmodeus felt himself forced to one knee, the half-fiend struggling against it and finding himself asking for help in the most unlikely of places.

All Father...I know I have ever been your enemy in the past, but hear me now...grant me the strength to cast off the dead god's shackles, and I shall spend my life atoning for the sins of my past...

"HOW DARE YOU!" came the wailing cry of Necros, for as the All Father heard the half-fiend's prayers the dead god knew at once, and in that moment the unseen restraints that bound Asmodeus, son of the Fallen One, to his service were stricken from him.

Asmodeus slowly stood from where he had knelt.

"KILL HIM!" Merrek shouted, the two demons looking to each other with panicked expressions.

Asmodeus reacted faster than either of them could have expected. Crouching down briefly, he leapt towards the one to his left, delivering a back-spinning heel kick to its throat that sent it staggering backwards. In that instant, the one to the right reacted, advancing towards him with its massive hands open as if to restrain him. But Asmodeus was prepared, and as the demon lunged for him he slid deftly beneath its legs, reaching up and grabbing hold of its oversized member. Standing quickly, he placed his right foot on the small of its back, and simultaneously pushing forward with his foot while pulling back with all of his might, ripped the demon's sex from between its legs. The creature let out an unearthly howl as blood spurted in gushes from where its member once was.

As it collapsed to the ground, Asmodeus tossed the lifeless piece of flesh aside, turning his glare upon the other, just as it watched on in horror while its counterpart bled to death on the ground. Roaring furiously, the other demon stepped forward, crouching low to defend against the same happening to it. Once more, Asmodeus was on the move in an instant, stepping in and swatting the demon's hands away as it grasped at him. Turning his back to it, he delivered a strong blow to the demon's stomach, the creature doubling over as Asmodeus drove the point of his elbow into it just above its waist. Then, reaching up with both hands, he grabbed hold of the creature behind its neck, and in a single motion crouched down to a kneel, twisting and pulling the demon down with him and tossing it over his right shoulder. Landing in front of him, it was a simple matter of reaching forward as it sat up, wrapping his right hand around the front of the demon's head and placing his left on the back of it before a sudden twist and a sharp snap brought the demon's life to an abrupt end.

With one dead and the other dying on the floor, Asmodeus stood, turning his attention to Merrek. Letting out a feral snarl, Merrek held his hands together, and when he pulled them apart a hellish looking sword materialized between them. Grasping it in his right hand, he pointed a clawed fingertip at Asmodeus.

"Your soul will lament in the darkest pit of the abyss…just like your whore mother's."

"Tell me, father…what was it like, falling from the grace of Mithos? Did you feel pain when he struck you down from his paradise for your vain arrogance?"

His eyes growing wide, Merrek bared his fangs, drawing his blade back into a ready position. Yet still Asmodeus continued to speak, slowly circling Merrek and forcing him to do the same to keep his footing.

"You were beautiful once, yes? All angels are, from what I'm told. How it must have devastated you…once such a gorgeous thing to behold…twisted into a perverted mockery of a scraph."

His rage building inside him, Merrek's chest heaved in deep breaths, the voice of the dead god spurring him into action.

"Kill him…"

With a bestial roar Merrek leapt forward, lashing out at Asmodeus with a flurry of swipes from the sword in his right hand and the claws on his left. Expertly dodging and sidestepping each one, when Merrek overextended with a swing of his sword, Asmodeus moved in. Wrapping his left arm around Merrek's right, Asmodeus grabbed hold of Merrek's wrist with his right hand, a sharp twist and push forcing the sword from it and sending the weapon clattering to the ground. Merrek howled in frustration, wrenching his arm away from Asmodeus. But the half-fiend released it willingly, and with a swift movement had collected the weapon and repositioned himself for the offensive.

Then came the half-fiend's turn, the blade flashing in his hand as fist, feet, and blade lashed out. Merrek soon found himself unable to match his son in terms of sheer speed. Then , with a wide sweep of his arm, Merrek caught Asmodeus unaware, knocking him aside and sending him sprawling to the ground. Catching himself as he landed, Asmodeus was back on his feet in an instant, but when he spun around, Merrek had already descended upon him, reaching out and grasping at the top of the half-fiend's head with one of his monstrous sized hands. Asmodeus ducked out of the way, but Merrek still managed to get a hold of one of the small horns that crowned his skull, snapping it off with a forceful twist and tossing it aside.

Staggered momentarily as pain shot through him, Asmodeus saw Merrek closing in on him again and was spurred to action. He narrowly ducked out of the way as Merrek lunged for him again. It was as Merrek turned to round on him that Asmodeus spotted his opening, risking being crushed by the Fallen One's gigantic muscular arms on a single killing stroke.

Lunging upward and putting all the strength of his legs behind him, Asmodeus took the handle of the blade in his left hand, grasping it upside down and bracing the pommel against his right palm. As the point of the blade found its mark, Merrek's eyes went wide. The cold metal slid up through his chin and continued on through the roof of his mouth. The point of the blade nicked the inside of the top of his skull once it had passed effortlessly through the brain matter.

As Merrek sank to his knees, Asmodeus withdrew the blade, taking it up in his right hand and grabbing hold of one of the horns that sprouted from Merrek's head in his left. Going to work immediately, Asmodeus hacked at the Fallen One's neck with the edge of the blade until finally it separated, the headless body slumping to the ground while the vacant eyes of Merrek stared lifelessly forward, his mouth hanging open from the last surprise of his life.

Covered in spats of blood, Asmodeus cast the sword aside, holding the head of his father in his hand and looking up…the motionless skeleton of the dead god remaining silent as the half-fiend tossed the head of Merrek at his feet.

It was as he was about to begin ascending the steps to dismantle the dead god's corpse that he suddenly began to fall, the gruesome scene of his father's murder fading into the horizon as if he'd been pushed out of reality itself and was floating helplessly away. All at once, the sensation of dread that accompanied the abyss fled from him, the voice of the dead god growing faint as it became increasingly distant.

"You…you are denied entrance…to my abyss, half-fiend…I hereby cast you out…forbidden from returning…condemned to wander the shores…between time and space…"

When he awoke, Asmodeus felt the unfamiliar yield of sand beneath him. Lying on his back, he opened his eyes. The sky appeared to be in its twilight hour, yet more unsettling was the vibrant orange and royal purple shades it was cast in. Glancing over to his right, a vast crimson ocean stretched out, the waves lapping at his shoulder where he laid.

Pushing himself up onto an elbow, Asmodeus looked over as the strangest looking creature he'd ever seen approached; crustacean in nature, it was the size of a large cat and appeared to have six claws, four of which looked shrunken and unused, with a pair of beady black eyes atop a pair of antennae that sprouted from its body. Scuttling past him it retreated into the water, and as he looked around the half-fiend spotted a large number of them.

It was then that he heard a voice, neutral in tone and completely lacking in any inflection, yet even as he heard it Asmodeus was filled with a great sense of awe, as if the very essence of his being were reacting to it.

"A child of both Temelachus and Colopatrion, cast upon the shores of time by a younger god. Tell me, child…what is your name?"

Searching for the source of the voice, Asmodeus found himself looking upon a featureless humanoid, with the narrow hips and broad shoulders of a male but seeming to be lacking in gender. White eyes peered down at him, with only a faint outline of a nose above thin lips parted in a welcoming smile.

"My name is Asmodeus…some call me son of the Fallen One…where am I?"

"A difficult question to answer entirely, but for now simply know that you are safe here."

"But where is here? I must know," Asmodeus pressed, pushing himself to his feet and brushing sand off of himself.

"It is called The Timeless Shore, though far more complicated than a name. You must have angered a younger god tremendously for them to exile you in such a manner."

Looking around, Asmodeus let out a sigh as he saw the crimson ocean spread out all around him as he stood on one of what appeared to be a limitless number of small islands of sand dotting the area.

Turning to the featureless humanoid with pale, glowing skin, Asmodeus tilted his head. "My apologies, but I'm afraid I'm a bit disoriented…may I ask who you might be?"

In response, the humanoid smiled, nodding as it answered. "I am The One Who Remains Neutral. You may call me Talgaroth."

THE END

DANIEL MITCHELL

Slayer of dragons and demons, charmer of princesses, hero to all mankind...all of these and more are some of the greatly exaggerated and often fabricated accomplishments of the author. Born in Columbus, Ohio, and quickly whisked away to the small town of Ashland where he was raised, Daniel was an only child and lived a quiet, happy life until he was 7, at which point the first of his three younger siblings was born. Now 30 at the time of The Second Crusade's publishing, Daniel resides in Wooster, Ohio, with his significant other and her accursed overweight cat. The Second Crusade is his second published work, being a prequel story to The Vlishgnath Chronicles. His hobbies (aside from reading and writing) include video games, Dungeons & Dragons (he prefers the Pathfinder system), and enjoying good beer with great friends.